MAHONEY

by

Andrew Joyce

MAHONEY

ISBN: 978-09981193-7-3

Published by William Birch & Assoc.

For

Suni Quintana

the sweetest little flower in all of España

My sincere thanks to:

Emily Gmitter
my editor extraordinaire

Peter Walsh
my Irish connection

Jere Swain
who helped out

&

Suzanne Brailey
in whose carriage house I wrote this book

It started as a dream ... a dream of a place where no one ever went hungry and fine Irish whiskey flowed from fountains ... a land of good and plenty. But first, the nightmare had to be endured.

Part One
Devin

1

In the second year of *an Gorta Mhór*—the Great Famine—MacMurragh stepped into Devin Mahoney's cabin but stopped short, just inside the door. There was not a stick of furniture present; everything had been sold off, one piece at a time, as the hunger grew. Devin had not eaten for five days, and then it was only a meager bowlful of cornmeal. Before that, he had gone three days without a single morsel of food passing his lips. Devin Mahoney, the descendant of kings, lay on the dirt floor of his small, dark cabin, waiting for Death to take him by the hand and lead him out of this world of misery.

≈ ≈ ≈

Near in distance, but leagues away in time, a lone horseman ascends a small windswept hill. He is wearing a bronze breastplate, but no helmet. A long-handled broadsword hangs from his left hip. When on the crest of the hill, he dismounts and looks about him. To the east, the green undulating hills roll on until they touch the pale blue sky in the far distance. To the west, the green carpet flows gently into an angry, grey sea. To the north and south—nothing but the green verdure of the land can be seen. It goes on forever.

The man's name is Màel Muad mac Brian. He is the master of all he surveys. He is *Ard Ri*, the High King of all of Ireland. There are many lesser kings, but there is only one High King. It is a tenuous hold he has on the crown. However, for the moment, he is ruler supreme.

Years later, his son, Cían mac Máelmuaid, chief of the *Cineal Aodha*, married Sadb ingen Brian, the daughter of Brian Bóruma mac Cennétig, the man who had killed Cían's father and became High King.

He and Sadb had a son, Mathghamhain, whose progeny would become the sovereigns of Southern Ireland and be forever known as Mahoneys.

≈ ≈ ≈

Devin Mahoney was too weak to sit up, but his eyes bored into the landlord's agent as he stood in the doorway, blocking the feeble light from a weak Irish sun trying to cast its rays through a grey and overcast Irish sky.

"I see y're still drawing a slim breath of life," said MacMurragh, the landlord's lackey.

"Aye. For a few days more, at least," whispered Devin.

Devin Mahoney was nineteen years of age and the last of his family left alive. His mother had been the first to go when the blight hit. She lasted only four months. She had always been a little on the frail side, but going days at a time without eating made her even more delicate. One night, she put on her finest dress and sat in her old rocker. She told her family that she was tired and needed a rest. The next morning when the family awoke, she was still seated in her rocker, dead.

The agent took a few steps into the dreariness and nudged Devin's leg with the toe of his boot. "I be wanting to talk to y'."

"Speak, damn ya. Then be gone and leave me die in peace."

"You'll not be dying this day, Mahoney. Lord Feilding has sent word that he will pay yer way to America if that's what y' be wanting. If it was up to me, I'd let you die and then we'd be rid of y' for good."

"Why would he be wanting to send me to America? He has never given a tuppence worth for any of us Mahoneys."

≈ ≈ ≈

Months earlier and nearly four hundred miles due east, on an estate comprising two hundred and eighty-four acres in Warwickshire, England, the Seventh Earl of Denbigh, William Basil Percy Feilding, sat in the library of his ancestral home, Newnham Paddox. With him were three of his closest friends: Lord Beckham, Lord Beaumont, and his old school chum, Francis George Hugh

Seymour, the 5th Marquee of Hertford, also known as Pinky to a select few.

They had just adjourned from the dinner table, leaving the women free to get on with their gossiping. The men had important matters to discuss. There would be no talk that evening of cricket scores or the latest method of cattle breeding.

Having served the gentlemen their port, the manservant quietly departed. Left to themselves, the four men, sitting in high-backed, leather-covered chairs, clipped the ends off their cigars and soon the distinct rich aroma of West Indian tobacco filled the room. At length, Lord Feilding cleared his throat and said, "Gentlemen, what are we to do about this damnable Irish problem?"

Lord Beckham leaned forward and seemed on the verge of saying something. Instead, he sipped his wine and leaned back into the warm embrace of the overstuffed chair.

Lord Feilding sighed. "All of us here have landholdings in Ireland. What are we to do about the tax? That damnable tax will ruin me! If the blighters over there are starving, why doesn't the government send them food? Why tax us?"

The 5th Marquee of Hertford rose from his seat and picked up the decanter from his friend's desk. As he refilled his glass with the dark purple liquid, a wily smile played across his lips. "If I remember correctly, Bill, you were the one always so sure you'd be sent down for failing an examination while we were at Oxford."

"That was a long time ago, Pinky. I do not believe for one moment that I am overstating the severity of the situation when I say the tax on the number of our tenants will be the ruin of us."

The Marquee tilted his head back, blew out a stream of blue-white smoke, and sipped his wine before addressing his friend. "If I understand you correctly, you have two questions you would like answered."

Lord Feilding nodded.

The Marquee continued.

"First of all. One cannot just feed people when they are hungry. They must work for what they receive or else they will become indolent, and the Irish are already a languid and indolent lot. Rest assured the Prime Minister knows this, hence, the creation of the work gangs and workhouses. However, someone has to pay for

3

those things, and Her Majesty's Government has decided that it should be us. I agree with the concept in essence, but not with who should pay for the program."

"I don't care who pays for it as long as it's not me! I can't afford the tax. It will ruin me," said Lord Feilding.

"You just built a third story onto your house. At how many thousand pounds sterling?" asked his friend, the Marquee. "You used to have thirty-four hearths throughout the house. How many have you now? You needed a third floor like you needed another head. My point is we can afford just about anything. However, that being said, why *should* we pay the tax?"

Lord Beaumont, who had yet to speak, stood and reached for the decanter. "We will pay the tax because we have no alternative. If those damn Irish did not breed like rabbits, then perhaps this year we would make a profit from our farms. The rents I collect do not come anywhere near what I'll be paying in taxes."

Having had his say, Lord Beaumont relinquished the floor by sitting back down with a full glass of the best port to be had in all the British Isles.

The Marquee eyed Lord Beckham. "Have you anything to say?"

"Yes, by George. May I have a spot more of that splendid port?"

The Marquee filled Lord Beckham's glass. Then, eyeing his three peers, he said, "We would not be in this pickle if we had not subdivided our land to the extent we did. When the law was passed giving us one vote in the Irish Parliament for each tenant farmer on our land, we got greedy for votes, not to mention the additional income the new tenants would bring. When the famine came, the additional tenants became more a liability than an asset. Prime Minister Peel and the Colonial Secretary, Lord Stanley, in their zeal to be seen as properly addressing the problem, have deemed it necessary to tax us landlords for the creation of workhouses and work gangs."

The others in the room vigorously puffed on their cigars in silent agreement.

The Marquee continued: "My only concern is to remove the tenants from my land with the least possible fuss, and I think I have found a way to do so without throwing the poor buggers off onto the road to starve to death. That might not look so good and it may have

4

unpleasant repercussions. You can push a people only so far before they will rise up against you. Look what happened with the colonists under King George's rule."

The others nodded and leaned slightly forward with keen anticipation for what the Marquee would say next.

"I have given the matter a thorough and full consideration and I believe I have come up with a solution." He interrupted his discourse to avail himself of the enticing port.

"Out with it, Pinky!" implored Lord Feilding.

The Marquee smiled at his old friend. "The solution is simple. We send them all off to America."

"What?"

"It is less expensive to send a family of six to America than it is to pay the tax on them. I have spoken with a few ship owners and they have all agreed to take the tenants at reduced rates if we use their ships exclusively. It's not much different than shipping cattle," said Francis George Hugh Seymour, the 5th Marquee of Hertford.

"I think you've got it," said a smiling William Basil Percy Feilding, the 7th Earl of Denbigh. "Let's finish our port and rejoin the women. And, Pinky, I'll be wanting the names of a few of those ship-owners of whom you spoke."

≈ ≈ ≈

Looking down at the recumbent Devin Mahoney, MacMurragh said, "Y' ask me why His Lordship would send ya off to America. Well, I ask no questions. I do as I am told. Do y' want to go or lie in yer own filth and die? The ship leaves from Cork in two weeks."

Devin forced himself to sit up and leaned against the stone wall of the cabin. The agent was no more than a dark silhouette against the soft brightness streaming in through the door of the windowless cabin. Addressing the gloomy specter, Devin said, "I could not walk out that door behind y'. How am I to get to Cork? And how am I to live for two weeks more with nothing to eat?"

"If y' agree to go, I'll send the cook down with a little food to get y' back on yer feet. When y' leave, y' are to be given enough to keep y' alive until y' board ship. Once at sea, y'll have nothing to worry about. And once in America, y'll have less still to worry about. In America, employment is plentiful and everyone is rich."

5

"Again, I'll ask y'. How am I to get to Cork?"

"Y'll walk, be damn'd. Y' don't expect the master to send y' off in his fine coach, do y'?"

"I'll go. Send down the food."

Devin had agreed to go to America only as a way to get something to eat. He had to think on what his next move would be. The agent would probably allow him food until he was strong enough to make the trek to Cork. Then he would be given a sack of meal. But what if he did not board the ship? Whatever he decided, he would no longer be living on the farm on which he was born.

He lay back down and thought of his father and two brothers. His sister, Hannah, was safe, thank God. She had married before the famine struck and moved to the North where the suffering was not as widespread, at least not yet.

A few months after his mother died, Devin's father and brothers had checked themselves into a workhouse. It was a decision of last resort, made when it became apparent they would all starve to death unless something was done. The three older men would subject themselves to the indignities of the workhouse: the wearing of a uniform, the bad food, and the twelve-hour work days. At least in the workhouse, they would be fed twice a day.

The salary wasn't much, but what there was would be turned over to Devin who would stay on the farm to protect the tenancy. When the famine was over, the Mahoneys would check themselves out and return home. That was the plan.

What they had not planned on was being exposed to disease. Bathing and cleanliness were practically nonexistent in the workhouses. Most of the inmates were infested with lice or worse. Two months after entering, all three of the Mahoney men came down with typhus. Within three weeks, they were all dead. And now here lay Devin, close to death himself.

A little while later, the cook from the manor house came in with a bucket of stirabout.

"Here, this will give ya strength," she said.

Devin struggled to sit up. Once he was leaning against the wall, the cook placed the stirabout within his reach.

"Now you go easy, with ya. If you eat too much, too fast, you'll make yourself sick, sure enough." She pulled out four slices of bread and a spoon from the big pocket in the front of her apron. "I wasn't supposed to give you bread, so let's keep this between ourselves." Devin smiled up at her. His first smile in many, many a day. The cook smiled back, then left him to eat his stirabout alone.

Devin first ate a slice of bread. Before the famine, he had never thought of bread as having any flavor. However, as he chewed, his taste buds awoke with the sensation of slight but intense explosions. The coarse brown bread was the most wonderful thing he had ever eaten in his life.

With the bread settled comfortably in his belly, Devin dipped the spoon into the still-warm porridge. After three spoonfuls, his shrunken stomach was full and he lay back down to wait for his strength to return.

If MacMurragh had just a spark of human decency, he would have let Devin work around the manor house in exchange for food. However, the man hated the tenants and did everything he could to make their lives miserable. The cook was a good woman and used to give the Mahoneys a little food at the start of the famine. But MacMurragh had caught her at it and threatened to terminate her if she did it again. She, being a widow and having a small child to look after, had no choice but to cease her philanthropic ways, though it broke her heart to do so.

As he pondered his future, Devin fell off to sleep and dreamt of his past. During the week, there had always been cabbage and potatoes, and maybe a little milk. Sometimes the potatoes were fried, sometimes boiled together with the cabbage, and sometimes roasted in the fire. For most Sunday dinners, there would be meat on the table, usually pork. And at Christmas-time, there was always a pudding. As a child, he and his siblings awaited Christmas with wild anticipation. There were never any presents; the family was too poor for things like that. But they always had a pudding. It was the high point of the year.

Devin slept through the night. And as he slept, his body absorbed the nutrients from what he had eaten. In the morning, he was strong enough to stand and go outside. But first he ate his fill of cold porridge, which had congealed in the bucket. For dessert, he had a slice of bread.

He met MacMurragh outside the cabin.

"I see y're strong enough to move about. Would y' be leaving us today?"

"Y' said the boat doesn't leave for two weeks. I'll need a day or so to get my strength back. I can make it to Cork in five days. So don't worry, *Your Lordship*. Y' just keep up your part of the bargain and I'll be on my way as soon as I'm able. There's no longer anything to keep me here."

"When y're ready to go, see the cook and she'll give y' enough food to get ya to Cork. The name of the ship is the *Archimedes*. Tell the captain yer name and that y' are a tenant of Lord Feilding; he'll have a place for y'. I'll expect y' to be gone on the morrow before I get back from town. I'll be wanting to burn that hut of yers, to be rid of the stench."

Devin had never liked MacMurragh. If he had been at the top of his form, he would have punched the agent right in his big, fat, ruddy face. Instead, without a word, he went back into the cabin and thought of better times.

Over there had stood the table where so many family dinners had taken place. Before the famine, dinner had been the best part of the day. It was a time to come together as a family and discuss things of great import. Such as Hannah's insistence that she needed a new dress. *"How do y' expect me to attract the boys if I have to wear this raggedy old thing?"*

His father had patted her hand and said, "We'll see what we can do right after the harvest." She got her new dress and she got her husband.

Devin smiled at the memory.

Over there, against the south wall, is where he and his siblings had slept. During the winter, he and his brothers would take turns keeping the fire lit throughout the night. He could still hear his eldest brother, John, yelling at him in the darkness. *"Devin, y've let the fire die down. It's yer turn. Get yer arse out of bed and do yer duty!"*

Again, Devin smiled.

His parents had slept in the adjoining room, the only other room in the cabin. As a young boy, Devin had once asked his father why he and his mother did not sleep by the fire in winter. Remembering his father's answer caused another smile to play across his lips. *"Yer mother is all I need to keep me warm during the night."*

Now the cabin was as empty as his heart.

It was at that moment Devin made up his mind. He *would* go to America and become a very rich man. He would return, buy the land from Lord Feilding, and find himself a good, strong Irish lass to bear him many children. He would live out his days as lord of the manor, surrounded by his children and grandchildren. Never again would a Mahoney go hungry!

He lay down on the earthen floor, next to the cold fireplace, to spend his last night in the only home he had ever known.

In the morning, he knocked on the kitchen door. Shortly thereafter, the cook appeared and handed him a canvas sack. "Here. This will keep yer body and soul together until y're on the boat. There's five pounds of meal and two of oatmeal. I've also given y' a small kettle and some matches."

Devin thanked her and turned to leave, but was stopped in his tracks. "Wait a minute. I'll be right back." It was a cold November morning, and she had noticed that he was shivering in his tattered rags. She was soon back, holding a gentleman's overcoat.

"Take this and be gone with y' before Mister MacMurragh returns. It is the master's coat and I would surely be put out upon the road if it was known that I had given it away."

"I cannot take it. Y' and your child would starve if y' were thrown out."

"Do not worry. The master will never miss it. He has three more just like it. The only danger is if Mister MacMurragh sees y' wearing it."

Devin leaned in and kissed her on the cheek. "Y're a good woman, Aife Meehan. When I return from America, I'll build y' the grandest house County Kerry has ever seen, and y'll never have to work another day as long as y' live."

She said nothing, but a single tear rolled down her right cheek as she closed the door.

Devin put on the coat and hefted the sack over his shoulder. The sun was trying to assert itself over the eastern horizon—a new day in more ways than one. As he stepped through the gate and out onto the road that would lead him to Cork, and ultimately to America, he thought of something his parish priest had once said in a sermon.

The journey of 1,000 miles starts with the first step.

2

An ancient road it was. The Roman Christians had used it in the fifth century to spread The Word and baptize an entire nation. Then the Danes—or Vikings as they were known at that time—who had come to conquer the isle late in the eighth century deepened the wheel ruts laid down by the monks. Along its length, from the Celtic Sea to the Atlantic Ocean, they had built their castles. By the time the Normans arrived in the twelfth century, it was a well-worn track. In the sixteenth century, Henry VIII's soldiers used the road in their subjugation of an unruly people. Three hundred years later, Devin Mahoney, in solitary desolation, followed the wheel-rutted lane to an uncertain future.

To the east, horizontal bands of orange lightened to pink then to white as Devin made his way into the face of the rising sun. As the miles slipped away, he saw no children playing in their yards as in years past. Occasionally he would see a work gang, but for the most part he had the road to himself.

As he approached the town of Coom, he came across the body of a dead man lying in a ditch. There was little doubt that he had died from starvation. The body was barely more than a skeleton. It was not the first dead person Devin had ever seen. Over the last fifteen months, he had seen many. Devin wore no hat to doff, but as a sign of respect, he nodded toward the inert form as he passed by.

He made it as far as the outskirts of Glenflesk before deciding to stop for the night. He went into the woods off to his right, while the last rays of the setting sun reflected off the somber grey clouds to the west, momentarily turning their edges pink. After a few steps, he came across a small clearing. *This will do*, he thought.

The road followed the River Lee, so water was easily accessible. He had not stopped during the day to eat, for his strategy was to make what he carried in the sack last as long as possible. Besides, he was used to going without food. Nevertheless, he now keenly anticipated a bowl of cornmeal, bland though it be.

After collecting what dead branches he could readily find, he made a space for his fire. Once he had the fire going, he reached into the sack and brought out the kettle and the larger of the two bags of food, figuring it to be the cornmeal.

At the river, he drew the kettle half-full with water. On the way back to his camp, the thought suddenly struck him that Missus Meehan had made no mention of a spoon. How was he to eat his stirabout?

He need not have worried. Missus Meehan was a good woman, indeed she was. He found a large, wooden-handled spoon at the bottom of the sack.

He held the pot of cornmeal over the fire using a short branch and waited for the concoction to start its contented bubbling. Before long, he would eat.

Devin's eyes were fixated on the mesmerizing flames. Doubt about what he was doing crept into his contemplations. It was a long way to America. Did he really want to leave the Auld Sod? But if he stayed, what hope would there be for him? Half the country was slowly starving to death.

His thoughts were interrupted by a thrashing noise behind him, off to his left. He turned to see a man coming his way, wearing a smile, his hat in hand. " 'Tis only I, Tom McNevin from Kinsale, County Cork. I saw yer fire and thought y' might be wanting company on this grand night."

"Come in, Tom McNevin. Come and sit by the fire," invited Devin.

McNevin squatted opposite his host and held his hands over the fire to warm them. The firelight revealed a gaunt face. He looked to be about forty. His hair and beard were dark, but carried a little grey. His eyes were laughing eyes, merry eyes. His clothes were little more than rags. He sported no overcoat, he wore no shoes. McNevin looked across the fire at Devin and saw a young man with a sparse brown beard and stormy blue eyes. He was a good-looking lad and his welcoming smile made Tom McNevin feel right at home.

" 'Tis a grand night to be sitting by a warm fire such as yers, and in such fine company," said McNevin.

" 'Tis so. I'm Devin Mahoney."

12

Devin noticed McNevin eyeing the pot he held over the flames. "Have y' eaten recently?" he asked.

"I cannot say that I have. But I have not come to eat yer food. 'Tis a cold night and yer fire looked inviting."

"Y' are welcome to anything I have. I, too, know what it's like to go without eating."

Devin handed the stick holding the kettle to McNevin. "Here, hold this. Keep it atop the flames. I'll do the stirring and soon we'll be eating like kings, we'll be."

As Devin stirred the cornmeal, he asked of McNevin, "When did y' last eat?"

"Like many of our fellow countrymen, it's been a little while since a bit of food has passed these lips. A day or two days, 'tis all the same. Since the blight came upon us, one day seems like all the others. I don't count time by days anymore … or even hours. Time is the distance from one meal till the next."

When the stirabout was ready, McNevin placed the pot on the ground next to the fire and eagerly looked in Devin's direction. He was trying to be polite, but the pain in his stomach willed him to inquire, "Do y' have two spoons?"

"Only the one. Y' are my guest, y' eat first. When y' have had yer fill, then I will eat."

They took their turns and when the pot was empty, McNevin insisted that it would be he who took it to the river to be cleaned. While McNevin was at his task, Devin searched out more firewood. It was a cold night and they would have to keep the fire going. Devin would be warm enough in his heavy coat, but McNevin would need the warmth of a fire.

With their respective chores taken care of, the two men sat down next to the fire, one on each side. They were grateful to have eaten this evening. Tomorrow would bring what tomorrow would bring. But for the moment, they were two contented Irishmen.

Devin asked, "Are y' going or coming from Kinsale?"

"I've been to Dublin. I'm going back to Kinsale, but there's little of any worth there for me, no more. These days there is very little for me, and people like me, anywhere in all of Blessed Ireland."

"Y're slightly out of yer way."

13

"When I left Dublin, I thought I'd roam a ways to the west and see if there was any work for an able-bodied man. I've been all the way over to Glenbeigh. There *is* no work, and very little food that I've come across in me travels."

"I'll tell y' true, Tom McNevin, there is very little for us poor folks here in Ireland. The land of St. Patrick, fairies, and the little people. The land of ruins. Of standing stones that have stood since the beginning of time. The land where my ancestors vanquished the Danes and ruled all this land hereabouts. I tell y' true, Tom McNevin."

McNevin moved a little closer to the fire.

Devin threw on a few sticks to build it up. "Tell me, Tom. What is it like in a big city like Dublin? Are there hungry people there, too?"

"If y' are not ready for sleep, I'll tell y' what I've seen from Kinsale to Cork to Dublin and back. Methinks that somehow we Irish have angered the gods. What misery I've seen.

"But before I tell me story, y' must tell me what it is that y' are doing out here on a cold night, mixing stirabout, wearing a fine gentleman's overcoat. I would think that y' could afford to stay at an inn."

Devin laughed. "The coat was given to me by a kindly woman. Underneath, I am dressed much as y' are." He then told his story and ended with, "I'll be going to America now. When I return, I'll live in as fine a manor house as y' have ever seen and have a coach-and-four to draw me to and fro as befits a man of my standing. No longer will I be walking from town to town."

McNevin warmed his hands over the fire. "I'm sorry about yer family. Me, I never had much of a family. Me mum died bringing me into the world and, for one reason or another, I never married. Perhaps it was for the best. I don't know how I'd survive having my whole family wiped out in a trace."

Devin said, "My sister is safe up in the North."

"'Tis good to hear."

"Now, y' tell me what is happening outside of County Kerry, in the rest of Ireland."

McNevin leaned back as the flames flared up. "I'll get to telling y', to be sure. I am a *seanchaí* of renown. An Irish teller of tales am

14

I. Y' make yerself comfortable and I'll pay for me supper this night with a tale that y' will remember and pass down to yer grandchildren as they sit upon yer knee in that fine manor house y' will one day be building."

Devin pulled his knees up, wrapped his arms about his legs, and waited for the *seanchaí* to begin his story.

"I had six acres that I planted every year for twenty years. The crop fed me with enough left over to sell at market and keep me steeped in whiskey for a few weeks after harvest. Me rent was always paid. But then the blight struck. The leaves withered, the stems rotted, and me beautiful praties were covered with dark and black patches. It all happened so quickly.

"Without a crop, me rent I could not pay. The owner's middleman badgered me daily and told me I'd be thrown out onto the road unless I came through. This, after twenty years on the same plot of land. I had always paid me rent, but would the landlord give an understanding to the blight and what it has done to this country? No, he would not. He wanted only his money and his tenant of twenty years be damned! I told the middleman that y' cannot get blood from a turnip.

"As a result of the agent's badgering, I took myself off and joined one of those work gangs that the government had set up. We went out at dawn each day to dig holes. There was no rhyme nor reason for those holes, but if we wanted to be paid, we'd have to dig them damn holes. The next day we would go out and fill in those very same holes. Sometimes we would build stone walls that enclosed nothing or made an existing wall higher by two feet or more, only to keep us working.

"At least we were fed twice a day. Once at ten and again at four. But it was very poor gruel they gave us, it was. And y' had to work the full ten hours to be given even that.

"At the end of the week, I would turn my pay over to the middleman to keep a hold on my farm. But he always told me I still owed. Finally, I had had enough. I was working ten hours a day, six days a week, for two miserly meals a day. And after all that work, I still went hungry on Sundays!

"The summer of last year I gave up my farm and left Kinsale. I thought I could find work in Cork, loading boats. It was on my first day out that I saw my first horror. I came across a woman walking my way, holding a bundle in her arms. Like me, she was dressed in rags, and like me, she was thin, her face drawn. I could tell she had not eaten in many a day. But unlike me, she had a look about her that I cannot describe.

"When we came abreast of one another, I stopped and asked, 'Are y' alright?' She looked at me with a blank stare and says she: 'I do be alright, but my baby is hungry. Can y' spare a morsel of food for the wee little one?'

"I had a biscuit in me pocket that I was holding for dinner. But how could I say no to her plea, even if I had wanted to? I withdrew the biscuit and held it out to her. She says, 'Y' give it to him.' She unwound the swaddling to reveal her child. It was horrible, it was. The infant was dead and, it was plain to see, had been so for some time. I looked at the woman smiling down at the lifeless baby as though he was still alive. She had lost her mind either from hunger or grief … or both."

Devin exclaimed, "That's horrible. What did you do?"

"I did the only thing I could do. I pressed the biscuit into her hand, saying, 'Y' feed him and have some for yerself.' She did not try to feed her baby and she did not raise the biscuit to her own lips. She thanked me and resumed her slow wanderings. I stood in the middle of the road, watching until she was out of sight."

"Yesterday, I came across a dead man lying on the road just outside of Coom," said Devin.

"Aye. Corpses lay thick upon the countryside these days, they do. I've seen a few myself. A month back, I stepped into a burying ground to avail myself of a little shade from the beech trees lining its walks. I stumbled upon a funeral taking place and decided to linger until the service was over. After the mourners had left, the burying men placed the coffin over the dug grave. One of them pulled a string and a spring mechanism popped open the bottom, and the body, wrapped in old potato sacks, fell six feet to its final resting place. I asked about it. 'We have run out of wood for the making of coffins. There are just too many dead. Undertakers all over Ireland are doing the same,' I was so informed."

" 'Tis a sad day for Ireland, indeed. Now tell me true, Tom McNevin, what is life like in the big cities of Cork and Dublin?"

McNevin leaned toward the fire, his face a ghostly pallor from the reflecting flames. "'Tis a little better than the country, but not by much. There is no work to be had in either place. People in from the country have crowded the streets looking for work and the police do not like it. But they arrest no one because then they'd have to feed them. What they do is give beatings, hoping that will drive them back to the country. I have been on the receiving end of a few of those beatings myself."

"Do they beat the women as well?"

"To be sure, I have seen it done, so I have."

"Then it's glad to be off to America, I am," said Devin. "What else have you seen? I want to know so I can tell the people of America the true story of what is happening here. They are a rich people, and a kind people. They would send relief if they only knew."

McNevin threw a few more sticks onto the fire. When they had caught, and the flames flared up to dance about in the slight wind coming in from the north, he said, "'Tis to be a cold night this night. I am grateful for the warmth of yer fire, and I will tell y' of more things that I have seen. I cannot understand how we have fallen so low."

Devin braced himself for what he was about to hear.

"From Dublin, I walked west to Galway. 'Tis on the coast that I saw what cruelty really is. There were two women collecting seaweed and putting it into baskets. Having nothing better to occupy me time, I approached with an Irish greeting, '*Dia dhuit.*'

"'Hullo to you,' answered one of the women.

"They had a few years on me. Grey-headed and dressed in rags, they were. One of 'em had a ratty old red shawl about her shoulders. The other one's dress was in such tatters that it was cut off above the knees. Their clothes were heavily patched and neither of them wore shoes.

"They continued with their work, picking up seaweed below the high-water mark as we walked along the beach. 'There be plenty of what yer after just a few feet away, at the high water line,' says I. 'Why do y' scavenge for the scraps when the bounty lies within reach?'

17

"'We dare not,' said the one with the shawl. ' 'Tis the landlord's property above that line.'

"The wind was blowing in off the ocean and felt good. A warm June day it was. We were walking in that manner for a short while, when, from the north, three policemen came running towards us, making heavy footprints in the sand. As they got closer, I could see that one was a sergeant, the other two, privates.

"When they caught up with us, the two privates pulled the baskets from the women's hands. The sergeant said, 'I arrest you for thievery. You three are to come along with us. And come peaceably if you know what's good for you.'

"I was shocked at the turn of events. Not so much that I was being arrested, but by the fact that it was against the law to collect seaweed. Since when?"

Devin shrugged his shoulders.

McNevin answered the shrug. "I'll tell y' since when. Since those damn English came here with Henry II hundreds of years ago. The English think they own the whole damn island and all of us, too! But enough of that. Back to my story."

Devin broke a dead branch in two and threw the pieces onto the fire. "Please continue," he urged.

"The women told the police that they took seaweed only from below the high tide mark. 'That is surely not against the law,' they pleaded.

"Apparently it *was* against the law. The sergeant's response was short and to the point. 'One of the landlord's drivers saw you and reported you. There is nothing we can do here. You must face a judge in a court of law. But why were you collecting seaweed a' tall? You do not look like you have a crop that needs fertilizing.'

" 'We was gathering it to eat,' says the woman with the torn dress. At that point, I spoke up. 'I was not stealing seaweed, merely walking along with these two grand ladies, enjoying their good company. Y' do not see a basket in my hands.'

"The women corroborated my words. And the sergeant, being a fair-minded individual, said, 'Seeing as how the report was about two women and no mention of a man, you be on your way now.'

"I continued down the beach until I came to a path that led back to the road. I'll tell y' true, Devin Mahoney, there have been times

18

since then that I wished I had allowed myself to be arrested. At least I would have been fed twice a day while in jail."

"'Tis a sorry thing to hear," said Devin.

"Aye, 'tis," agreed McNevin.

Devin laid more sticks on the fire. "We should get some sleep. We have a good walk ahead of us tomorrow."

"Are y' suggesting that I travel the road with y'?" asked McNevin.

"Sure. You are my *seanchaí*. As we walk, y'll be telling me tales of things y've seen in this last year and I'll be sharing my food with y'."

"It will give my head peace to travel with y'. May your blessings outnumber the shamrocks that grow on our beloved island."

"Thank y', Tom. There's enough wood to sustain the fire throughout the night, but I'll have to depend on y' to keep it going. According to my dear departed brothers, I am not very good at that sort of thing."

"I'll see y' on the morrow, Devin Mahoney."

"God willing."

3

In the morning, the two men shared a modest serving of porridge and started on their way. Overnight, grey storm clouds had moved in from the north, bringing with them a cold and bitter day.

Stone walls, three to four feet high, edged the road. Mile after mile, the ground lay fallow; the rich black soil uncultivated. Here and there, the remains of a stone dwelling could be seen. Its thatch removed, its walls tumbled over.

"'Tis a desolate sight," observed McNevin.

"'Tis that," agreed Devin. "Why are the houses tumbled? Where have the people gone?"

"The landlords are running people off the land, or they're getting rid of 'em by sending 'em to America. Either way, there'll be less planting in the spring and fewer crops come the harvest," said McNevin.

After a moment's thought, he continued. "Y' asked why the houses are tumbled. I'll tell y' why. When a landlord gets rid of a tenant, the houses are destroyed so the landlord can expand his pasture land. People are cleared to make way for the raising of sheep and cattle. There's more money to be had that way because the landlords pay no tax on cattle, only human beings."

≈ ≈ ≈

In the first year of The Great Famine, on a fiery August day, the sun splitting stones it was, Andrew Fitzgibbons' world ended and his hell began.

Like most, his potato crop had failed, but unlike most, his family was eating, thanks to his son's vegetable garden. And his rent was paid up to date. He did not know how long that would last, but for now he was holding on.

His wife was kneeling over the peat fire, boiling a cabbage for their noon meal. Andrew's oldest son, Daniel, fourteen years of age, was tending his garden with love and care. The boy had the gift of *a bhfuil ordóg glas*. A green thumb, as the English would say. The younger children were playing near the house, under Andrew's watchful eye.

Yes, things were bad in Ireland and getting worse as far as Andrew could tell, but for the moment, all was well for him and his. Then the clock ticked one tick and the fateful moment arrived.

A gang of the landlord's drivers came up the stone path that Andrew's father had laid when Andrew was but *leanbh beag*, a small child. There were seven in number, led by Thomas Cohan. Andrew knew him well. Tommy was the town bully and a thoroughly unpleasant man. He was tall, almost six feet, and his arms were thick with muscles. His smirk announced to the world that he was enjoying himself.

Cohan got right to the point. "Y' have ten minutes to gather yer possessions and yer rabble, Andrew Fitzgibbons. His Lordship is increasing his pasture lands and y' and yer hovel are in the way."

"What do you mean, Tommy Cohan? My rent is paid."

"'Tis no concern of mine," said Cohan. "I've been told to move y' off the land and that is what I'll be doing. Yer ten minutes start now."

Andrew was dumbfounded. He could not think straight. This was too much to take in all at once. His mind was reeling off the possibilities. Could he fight the seven men before him and drive them from his house? No. Could he plead for time so that he might beseech the landlord to reconsider? The look in Cohan's eyes said no. Would God send down a lightning bolt to strike Tommy Cohan where he stood? Probably not.

"Y' now have nine minutes."

Andrew called to his son. "Daniel, gather the little ones and bring them inside. Hurry!" He went into the house and told his wife to stop what she was doing and gather up all that she could carry of their belongings and take them outside. "Then come back for more."

She stood immobile at the fire with her stirring stick in hand and a questioning look on her face.

"I will explain later, but right now y' have to do as I say."

The children came in and Andrew told them the same thing he had told his wife. Daniel had overheard the conversation with Cohan, so there was no hesitation on his part. The younger children thought it a grand game and readily joined in. His wife, seeing the fear in her husband's eyes, placed the spoon into the pot of cabbage, picked up a rag, and took the pot off the fire. She took it outside and placed it on the ground. She was surprised to see Cohan and the other men, but said nothing and hurried back inside.

When everything they owned, which was not much, was outside the house, Cohan gave the order to remove the thatch. The family had to stand by and watch the destruction of their home.

Andrew's wife huddled with her three small children, ages nine, seven, and five. Daniel stood next to his father. With the roof reduced to a pile of hay, the drivers started in on toppling the walls. Missus Fitzgibbons began to cry.

With the destruction complete, Cohan told Andrew that the family was to be off the land by sundown. "Thems me orders," said Cohan. "And I'll be wanting no trouble from y', Andrew Fitzgibbons."

"Where are we to go? What are we to do?" demanded Andrew.

"Again, 'tis no concern of mine," said Cohan.

Daniel, knowing the family would be needing food, ran to his beloved garden and started picking anything that was anywhere near to being ripe.

Cohan yelled, "Y' there, stop! That be His Lordship's property."

Daniel ignored the command. An enraged Cohan ordered two of his men to restrain the boy and hold him. To another he said, "Y' go along into town and bring back a constable."

Andrew pleaded with Cohan to release the boy and they would be on their way. But Cohan was deaf to Andrew's entreaties.

The constable arrived shortly thereafter, and, based on Cohan's testimony and the law that stated a landlord owned everything on his land, he promptly arrested Daniel for thievery and destruction of property. He was not moved by the crying of the boy's siblings nor the pleas from his parents.

The next day, Daniel went before a judge and was sentenced to two months in jail for his crime against the landlord.

≈ ≈ ≈

As the sun rose higher in the sky, the temperature climbed a wee bit, but still, a bleak, cold day it was.

Except for the fact that he was not wearing a hat, Devin could have been mistaken for a gentleman in his grand overcoat. He looked over at McNevin, dressed in rags and barefooted. He did not seem bothered by the weather, but Devin thought he would offer the use of the coat. For a little while, anyway.

"No thank y', Devin Mahoney, and may the saints preserve y'. I am fine the way I am. Winter's on its way and I must prepare for the onslaught. This is balmy weather compared to what is coming," said McNevin, his eyes still smiling.

With the sun directly overhead, Devin suggested they rest for a while. "Aye, 'tis a good idea," agreed McNevin. "There be a small hill over yonder. Why not climb its summit and look over the land? This may be yer last look at County Kerry 'til y' return from America. The line for County Cork is just ahead."

They scuttled over a low stone wall and made their ascent. Atop the hill, they spied squares of green pastures intermingled with dark patches of deserted and forsaken farms. On the far side, in a picturesque meadow with many shade trees, the two men observed people milling about, dressed in their finery and surrounded by colorful flowers.

"What is that about?" asked Devin.

McNevin's face grew hard as he explained. "I heard about this, but I thought with all that is going on, they would have cancelled it."

"Well, what *is* that down there?"

"'Tis the Ballymakeery Flower and Cattle Show."

"How are flowers grown in this weather?"

"They're grown in greenhouses."

McNevin could see that Devin was getting angry.

Pointing to a small parcel of land that had once been someone's home, Devin said, "Y' mean to tell me with all this going on. With tumbled-down houses not a stone's throw from here. With people being run off their farms. With the dead of their fellow countrymen clogging the highways—with all *that!*—these people can gather to celebrate pretty flowers and fat cattle? Is that what y' are telling me, Tom McNevin?"

"Sure, 'tis what I am telling y', Devin Mahoney. And I can see it in yer face. Y' want to run down there and clomp a few of those that be in attendance. Is that not right?"

"That is so."

"Before y' do, I want y' to know this. I've been to Cork and Dublin. I've been on the docks, seeing ships being loaded with good Irish produce and Irish wheat. Not to mention Irish cattle. 'Where's it going?' asked I. 'To England,' I was told. 'With people starving to death right here in Ireland?' ventured I. ''Tis none of yer affair. Now be off with y,' I was told.

"I, for one, am glad we happened upon that sorry spectacle down below. And 'tis a good thing I told y' about the food leaving Ireland. I hope it gets y' good and angry. Now, take that anger to America with y'. Store it deep within yerself and hold it dear. And when y' make yer wealth, y' come back and do something for those that need it!"

Devin's desire to punch someone in the face subsided a bit, but the anger remained.

The two men continued to stare at the offensive sight, pondering the insensitivity of man. In time, and in silence, they resumed their journey.

As they made their way eastward, the sun continued its advance to the western sea. As it slid beneath the horizon, the edges of the grey clouds turned a vibrant orange, then pink, and then back to grey.

The travelers came upon the town of Macroom about then. They passed through quickly to avoid drawing the attention of the constabulary. On the far side of Macroom, they came across a tumbled-down house with part of one wall still standing. "This is where we'll spend the night," said McNevin. " 'Tis close to that stream we just passed. We'll have water for our stirabout, and a little protection from the wind."

They stepped carefully over the fallen stones and made their way to the standing wall. At first they did not see the huddled figures, two of which were children.

"Will y' look at that," exclaimed Devin. " 'Tis a woman and two little ones."

The woman pulled the children close. In a faint, hoarse whisper, she pleaded, "Please, Your Lordship. We need shelter for this one night only. We'll be gone in the morning. Y' will never see us again."

Devin touched McNevin's arm, indicating that he would handle the situation. He took a few steps forward and knelt down on one knee in front of the woman. She shied away, hugging her children more tightly.

" 'Tis alright. We're friends. My name is Devin. That fellow standing over there is Tom. We have come here seeking shelter from the night, as you have."

The woman relaxed a little. "My name is Bridget O'Brien and these are my daughters. We were on our way to Dromagh to be with my sister."

Devin said, "Would y' and yer two pretty lasses care to join us in a bit of stirabout?"

The woman burst into tears. Devin, thinking he had done something wrong, stood and took a step back. He turned to Tom for guidance, but all he received was a shrug.

He stood there helpless, looking down at the woman as her shoulders heaved and her sobs reverberated in the night. Eventually, the sobbing subsided enough for Bridget O'Brien to say, "I beg your pardon, sir. 'Tis three whole days since any of us have tasted 'ere a morsel of food. We had not the strength to continue our journey. Sure, I'd come to thinking the journey alone would finish us."

Devin tenderly placed his hand on Bridget's shoulder. "Ye'll have food this night, ye will. Tom and I will attend to the fire and the stirabout. We'll be eating soon enough."

Devin tossed the matches to McNevin and said, "We can use the thatch poles for firewood. If y'll break up a few and start the fire, I'll retrace our steps to the stream and fill the kettle."

McNevin nodded and set about his work. Devin retrieved the pot from the canvas sack and started out. After two steps, he placed it on a square stone and took off his coat. He laid it over Bridget and her children as one would a blanket. "Here, this will warm y' till we get some food inside y'."

25

When he returned, he brought the kettle to Bridget and bade her to "sip gently."

"My children are as in need of water as I am. Let them drink first."

Devin held the pot for the girls and allowed them to drink their fill, then held it for their mother until her thirst had also been quenched. With that accomplished, Devin set about mixing the cornmeal.

Bridget and her children inched closer to the fire for warmth. The two girls were captivated as they watched the cornmeal being stirred. Their eyes followed the spoon as it made its slow circuit around the pot. Around and around, and every pass bringing the yellow ambrosia closer and closer to their watering mouths. They licked their lips in agonized anticipation. They gave furtive glances at their mother, as if asking how long before the bounty would be ready.

Devin noticed their interest and said, "In the twinkling of a fairy's eye, you'll be eating this grand food. In the meantime, please tell me your names."

The girls averted their gaze and looked down at their bare feet. Their mother spoke on their behalf. "With all we've been through since my husband's death, my daughters are a little shy. The older girl is Ellen. And the little one is named Margaret."

The girls raised their faces to Devin. They were not smiling; they were too hungry for that. But the fear had left their eyes. Tom was standing behind Devin and looked at the girls in their raggedy clothes. Seeing their worn faces broke his heart. Being a *seanchaí*, he decided he would tell them a story after they had eaten. It would keep their minds off their troubles. At least for a wee spell. It was all he had to offer.

When the stirabout was ready, Devin placed the kettle on the ground near Bridget and handed her the spoon. "Ye eat first."

She gave the spoon to her youngest daughter, Margaret. "Take but two mouthfuls and pass it on to your sister." In like manner, the spoon was passed among mother and daughters until they had eaten their fill. Devin and McNevin made quick work of what was left.

26

The heat of the fire reflected off the remaining wall, warming the five sojourners as they sat in silence, savoring the feeling of the meager meal resting in their bellies.

At length, Devin addressed Bridget. "I'm going to America and I want to tell the people there what is happening here. If you do not mind me asking, I'd like to know how y' came to find yerself in such a dire situation. There is much going on, and I am beginning to think the famine is only part of the problem."

Bridget adjusted herself to get comfortable; Margaret and Ellen were hugging her close, trying to keep warm under the heavy coat. She looked across the fire at Devin and, for the first time in a long time, she smiled. "Ye two have been the saving of us. If not for yer kindness, we almost certainly would have died along the road. Yes, I will tell y' my story and y' will tell it to others. Maybe it will help to bring an end to all this suffering."

Devin leaned forward, his eyes ablaze in the firelight.

Bridget began her story.

"When the blight first came and our crop failed, my husband, James, did not dally. He took himself right up to Cork and found a job as a cooper's assistant. He was always brilliant when he worked with wood, and he was a grand barrel maker, he was. It was a two-hour walk to Cork and another two hours back, but we ate every day. As the famine deepened, the demand for barrels became less and less. Finally, the cooper had to let James go."

At the thought of her husband, Bridget hugged her daughters all the closer.

"James still went out every day and most days came home with something to eat, a few morsels. Some days not. He would not speak about where or how he had acquired the food. And he seldom ate with us. He always said he had eaten his share on the way home. That was not like him, but I did not question it.

"We were all getting thinner and thinner, but James more so. Then one day he was too weak to go out. He lay in bed as a fever crept over him. I thought a little tea might soothe him, but we had none. It hurt me to do so, but I took my mother's brooch, which she had given me on my wedding day, into town to see if I could exchange it for a tin of tea. Soon after I left, James sent Ellen to

27

fetch the parish priest. By the time I returned, the priest had already given James the holy sacrament of Extreme Unction.

"As my sweet James lay a dyin', he confessed that he had not been eating. All the food he had come by, he gave to us."

Devin said, "I am so sorry." McNevin wiped away a tear.

"A good man was he," lamented Bridget. "And he'll be feeling hunger no more."

McNevin threw a thatch pole onto the fire, sending a whirlwind of angry cinders into a cold November night.

Bridget waited for the glowing maelstrom to subside before continuing with her story. "We buried him the next day. There was no money for a coffin, and I cried buckets of salt-tears as he was placed into the ground." She grew quiet and stared into the fire, reliving her husband's funeral. At length, she whispered to herself, "I don't think James minded not having a coffin."

"What did y' do then?" asked Devin.

"If I had not the little ones to look after, I would have gladly followed James into the grave. Instead, I sold everything we still owned so as to bring sustenance into our house. When I had nothing left to sell, in desperation I went to our priest and asked what was I to do. He told me of a relief office north of Cork where I could get an allotment of food. It was a two-hour walk each way, but that did not matter. The three of us set out early the next morning.

"When, at last, we located the office, the gentleman told me he was closing for the day and that we would have to come back on the morrow. It was a forlorn walk back to our home, it was. That night, two nights ago, we huddled by our fire, me telling the girls not to worry, the next day we would eat.

"Again we walked the two hours, but the office was closed. It being only middle morning, we waited until dark, hoping someone would come to open the place. But no one ever did. So we returned home." Bridgett heaved a sigh. "I don't think we'll find any help there. This morning, the girls and I set out for my sister's. She and I have not spoken in nearly three years, so I do not know what will be waiting for us when we get there."

Bridget grew silent. All was quiet. Even the wind had temporarily hushed its howling in muted admiration for a durable woman.

McNevin clapped his hands to get Margaret and Ellen's attention. "Have I ever told ye about the time I captured the king of the little people and forced him to turn over his pot o' gold? Of course not, we have just met. Well, listen, my colleens, and ye shall hear a tale such as ye have never heard before."

Margaret and Ellen, wide-eyed, leaned forward, not wanting to miss a word.

" 'Twas a dark night, the blackest of pitch nights as ever a night had been …"

4

The fire burned brightly throughout the night; McNevin had made sure of that. In the wee hours, with the sky greying and the stars beginning to fade into the greyness, the travelers, one by one, came out of their sleep.

Devin prepared the stirabout and everyone had, what was for them, a large breakfast. When it came time to go their separate ways, Bridget held out the overcoat to Devin. "I'll be thanking y' for its use," she said.

Devin made no move to accept the coat. "Y' keep it. 'Tis better to comfort three than one, Bridget, and I'll hear no more of it. Y' have the welfare of two souls as well as yourself to look after." Holding out the bag containing the cornmeal and cooking implements, he added, "Y' take this also, *a chroi*. Y' have the makings of at least a two-day hard walk afore y' set eyes on Dromagh. Sure enough, those girls' spirits will need lifting during such a journey and a full belly will go some way to doing that. Indeed, ye three will be needing to eat heartily if ye're to get there a'tall."

Bridget's eyes moistened; her voice quivered. "I be weak, sure enough, Devin Mahoney. 'Tis weak with emotion, I am, in the face of such kindness." She composed herself and spoke a bit more forcefully. "Aye!" she exclaimed, drawing her frail shoulders back. "For the sake of my girls, I'll accept the kindness of Mister McNevin and yerself, but I'll have y' know that I'll not be forgetting what y' have done for us. Yesterday had a mother's heart so low as being ready to give up and die in this place. Today finds me stronger of heart and knowing that all will be right. God surely would not have had our paths cross if He had not designs for us to live to a greater purpose."

She reached for the sack, but at the last moment, grabbed Devin's hand and kissed it, her warm tears falling in abundance like salty raindrops.

The men waited until Bridget and her daughters were safely on their way before resuming their journey.

It was not long before McNevin said, "Y' are indeed a generous man, Devin Mahoney. First y' share what little food y' have with me, and then with Bridget and the two little ones. Next y're giving away your fine, warm coat. Methinks there is a grand place awaiting y' when y' get to Heaven."

"Be silent. Was it not y' who told me this weather was balmy? Well, 'tis. While walking, I was working up a mighty sweat under that heavy coat. 'Tis better used as a blanket for Bridget and her little ones."

McNevin said nothing more.

The day warmed as their shadows grew short. In the late afternoon, as the shadows grew long again, McNevin said, " 'Twill be dark before long and this pleasant weather will take itself away with the sun. I don't suppose y' kept a match or two?"

Devin shook his head. "Bridget will find far more use for them than us, *a chara*."

"Just as I thought," said McNevin. "But it matters not. I know of a place up ahead where a weary traveler can rest his head for the night and perhaps partake of a wee bit of food to boot."

Devin asked no questions as he marched towards his future, leaving his past farther behind with every step.

As they drew near the town of Ballincollig, and with twilight gently descending from above, McNevin asked in a conversational manner, "Are y' familiar with Lord Beckham?"

Devin was cold, tired, and hungry. He answered with an indifferent grunt.

McNevin, who was not to be put off by a curt reply, continued, " 'Tis no reason y' should know him. Or even know *of* him. But he has a grand estate in Ballincollig."

" 'Tis delightful to know," said Devin rather sarcastically.

"I only mention that small fact because we'll soon be passing it by. As I've said, it's a grand estate … and very inviting."

Devin abruptly stopped in his tracks. "Y're up to no good, Tom McNevin, sure y' are. What are y' schemin' about?"

McNevin, likewise, ceased his forward motion. "I've been thinking. Why not avail ourselves of Lord Beckham's hospitality?

His grand estate is right up the road and I hear he's not been seen about lately."

"And how is it that you are in possession of such information? Are you a personal friend of His Lordship?"

"Not a'tall. Not a'tall. I never met the man. But when last in the vicinity, I still had a few bob in me trousers, so naturally I took me self off to the local pub. 'Twas while enjoying a welcomed pint that I overheard a most interesting conversation."

Darkness was rapidly approaching and Devin felt they should move on. "Can y' tell me about it as we walk? It's getting colder."

"I can, for sure I can."

Side by side, shoulder to shoulder, the two men resumed their trek down the age-old road. It was Devin who spoke first. "Before y' tell me of yer conversation, we should find shelter for the night. Perhaps there is a tumbled-down house soon up ahead."

McNevin's eyes sparkled as he said, "Are y' daft, man? I just told you we can be the guests of Lord Beckham this night."

"Y' said no such thing. Y' were telling me about your adventures in a pub."

McNevin rubbed his chin in puzzlement before slapping his forehead. "Y' be right. Now listen to me and do not interrupt and I'll tell y' something to warm the cockles of yer heart.

"In this pub, I was. The two gents at the next table were talking about one of their neighbors. Says the first gent: 'He's getting on in years. 'Tis a good thing it is that his lordship has not visited recently. The grounds are unkempt and poachers have free reign.' The second gent nods his head and adds to the conversation: 'Poor Paddy's hearing is almost gone and his eyesight is not much better.'

"Now, hearin' that, I become as interested in ol' Paddy as if I'd known him all me life," said McNevin with a wicked smile.

In spite of himself, Devin found he was becoming engrossed in the story. It took his mind off his empty stomach and the coldness embracing his being.

McNevin went on with his tale. "It turned out that ol' Paddy is the groundskeeper for Lord Beckham's Ballincollig estate. He lives in the gatehouse, alone, but he spends most of his time at the pub. 'Twas useful information indeed."

"Useful? Useful in what way?" asked Devin.

"Useful as in providing a roof over me head and a meal in me belly."

It was now full dark and the wind had picked up, bringing with it a chill from the north. There were no buildings—tumbled-down or otherwise—along that stretch of the road. Nowhere to get out of the wind.

Devin's teeth began to chatter, his body trembled from the cold. He could not understand why McNevin was not doing the same.

A few minutes later, McNevin announced, "There 'tis! Up there ahead, on the right. Can y' make it out?"

The stones that made up the wall were limestone and readily reflected the light of the waning moon. Devin had no trouble making out the run of the wall.

"Let us walk by the gatehouse to see if there's anyone about or if a light shines from within," suggested McNevin.

Devin wrapped his arms about himself trying to get warm. It helped, but not much. "Now y' tell me an' tell me straight, Tom, what it is that y' have in mind. I think y' intend to go onto the estate."

"Of course I intend to go onto *His High and Mighty's* estate. I've done it afore when I was here last. And then it was never half as cold as 'tis tonight. There be a coach house with hay that we can sleep on, with horse blankets that we can sleep under. There are stores of oats for making porridge. We'll be having hot food in our bellies this night, sure as me name is Tom McNevin."

Devin was aghast. "That'd be trespassing *and* stealing! If caught, we'd sure to be arrested."

"Aye, *a chara*, and we could also freeze to death this night. Now you listen to me, Devin Mahoney. Y' gave away a fine coat and all yer food. If y' did not share what little y' had with me, I might not have made it this far. I am sure that Bridget and her daughters find themselves in far more comfortable circumstances this night than y' because of yer generosity. So I'll hear no more from y'. Now come with me. We'll avail ourselves of his Lordship's hospitality, sure it would be unsociable of us not to … downright unfriendly I'd say."

Devin was too cold to take the argument any further. "Y' be a bad influence entirely, Tom, but lead on. Let's see if Paddy is home or not."

The estate was a large one. The front wall ran almost a mile in length, with the gatehouse situated dead center. The big iron gates were closed, and fastened about the iron bars where the two sides met were a lock and chain. No light showed from within the gatehouse. It looked as though Paddy was at the pub.

"What now?" asked Devin. "The gate is locked and those walls are eight feet high."

McNevin touched his nose with his index finger and winked. "Follow ol' Tommy-Boy; he knows a way in."

They made their way down the road to where the wall turned and ran along the eastern border of the estate. "There's an old tree up ahead with low-hanging branches, accommodating they are. 'Twill be no bother to climb over," said McNevin.

Once over the wall, McNevin walked by the coach house without slowing down. But Devin stopped. "This looks to be a coach house," he said.

McNevin called over his shoulder as he kept walking. "Aye, lad, that it is. But we'll not be taking advantage of its accommodations this night."

After a few fast steps, Devin caught up. "What are y' up to, Tom? I thought y' said we'd be spending the night in a nice warm coach house."

"I did, but 'twas an untruth I told. If y' knew I intended to stay in the manor house, y' never would have come over the wall with me. Is that not so?"

"Sure enough y' be right about that. I'll not break into another man's house. Not even to get out of the cold and feed my belly."

McNevin chuckled. "Y'll not be breaking in. Half the windows are unlocked. At least they were the last time I was here, and I don't think Paddy's improved in his job since then. We'll go in through a window, start a fire in the stove, make some stirabout, and enjoy His Lordship's hospitality for a few hours."

Devin gave in. His skin was turning a nice shade of blue and if his stomach growled any louder, Paddy would be able to hear it all the way down at the pub. Sitting next to a warm stove had more allure than lying on the damp, cold ground and shivering throughout the night.

They found an unlocked window on the side of the house, next to the kitchen, and entered.

"There should be a supply of wood by the stove. We'll have a fire going in no time," assured McNevin.

"I only hope that Paddy's not around. I would hate to miss my boat to America on account of being in jail," said a nervous Devin.

The ambient light was sufficient to find what was needed to get a fire going. With the stirabout starting to bubble, the two men sat close to the stove and enjoyed its warmth.

Devin had been astonished to see a pump inside the house. He had heard of such a thing but had never seen one. He asked McNevin if he had ever seen an inside pump before.

"To be sure I have. 'Twas the last time I was here. And that's not all. There be a loo right inside this very house!"

"Go on with y'. Pull my other leg, Tom. I do not believe y'."

"First let's have our stirabout, then I'll show y'. 'Tis a wondrous sight indeed."

Afterwards, they cleaned the kettle and the spoons, and put them away so there would be no sign that anyone had been there. If Paddy looked closely enough, he might notice that the stack of wood was down by a few pieces. But there was nothing they could do about that.

They then went up the stairs to see the wonder of wonders. As they walked down the long hallway, Devin remarked that McNevin must have given the house a thorough inspection on his last visit.

"That I did. I thought it best to know the lay of the land. Did y' know that the loo has its own silver candlesticks? Two of 'em?"

"How would I know that?"

"My point is that when we get there, I'm going to light a candle so that you can have a proper look-see."

"Y' can't do that! The light will be seen from outside."

"We're in the middle of an estate of God knows how many acres. And we're surrounded by an eight-foot-high stone wall. Don't y' worry, no one will see a light. Now come on, y' must see this marvel in all its splendor."

When they reached the dark brown oaken door at the end of the hall, Devin asked what he thought was a sensible question. "Did y' think to bring matches up from the kitchen?"

McNevin's eyes crinkled in a smile. "Y' be worrying too much. Stay here while I go in and light a candle." A moment later, he was back. With a flourish and a pronounced bow, he stepped aside so Devin could enter the holy of holies … the inner sanctum, so to speak. He was duly impressed and, after a short inspection, asked, "Where does the … um … *y' know* … go?"

"Of that, I am not sure. I believe there is piping that carries it out of the house."

"Do y' think they have anything as grand as this in America?"

"They must. Everything in America is grand."

Devin extinguished the candle and closed the door. "Now let us go downstairs and lie down next to the stove for a few hours. In the morning, we must be out of here while it is still dark."

McNevin hesitated. In the semidarkness, his face was hard to read, but his unsteady voice betrayed him. "I have something to confess to y'. I did not bring y' to this house only to get y' warm and to steal a few oats. I brought y' here to make a proper thief of y'."

McNevin hurried on before Devin could say a word. "Let me finish before y' say anything."

Devin waited.

"Y're half my age and I've seen a bit more than y' have. Y' are going to America; are y' planning on wearing those rags? Have y' given thought as to how y'll live until yer boat leaves? And surely the captain won't let y' onboard until just before sailing time. I be not a thief by nature, but y' need clothes and a few bob to hold y' over. And landing in America with a few pounds in yer pocket would do y' no harm." McNevin said all that in a rush as though he'd been holding it in and wanted to get it out as fast as possible.

Devin decided it was time to speak out. "Y' are right about the clothes. I would like to land in America not looking like this. And I think a coat would be of use on the voyage over. Are y' suggesting that we rob His Lordship?"

"As I've said, I was here before and looked around, but took nothing. Things are different now. I have no shoes and y' have no coat. The man who owns this house hasn't been here in two years and he has a wardrobe brimming with clothes. I say we help ourselves out of necessity, not out of greed. Most likely His

Lordship does not know what he owns. He'll never miss the few articles of clothing we appropriate."

Out on the road, less than a mile away, Paddy was making his way home with his best friend, Clancy, whom he had invited to the gatehouse for a little nip before saying goodnight to one another.

Devin had been convinced. "Let us see what His Lordship has in the way of clothing. Then let us be rid of this place. With warm coats, we can sleep by the roadside in some comfort. We'll bring matches and build us a fire."

McNevin slapped him on the back. "Now yer talkin', lad. Follow me." They entered an adjacent room and McNevin lit a candle. Pointing toward the wardrobe, he said, "Help yerself. And don't take just a coat. Y' could use trousers, a shirt, and, of course, an overcoat. A new pair of shoes would not hurt yer appearance neither."

As Devin made his selections, McNevin stood by a desk. "There is a humidor here with very nice cigars in it. Would y' care to partake of one?" he asked.

"Don't be daft, man. I do need the clothes, but I do not *need* a cigar."

After Devin was properly dressed, McNevin selected a few items of clothing for himself. They bundled up their old clothes and started down the stairs just as, unbeknown to them, Paddy and Clancy were approaching the front gate.

"Do y' smell that?" the groundskeeper asked of his friend. "It smells like a wood fire coming from the manor house. It cannot be His Lordship; he surely would have had me open the house and have everything ready for him."

"Yes, I smell it. What do y' think it is?"

"I do not know. But I'm getting me shotgun and a lantern and I'm gonna find out. Y' take yer self off and bring back the constable. It's probably a brazen poacher cooking his thieved rabbit right here on the estate. They think they know ol' Paddy so well. I'll show 'em. Now make haste and be off with y'."

Devin and McNevin were breaking up the fire in the stove and making sure everything looked as it did before they came in. They were just about to go out the same window they used for their ingress when they saw a lantern coming down the path.

McNevin whispered to Devin to drop his old clothes. " 'Tis no good. They're gonna know we were here. We're gonna need our hands free if we are to get out of this." They hid in the shadows of the room and awaited further developments.

Paddy went straight for the kitchen door and unlocked it with his key. Holding the lantern high, he looked about. Everything seemed in place. Everything, that is, but the stove. It was warm to the touch. He placed the lantern on the table and put the stock of his double-barrel shotgun against his shoulder, the business end pointing directly in front of him, his finger on the triggers.

With the bravery of many pints of Guinness, Paddy shouted, "If y're still here, come out. 'Tis better than being shot like a lowly cur."

No one answered. No one came out.

Even though fueled with Guinness, Paddy was no fool. He was not about to go through a dark house by himself, looking for an intruder, shotgun or no shotgun. He would wait for the constable.

McNevin moved silently toward the window and quietly raised it. He motioned for Devin to follow. They landed on the ground outside without making a sound. McNevin whispered, "Let's make for where we came in and we'll be up the tree and over the wall before Paddy knows we're gone."

Devin took off running and promptly ran into the constable and Clancy, knocking them both to the ground. McNevin yelled, "Don't stop. Keep going!"

When they reached the tree, they could hear the yelling and commotion back at the house. It sounded like Paddy, Clancy, and the constable were marshaling their forces for a pursuit.

Devin was reaching for a branch when McNevin grabbed his arm. "Wait, Devin Mahoney. If we both were to go over that wall, they'll have us on the road before we've covered a furlong. One of us has to stay here and lead them on a merry chase through the grounds, and I've decided it shall be me."

Devin, horrified at the thought of leaving his friend behind, said, "I'm not deserting y'. We both go or we both stay."

"Now y' listen to me, Devin Mahoney. It was always my intent to get myself arrested for the winter. I'll just be doing it a few weeks earlier, that's all. In jail, I'm fed twice a day. I'll not be feeling the cold, and I don't have to work like a donkey, like I would in a workhouse. Y're on your way to America, but y' will never get there if y' are arrested this night. Go on with ya! Go become an American millionaire and do ol' Tom McNevin proud!"

Devin could hear their pursuers beating the bushes, searching for the intruders. They were close by. Despite the cold, his brow was damp. His eyes darted left and right, expecting Paddy or the other men to leap out of the darkness at any moment. He was truly fearful, but did not want to leave his friend behind.

McNevin spoke forcefully. " 'Tis what I want. Y' go! But first take this." McNevin reached into a pocket of the coat he was wearing and pulled out a stack of folded pound notes. With a wide grin, he said, " 'Twas in the box with the cigars. I was going to give it to y' when we split up. It will keep y' going until the boat leaves, with a little left over for when y' get to America. Now be gone with y'. I've got a game of hide n' seek to play with Paddy and his friends."

Devin accepted the money, shook McNevin's hand, and with a heartfelt smile of thanks, he was up the tree and over the wall. He landed softly on his feet and continued his journey, one step at a time, along the ancient road that would eventually lead him to The Promised Land.

5

A dense fog lay thick upon the ancient city. Its buildings shrouded in a white mist, its citizens appearing as ethereal forms through the diaphanous vapor. Into this all-pervading whiteness stepped Devin Mahoney. The sun had not yet arisen from the Celtic Sea, yet a few shopkeepers were sweeping the footpath in front of their shops. Others, just arriving for the day's work, were unlocking their doors. Cork City was preparing for a new day.

The shop owners were not the only ones on the street that morning. Devin passed many a doorway with people huddled together against the cold. Their clothes were old and tattered, very few wore a coat. Most of them averted their eyes as he passed by. At first this perplexed him, but he soon realized that he was dressed as a gentleman, hence he was perceived as such. The poor wretches had troubles enough. Surely, they did not need to anger a man of his obvious social standing by making eye contact.

Devin's first order of business was to find his way to the harbor and speak to the master of the *Archimedes*. He stopped to ask a constable for directions. "At the second street go left. That will take y' to George Street. Turn left again and it will take y' right to the port."

"Would y' mind a passing stranger asking who are all these good people I see crowding these city streets on such a cold, damp morning?"

"Country folk sure enough, come looking for work or to be fed at the soup kitchens set up by the Quakers and Baptists. The blight is a terrible thing! May the Holy Mother take the harm of the years away from them!"

"Amen to that, *a chara*," said Devin.

On George Street, the number of destitute people only increased. Devin was feeling a little guilty being dressed in clean, warm clothes and having a pocketful of pound notes nestled next to his bosom while those he passed shivered in their rags.

40

By the time he found the quay, the sun—a feeble white orb trying to assert itself through the dense fog—hung low in the eastern sky.

As luck would have it, only three ships were berthed on the wharf that day and Devin had no trouble locating the *Archimedes*, a square-rigged barque of one hundred and twenty-two feet.

He went straight up the gangway and at the top was met by a man sitting at a small table.

"What can I do for you, sir?"

Devin was momentarily taken aback. Never in his life had anyone addressed him as *sir*. However, he quickly recovered. "My name is Devin Mahoney. I believe Lord Feilding has arranged for my passage to America."

"Yes, sir. Let me check the book."

The man turned a few pages in a leather-bound accounts book lying open on the table. "Ah, here it is." He looked up at Devin. "Are you a friend of His Lordship's?"

"No, I am one of his tenants."

"If you don't mind me saying, you are not dressed as the others who will be making the voyage."

Afraid he might be denied passage if he could not prove he was a tenant of Lord Feilding, Devin said, "You must believe me. I've lived on his land all my life."

The man's demeanor changed. In a gruff voice, he said, "We sail in six days on the morning tide. Be here the afternoon before for your medical exam. Now be off with you."

Devin was puzzled by the man's abrupt change of attitude and stayed where he was.

"I said, be off with you. It's bad enough that I have to be cooped up with you Irish trash while at sea, but I'll be damned if I'll put up with it one moment longer than necessary."

Devin asked, "Are y' the captain?"

"I'm the first mate."

A glint came into Devin's eyes. The man had gotten his Irish up. He was obviously English and Devin had no use for the race. They had stolen his people's land. They were in the process of stealing their produce and beef and shipping it off to England, while thousands, if not tens of thousands, of Irish men, women, and children were dying for lack of food. He told the mate to stand up.

"I beg your pardon?" said the mate, unsure of what he'd just heard.

"I'd be obliged if y'd be standing afore me!"

"And why would I be doing that?"

"Because I'm not in the habit of hitting a man while he's sitting down."

Before the mate could respond, a large man came up through a hatch and approached the table. His hair and beard were grizzled, his lips, thick, his skin leathery and brown from years at sea. He said to Devin, "My name is Robert Hood. I am the master of this ship. I heard you say that it was your intention to hit my mate. Is there a problem?"

The mate started to say something, but Hood cut him off. "I'll hear from the gentleman himself."

"Your mate has put an insult on me and the people of Ireland. I was just about to show him what I thought of him."

Hood almost smiled, but caught himself. "You'll have to excuse Mister Marks. He's been on duty since last night. He must be tired. I was just about to relieve him."

Devin did not care how long the man had been on duty; he still wanted to have a go at him. Hood spoke to his mate. "You go below and get some food into you. And then get some sleep. I'll take over here."

"Yes sir," said the mate. As he made for the hatch, he gave Devin one last, nasty look.

Captain Hood sat in the vacated chair and asked, "Now. What can I do for you?"

Devin repeated what he had told the mate.

Hood checked the book. "Yes. You are booked for passage. We leave in six days, Sunday morning, on the tide. You must be here the afternoon of the day before for your doctor's examination. It's the law. And there'll be no lingering around the docks until sailing time. So I'll see you back here on Saturday afternoon."

Devin looked up at the mainmast and saw the Union Jack fluttering in the breeze. He thought he'd be sailing on an American ship. But the die was cast; he would be taken to America by the English.

Before he turned to go, Devin asked, "How long will it take us to get to America?"

"With a fair wind, we should come upon the Gulf of St. Lawrence in forty-five days or so. Then it's only a few days' sail up the river to Québec City."

Devin was appalled. "I thought Lord Feilding paid for passage to America!"

Hood set him straight. "And where do you think Canada is located?"

"But I want to go to America … I mean, the United States."

"Then you can do what many a man before you has done. You can walk south and cross the border into the United States. I'm told it's no more than a hundred or a hundred and fifty miles. For a strapping young fellow like yourself, that should be no problem."

The next five days went by quickly. Devin had found lodging with a woman who took in boarders. It was less expensive than staying at an inn. He was trying to save his pound notes for when he got to America, although he did buy himself a hat to keep his head warm. He also converted a few notes into shillings in order to have coins in his pocket as he walked the streets of Cork.

When he came across a particularly destitute person, he would press one of the coins into their hand and walk on, without saying a word.

It was a bittersweet time for Devin. He was anxious to get to America and make his fortune, but at the same time, he was sorry to be leaving the Auld Sod. His heart and his soul were embedded in the land. His ancestors had ruled Southern Ireland. And even though the Mahoneys had fallen in rank, they were still a proud and noble people.

For now, Devin was the last of the line, but not for long. When he became rich, he would return and start a dynasty. It would not be as of old, when they were kings. No, those days were gone. The new Mahoney dynasty would consist of men of property and of industry. He and his descendants would produce food to help a starving nation. His children and their children would be elected to parliament and fight for Irish independence, and Ireland would be a free state one day. Devin Mahoney's progeny would see to that!

On the appointed day, at the appointed hour, Devin Mahoney walked up the gangway of the *Archimedes* where he was met by a common seaman. "Are you a passenger for America?"

"Aye. It's off to America, I am," said Devin with an enthusiastic grin.

Pointing to a group of people lined up on the starboard deck, the sailor said, "Go over there, and the doctor will examine you."

Devin did as he was told and got in line. There were forty to fifty people in front of him. The children were squirming about, and every once in a while, one would make a break for freedom, only to be pulled back into line by his or her parent.

The queue moved forward rapidly. As Devin neared the front, he saw the reason why. The "medical exam" consisted of nothing more than the doctor asking the person their name and if they felt sick. If one *were* feeling ill, he or she would not admit to it. To be judged so, one would be denied passage to The New World. It was the law. A law that was easy to circumvent. It had been instituted at the behest of the Canadian government, but the entire process was a sham. The authorities wanted as many people as possible to leave the isle, hence the perfunctory medical exam.

Once an emigrant answered in the negative, the doctor would tap that person on the shoulder and say to the assistant standing next to him, "This one passes." A notation was then made into a ledger book and the next person in line stepped up to be "examined."

After Devin had been deemed fit, he was told to go to the bow and join his fellow passengers.

When the doctor had examined the last person, he turned to his assistant and held out his hand without saying a word. The man closed the book and gave it to the doctor, also without saying a word.

A few minutes later, the Captain and his first mate walked out on deck.

"All fit, as usual?" asked Hood.

"Not a sick person among the whole lot."

"Thank you, Doctor."

After wishing the Captain a bon voyage, the doctor and his assistant disembarked the good ship *Archimedes*, only to be swallowed up by the swarm of people milling about on the wharf below.

Hood stepped up onto the forecastle and looked down on the group of emigrants standing on the foredeck. He held up his right hand for quiet. While waiting for complete silence, he stood with his arms folded across his chest, neither smiling nor frowning. Soon, the only sound heard was the screeching of seagulls as they flew overhead, awaiting the dumping of the ship's garbage.

Hood unfolded his arms and began to speak. "First of all, I'd like to welcome you all onto the *Archimedes*. My name is Robert Hood. I am the captain of this fine vessel and I take great pride in her. Anyone caught intentionally doing damage to her will be put in chains. You men and boys, if you feel inclined to carve your names on something, wait until we get to America. There you'll find plenty of trees on which to do your woodworking.

"Every adult will be given seven pounds of food per week and two quarts of water per day, the children a little less. Your food allotment will consist of oatmeal and biscuits. Once a week, on Sundays, everyone will be given a portion of meat until it runs out.

"There will be two fires on deck where you will do your cooking. They will be attended to by my sailors. Each family will have a few minutes at the fire. Remember, there will be others waiting their turn, so do not dally.

"Space is tight. Each passenger is allowed one small bag of personal items. Anything more than that will be thrown overboard. Do I make myself clear?"

Most of the emigrants nodded their heads. Captain Hood went on with his speech. "Our tally says there are two hundred and fifty-three of you. That presents a slight problem. There are only two hundred bunks down below, so some of you will have to double up. Single men will get first choice.

"You may or may not have heard that the crossing would take three weeks. Well, I'm here to tell you that is not true. However, we should sight the banks of Newfoundland within forty-five days.

"One last thing. You will be allowed on deck only while you are cooking your meals. I cannot have you interfering with my sailors."

45

He did not ask if anyone had any questions.

"Mister Marks, take over."

Marks was now in charge.

"There will be no leaving the ship. It is now one bell—four o'clock to you. At four bells—six o'clock—you'll come up to cook your dinner in an orderly fashion. This will be the one and only time you'll all be allowed on deck at the same time. Once we are at sea, you'll come up in lots of fifty."

The space the emigrants would call home for the next forty-five days was one level below the main deck. Bunks ran down both sides, up against the hull. Tables occupied the middle ground. The bunks were narrow and tiered four-high. Thirty inches separated each bunk. The top bunk was only twenty-six inches from the ceiling. Despite Devin's having lived all his life in a small cabin, shared with five other people, he was not prepared for the extremely confined conditions he encountered. If not for the tables, he would have thought he was on a slave ship.

Devin chose a top bunk hoping it would afford him a modicum of privacy. The bunks had not the luxury of a mattress; the wooden slats were instead covered by a thin layer of straw. He left his hat on the bunk and climbed back down onto the deck.

The children were having a wonderful time exploring their new home and making friends. But the dimly lit space, with its restricting and creaking walls, filled the adults with foreboding.

A sailor stuck his head through the overhead hatch and yelled down, "All those who want to come up on deck at this time may do so."

As they emerged into the night air, the emigrants were ordered to stay away from the afterdeck. They were given one wooden bowl and one wooden spoon each. "Hold on to these. They'll be yours throughout the voyage. If you lose them, they will not be replaced."

Devin was glad to be back out in the fresh air. It was stifling down below. Two fires were burning, one on the starboard side of the forecastle and one on the port side, each enclosed in a wood case lined with bricks. An assortment of metal pots stood ready for the passengers' use. Sailors passed out rations of oatmeal, along with one biscuit per person, including the children.

After everyone had eaten, the emigrants were told to go below. It was then that a few of the women leaned into their husbands and whispered a few words. The men nodded, and one of them asked the third mate, "Excuse me, sir, but where are we to ... I mean, where ... y' know ... relieve ourselves?"

"There are buckets down below. Use those, and when they're full, you men take turns bringing them up here and heaving what's in 'em overboard. Be careful. First know the direction of the wind. If you throw the contents into the wind, you'll be very sorry and so will anyone that has to stand next to you."

One woman jabbed her husband in the ribs and said something in a low voice. He, in turn, asked a pertinent question. "Y' mean to say we'll have no privacy?"

The third mate knew the question was going to be asked and had a ready answer. "On your deck, you'll find a section of old sail abaft. It's crammed into the port corner. You can hang that from the beams and use it as a curtain. There are nails already in place for that purpose."

That first night, as Devin lay on his bunk with the ceiling just inches from his face, he thought, *So this is what it'll be like, lying in my coffin.*

Regrettably, the ship that was to take him to America—and many more like it—would come to be known as coffin ships ... and not because of the tight spaces between the bunks.

6

"Cast off!" came the cry from the afterdeck. The white sails of the foremast fluttered in the light wind before filling with air. The bow of the great ship slowly pulled away from the wharf as Captain Hood gave the order for the mizzen to be raised. The mainsail remained furled on the yardarm. The tide and the billowing sails carried the *Archimedes* eastward on the River Lee, eastward into the rising sun. Silence reigned below decks. The emigrants seemed to be holding their collective breath. There was no turning back; they were off to a new life in a new land.

The ship glided into the large expanse of water known as Loch Machain, where she could stretch her wings. Tacking to the southeast, she made her way to Passage West and once again entered the confines of the River Lee. Then it was due south and around the tip of Great Island. At Roches Point, with the Celtic Sea dead ahead, Hood ordered the mainsail raised and allowed the first of the passengers up on deck to prepare their morning meal.

People lined up with their bowls and spoons. The first fifty in line were permitted up onto the deck and into the sunshine. The rest would have to wait.

Devin did not mind. He thought it a good opportunity to get to know some of his fellow passengers. He made his way over to three men gathered around the nearest table and introduced himself.

"Hullo. My name is Devin Mahoney from County Kerry."

The tallest of the three, as tall as Devin at six feet, two inches, held out his hand. "I'm James Farrell." He nodded towards the man to his immediate right. "This is Timothy Dunne and the gent next to him is Patrick Burke."

Farrell had a wide, kind face with a thatch of sandy-colored hair draping to his shoulders. Dunne was stout, but not fat, his hair thinning and red in color, his smile, inviting. The third man, Burke, stood almost as tall as Devin but lost out by an inch or two. His hair, or what was left of it, formed a grey fringe at the sides and back of

48

his head. He was the oldest of the lot, nearing sixty years of age. The other two were in their mid-thirties.

Burke said, "We three are from Dromahane. Our landlord gave us the option of going to America or remaining in Ireland, but we wouldn't be on his land if we stayed, said he."

"Ah sure," said Dunne, " 'twas either to be on this boat or to be living in a scalpeen under a bridge. And me with a wife and three little ones to look after."

"My wife and I have two fine boys, twins they are," chimed in Farrell.

Devin looked at Burke as though asking, *And yer family?* "My missus died last Christmastime from weakness brought on by the famine … and we never did have any children."

"What about y', Mister Mahoney?" asked Farrell.

"My family is all gone, save for my sister," answered Devin. "But I'd like to meet yer families, Mister Farrell and Mister Dunne."

"It's to be a long voyage, Mister Mahoney, and we'll be at close quarters for most of it. Why not call each other by our Christian names?" offered Farrell.

Farrell went on: "The older children are sitting around that last table in the back. My boys are there, as are Timothy's three darling children. My wife is feeling a little sickly, she's in her bunk. Timothy, where is yer wife?"

"She's two tables over. That one with all the women around it. They've been over there gabbing since we set sail." Farrell casually nudged Burke and, with a roguish glint in his eye, proclaimed, "Those that gossip with ye will gossip of ye."

"Aye, sure enough!" said Burke. "A silent mouth is sweet to hear."

Dunne said, "We'll all sit together while we eat, and y' must join us, Devin. Y'll get to know us and our families then."

"I'd be honored to eat with ye, but right now, I've a thirst on me that would shake the Devil. Would any of ye know where I could come by some water?"

"Water, is it?" said Burke, "And ye call yerself an Irishman!"

"Take no mind of him," said Farrell, "or the journey, long as 'tis, will seem longer still. But as to water, we were told 'twas to be given out three times a day. Sailors will bring it down to us in buckets and ladle it out into our bowls. My wife has been asking for a sip of water for hours now. I went up on deck to fetch a bowlful but was informed I would have to wait until it was brought below, there would be no exceptions."

The first of the first fifty passengers started coming back down through the hatch, holding onto the ladder with one hand and their bowls of porridge with the other. People rushed to take their place up above. Devin stayed where he was. He wanted to be in the last group going topside in the hope he might be allowed a few extra minutes in the sunshine if there was no one else waiting to come up.

After everyone had eaten, two sailors, each holding a bucket of water, came down the ladder and instructed the emigrants to line up and have their bowls ready. Farrell rushed to his bunk, grabbed his and his wife's bowls, and got in line near the front. At first, the sailor refused to fill the second bowl, but when Farrell explained that his wife was too sick to stand in line, he relented and begrudgingly ladled out the water.

For the afternoon meal, Devin was again among the last group of emigrants up on deck. He was hungry but did not approach either of the fires; too many people were jostling to get their pots over the flames. He would wait his turn. To starboard lay Dursey Sound and the rolling green hills of Dursey Island. The last bit of Irish land— the last bit of any land—that he and his shipmates would see for many a day. It was with a sigh and a heavy heart that he turned his back on his beloved emerald isle and looked out to the open sea where the setting sun had set the western sky aflame.

Lines of white birds, flying in V-shaped formations, swooped in low over the ship on their way home after a day foraging the sea's bounty. Devin marveled at the sight and thought what a beautiful world God had created.

'Tis men who have made it ugly.

As though to prove his point, the first mate, Marks, came up and stood next to him. "I see you made it onto our ship, *paddy*."

"My name is not Paddy."

"You're all potato-eating paddies to me."

Devin gave no voice to his anger. *If I start a fight with the blaggard, I'll be put in chains and not see the light of day until we land in America.*

"Y' right. There's no denying that we Irish like our potatoes."

Before Marks could respond, Devin left the first mate where he was standing and went to one of the fires to prepare his stirabout. Marks was sorely tempted to give chase and continue his needling but remembered the Captain's admonishment not to unduly antagonize the emigrants.

With his cooked porridge and a biscuit, Devin went below and sat down at a table with his new-found friends. "Hullo, Devin," greeted Farrell. "I'd like y' to meet my two sons." Farrell's boys were twelve years of age. Devin had been told they were twins, but they were not identical. One boy was a little taller and had dark hair. The other's was light, neither ginger nor blonde, but a combination of both. Slapping the shoulder of the dark-haired boy sitting next to him, Farrell said, "This is Eamon and that other handsome lad sitting across from me is Emmet."

"And yer wife, James, is she still feeling poorly?"

"That she is. At first I thought it to be seasickness. But now she has a slight fever. I got her to eat a biscuit, but that was all. It's water she's wanting. Perhaps the fever will break tonight, and she'll be sitting here with us in the morning, sure enough."

Dunne sat on the other side of Farrell with his wife, Johanna, and their three children. The oldest daughter, Cara, fourteen years of age, smiled demurely as she ate her porridge. Their son, Matthew, age eleven, was absorbed in a quiet conversation with Emmet Farrell. Hannah, a cute little lass of seven, sat next to her mother and daintily broke off pieces from a biscuit before mixing them in with her porridge. Burke sat at the end of the table, talking with a man who sat opposite him.

The next few days were more of the same. The monotony was setting in early. Twice a day the emigrants were called topside to cook their meals and then driven back down below after only a short time in the sunshine and fresh air. Three times a day, sailors would arrive with the water ration—two ladlesful per adult, one per child.

Farrell's wife's condition worsened.

On their fourth day at sea, Devin stood at the rail, looking out at the grey-green ocean while waiting for a space to open up at one of the fires. It was a fine morning; the ship rode the waves with the never-ending, up-and-down rolling motion he had become

51

accustomed to, and he was content. Soon he would be in America. Soon he would be a rich man. Soon he would return to Ireland. But he would travel as a gentleman with first-class accommodations. Not as part of a herd of human cattle.

Farrell came and stood next to him but said nothing. He stared at the rolling waves as though mesmerized. At length, he hung his head and beat his closed fists on the oak railing.

"What troubles y', Jamie?" asked Devin.

"My wife, my beautiful Sarah, has only gotten worse. She cannot eat. She has chills and spends her days in great agony. And now, this morning, she has a dark red rash creeping across her skin. I just spoke with the first mate. I asked him if there was a doctor among the crew or at least someone with medical knowledge. 'No, there is not,' was his answer. He did not ask what need I had of a doctor. I'm getting the feeling that we are no more than cargo to the master of this ship and his crew."

Devin did not tell Farrell what he was thinking; it was too dreadful to even contemplate.

Back down below, Devin ate silently, not contributing to the conversation of his tablemates. He was worried. He replayed in his mind what Farrell had said. *"She cannot eat. She has chills and spends her days in great agony. And now, this morning, she has a dark red rash creeping across her skin."* He came out of his thoughts and looked across the table at little Hannah Dunne. The girl was beautiful. Her blonde hair and sky-blue eyes signified she had a wee bit of Danish blood coursing through her veins. She had been staring at Devin but averted her eyes when he looked up at her.

"Hullo, Hannah. My name is Devin, in case y' have forgotten."

The girl's eyes were focused on her bowl of half-eaten stirabout. She raised her head slightly; from under incredibly long eyelashes, she peeked out at Devin. "I remember yer name, sir."

"Hannah is a beautiful name. My sister is named Hannah. I believe it's a name saved for only the prettiest of girls."

Hannah's translucent, milk-white cheeks turned a bright pink as she smiled from ear to ear. Devin had just made a friend.

"Where's yer family?" enquired Devin.

Hannah pointed to her right. "At that table down there."

"Why aren't y' with them?"

"Sometimes I need to be alone."

"I'm sorry if I'm intruding," said Devin.

"No! That's not it, Mister Mahoney. Sometimes my brother and sister tease me a little too much and I need to be away from them."

"Please call me Devin. It's more friendly."

The girl nodded and went back to eating her porridge.

Farrell walked up and sat down. He wore a worried look on his face. "I'm growing more concerned for my wife. She's getting worse."

"May I see her?" asked Devin.

"Why do y' ask? Do y' know medicine?"

"I will tell y' what I know after I have seen her."

Sarah Farrell's bunk was third from the bottom, hence Devin did not have to climb or crouch to look into her eyes and see the fear and pain residing there.

Farrell introduced him. "This is Devin Mahoney. He has come to pay his respects. He wanted to meet y' because I have spoken of y' so often."

Devin said, " 'Tis good to meet y' at last, Missus Farrell, sure enough. Please do not talk. I can see that you are sickly. I have come only to pay my respects, as Jamie has said. I'm sure y'll be up and about in no time. I'll now leave y' to rest."

Devin had confirmed his blackest thoughts and now he needed to speak with Farrell, alone. He began hesitantly. "I hope I'm wrong, but it looks like your wife has typhus."

Farrell's eyes widened. Defiantly, he asked, "And how would y' be knowing that?"

Devin met Farrell's gaze. "My father and my brothers all died from it. They had the fever, the dark red rash, the pain, and the loss of appetite. If I'm not mistaken, she'll next be out of her head, not thinking right. I pray that I'm wrong, but I've seen it up close, too many's the time."

Farrell's legs went weak. The room crowded in around him. He needed to think. He sat down on the closest bench with his back to the table and stared straight ahead, seeing nothing. All he could think of was Sarah on their wedding day and how beautiful she looked: her laughing eyes, the flowers in her hair. After a few moments, he cried out, "I must see the Captain!" and ran for the ladder.

If it was typhus, then it would spread like it had in the workhouse. Devin looked about at his fellow emigrants, all of them eagerly anticipating their new lives in America, and wondered how many would survive to live those lives.

Farrell returned. "The Captain said no matter what is wrong with my wife, there is nothing to be done about it. He said I was not to alarm the other passengers, to keep my suspicions to myself. When I asked if I could have extra water for Sarah, he informed me that there was only enough to get us to Canada and not a drop to spare. If he were to dole out water every time someone took sick, we would run out of it long before we reached land."

Devin rested his hand on Farrell's shoulder. "Sarah can have half my water ration."

"God bless y', Devin Mahoney. The earth has men like you all too few."

What Devin had feared soon came to pass. The cries and the moans of those with typhus filled the confined space of the lower deck. Farrell spent most of his time attending to his wife, mopping her brow and meting out what water he had saved from his allotment and what Devin had given him.

The first to die, however, was not Missus Farrell. An older woman who had been traveling alone was the first to go. She went fast, only a few days after contracting the disease.

Mister Marks came down and was about to ask for two volunteers to carry the body topside. But when he noticed Devin, he said, "*You* ... and one other man. Bring her up." Dunne volunteered. The rest of the emigrants were told to stay where they were.

Sunlight reflected off the water, the wind was light. The sea rolled under the ship, gently lifting her to the top of a wave, and just as gently depositing her back down in the trough of the following wave.

The woman's body lay on a small remnant of sail. A sailor placed a few pieces of pig-iron at her feet so the corpse would sink, then wrapped her in the canvas and bound the inert form with rope.

Marks had been overseeing the process and did not notice that Devin and Dunne had not gone back down below. When he saw them, he ordered them to clear the deck. Dunne started for the hatch, but Devin stayed where he was. The woman had no kin onboard and Devin had decided to stand in for the last family she had known—her fellow emigrants—and said as much to Marks.

Marks shoved Devin to get him moving. Devin did not budge. Marks gave him a second, harder shove, pushing him a few steps back. Devin balled up his fists and planted his feet wide apart. If Marks touched him again, he was prepared to lay him down.

The Captain called out. "That will be enough, Mister Marks. The gentleman is right. The woman should have someone at her funeral besides us old Jack Tars."

He gave the order to lift the corpse to the railing above the gunwhale, then asked Devin, "Have you any words you would like to speak?"

"I did not know her. I don't even know her name, but I would like to say I'm sorry that she will never make it to America. 'Tis a sad thing, it is."

Captain Hood nodded towards the two men holding the corpse. They heaved it over the railing and into the green-grey Atlantic where it bobbed on the surface for a moment before sinking, feet first, to its final resting place.

Two days later, Dunne and his wife came down with the disease.

A day after that, Farrell himself fell sick. By then, a total of thirty-two emigrants were suffering from various stages of typhus.

On the day of Sarah Farrell's death, an icy wind pushed the *Archimedes* westward. Farrell was too weak to get out of his bunk, much less go up on deck. The task of accompanying the Farrell twins, Emmet and Eamon, fell to Devin. The boys were stoic and held their sorrow close as they watched their mother made ready for her long sleep beneath the waves.

She was prepared much as the woman who had died before her had been. However, instead of lead ballast, a small length of chain was placed on her chest before she was enclosed within a fragment of sail.

Once again Devin spoke the words that would send a soul to heaven and a body to the depths of a cold, cold ocean. With the twins standing next to him, one on either side, his arms around their shoulders, he spoke loud and clear into the strong wind. "I speak for these two young boys who are too grief-stricken to speak for themselves. I pray that God will take Sarah Farrell to his bosom and protect her with His love until the day she is reunited with her family."

As Sarah Farrell's body sank beneath the waves, the first of the sharks appeared.

Typhus was not the only disease ravaging the passengers. Many came down with dysentery. The poor souls were too weak to get out of their bunks to use the slop buckets. Those suffering from diarrhea lay in their filth. They were beyond caring.

People started dying at an alarming rate. One or two a day. Jamie Farrell was gone; his sons, the twins, had come down with typhus and were barely hanging on. Dunne and his family were all sick, except for Hannah. Devin took her under his care. He made sure she received her water allotment and cooked her stirabout for her.

By the beginning of the fourth week, things had gotten so bad that the Captain would not allow anyone to attend a funeral, regardless of their relationship to the deceased.

The dead were no longer weighted down because there was nothing left on board to weigh them down with and no material in which to wrap the bodies. Two sailors would bring the dead body up above and immediately throw it overboard, like so much garbage. But there was no fear of the corpse floating in the ship's wake for very long. For by then, at any given time, there were thirty to fifty sharks following the ship. They had been feeding off the dead for weeks.

On a clear, blustery day, Devin stood at the bulwark while waiting for his turn at the fire. He held Hannah Dunne in his arms so that she could see over the railing. Both enjoyed the salt spray striking their faces as the ship plunged from the top of a wave into a watery valley.

"Do y' think my family will get well?" she asked.

"That is in God's hands. Y' keep up with yer prayers, little one, and I think He'll hear y'."

"Why is it up to God who lives and who dies?"

"He put us here, so I think that gives Him the right to take us from this world when He so pleases."

"It doesn't seem fair."

Thinking of his own family, Devin replied, "No, child, it does not."

Three days later, Hannah's brother died. The day after that, her sister was gone. And the day after that, she was made an orphan.

The ship was still sixteen days from the banks of Newfoundland. It was then that things got worse, if that were even possible.

7

Fifteen days from Newfoundland, Devin overheard two sailors talking about three of their shipmates who had come down with typhus. Devin, wanting to escape the confines below deck, thought perhaps Captain Hood would let him fill in for one of the ailing sailors.

While preparing his and Hannah's meal, he noticed the Captain at the taffrail, looking out to sea. It was forbidden to approach the afterdeck, but Devin was bound and determined. He told Hannah to keep an eye on the stirabout, took a deep breath, and stepped over the imaginary line separating the afterdeck from the rest of the ship.

"A fair and good morning to y', Captain, sir."

"You are not permitted here. Please remove yourself to the foredeck," said the Captain, still looking out to sea.

"Beggin' yer pardon, Captain, sir, but I've come to offer my services. Word is that y' are shorthanded on account of the illness stalking your ship. As of yet, I am able-bodied and fit as a spring lamb. Y' give me a task and it will get done, sir!"

Hood thought for a moment. His options were limited; another able-bodied hand had come down with typhus just that morning, making it a total of four.

He turned to face Devin. With a look of doubtful appraisal, he asked, "Have you ever been to sea before? I mean as a sailor."

"No, sir, I have not. But I will perform any job to yer satisfaction. The only wage I ask is an extra ladleful of water a day."

Hood's stance stiffened and his eyes veiled. Devin hurried on. " 'Tis not for me I'm asking, Captain, sir! There is a wee lass of only seven years down below. Her whole family has been taken by typhoid, sir. I'm thinking, maybe, if she has enough water to drink, she might not get sick."

The Captain softened. "You would have to work with Mister Marks. Can you do that without hitting him? Because if you do, I'll throw you in irons."

"I'd work with the Devil himself to be out in the fresh air."

"Fine. I'll tell Mister Marks to work you hard, but not to abuse you. I'll assign you to the first dog watch. When you hear eight bells, you come up and report for duty."

Devin returned to Hannah just as the stirabout was ready.

"Aren't y' the good girl to have done that all by yerself," said Devin.

After they had eaten, Devin sought out Patrick Burke.

"I'll soon be going topside for a while. When I do, can y' keep a watch on Hannah for me?"

"'Twould be my pleasure."

At eight bells, signaling the end of the afternoon watch and the beginning of the first dog watch, Devin was up on deck awaiting his orders.

Mister Marks did not keep him waiting long.

"You there, paddy. Do you know why we're called Jack Tars?" Marks did not wait for an answer. "Because the rigging and lines on a ship must be tarred."

Devin had no idea what Marks was talking about, but he held his tongue. He figured Marks would eventually get to the point.

Marks nodded towards the foremast. "That rigging needs tarring, and you'll be doing it." He called to a nearby sailor. "Get this lubber aloft. Tell him what's expected of him."

With one last derisive look in Devin's direction, Marks turned and walked off, quite pleased with himself.

A northeasterly wind pushed the *Archimedes* farther into an endless sea. The sky was an infinity of blue, save for a few distant clouds dotting the horizon. How small Devin felt, being on an insignificant ship in the midst of so much ocean and sky.

'Tis here a man can truly appreciate the majesty of nature.

"Come with me," said the sailor.

Devin awoke from his musings and followed the man along the gangway.

When they stood before the foremast, the sailor pointed to a small bucket and explained, "This is what we call tarring down. You'll take that bucket and a length of oakum aloft."

Devin craned his neck skywards. The top of the mast looked a long way off, at least eighty feet, he guessed. He brought his gaze back down to look the sailor square in the eye.

"Are y' saying that I should take that bucket in one hand and a short piece of rope in the other and scurry up to the top of the mast? How am I to hold on with my hands full?"

The sailor smiled through his beard. He was thirty years of age, eleven years older than Devin. His skin was brown from the sun, but not as leathery as the Captain's. "My name's Jim. And who would you be?"

"My name's Devin Mahoney."

"Well, Devin Mahoney, I understand that you volunteered for this. But not to worry. I'll be right here with you."

Devin nodded and felt a little easier, but not by much. Jim proceeded to enlighten Devin on the finer points of tarring.

"Aye, lad, you do go aloft with the bucket and that 'short piece of rope'. But this is how you do it. Put the oakum in the bucket and slip the handle over your forearm. That will free up your hands so that you can climb the ratlines to the masthead. Then all you have to do is smear the tar onto the shrouds using the oakum."

Devin again looked heavenward. "What are shrouds?"

"Those ropes steadying the mast."

"How am I to get out to the shrouds, and why do they need tarring?"

Jim laughed. "You *are* a lubber, indeed. First of all, we tar the shrouds and stays because they're made of hemp, and hemp will rot out here in the salt air unless tarred.

"As to how you get out to the shrouds, we use a gant-line. That's this line here. It runs up to and through a halyard at the masthead. When you get up there, put your foot through the loop and swing out. You'll be 'twixt heaven and earth, but don't worry, Jimmy-Boy here will be minding the line. I'll be lowering you down as you do your tarring. It's called riding down."

For a moment, Devin thought about going back down below decks. But then said, "All right, 'Jimmy-Boy'. Y're right, sure enough. I did volunteer."

With the bucket hanging on his forearm, Devin started, warily, up the ratlines. Before he was out of earshot, Jim yelled, "Be sure to

60

leave no holidays or you'll have to do it all over again. And be mindful not to drop tar on the deck, or we'll spend our time later scraping it off."

At the top of the mast, hanging on for dear life, Devin looked down and shivered. *If this rope slips or I lose my hold, I'll never see America. Worse yet, I'll never see the Auld Sod again.*

He made it through the watch, although very little tar had been applied. The time was used mostly in learning the technique of hanging in midair while trying to smear a sticky substance onto a rope that stayed just out of reach. But by the end of the watch, Devin had mastered the finer intricacies of tarring. Tomorrow, he'd be sure to get more done.

Jim had been patient with the lubber, and Devin had warmed to him easily. As they were scraping up the tar that had fallen onto the deck, Marks walked up and stood with his hands behind his back, observing the two men down on their knees. At length, he said, "You there, Jim Darby, the potato-eater dropped the tar, and *he* will clean it up. Four bells have sounded. Your watch is over, be gone with you now."

Devin's jaw tightened, but he uttered not a word. With an embarrassed look, Jim gathered his tools and left Devin to the mercies of Marks.

Marks said nothing further, but hatred glowed in his cold brown eyes.

Devin removed the last of the tar from the deck and returned below. Hannah was sitting at a table with Burke. "We saw you dangling from the sky while we were up on deck cooking our meal," said Burke.

Hannah asked what was on his hands.

"'Tis tar, Little One."

A sailor came down the ladder with a water bucket. Devin suggested to Hannah that she should retrieve her bowl and get in line.

When she was gone, Burke said, "You missed your afternoon meal."

"Matters not. I'm not hungry. I'll tell y' true, being above decks made me forget for a little while how miserable it is down here. Has anyone else died in the time I've been away?"

61

"No. But as you can hear from the din, there are still multitudes of the sick."

"How many dead so far?" asked Devin.

"I have not been keeping a tally, but my best guess would be nearing fifty poor souls have left us for greener pastures."

"And four of those souls were Hannah's entire family."

"Indeed. It is too sad."

"I pray the dying is over, but I do not care to wager on it. The sailors are starting to come down with the sickness." With a rueful look, Devin added, "We are two weeks from Canada, and I must keep Hannah safe until then."

"What will you do with her once we're there?"

"I've never a notion, truthfully, *a chara*."

The next day and the day after that, Devin was assigned to the forenoon watch and continued with his tarring duties until the shrouds of the foremast were finely coated in a thick layer of the black substance. In that time, two more emigrants died.

On the morning of Devin's fourth day as a sailor, Marks, in his usual manner, ordered him to swab down the port deck. "And if it's not done to my satisfaction, you'll do it again," he hissed, menace dripping from every word.

A light breeze had come in from the north, and the yardarms were braced to catch what little wind there was.

A short while later a silence befell the ship. Sailors were lined up along the starboard rail, looking north. A few whispered among themselves, some pointed northward. One man blessed himself.

Marks walked up and berated the men, yelling for them to get back to work, but stopped in mid-tirade as he followed their gazes out to sea.

Off the starboard quarter, a threatening mass of darkness, a cloud of immense size stretching across the entire horizon, headed their way. It seemed to come straight up out of the ocean. White streaks of lightning split the black sky and rained down into the sea.

Over his shoulder, he shouted, "Captain!"

"I see it, Mister Marks," said Hood. "Have those men stop their gawking and set to work battening down. Send men up to reef the mizzen and foresail and furl the main. It looks like we're in for a decent blow."

The emigrants who were on deck cooking their morning meal were quickly herded below and the fires put out. Jim came up to Devin, holding various lengths of rope. "Stow your bucket and mop and come with me. We're to batten down the water casks."

The water casks were two decks below, aft of the forecastle. Arriving there, Devin observed that the casks were already tied down with a stout rope.

"They need more securing. The blow that's coming our way would rattle ol' Mister Hob himself," said Jim. Handing Devin a length of rope, he continued: "We don't want these barrels to come loose or it would be the death of us. You put another line around those over there, and I'll handle these. And lash 'em down tight, lad."

Devin noticed two of the casks were standing in pools of water and called out, "Some of these casks are leaking."

"We can't worry about that now," said Jim with a wave of his hand. "Hurry up. We have to go topside and help with the battening down."

When they re-emerged on deck, the sun was hidden by thick, steel-grey clouds. The wind had picked up considerably.

Lightning danced across the water off the starboard bow, followed by low rolls of thunder. The waves grew higher, the valleys, deeper.

Devin followed Jim along the port gangway, working quickly. Fastening, tightening, and securing anything that might work loose. When they had finished, Devin scanned the deck. The sailors were milling about, taking one last look at the storm before going below to ride it out. The preparations were complete. The sails were reefed, anything that could conceivably come loose had been tied down, and all that was left to do was await the storm heading their way.

Jim advised Devin to go below. "Warn your fellow passengers. Tell them things will get a little rough, but not to worry. The captain knows his ship. He's one of the finest seamen I've ever sailed with."

Devin nodded and Jim disappeared through the hatch to the crew's quarters. Devin was about to lift the hatch leading to the emigrants' deck when Marks came up behind him. "Where do you think you're going?" He was holding a slicker and tossed it to Devin. "Put it on," he ordered.

"And why would I be doing that?"

"I'll be at the helm when the storm breaks, and you'll be standing right next to me."

"Why would I?"

"Because you are now a member of the crew and you'll take orders like everyone else. Unless you want to go below and huddle in fear with the rest of the cattle."

Devin had wanted to be below with Hannah to comfort her during the storm, but he knew that, in his absence, Burke would look after her.

They went to the afterdeck where Marks relieved the helmsman. Four slickered sailors stood amidships—two to port and two to starboard—holding tight onto the railings, their knuckles white. The Captain paced the bow, soaking in the salt spray. Otherwise, the deck was deserted.

Captain Hood made his way back to the helm, steady-footed on an increasingly tossing deck. When he saw Devin, he said, "Mister Marks, what is this man doing here?"

"It's still his watch, Captain. If something goes wrong and I have to get a message to you or call hands up on deck, I'll be needing him."

Hood nodded. He knew what Marks was up to. He wanted to put a scare into the Irish lad. *Well, let him have his fun. By the looks of things, this storm is going to be one for the books. It'll be a story the boy can tell for the rest of his life.*

"You have the helm, Mister Marks. Keep her steady as she goes. We are running before the wind with the Devil at our backs." With a final nod to Devin, accompanied by a faint smile, Hood took his leave.

"Now it's just you, me, and the storm, my Irish friend," laughed Marks.

"Do y' mind if I ask y' a question, *Mister* Marks?"

"You better ask it afore the storm hits."

"Why do y' hate the Irish so? What have we ever done to y'?"

Marks looked Devin hard in the eye. "My brother was killed by you Irish."

Devin waited, but no other explanation was forthcoming.

64

The sky grew darker with each passing minute. The clouds thickened. The wind wailed. The waves grew mountainous. Seafoam crashed over the deck and swiftly slid back out to sea. The ship dipped into valleys as deep as its mainmast was high.

The black cloud moved in, extinguishing all light except for the blinding flashes of lightning. A torrential, drenching, cold rain poured down as Devin hugged the binnacle, trying with all his might not to be washed overboard. He prayed to his God in heaven, to Jesus, Mother Mary, and all the saints, that this would not be his last day on earth.

Effortlessly, without concern for those onboard, the sea tossed the ship from side to side and from stem to stern. A clap of thunder shook the ship right down to its keel. Flashes of lightning intermittently illuminated the deck to show that three of the four sailors who had been amidships were now nowhere to be seen, presumably washed overboard. Devin informed Marks of the missing men by pointing to where they had been.

Marks yelled into the wind. "Don't you worry about them, paddy. *You* hold on. This will all be over afore you know it."

Marks had barely uttered those words when there was a tremendous flash followed by a thunderous crashing sound. Lightning had struck the mainmast! Devin watched in horror as the mast toppled over. It came to rest on the starboard gunwale, most of it in the sea, but still attached to the ship by its rigging.

"Quick!" yelled Marks. "Get below and have the men get up here. Tell them to bring axes to free the mainmast before it drags us down. Then go and get the Captain."

Before Devin could make a move, a monster wave washed over the ship, almost capsizing her. The wheel spun heavily, throwing Marks onto the deck. He was sliding towards the port gunwhale and certain death in a raging sea when, at the last moment, his movement was impeded. Waves washed over him, momentarily obscuring his vision. But then, with one blinding flash of lightning, he saw what was keeping him from a watery grave. The potato-eater had a hold of his ankle.

They stared into one another's eyes. Each knew what the other was thinking.

I should let him go. The world would be better off without him.

I wouldn't blame him if he released his hold on me.

But there was no real debate within Devin's soul. He had to pull Marks back to safety, and that's all there was to it.

Captain Hood had felt the ship veer out of control when Marks fell away from the wheel and had come up on deck. He had control of the helm as Devin pulled Marks back onboard. He said nothing about that. Instead, he yelled to Marks over the howling wind, "Get some men up here to cut away the mast." He then ordered Devin below. "You've done good, boy. But now you have to leave things to us real sailors."

Devin was happy to obey the order and made his way forward on shaky legs, holding on to the railing with all his strength as peals of thunder reverberated through the rigging, as sea-water washed over him, as a vengeful sea laughed at his pitiful plight.

8

Below deck, the emigrants were holding on to anything they could to prevent being flung about as the ship viciously rolled in the rough seas. Some of those down with typhus and too sick and weak to get out of their bunks had been tossed to the deck where they were left for the time being.

One by one, the lamps went out as they ran out of fuel. Soon, the only source of light came from a single lantern swinging wildly about, creating a macabre dance of shadows and light that played across the walls and deck.

With every wave that knocked the ship on its side came a chorus of screams. People were throwing up until there was nothing left to throw up. The slop buckets had long ago tipped over, their contents flowing freely across the deck as the ship pitched from side to side.

Devin sat at a table, holding Hannah tight with his left arm, his right arm wrapped around a support beam. He was thankful the benches and tables were secured to the deck. Burke sat across from them, gripping the table with both his hands, his face white with fear.

In an attempt to put both Hannah and Burke at ease, Devin joked, "Do y' think they'll be bringing us our biscuit ration anytime soon?"

Burke gave a weak smile. Hannah hugged Devin all the tighter.

Soon the solitary source of light went out, and the emigrants were made to endure the storm in total darkness. By that time, most of the people were so seasick they just wanted to die and get it over with. At one point, the ship was laid over on her side, and clusters of people slid across the deck. When the ship righted herself, they fell back to where they had been.

An eternity later, the *Archimedes* settled on an even keel.

Devin sat Hannah on the bench and yelled out into the darkness. "Stay where you are. I'll go and fetch oil for the lanterns." He felt his way to the ladder and came out onto the main deck, grateful to take a breath of fresh-smelling air. Night had fallen, clouds covered the stars; not a breath of wind moved across the deck. The sea seemed eerily silent and calm in the aftermath of such an intense storm. The mainmast was gone and the sails of the other two masts were in tatters.

Devin spied Jim cutting away what was left of the mainmast shrouds. He made his way over and asked, "Can I get some whale oil for the lanterns below? We're in darkness down there."

"I'm sorry, lad, but you'll have to ask one of the mates or the Captain. I am not allowed into the stores unless ordered."

Marks walked up and told Jim to get back to work. To Devin he said, "And what do you want?"

Devin squared his shoulders, ready for a fight. "I be wanting a little oil to light that stink-hole down below."

"Darby, get this man what he wants, and tell the cook to send down biscuits for those able to eat. It's been a while since they've had any food. And you bring them water." Saying nothing more, Marks quickly walked away.

Devin got the lanterns lit. The men who had volunteered to clean the decks of vomit and the spill from the slop-buckets were sent above to procure the salt water needed for the job. When things were relatively ship-shape again, the biscuits and water were brought below and apportioned.

As Jim was ladling out water, Devin asked, "With a broken mast and no wind, what's to become of us?"

"Well, we still have the mizzen and foremast. But you're right. We do need wind, and that is something we cannot control. Worse yet, we've been blown off course, probably by many miles. And with clouds obscuring the stars, we cannot take a fix. We're somewhere south of where we should be. Perhaps in the morning the skies will clear, and a noon sighting can be taken using the sun. But I think we have a bigger problem. Those casks that you said were leaking were almost empty when I went to fetch the water. I told Mister Marks, and he and the Captain went below to inspect the water supply."

Three sailors had been washed overboard during the storm, which left Captain Hood more shorthanded than ever. Hence, Devin was assigned two watches per day.

The morning after the storm found the ship shrouded in fog and still becalmed. When Devin reported for duty, Marks said, "Let's go forward where we can have a little privacy."

Marks leaned his hands on the railing and looked out into the grey, gossamer-like fog. He seemed to be searching for something—perhaps the right words. He lowered his head and stared at the deck. In a soft voice, he asked, "Why did you save me?"

Devin, looking not at Marks but into the fog, said, "I do not know. I acted without thinking."

"You may have acted without thinking at first, but then you had a choice. I saw it in your eyes. You were debating whether to release your grip on me or pull me to safety."

Devin did not want to have this conversation. He did not think Marks would understand; hell, *he* didn't understand why he did what he did. To change the subject, he said, "Y' told me that the Irish killed yer brother. Well, I'm Irish, and I never knew yer brother. But still y' treated me like a dog. So tell me. What makes *y'* do what y' do?"

Marks let go of the forestay and leaned against the railing. This was hard for him, but he was seeking atonement and to atone for one's sins, one must serve a penance. "I owe you at least an explanation." With one long, sad sigh, he began telling his story.

"My brother and I were close. His name was Charles. He was four years my senior and I looked up to him. He was my hero. When we were young, I'd follow him around like a lost puppy."

Marks smiled at the memory.

"Two years ago, he met a woman in East London. To escape the famine, she had come over from Dublin looking for work as a housemaid. Somehow, Charles met her, and he fell in love. I don't know all the details because I was at sea at the time. I had to piece the story together by talking with his friends and from what the constables had told my mother.

"Then, for some reason, the woman suddenly returned to Ireland. Charles held out for three long weeks, but then followed her to that vile island."

Devin turned his gaze from the sea and looked dead-on at Marks.

"I'm sorry. I did not mean that. It's just that until recently—until very recently—that's been my thinking."

Devin nodded.

Marks continued. "Charles wanted to marry the woman. She took him to meet her family and that's when the trouble started. The famine had taken her father. The head of the house was now her elder brother and he had no love for the English. But that wasn't all of it. They were a Catholic family, and my brother, of course, was of The Church of England. Her brother forbade the marriage on religious grounds."

The fog began to thin as Marks continued with his tale.

"That did not deter Charles. He asked the girl to meet him at the inn where he was staying. He wanted to convince her to marry him in spite of her brother. They were in love and they had natural urges. Well, her brother had followed her to the inn and burst in while they were in bed. Without warning, he drew a pistol and shot my dear brother dead."

Devin couldn't help himself. He put a hand on the man's shoulder and said, "I'm sorry."

Marks acknowledged the kindness with a half-smile.

"By the time I got there, the brother had absconded to America, and I didn't have it in me to kill the woman, even though she was the cause of Charles' death. She had loved him, after all. I left Ireland with a deep hatred of its people. A hatred I have nourished for these two long years. But now, thanks to you, I am free of that hatred."

The two men stood at the bow of the *Archimedes* staring at one another, much as they had the night before when Marks had looked into Devin's eyes and wondered how long before the paddy would loosen his grip and let him fall into the raging sea. In due course, Marks said, "The Captain has put you in charge of the passengers. You'll ensure that they come up in orderly lots to cook their food, and you'll bring them their water. That will free up a man to do things that you can't."

Devin laughed. "Did I not tar the shrouds to yer satisfaction?"

"I'm sorry about that. To put a landlubber up a mast is a mean thing to do. But I have to say, you did it without complaint."

"I did, sure enough."

Marks' smile faded. "Here's the thing. We're low on water. Even with all the deaths we've had, we might not have enough to get to Canada. We're going to half rations for everyone—sailors and passengers alike. You'll have to explain that to your people. If there's any trouble, let me know, and I'll settle it. One thing, though. The Captain did say the girl, Hannah, could still have an extra half ration."

"So, how do I get started?" asked Devin.

"First, get your people up here to start their fires. Then, fill two buckets and bring them up. Dole out the water so they can cook their porridge, but be stingy with it."

The fog fully lifted in the late afternoon. But still there was no wind.

That evening, sitting below at a table with Burke and Hannah, Devin said, "I'm told that, because of the water shortage and being so far south of where we should be, the Captain has decided to sail for New York instead of Canada."

"Wouldn't be a bad thing," said Burke.

Devin looked at Hannah and asked, "Would y' like to go to New York?"

She scrunched up her face as though in deep thought, then said, "If I can't have my mommy and daddy back, I don't think it matters. But I would like to be with you, Devin, wherever you are … if I can."

"Yes, Little One. Y're going to stay with me, and we'll take grand care of one another. Then one day, we'll return home where y' will have the handsomest of men at yer feet, begging to escort y' to the finest balls and the fanciest of parties."

The next two days were as still as the one before, not the slightest sign of a breeze. But no one else died among the emigrants. The water situation only grew worse. At their present rate of consumption, they would run out of water in one week's time.

The ship was nigh crippled without its mainmast; the best that could be expected with a fair wind was nine days' sailing time to New York. The captain ordered a further reduction of the water ration.

At long last, after four days becalmed, a slight gust of wind came out of the east. The sails half-filled with air and lightly luffed in the breeze. Shouts of joy were heard from emigrants and sailors alike.

At two bells, Devin started to go below to get water for the emigrants' stirabout when he was stopped by Captain Hood. "Hold on there, boy. You won't be needing to do that. There'll be no more cooking on deck. We can't afford water for your people's porridge. Water is too precious right now. Until we get to New York, water will be further rationed; only one ladleful per day, per person, myself included. For small children, it'll be half that much. You go and see the cook; he'll give you biscuits to distribute to the passengers. One of my sailors will fetch the drinking water."

Devin asked, "Does the rationing include the little girl I'm looking after?"

"I'm sorry, son, it does."

Even though there was no more cooking to be done, the Captain allowed the emigrants up on deck in small numbers once a day. Each group had an hour to spend out in the open before going back down below.

At one such time, Hannah was sitting on the forecastle, speaking quietly with another young girl. Devin and Burke stood at the rail, watching dolphins playfully riding the bow waves. They were a welcome sight. Whenever dolphins were around, there were no sharks to be seen.

Burke leaned heavily on the rail, his head lowered. "Wasn't I the fool of the world. I thought we Irish could be no worse off than when the famine came and people started dying. But now I know different."

"What are you talking about, Patrick?"

"Look about you. By my count, sixty-one people have died. And I'm not counting the sailors. Hannah's entire family is gone, she's an orphan now. And what about Timothy Dunne and his family? No, Devin, I think we should have stayed in Ireland and fought the landlords. Maybe burn down a manor house or two. Do as Saint Patrick did with the snakes ... run a few of their lackey agents into the sea and be done with them."

Devin turned and faced Burke. "Perhaps what y' say is true. But we're here now and must make do. Once in America, we will become rich, sure we will. Then return to poor ould Ireland and do some of the things y're saying."

Burke disagreed. "I'm nearing sixty; I'm not ever going to be rich. What I am *going* to do is get work in America doing whatever I can and save my money to return home. I may burn down a manor house or two when I get there … I don't know. But I *am* going home because, when my time comes, I want to be buried under the soft green grass of Ireland, with shamrocks growing on my grave. And I tell you true, Devin Mahoney, I'll not be sailing on a coffin ship like this when I return."

The next day, the water situation worsened yet again.

Jim Darby and Devin were in the hold getting the emigrants' water ration for the day. The ship was down to the last two casks, but they were large casks. If no other misfortune befell the *Archimedes*, the ship should arrive in New York just as the water ran out.

Darby held the lantern high and Devin removed the top of one of the casks. Right away, he knew something was amiss. A strange smell wafted up from the barrel.

"What do y' think of this, Jim?"

Darby moved closer and asked Devin to hold the lantern. He cupped his hands and dipped them into the barrel. Bringing the water to his mouth, he took a sip and promptly spit it out.

"Here, give me that lantern."

Holding the lantern low, he read the words stenciled on the side of the barrel: *James & Sons, Winemakers*.

"Damn! They used old wine barrels. The wine must have soaked into the wood and now it has leached out and mixed with the water. It's drinkable, but it's not going to taste very good."

The emigrants did not complain. Their spirits were already as low as they could possibly be. Sixty-one of their number had died and another thirty were down with various sicknesses. The stench of their living quarters was beyond description. They had been existing on nothing but bread and water for days now, and very little at that.

People had stopped dying, and that was a good sign. Maybe the corner had been turned on the typhus epidemic. That, and the fact that they were nearing the Promised Land, kept the emigrants going. If only they could hold out for a few more days.

73

Devin was still assigned to two watches. The forenoon watch, where he passed out the biscuits and water to his fellow emigrants and performed other duties given him. And the middle watch, which was from midnight to four o'clock. Devin liked that watch. Things were quiet and his sole duty was as a lookout. He just had to make sure he didn't fall asleep, or there'd be hell to pay.

Marks always came and sat with him for the first hour. Devin had learned that Marks had a family—a wife and two boys. He did not like being away from them for such lengths of time, but being a sailor was the only way he knew to make a living. He hoped to become a captain one day, which would allow him to share in the ship's profits and perhaps retire to that country home he and his wife envisaged, sooner rather than later. Much like Devin, Marks, too, had a dream.

According to the Captain, they were now three days from New York, wind permitting. Devin was ladling water into the emigrants' bowls when he noticed Hannah was not in line to receive hers. He called to Burke and asked where she was.

"She's in her bed. She says she's tired. I don't think it's anything serious. She has none of the signs of typhus. It's been a hard voyage. I think it has all just caught up with her."

Devin nodded, but still he was worried. He asked Burke to bring her allotment of water to her and see that she drank it, despite the taste.

After Devin finished doling out the water, he went to Hannah and knelt by her bunk. She was awake, but sickly pale.

"How are y' feeling, Little One?"

"I'm fine. Just a little tired, is all."

Devin smiled a big Irish smile and stroked her hair. "Y' know, we'll be in New York in a few days. It's the grandest of grand cities, *a chroi*. I have a wad of pound notes on me. We'll stay at the finest inn the city has to offer. And we'll dine at the finest restaurants as befits a young lady of grandeur, such as my fair Hannah. Does that not sound grand?"

"Yes, Devin, to be sure, it does."

"Alright, then, y' get some rest. I'll soon be bringing y' a biscuit and we'll let on like we're sitting in a fine restaurant, and y're wearing a dress I'll buy y' as fancy as y've ever seen."

Devin leaned over and kissed Hannah on the forehead before leaving her and searching out Burke.

"I think y're right, Patrick. I see no sign of typhus about her. She's sure to be tired, and who could blame her? She's borne more than her share for such a young heart. I lost my family also, but I was a grown man. That poor wee girl has had her whole life torn asunder overnight."

Devin Mahoney, too, was tired. But he could not slacken. He owed too much to too many. His father and brothers had died that the family farm might be saved. And there was Missus Meehan, who had given him a gentleman's coat to keep him warm on the first leg of his journey. Tom McNevin, who had shown him the wonderful machinations of an inside loo and had offered himself up to arrest so that Devin could continue on his way to America. And now he had little Hannah Dunne depending on him.

With a weary sigh, he raised himself from the table. It was time to see the cook and get the miserable, worm-ridden biscuits that would feed and sustain him and his fellow travelers until they were off this accursed ship.

After he had distributed the biscuits, all save two—one for himself and one for Hannah—he went to Hannah's bed. She appeared to be asleep. He was about to turn away when he noticed her chest was not rising and falling. *Oh dear God in heaven, please let her be breathing.* He shook her shoulder, pleading with her to open her eyes. Then he felt her cheek. She was cold to the touch.

He screamed for Burke to come over. *"She's not breathing ... help me ... help me!"* he cried. Burke pushed Devin aside and knelt down. He raised the girl's eyelids, looking for life. Finding none, he said, "I'm sorry, Devin, she's gone, lad. Gone to be with her mommy and daddy."

"Why, Patrick? Why? 'Tis not right! She didn't have the sickness."

"Perhaps it's God's will, or perhaps she missed her family so much that she decided to join them."

Devin held Hannah's hand in his and said a prayer for her eternal soul. He beseeched God to take her to her parents and to please look out for her, seeing as how he no longer could. He then tenderly wrapped her lifeless body in a blanket, took her in his arms, and carried her topside.

The Captain was on deck speaking with Marks.

"Please, sir. I couldn't bear the thought of the sharks getting to her. Might I have something to weigh her down?"

Hood eyed the small, blanket-covered form and asked, "Is that the little girl you were looking after?"

Devin nodded.

Marks stepped forward and said, "Sir, there is a short length of chain in the fo'c'le that weighs three times what she does. It will send her little body straight to the bottom, too deep for the sharks to get at her."

"That will be fine, Mister Marks." To Devin, Hood said, "You officiate at her burial. If you wish, I'll have the men who are not on watch turn out to give her a proper send-off."

"No, thank y', Captain. If y' don't mind, I'd rather do this myself."

Teary-eyed, Devin brought Hannah to the bow and bound her in the chain. He took long minutes delaying the inevitable. Then, lifting her over the gunwhale, he lowered her body as far as possible before letting go. Mercifully, her body did not bob about, but sank right off. He found it hard to take his eyes off the spot where she had slid beneath the waves.

That night—during the middle watch—as Devin looked up at the countless stars overhead, he tightened his hands into fists and brought them down hard on the railing in frustration and despair, time and time again.

Marks noticed and came to him. "Do you want to talk, my friend?"

"There's not much to say. But yer company would surely be appreciated."

The two men leaned on the rail and looked down into the sullen, black sea. They watched as green phosphorescence floated alongside the hull, only to be lost in the ship's wake. At length, Devin said, "That's beautiful. I'm of a mind to be thinking it's Hannah's soul floating off to Heaven."

Marks straightened. "Yes, it is a sight. But I have to tell you, I've come to a decision. I'll not serve on a ship such as this any longer. The Captain is a good man, but the lords who are paying the ship's owner to bring you Irish to America never pay enough to allow you to be fed decently. And there should be a doctor on board, costing those blac'gards even more of their precious money than they'd be wanting to part with. I'm going to sign on with a ship that plies the waters between England and Ireland. I'll be home every few days. I'll be with my wife, the good woman that she is. And I'll be able to watch my boys grow up."

"Yes," said Devin. "Be with your loved ones and cherish them while y' can."

Early the next morning, the lookout sighted land.

Later that day, the *Archimedes* limped into New York Harbor and dropped anchor. The date: December 21, 1849.

9

The faint winter light from a somber sky fell across the *Archimedes* as the dory approached. Four strong men rowed while a fifth sat at the stern, arms folded. He was the Master of the Harbor, and this ship, with its missing mast and torn sails, had no clearance to anchor in *his* harbor, impeding lawful shipping.

"What are you doing?" demanded the harbor master. "You cannot anchor here."

Captain Hood looked down at the small boat from the port gangway and spread his hands wide. "We have sick aboard. We have no water and very little food. And as you can see, our mainmast is gone. You cannot turn us away."

The harbor master's back straightened. "Sick, you say?"

"Yes. Half the passengers and a few of my sailors."

"Then consider yourself quarantined. I'll send out the health inspector. If you need water, have a few barrels ready to lower onto the inspector's boat. I'll have them filled and brought back out to you. We'll worry about the food later, after I get the inspector's report."

Hood had allowed the healthy emigrants up on deck to glimpse their first sight of The New World. They had all heard the exchange between the Captain and the American official. Devin was standing next to Burke and exclaimed, "*Quarantined!* He can't do that!"

"Aye, he can. As harbor master, he's well within his rights. Worse still, we'll most likely be told to cast off for Canada, seeing as how that's where we were headed to begin with."

The emigrants were ordered below to await the health official. But Devin lagged behind; he needed to speak with Marks.

Marks was amidships, overseeing the barrels being brought up.

"Mind if I talk to you?" asked Devin.

"Aye, lad, wait for me at the bow. I'll see you when I'm done here."

Devin paced about until Marks joined him. "I've got to get off this boat. I never did want to go to Canada. I'm so close." Pointing over Marks' shoulder to the buildings along the wharf, he almost shouted, "I can see America, I can. 'Tis right there!"

Marks put his hand on Devin's shoulder. "If you'll calm down, maybe I can help you."

Devin took a deep breath and nodded.

"The health inspector is sure to do a head count of those that are healthy and those that are not. That will include sailors too. Before we're allowed to leave the harbor, another count will be taken. If anyone is missing, it will mean trouble for the Captain."

Devin had grown to like Captain Hood. He did not want to cause him problems with the authorities. He started to say something, but Marks held up his hand and said, "Let me finish."

Again, Devin nodded.

"This is what we'll do. You go down to where the water barrels are stored and you stay there. With the many deaths we've had, one person more or less is not going to be missed. And the Captain will have his hands full with the inspector and the harbor master to pay too much attention to what we're doing."

"But if it's going to cause the Captain difficulty, then I'd rather stay onboard and walk back down from Canada."

"No one will know. After we're on our way north, I'll tell him what I've done. I don't think he'll pay no mind. His main concern right now is to get to Canada and discharge his passengers. No offense, but he'll be glad to be rid of you. You'll be one less person he has to worry about."

"What's yer plan?" asked Devin.

"Just before the first watch ends, I'll come and get you. The men are well tired and will waste no more time than is necessary above decks this night. I'll have those on watch doing duties either below or on the afterdeck. Make your way to the bow and slip over the side. Then swim for the wharf, but make sure no one sees you coming out of the water or we'll all pay the piper!"

"Will not someone on the ship hear the splash when I hit the water?"

"There will be a line over the side so you can ease yourself in. Be prepared. It's going to be cold."

79

Devin shook Marks' hand and asked if he could go below to say goodbye to Burke before he went into hiding.

"Just be quick about it. You don't want to be caught below when the inspector gets here."

Devin found Burke lying on his bunk and asked him to join him at a table. Once seated, Devin leaned across and whispered, "I'll be leaving y' this night and I wanted to say goodbye and Godspeed."

Burke was not surprised. He reached out his hand and said, "I expected nothing less from you, Devin Mahoney. If any man can, I know you'll make your fortune and return to Ireland a wealthy man; and when ya do, look up ol' Patrick Burke. I'll be somewhere around Dunboyne. It's just outside of Dublin, to the north. It's where I was born, and it's where I plan to die."

Devin grabbed Burke's hand and gave it a vigorous shake. With no further words between them, Devin took his leave and retired to the darkest recess of the hold where the water barrels were stored.

The health inspector made his inspection and yellow-jacketed the *Archimedes*. The ship was permanently quarantined. No one would be allowed off. The American officials would provide enough water and food to get the ship to Quebec City. As soon as provisions were delivered, the *Archimedes* would be sent on its way.

Five minutes before midnight, Marks came for Devin and led him up on deck. They shook hands at the hatchway. "I'll stay here and keep an eye out. It's been a pleasure to have known you, Devin Mahoney."

"Y' too, Mister Marks."

The water *was* cold. He swam up under a wooden pier and looked around for a way to get out of the water unobserved. It did not look good. He tried to shimmy up one of the pilings but cut himself on the barnacles growing thereon. Besides, the piling was coated with tar. He would have to find another way out. And it would have to be fast; he was shivering, his teeth were chattering from the cold.

He swam south along the dock. Just when it seemed totally hopeless, he spotted a ladder up ahead that had been nailed to a piling. *Clearly, I be not the first soul looking to get out of this cold water.*

He made his way up and onto the dock, which was deserted at that time of night. The air was colder than the water; he had to get out of the wind or he'd surely catch his death. He found shelter in an alleyway littered with trash and spent his first hours in America huddled behind a pile of old lumber, shivering in the cold. But no matter, he was on his way to fulfilling his dream.

He could not go to an inn soaking wet, but as soon as his clothes dried, he would go in search of proper shelter. For now, he found several old newspapers lying about and covered himself as best he could, seeking a little warmth. Without meaning to, he slept.

He awoke to daylight and dry clothes. Men were rushing about. Ships were being loaded and unloaded by big, brawny men, some of them Negroes. This was the first time Devin had ever seen a black man. And it was also the first time he had seen a boat run on steam. A river boat was passing by, belching thick black smoke against a cobalt-blue sky. Its whistle sounded a lonely cry that was soon carried away on the wind. America was indeed a wondrous place.

Devin had no idea where to go. He thought it best to get away from the wharf. A constable might inquire from what ship he had landed. He walked west a few blocks, then turned north and kept walking. Everyone he passed was well dressed and some looked at him suspiciously. Gradually the neighborhood changed. The people weren't as well dressed, but still their clothes were in better shape than his.

He continued walking north, looking for a neighborhood where he would not be as noticeable. He was afraid the police would question him and, because of his accent, eventually discover he was off the *Archimedes* and haul him back to the ship. The neighborhoods continued to deteriorate as he made his way north. Eventually he came to an avenue teeming with people. He stood taking in the scene before him, mouth agape.

Most of the people were as shabbily attired as he. Men with pushcarts lined both sides of the street, selling fruits, vegetables, milk, and even oysters. The street itself was filled to capacity with human bodies. Up and down the street, tethered or hobbled horses looked on with curiosity, or maybe amusement, at the seething mass of humanity parading before them. The few horse carts on the thoroughfare had trouble maneuvering through the crowd. Devin

81

would have to be careful where he walked to avoid stepping in the ubiquitous horse manure. Close by, two dogs gnawed on the remains of a bloated pig that lay in the gutter.

The only good thing he could discern from the hectic scene was that everyone spoke in different Irish dialects. These people were from all over Ireland. Some even conversed in Gaelic. He took a tentative step into the throng, taking in snatches of conversations as he made his way through the human tide.

"'Tis myself I be thinking of."

"Bould as y' please, he ..."

"Thems that I heard it from said ..."

"Himself would do it in a trace if only ..."

"Sure y' be right, but ..."

Two- and three-story-high buildings lined the street, their ancient, unpainted wood facades caked with grime. A few buildings were made of brick, but still wore the grime of the city like a badge of honor.

People leaned out of windows, conversing with individuals in the street below by yelling down at them. Horses whinnied, pigs squealed, and roosters crowed. The incessant barking of dogs only added to the cacophony of mixed sounds.

By then, the sun was nearly overhead, and Devin realized he was hungry. He approached a pushcart vendor and inquired, "Might I purchase one of your fine apples, sir?"

"Aye, to be sure, 'tis why I'm here. Ye'll never find a better apple in all the city!"

Devin picked out a big, enticing, red one and asked how much was owed.

"That will be three cents, sir."

Devin handed over a pound note. The vendor looked at it and quickly handed it back, saying, "You must be right off the boat, lad. I cannot change that. I could not change that in a month of Sundays."

Devin put the apple back on the cart and turned to leave.

"Hold on there," called the vendor. "Y' take it and pay me when y' can ... and welcome to America."

Devin accepted the fruit with gratitude.

A nearby man, leaning against a building, arms folded and ankles crossed, overheard the exchange between Devin and the vendor. He was dressed better than most of the people milling about. He wore a tan jacket over a spotless white vest. His white trousers were held up by black suspenders. The hat sitting upon his head was a low-crown, short-brimmed affair, with sides that flared slightly upwards. He wore it angled down to the right, giving him a rakish look. His black boots were polished to a high shine.

As Devin walked by, he called out. "Boyo! A moment of yer time, if y' please."

Devin, thinking he must be calling to someone else, turned around to see who was behind him. There was no one there.

"'Tis yerself I be addressing, sure enough," said the man. "The name's Michael Cudahy from County Mayo, the fairest county in all of Ireland. And may I ask, to whom do I have the pleasure of addressing?"

"I'm Devin Mahoney from County Kerry. 'Tis a pleasure to meet y'."

"Well, now, Boyo, y' must excuse me, but I couldn't help but overhear yer conversation with ol' Denis Doheny. He's been selling apples from that cart for a while now and doing well here in America. He's from County Kerry too, don't y' know?"

Devin was willing to take Michael Cudahy's word for it.

Cudahy leaned in a bit and whispered, "Not meaning to pry, *a chara*, but I noticed that stack of pound notes y' pulled out. No offense meant, but if'n y' were smart, y'd do well not to let too many folk 'round here see what y're carrying. They can't all be as fair and honest a soul as the bould Michael Cudahy, try as they might. From what I've witnessed, this part of the city would harbor more'n its fair share of bad apples, a place rife with thieves and no-gooders. A man'd do well to keep his wits about him an' tread careful, sure enough."

"Thank y'. I'll be sure to keep that in mind," vowed Devin.

Cudahy slapped him on the shoulder and laughed good-naturedly. "I have no doubt that y' will. Y' look like a smart young man. Might I ask what yer plans are?"

"I've only just arrived in this fair land and my only plan is to find an inn that I can call home until I get my bearings."

"Then y're in luck, Boyo. I know just the place. Clean, and good people be yer neighbors. But I must tell y' something. It's not exactly an inn. They don't have inns here in the city. They have hotels."

"Is it a hotel y' be wanting to take me?"

"I would surely, and ye'd be deservin' of no less, but most of us Irish are not allowed such luxuries, *a chara*. Hotel doors don't hinge the right way for us Irish, if ya catch me meaning."

"And why not?"

"Look around y'. These people cannot afford the expense of a hotel. Most of them are, like you, just off the boat with nary a bob between 'em. Look how they're dressed. American hotels are grand affairs, like palaces they be." Pointing his chin at a crowd of people milling nearby, he continued, "The hotels I've been to would not let the likes of them through their front doors."

"Even the finely heeled and brass-pocketed?"

"Aye, sure enough, well-heeled and brass-in-pocket. If y' have money, y' can do anything in America. The clothes proclaimeth the man. As you can tell by my clothes, I am a man of means. I could bed down in the finest of hotels, on the softest of pillows, but I prefer the company of me own countrymen. I try to help them get well-heeled and rich, like me, when I can. In the same light, if'n ye'll let me, I'll help y' find a place to live in time, so I will."

Devin said, "Well, for now, I'm not short, with my hands hangin' to me!"

"Aye, Devin Mahoney, I sees that sure enough, but look how y're dressed. Ye've tar on yer clothes, and y' look like y' slept in 'em. Y'd do better to stay where I will bring y', leastways 'til y' can get new clothes. Trust me, lad, 'tis a grand place I be bringing y' to. Might I enquire, is all yer money in pound notes?"

"Yes."

"And might I enquire also just how much y' have in pound notes?"

"Thirty-eight pounds."

A wide smile radiated from Cudahy's face. "Y' know y' cannot spend pounds in America? Y' must have dollars."

"Are y' telling me my pounds are worthless, then?"

"Not a'tall, Boyo. Y'll be havin' to exchange 'em is all."

"How do I do that?"

"Y' *could* do yer changing at a bank, but there be no banks in the vicinity of where we stand. And no self-respecting bank is going to let y' in looking as down-at-heel as y' do."

Devin looked down at his clothes and had to admit Cudahy had a point; they *were* a sight. He had been wearing them for almost two months and the journey across the Atlantic had been less than kind to them. They had come a long way since he "borrowed" them from Lord Beckham back in Ballingcollig.

"If I can't change my notes at a bank, then how do I change them?" asked Devin.

"Y' leave that to me, *a chara*. I know a man that'll do it for as wee an expense as is hardly worth talkin' about. As fer me, I'll not be takin' ne'er a red cent fer me trouble. Sure, the thought of helping one of me own is more'n payment enough, sure as God is me witness."

Cudahy rattled on, blessing himself in the process. "It'll give me head peace, no end, to help out a fellow countryman such as yer good self."

"Can we do it now?" asked Devin. "I'll be needin' new clothes, and I'll have to pay the landlord y'll be taking me to."

"Aye, sure enough, 'tis prob'ly best to get it done and over with so that y' can get yer start in America. If y'd just hand over yer pounds, then I'll be back in two shakes of a lamb's tail with dollars a plenty for y'."

The look on Devin's face betrayed his thinking.

Cudahy read the look, leaned in closer, and conspiratorially whispered, "I'll have y' know what we're doing is not entirely legal and above board here in America. If y' was to come with me, my friend would be fair slow to acknowledge me existence, let alone exchange money with me. He doesn't know y', but he's known me for donkey's years. He's a very careful man, he is." Cudahy stood a little taller and slowly and so very sorrowfully shook his head. "But if y' don't trust me," he declared, "then I'll be on my way with only the kindest thoughts and wishes towards y'."

Devin was ashamed of himself for what he had been thinking. Here's this man, out of the kindness of his heart, offering a helping hand to a wretch such as himself.

"Sure, y' be right," said Devin as he reached into his pocket and pulled out the precious pound notes. He peeled one from the roll. Holding it up for Cudahy to see, he said, "For luck, I'll be keeping this one to remind me of Tom McNevin, a true friend if ever there was one."

Cudahy accepted the bills. "The man's place is right nearby. Y' wait here and I'll be seeing yer palm creased with American dollars as quick as y' know."

Devin watched as Cudahy swaggered down the street and disappeared around the corner.

Now that he was alone, Devin bit into his apple. He had been too polite to eat it while speaking to an obvious gentleman such as Michael Cudahy. While he waited, he watched the parade of people pass by. It was good to be in America. Today he would find lodgings, tomorrow he would find work of any kind, no matter how meager the pay. He would work hard and save his money. When he could, he would move to a better part of the city and get a better-paying job. He would become prosperous, a man of distinction, and then he'd go home. America was the land of opportunity. It shouldn't take more than a year, at best, to accomplish his dream.

He kept looking to where he had last seen Cudahy. He should be coming back around that corner at any time now. But after half an hour of waiting, Devin felt the first slight twitches of dread. Surely it shouldn't be taking this long. He said he'd be right back. Could the police have caught him exchanging the notes? Is he being led off to jail at this very moment, as I stand here waiting for him?

Devin walked to the corner and peered down the street. There was no commotion, no police activity, just a throng of people going about their business. He walked back to where he had been standing. He should stay there. If Cudahy came back from a different direction, he would miss connecting with him if he was not where he was expected to be. Devin shuddered at the thought.

An hour later, with still no sign of Cudahy, Devin paced back and forth and fidgeted as he waited. He kept going to the corner, hoping to see Cudahy coming down the street. But the man was nowhere to be seen.

He looked about, not knowing what to do. Not far away, he spied the apple peddler. Cudahy had said he knew the man. What was his name? *Doheny! That's right, Denis Doheny.* Devin approached him and asked, "Might I have a word with y', Mister Doheny, sir?"

Doheny looked up from arranging his apples and the corners of his mouth turned up to form a smile. "Back for another apple, are ye?"

"No, sir. But I would like to ask a question of y', if I might."

Doheny's head bobbed twice, indicating that he was open to a question.

Devin pointed to where he had spoken to Cudahy and queried, "I'm a wondering, did y' observe me speaking to a well-dressed gentleman over there?"

All of a sudden, Doheny's apples demanded his immediate and full attention. He averted his gaze from Devin and frantically started rearranging his apples from big piles into small piles and small piles into big piles. Devin didn't understand. "He said he knew y'. He told me y' were from County Kerry, as I am. Do y' know him?"

Doheny's shoulders sagged and he quickly looked to his right and then to his left.

"I know him, *a mhaic.* For the life of me, I wish I didn't. He's of poor stock, so he is. Cudahy's a member of The Forty Thieves gang. A bunch of murderin' an' thievin' scoundrels as e'r shook hands with the Devil. I have to give 'em ten cents from me earnings, every day, or else they'll throw ammonia over me apples. They've done it before, they have. When I saw y' talking to him, I knew nothing good would come of it. What has he done to y'?"

Devin's vision clouded over for a moment. His legs felt rubbery, he couldn't think straight. Had he just been robbed?

Doheny saw the anguish in the boy's face and came around the cart to where Devin stood. Taking him by the arm, he led him over to the curb and told him to sit down. "Now, unburden yerself, lad, and tell me all about it."

Devin explained what had happened. When he had finished, Doheny cried out, "Thirty-seven pounds ... by all that's Holy! Did y' know that a pound is worth four dollars and fifty cents here in America? 'Tis a small fortune. Besides, 'tis not illegal to exchange notes for dollars."

Hearing that only made Devin feel worse.

"What are y' going to do now?" asked Doheny.

"I think I'll go looking for him and get my money back."

"Are ye daft, man? I told y' he was of the Forty Thieves. They look out for each other. If y' was to go up against him, y'd have the whole pack of jackals down around y' before y' knew it."

Devin hung his head in despair. This was not the America he had envisioned and yearned for. Not the America that he had crossed an ocean for.

Doheny took pity on the lad and said, "Y' come with me, *a mhaic*. 'Tis time to close up shop, anyway. Y' help me push my cart and I'll show y' where y' can lay yer head this night. Tomorrow will be a new day and, God willin', we'll get things sorted out then."

Devin looked into Doheny's smiling green eyes and thought, *Maybe America is not so bad after all.*

10

Devin pushed the cart as Doheny walked alongside and tried to explain how things worked in America—particularly on the Lower East Side of the island of Manhattan—in the year 1849.

"Look around y', what do y' see?"

Devin shrugged as best he could, considering his arms were occupied with pushing an apple cart. Doheny did not notice. "All these people came here to make a better life for themselves, like y' and me. They came here for a better life, they did. But look at how we ended up. Right off the boat we've been herded into this little section of the city where no self-respecting American would want to live."

Doheny was just getting up a good head of steam.

"Not only that. But if y' go walking up to the city proper and you pass a business with a sign in the window advertising for help, take a close gander at the bottom. More'n likely it'll say, *No Irish Need Apply.*"

Devin was listening, but the rumbling of his stomach took precedence over what Doheny was saying. Then he remembered something. "Mister Doheny, y' said it was not illegal to exchange pound notes. Is that not right?"

"Right y' are, *a mhaic.*" But before Devin could say anything else, Doheny said, "Though y' be young enough to be *mo mhaic* and I yer father, as long as we're going to be friends, why not call me by my Christian name, Denis?"

"Sure enough, Denis. But what I was getting at, by going the long way 'round, is that I'm still the proud owner of an Irish pound note. If y' knew someone that could change it for me, then we'd be eating like kings this night, don't y' know."

"Aye, there be such a man. An honest and sincere man who changes pounds for dollars for them just over from the Auld Sod. He charges a fee, but it's fair. We'll be passing where he lives up ahead.

89

When we get there, y' go in. I'll stay and keep the ol' cart company."

Devin got his dollars, four of them, and bought a large dressed chicken for fifty cents from a vendor they passed along the way. Leaving him the grand sum of three dollars and fifty cents with which to start his new life in America.

Doheny led him down a narrow alleyway that could barely accommodate the cart. At its end, he pointed to a house standing by itself, off in a small field. "Over yonder, there she be."

Devin's eyes widened. "That grand house is yers?"

" 'Tis not a house, and it's not that grand. Wait until y' get a closer look."

" 'Tis grand looking from where I'm standing. If it's not a house, then what ye'd be calling it?" asked an incredulous Devin Mahoney.

"It's a tenement."

"What does that mean?"

"It's a house that has seen better days. The owner has cut it up into small rooms. Whole families live in what, at one time, was a bedroom or a parlor. In that house over yonder, two families are living in the attic and three in the basement, with nary a wall between 'em. And then there's the rest of the house filled up with other families."

"And y' live there?"

"In back is a carriage house. That's where I be livin', with three other gents. 'Tis a tad drafty in winter, but I live there 'cos it allows me to keep an eye on me cart. And it's cheap. Now, let us cross the street and get to roasting that fine chicken y' bought. And we'll roast us a few apples to go with it."

With Devin's help, Doheny pushed the cart through the double doors of the carriage house and closed them tight behind him, making sure they were well secured. With the weather getting colder, it wouldn't do to have them blow open in the middle of the night. The three men who lived with Doheny were in residence, sitting around a small fire.

Doheny made the introductions. "Boys, I'd like y' to meet a young friend of mine. This is Devin Mahoney from County Kerry. He's just off the boat and he's bought us a fine, fat chicken with plenty of meat on its bones to celebrate his first day in America."

90

The men stood up and went over to shake Devin's hand and thank him for his largess. Fresh meat, other than an occasional stray rabbit, was rare indeed to these men.

Doheny once again did the honors. "This strapping fellow here is Joe McKennedy. In polite circles, he's known as Big Joe McKennedy." The man *was* big; he stood six feet, six inches tall. His shoulders were broad, as was his smile.

The other two men were brothers, Mack and Beau Bailie. They were tall, but not as tall as McKennedy. Then again, few men were. They were a little on the thin side and both had dark red hair. McKennedy and the Bailie brothers hailed from Dublin and had come over on the ship together.

After the introductions were out of the way, McKennedy said, "Come, set yerself down here by the fire. We've cabbage and a heap of carrots on the boil. I'll move the pot ov'r so we can get to roastin' that grand bird y' be holding, Mister Mahoney."

Devin held the chicken out to McKennedy. "Here, 'tis all yours. If y' don't mind, I'll happily watch y' and see how it's done. 'Tis been a long day for me." McKennedy accepted the chicken and the men got down to the serious business of preparing their feast.

Beau Bailie went to a stack of old, dried lumber resting against the back wall and fetched two lengths of board. He placed one on the fire, sending sparks swirling into the chilled air. "We requisitioned this 'ere lumber from a nearby collapsed house. We're hoping it will see us through the winter."

McKennedy used his folding knife to put a point on a stout stick. He then slid it through the chicken and held it just above the flames. The reflecting light of the fire danced in his soft brown eyes. The Bailie boys and Doheny licked their lips in anticipation of the feast to come. Devin pulled his tattered coat about him and moved closer to the flames for warmth. The smoke from the fire was quickly dispelled by the wind coming in through the gaps in the walls where the old wood had withered and warped.

When the chicken was almost cooked through and through, the pot was placed back on the fire so the cabbage and carrots would be done at the same time.

The crackling of the fire and the creaking of the carriage house as it was buffeted by the wind were the only sounds to be heard as the five men devoured the chicken, making sure to suck all the meat off the bones before tossing them into the fire.

McKennedy licked his fingers of chicken grease and leaned back with a contented sigh. "Well, Devin Mahoney, that was a meal fit for the High King of Munster hisself!"

Around the fire, four heads nodded in agreement. The men then took out their pipes and tobacco pouches. McKennedy asked Devin if he smoked.

" 'Tis not a habit I have taken up. But my father and brothers enjoyed a pipe as much as the next man." Devin could not help but think back to his father and brothers contently drawing on their pipes, when, after dinner, the family gathered around the fireplace and basked in its warmth … and the love they had for one another.

Doheny raised himself from the earthen floor and went over to where his belongings were stored, reached into a wooden box, and pulled out a large brown bottle. "*Uisquebaugh*, the water of life!" he proclaimed. "Begging yer pardon, me friends, old an' new. I've been keepin' this, though a wee dram it be, for an auspicious occasion. An' I believe this to be such as remarkable a one as any, to be sure."

He sat down next to Devin. "Y' being our guest, 'tis only fitting that y' take the first sup."

Devin accepted the bottle and removed the cork. "*Slàinte!* May the hinges of our friendship never grow rusty." After taking a small swallow, he handed the bottle back to Doheny and said, "Just what I needed. I'll be thanking y'."

Mack Bailie asked, "What would a lad such as yerself have planned, now that y're here in America?"

"I'm going to make my fortune. I'll be a wealthy man before too long, sure enough, returning to the Kingdom that birthed me. I love the ould country and every sod of it. And I'll be making my way back sooner than not."

Mack grinned, his brother chuckled, Doheny nodded sagely. McKennedy hefted the bottle in salute. "Sure y' know, we wish the same for y', but for now, what are y' going to do for work?"

Devin had no ready answer to that. He had been on American soil for less than twenty-four hours. He had but a few dollars to his name and they would not last long. He hadn't even a place to live yet. Surely that must take precedence over finding work.

"To be honest, I've nary a notion as to what work I'll be doing. I'll work at anything to get my start. But for now, I'd be happy to find a place to rest my head at night."

McKennedy held the bottle out to Beau Bailie, who downed a goodly portion of its soul-warming goodness and then handed it on to his brother.

While Mack Bailie was taking his sip, Doheny said, "Why, y'll be living here with us, don't y' know. Is that not right, boys?"

"We'd have it no other way."

"Yer welcome, sure enough."

"Make this yer home for as long as y' like."

Doheny explained the arrangement. "We each pay the landlord a dollar a week to live in this drafty barn. He comes on Friday night to collect his tariff. Y' just make yerself scarce on those nights and he'll never be the wiser. We're in luck, this being Saturday. We won't see hide nor hair of him for a week."

By then, the bottle was back with Devin. Instead of raising it to his mouth, he said, "What are y' saying? I'll not be sneaking 'round. I can pay my way, I can."

"To be sure, *a mhaic*. But the landlord is a miserable, snakey excuse for a man. How he packs those poor souls into that house of his, tight, like fish in a can, he does. And comes the time they can't pay one week, out on the street he throws them. *And* he'll keep a hold of their belongin's until they can pay what's owed. The privy we passed as we came in is overused and has overflowed. The landlord neither has it drained nor the filth carted away. 'Tis a disgusting affair, right enough. We have to make use of the field out back to do our business."

"Aye, sure enough, animals would fare better," offered Mack Bailie.

Doheny paid no attention to what Mack had said and continued with his diatribe. "For water, we must trudge half a mile to a street pump and then carry the heavy water-laden bucket back the entire half mile. And there be very little bathing in that house over yonder … or out here, I can tell y' that. Still, we have it better than those living in the block houses with their filth and darkness. No light

93

shines in them interior rooms whatsoever. 'Tis a sad spectacle, methinks."

Doheny eyed the bottle Devin was holding. Before going on, he said, "'Tis better yer money be spent buying a chicken now and then to share with the rest of us. Or better yet, a ham to be boiled. What a Sunday dinner that would make!"

"Or a fatted calf," quipped Beau Bailie, the whiskey already taking effect on his wiry frame.

Doheny ignored Beau's outburst. "Do not be aggrieved, *a chara*, y'll be paying your fair share. But to hell with the landlord."

The Bailie brothers and McKennedy voiced their approval of the plan with nods and wide Irish grins.

Devin relaxed, took his delayed swig, and passed the bottle to Doheny. No one spoke for a few minutes, but soon, Doheny proffered a question to McKennedy. "Joe, are they needing able-bodied men up where y're working?"

Before McKennedy could answer, Doheny said, "Joe's found hisself a spate of work up on Fifth Avenue, where grand houses are goin' up faster than the closing pocket of an Englishman's purse. Four and five storied, they be. Even the streets are being paved with bricks! And Joe's the man that hauls all them bricks for the bricklayers. Maybe he can get y' work doin' the same."

McKennedy groaned in faux exasperation. "Now that y've run yerself down, Denis Doheny, perhaps y'll allow me to answer the question y' asked so very long ago."

"If y'd please, Joe, me friend. I've been sitting here patiently awaiting yer answer for the longest of time, I have," said Doheny.

Both men laughed, then McKennedy said, "This being a Saturday, there'll be no work tomorrow. And whereas Tuesday is Christmas Day, we'll have to get y' up there bright and early Monday morn if we are to find y' work, Devin Mahoney. Hauling bricks is rough labor, but y're a fine specimen of Irish manhood. Y' should do alright."

"Why not tell Devin what it pays? He might not be so keen to work for such a lowly wage," said Mack Bailie, laughing.

Joe took a good-natured swipe at the older Bailie with the back of his hand, deliberately missing the lad before saying, "It pays a dollar a day, and y' get paid at the end of each and every day. If y'

94

watch the bricklayers closely and ask 'em a few questions now and then, y' might one day become a master bricklayer yerself. Then it's a grand payday y'll be having, sure enough. 'Tis truly a respected profession. One I hope to be joining afore too long."

"And what is it that yerself and Beau do?" Devin asked of Mack.

"We're what the Americans call longshoremen. We're loading and unloading boats over at the wharf. The pay is good, a dollar and fifty cents a day, but the work is hard. We told Joe he could get work there if he wanted, him being the big strappin' fella that he is. But he's set his mind on becoming a bricklayer. A trade of quality, no less, and we merely lackeys, so it seems," said Mack, winking at his brother.

"Answer me this," demanded McKennedy. "If y're making such grand money, *yer Lordship*, why is it ye'd be lessenin' yerselves to be living in a drafty old barn like this?"

"We're saving every cent we can. It's a livery business we'd be wanting to start. Up north around 57th Street, there's plenty of open land. We want to buy a parcel and put a barn on it, get a few horses and a coach. Then it's in business we'll be, don't y' know."

When it was time to turn in, Doheny gave Devin the loan of a blanket. Tomorrow, Devin would buy his own things: blankets, a set of clothes, a razor, if he could find one, and most importantly, a heavy overcoat. In his wanderings, he had seen many an immigrant in the streets, selling personal items out of a suitcase.

On Monday morning, while it was still dark out, McKennedy shook Devin awake. "Come. We've got an almost three-mile walk and y'll be wanting to be first in line for a job. Y're in luck, though. Not too many men will be out the day before Christmas looking for work, *a chairde*."

As they walked through the dark and empty streets, Devin was thinking how fortunate it was that he had purchased new clothes the day before. He had even found a razor that was relatively sharp and had shaved his beard but left the mustache. Now, with his new clothes and freshly shaved face, he was presentable. If there was a job to be had, he would surely be first to get it.

The hiring boss liked him right off. "Some of my layers are slowing down because when they reach for a brick, it's not there. It will be your job to take the bricks off the carts and bring them to the layers. Stack 'em nice and neat, within arm's reach. Your friend here, Joe, is a good worker. If you measure up to him, you'll have a job for as long as you want. Be here the day after tomorrow at daybreak. We work as long as there's light to work by."

Devin enthusiastically shook the man's hand and thanked him. As he started to leave, the foreman said, "I'm not one of them who think all Irish are lazy good-for-nothings. I give a man a chance and judge him on his performance. You have yourself a Merry Christmas, and welcome to America."

Devin thanked McKennedy for helping him find employment and left him in the process of taking bricks from a horse cart and placing them in a wheelbarrow.

The next day was Christmas Day, so Devin decided he'd spend what money he had left on a feast for his new friends. He procured a canvas bag from a man on Orchard Street for five cents and made his way down and over to Paradise Square. He strolled along, buying vegetables from the various vendors—cabbages, a small sack of potatoes, onions, carrots, and a few turnips.

Now all he needed was meat. He came across no one selling chickens. A ham would be nice. *Or a fatted calf*, he thought, smiling to himself. But again, it seemed meat was in short supply the day before Christmas. Giving up, he turned for home. A stew would have to suffice. But after the ravages of hunger he had experienced back in Ireland, a hearty vegetable stew would be a grand feast indeed.

On his way to the carriage house, he passed by a pub. There was no sign denoting it as such, but there was a wooden placard hanging over the door showing an image of a glass of beer with foam running down its sides. Devin had no trouble discerning its meaning and decided to stop in for a pint.

He stepped inside and was immediately assaulted by thick tobacco smoke, raucous laughter, and many voices speaking the language of The Green Isle.

He threaded his way through the crowd and asked the man behind the bar for a pint. "A pint, is it? Y're in America now, Boyo. Might as well speak the language. This 'ere elixir of liquid gold is called a *glass* of beer, no less."

Devin paid for his beer and looked around for a place to sit. He saw an empty spot on a bench over against the far wall. As he sat down, he nodded to the man on his right as their eyes met. Placing the bag of produce between his feet, he leaned back and took a sip of the warm beer. It tasted good and went down easy.

After a few moments, the man on his right introduced himself. "How's it goin', young fella, me lad? The name's Paddy O'Day. Who might y' be?"

"I'm Devin Mahoney from County Kerry."

O'Day smiled. "Just off the boat, are y', then?"

"How could y' tell?"

"Shure 'tis written all over y'."

A congenial conversation ensued. Devin asked about life in America and O'Day wanted all the latest news from home. Devin bought them each another beer, and when he handed O'Day his glass, O'Day hefted it in salute. "May the strength of three be in yer journey."

"Aye, and a fair wind always at yer back, friend," returned Devin. "But might I ask what it is y're mindin' in that crate ye've been resting yer feet on? I cannot see through the slats, but it sounds like y' have a bird in there."

"Yer not far off the mark, young Devin. There's not one bird a'tall, but two. Two turkeys, one for me family and one I'll be selling as soon as I quit yer gracious company. I should have been out on the street long before now, but 'tis so warm in here, and the company's the finest."

This was too good to be true, but could he afford a turkey? He had but one dollar and thirty-seven cents left to his name. "Might I ask what y'll be wanting for that turkey y'll be selling?"

Tipping his glass toward the front door, O'Day said, "I'll get two dollars if I get a dime out yonder. It's Christmas Eve and 'tis a seller's market, shure enough."

Devin had been leaning forward in anticipation, but now leaned back in disappointment.

O'Day saw the letdown in Devin's face and asked, "What ails y', Devin Mahoney? Did y' have yer heart set on a Christmas bird?"

"I was thinking of it, but 'tis not important."

"Have ye not the two dollars?" Then a twinkle came into O'Day's eyes. "What would y' be having in yer pockets on this fair day, might I ask?"

"Not enough to buy yer bird. I have but one dollar and thirty-seven cents."

O'Day rubbed his chin in thoughtful contemplation. "Too bad, *a chara*. But seeing as how I'm without funds until I sell me bird, would y' be so kind as to buy me another pint? I mean, glass of beer. Is it not funny how the Americans cannot call a pint by its rightful name?"

" 'Twould be an honor and a privilege to buy y' a pint, and I'll have one with y'."

Devin stood to go to the bar, but O'Day tugged at his sleeve and told him to sit back down.

" 'Tis alright, *a chara*. I have coin enuf in me pocket and love enuf in me heart for me fellow man on this glorious day before our Savior's birth. I was only seein' if y' were worthy."

"Is it coddin' me, y' are? What do y' mean, 'worthy'?" Devin had been insulted right down to the marrow of his bones. He stood to leave, but once again, O'Day pulled him back by the sleeve of his coat.

"Afore y' be running off, *a chara*, I have something for ye." O'Day bent over and untied the rope securing the top of the crate. Opening the lid just enough to slip his hand inside, he felt around, causing no small amount of squawking. He pulled out a fine specimen of a turkey. The turkey was none too happy about the whole affair, but O'Day was wearing a wide grin.

Holding the bird by its legs, he said, "Here y' go, *a chara*, with the compliments of Paddy O'Day."

Devin was taken aback. "I cannot accept that," he said.

"Of course y' can. Now, don't be daft, young Devin Mahoney. It will warm the cockles of me heart to see y' walking out of here carrying as fine a bird as ever was bred."

Devin relented and gingerly took the turkey in hand. "I be thanking y', Paddy O'Day. 'Tis a wonderful thing y' are doing. Ye've not only given me a Christmas to remember, but four others as well. The next time I see y', I'll buy y' that pint y' asked for."

Devin left the pub with the bird's wings a flapping.

Mack and Beau Bailie brought home two loaves of bread, a tin of butter, and a small sack of potatoes. McKennedy supplied a rather large jug of homemade spirits he had secured from one of his coworkers. Doheny had made a deal with a woman who baked him an apple pie in exchange for a bucketful of his apples.

McKennedy slit the bird's throat with his folding knife and drained it of its life-blood. Mack plucked it, Beau cleaned the insides, and Doheny roasted it over the fire. From the innards, a tasty broth was made in which to cook the vegetables. When all was ready, the five men sat around the fire and thanked the good Lord for the bounty He had bestowed upon them.

After all had eaten their fill, McKennedy brought out the jug and the men passed it around in jovial camaraderie. About the time the bottle was being handed around for the sixth time, Beau stood up and started to sing, softly at first, but his voice grew stronger as he went on. His haunting falsetto filled the confines of the carriage house. On the second verse, the other men joined in, and soon their drafty home reverberated with sweet melodic sounds as five Children of Erin sang as they had not sung since leaving the Ould Country.

Silent night, holy night
All is calm, all is bright
Round yon virgin, mother and child
Holy infant so tender and mild
Sleep in heavenly peace
Sleep in heavenly peace

11

Hauling bricks was hard labor, but Devin did not mind; he had grown accustomed to hard work over the years. He made up one part of a two-man team, consisting of the bricklayer and the man who brought him his bricks. The bricklayers worked fast and if a hauler slowed down, the "layer" would not be able to lay the next row. And that did not bode well for the foreman's frame of mind.

Life at the carriage house fell into a routine. Because the men returned from work at different times, eating was seldom a communal affair. The two Bailie brothers ate together, as did McKennedy and Devin. Doheny had his own hours and could come in at any time. During the week, they were all far too tired to do anything after eating but crawl into their blankets and fall off into a deep sleep, while thinking of the bright future just around the corner. Each man had his own dream.

Fridays and Sundays were different. On Fridays, Devin did not go straight home after work. He would stop off at the pub where he had met O'Day and linger over a few glasses of beer until he was sure the landlord had been and gone.

Sundays were the best. That's when they could sleep in, and dinner was always a grand affair. Devin bought a dollar's worth of meat as his contribution towards the rent, and everyone worked in concert preparing the meal. One was in charge of the fire; another, cooking the meat; still another, the vegetables; and so on. The most important job of all usually fell to Doheny. But in an emergency, such as Doheny's source had run out, someone else could be depended on to come up with a bottle or a jug. Life was good in the carriage house, such as it was.

After a month, Devin had saved fifteen dollars from his pay. He was on his way to becoming a rich man. And then it happened.

It was a Friday night, February 8th to be exact. Devin was in the pub, avoiding the landlord as he did every Friday night. He was sipping on a beer and conversing with his tablemates when his eyes settled on a man across the room. It was Cudahy!

He was dressed in his finest, his outfit immaculate, as opposed to Devin's dust-covered and torn work clothes. He was smiling and laughing and seemed to be holding court. The other three men at his table hung on his every word. He looked as though he had not a care in the world. Devin wondered how much Cudahy had stolen that day, and from whom, to put him in such good spirits.

Time slowed for Devin, it grew dark around the periphery of his vision. At that moment, the only thing that existed in all the world was a laughing, smirking Cudahy. Devin thought about the heavy, brick-laden wheelbarrows he pushed all day long. He looked at the thin layer of red dust that covered his hands and clothes. He thought of the money Cudahy had stolen from him, almost one hundred and seventy dollars! How many tons of bricks would he have to move to earn that amount? All those thoughts coalesced into a crimson curtain that momentarily obscured his vision. Anger overflowed his being.

Devin shook with rage. He had to force his trembling hands to be still. He willed himself to calm down. He had something to do and he could not do it unless he had himself under control. He finished his beer, took a deep breath, and stood up.

Purposefully, but calmly, he walked over to Cudahy's table and stood opposite Cudahy, who was in the midst of telling a humorous story. When he noticed Devin looming over the table, he nodded in his direction, thinking Devin just another admirer.

In a veiled voice that would have chilled the hearts of intrepid men everywhere, Devin said, "Y' don't remember me, do y'?"

A look of intense irritation passed over Cudahy's face as he brought his narrative to a halt. He forced himself to smile so his companions would see what a good and tolerant man he was. "Can't say that I do, Boyo."

Devin walked around the table until he stood directly over Cudahy. "I'm the man y' robbed. Y' stole from me, my first day in America, ya thievin' *cladhaire*, and now y'll fork out what you owe me … one way or the other."

Cudahy's eyes became slits. Who is this dirty beggar that dared confront him in public? Is this trouble or something he could talk his way out of? Then he remembered. His face lit up as though Devin was a long-lost friend. "'Tis yersel', Boyo! Y're a hard man to find, sure enough! Wasn't I the one had difficulty findin' me mano and exchangin' yer pound notes fer dollars with the soles near worn off me feet from the looking. An' sure weren't ya up an' gone by the time it took me to get back to y'. An' sure isn't it fate alone that I finally found y', at long last."

Devin was having none of it, but he would give Cudahy one chance. "By my reckonin', y' owe me one hundred and sixty-six dollars and fifty cents and I'll be havin' it now."

"Sure, y' know I have it. I've been keepin' it safe fer y' and 'tis all yers. But I wouldn't be fool enough to carry such an amount on me person. Y' never know what scoundrel y'd be likely to meet, who would take advantage of a righteous gent such as I. I'll see y' tomorrow, right here, with the full amount."

Just as Devin had thought. He reached out and grabbed Cudahy by the lapels of his fine coat and pulled him to his feet. One of the men at the table started to get up, but Devin halted him in midrise. "If ya don't want some of what he's about to get, I'd sit back down if I was y'." The man did as Devin suggested.

Now Devin could give his entire attention to Cudahy. He released his hold on the lapels and backhanded him squarely on the face. Cudahy fell back a step or two, but kept his legs about him, wobbly as they were. A trickle of blood ran down his chin and fell onto the wooden floor, one drop at a time. His tongue licked at the side of his mouth; the warm, coppery taste told Cudahy he was bleeding.

He steadied himself by planting his feet far apart. Leaning slightly forward, he hissed, "Good for y', Boyo." Devin started for him to give him another slap, but before he had taken two steps, Cudahy reached behind his back and brought forth a knife sporting a nine-inch blade. "Y' want some of this, then, Boyo? I'll be only too willing to oblige!"

Everything Devin had endured for the past year—the death of his family, the long periods of starvation, being thrown off the family farm, the sights he witnessed on his trek to Cork, the voyage on the coffin ship, having to swim in freezing water to land in America, and being robbed his first day in the Land of

102

Opportunity—all those emotions, all that pent-up anger came to bear. He had had enough.

He charged Cudahy, surprising him. He grabbed the hand holding the knife and brought it down hard on the table. *SNAP!* Devin had broken the man's wrist. Cudahy let loose of the knife as he screamed out in pain. Devin snatched up the knife and glared at Cudahy's comrades, daring them to make a move. No one did. He turned back to Cudahy, who was now bent over and holding on to his forearm just above the broken wrist, whimpering in pain.

Devin knocked Cudahy's hat off his head, grabbed him by his greasy hair, and pulled his head up so he could look him dead in the eye. Holding the knife close to Cudahy's face, he said, "I just broke yer right wrist. If you don't want me to cut off yer right ear, y' will, with yer left hand, reach into yer coat pocket and come out with yer purse. I'm leaving here with that purse no matter what y' do. What y' have to ask yerself is do *ya* want to leave here with only one ear. Though from the look of y', it might be a welcome improvement. Your choice."

Cudahy did as commanded, but in a feeble attempt at saving face, he tossed the purse on the table rather than handing it over to Devin. Devin let go of Cudahy, and pushed him back down into his chair. "Now I want yer folding money."

Cudahy started to say something, but before he could utter a single syllable, Devin pushed the knife up under his chin and said, "Just one word … just one miserable word from y', and sure enough, it will be the last one y'll ever speak." Cudahy swallowed hard and reached into the pocket of his trousers. He withdrew a roll of bank notes and held it out for Devin to take. No heroics his time. Leaving the knife where it was, Devin put the roll into his coat pocket and took the purse from the table. It was heavy. Gold coins, most likely.

Cudahy was a beaten man, at least for the moment, so Devin removed the knife from under his chin and turned his focus to Cudahy's three comrades. "Ye boys might have a yearnin' to follow me out of here for yer own reasons, and I would welcome ye to do so, I would. I think it's fair play to tell ye that the first one to get to me will get this blade in his gut." Devin held up the knife for emphasis. "The other two may very well take me down, but not easily. And just a reminder: Number one goes down with me. So. Who wants to volunteer to be number one? Think it over and I'll be seeing ye outside, I will."

He backed away from the table. Cudahy's comrades stayed where they were.

When Devin had first confronted Cudahy, the room had gone silent. Everyone watched in amazement as the crazy paddy dug his grave even deeper by holding a knife on a member of the Forty Thieves gang. The men standing behind Devin parted and made a wide path to the door. No one wanted to get involved one way or the other.

Devin nodded to the room in general before walking out into the cold night air. He had no fear that someone would follow and confront him, but feeling the way he did, he wished someone would at least try. Adrenaline was flowing in his veins like a fast-moving train. He did not think he had punished Cudahy nearly enough. But he got some of his own back and that would have to suffice for now. He did not stop to count the money. That wasn't important. What was important was the fact that he had decided he would never again allow himself to be stepped on or taken advantage of. No matter how long he lived.

He could not wait to get back to the carriage house and tell the boys what had happened. He was sure there'd be a celebration, pats on the back. That he'd be told what a grand thing he had done. Someone was sure to bring out a bottle to toast his magnificence. But that's not what happened a'tall.

Doheny was beside himself. "Y' did *what*?" he demanded. "Y' beat up a member of The Forty Thieves? Are ya daft, man?"

McKennedy was a bit more sanguine about the matter. "I admire yer spunk. I might have done the same thing, but then I would have made for parts unknown, not come back here. Them Forty Thieves are a thick-knit bunch, sure enough."

The Bailie brothers stood off to the side and shook their heads, wondering if they should make for 57th Street now, before the Forty Thieves descended upon the carriage house and they got caught up in the carnage that was sure to follow.

No one broke out a bottle in celebration.

104

When things had quieted down a bit, Doheny explained the facts of life to Devin. "'Tis a good and brave thing y' done, sure enough. But I'm of a mind to be thinkin' y'd do well to move on unless y' intend on celebrating yer victory posthumously. Do y' understand?"

No, Devin did not understand. What was this all about? Surely he had beat Cudahy easily. What was there to fear? If Cudahy showed up looking for revenge, he'd best him again and he'd enjoy doing so.

Doheny said, "Yer not seein' the whole picture, *a mhaic*. I'll try and fill in the blanks for y'. Come, rest yer bones by the fire. Joe, fetch out the bottle. 'Tis shaping up to be thirsty work, I'm thinkin'."

The four men, Doheny, McKennedy, and the Bailie brothers, liked Devin. They liked him enough to try to save his life. Beau built up the fire and when it had warmed the carriage house a wee bit, Doheny spoke. "Let me tell y' how it is, *a chara*. Here in the Sixth Ward, we have no law to speak of. The Forty Thieves and The Dead Rabbits gangs run the Lower East Side. They've deep pockets, to be sure. And the politicians and police are fist-deep in 'em. They are quick to turn a blind eye to their shenanigans, lad, including murder. Scum of the earth they be, sure enough. 'Tis a crooked game, *a mhaic*, and they hold all the aces.

"So it won't be the police y' can go to when they come looking for y'. And come they will, make no mistake about that. No, not tonight. 'Twill take time to find y'. They'll be down to the pub tomorrow talkin' to anyone who might know y'. Surely y've spoken to a few of yer fellow countrymen, maybe even mentioned where ya hang yer hat. Some have seen yer comin's an' yer goin's, sure enough. An' mark me words, Devin Mahoney, they'll tell if squeezed, 'cos everyone fears the gangs, an' with sound enough reason, I believe."

Devin interrupted. "I'm not in fear of a one of 'em."

"A brave man y' be, but a foolish one, too. There is no way to high heaven y'll take on and defeat the ten or so they'll surely be sendin' here ta murder ya. As long as y're on this island, they'll hunt ya down and slit yer throat sure as anything. They've a reputation to live up to, and they can't be seen to be bested by a young lad such as yerself. Or sure enough every other upstart tryin' to make a name for themselves will be aiming to take over their patch."

Doheny looked for support from the others. "Is that not the way of it, lads?"

McKennedy spoke up. "As the auld cock crows, the young cock learns, Devin Mahoney. Y're no fool, lad, so don't set about to be proving us wrong."

Devin did not look any too happy with what he was hearing, but decided to keep his tongue, for the time being.

Doheny continued: "An' sure, y' did not come here to America to get yerself killed now, did y'?"

Devin said nothing.

"That's right, y' did not. Y' came here to make yer fortune and return to the Ould Sod a rich man. Y' can't do that if y're out there lyin' in a burial ground, six feet under. Surely, the devil's tail goes before y', *a mhaic*."

Doheny, in his own way, was making sense.

Doheny continued with his counsel. "New York is not the only place to make yer fortune. Have y' not seen those bills pasted to the sides of buildings asking for good, strong Irishmen to come to Pennsylvania to work on the railroad? They say the pay is good. But for y', the best thing is that y'll be a far reach from Cudahy and his bunch of cutthroat friends."

Devin reached for the bottle and took a long, slow pull. "I worked up a right thirst listenin' to all yer talkin', Denis Doheny."

"Aye. The well's not deep enough, me young friend."

When the bottle was safely back on the other side of the fire, in the capable hands of Mack Bailie who knew what to do with it, Devin asked, "And where might Pennsylvania be?"

"It's out west somewhere is all I know. I did speak with a gent once who had gone there to work on the railroad. I met him when he came back to get his family. He was going to settle them in a town called Philadelphia. Perhaps that's where y' should be going. He did say a railroad runs from New Jersey to Pennsylvania, straight as an arrow."

Devin asked the obvious question. "And how would a fella get to New Jersey, if he was of a mind to go there? This being an island, or so I hear."

"Y' heard right, *a mhaic*. But if y' were to go down to the south tip of this island, y'd find a fine fleet of boats tied up at the docks. I'm sure any one of the men owning any such boat would be more than happy to ferry y' across the water to New Jersey ... for a price."

Devin still thought leaving New York would be tantamount to running away from a fight and he was hesitant to do so. But what could he do against an entire gang of cutthroats? Then a thought occurred to him. "What about ye? When they come looking for me and I'm not here, will they not take their anger out on ye four?"

McKennedy answered. " 'Tis y' they'll be wanting. Besides, we'll be ever so helpful. We'll be tellin' them how y' ran in here all wide-eyed an' rabbit-like and grabbed yer things and told us where y' were planning on heading. Of course, we'll tell them exactly where y've gone. They will thank us and be on their way, trying to get to y' before y've traveled too many miles."

"Ye'd tell them where I've gone?" asked Devin, a touch of disappointment in his voice.

"Aye. Y've gone to Québec. To where y' were going afore yer ship lost its mast and got blown off course."

Devin looked at the Bailie brothers. "And what say ye?"

Without consulting his brother, Beau said, "It's as Joe says. The Forty Thieves' fight is with yerself and not with us innocent and helpful souls. Y' should have been away by now. Y'll be killed dead as a doornail if they catch up with y', and nothing surer."

"Enough of this," barked Doheny. " 'Tis time y' be a-leavin'. How much did y' get back from Cudahy?"

"I've not yet taken the time to count it."

"Well then, get to counting. And when it's tallied up, be sure to put most of it in yer boot and the rest in yer pocket."

Devin asked, "And why would I be doing such a thing?"

In exasperation, Doheny said, "May the Saints preserve us! If y're robbed, God forbid, they'll be getting only a small part of yer purse."

"I've no intention of letting anyone rob me ever again," Devin muttered under his breath as he counted the bills. When he had finished, he let out with a low whistle.

"What is it?" asked Doheny.

"There's over two hundred dollars here! Two hundred and eleven, to be exact."

Mack Bailie said, "If they had no reason to come after y' before, they'll sure enough have reason to now."

Devin was dividing the money into two stacks when he remembered Cudahy's purse. "Hold on," he announced. "I almost forgot." He took out the purse, opened it, and tilted it upside down. Eight double eagles fell onto the dirt floor, throwing up dust as they landed. Firelight gleamed off the yellow coins. "Gold!" shouted Beau Bailie.

Doheny picked one up and looked at it reverently. It was the first gold he had ever seen, and it was worth twenty dollars! It said so on the back. The single coin he held in his hand was more money than he made in a month and a half of selling apples. And there were seven more just like it, lying at his feet. He handed the coin over to Devin. "'Tis a good start y' have to accumulating yer fortune."

Having finally seen the merits in Doheny's argument, Devin decided to go to Pennsylvania. He changed into his good clothes and slipped the two stacks of bills into his boots, one in each. He picked up the coins from the floor and put four of them into his pocket. He then went to each man and placed a gold coin in his hand. He gathered his few possessions into a canvas bag and said to his friends, "Seems I've little choice but to be taking my leave earlier than expected. But from the bottom of my heart, 'tis no lie when I say 'twas a pleasure to have known ye. May St. Patrick guard ye wherever ye go, and may the good saints bless ye, one and all."

Each man shook Devin's hand and wished him well. Doheny was the last. "I'll be thinking fondly of y', Devin Mahoney, and I'll be sorely missing yer company."

"Come, see me out, Denis, if ya'd be so kind as to point me in the right direction."

With a final nod good-bye to the others, Devin walked out of the carriage house, followed by Doheny. After a few steps, he stopped and said, "That's alright. We're grand here, I know which way to go, I'll find the dock. I just wanted to thank ya, Denis, for being my first friend in America. I'll not be forgetting ya." Placing a double eagle in Doheny's hand, he added, "Take this to put toward that shop ye're sure to be opening one day."

Emotion welled up in Doheny's heart as he said, 'Y've already given me one of these."

"So I have."

The last Doheny saw of Devin Mahoney was the white of the canvas bag that hung from his shoulder as he walked into the dark night.

12

Devin found a man willing to row him across the river. The agreed upon price: one dollar. As they neared midstream, Devin asked the oarsman if he knew about a train that went all the way to Pennsylvania.

"I do know there is a station in Jersey City. As to where the train goes, I have no idea. South, I believe."

"Where might I find Jersey City?"

"That one's easy. Right near where I'm going to land you. Ask anyone you meet, and they'll put you straight."

It was getting on to midnight when Devin found the station. But the place was closed, and he would have to wait until morning. He sat down on a nearby bench and pulled his coat tight about him to ward off the cold.

In time, he fell into a restless sleep, sitting upright on a hard wooden bench, alone, on the outskirts of Jersey City. Three thousand miles from his beloved Ireland.

When he next opened his eyes, it was six hours later, and people were bustling and milling about. A line of people stood in front of the ticket window, which was now open for business. Devin went to the end of the line and waited his turn to purchase a ticket to the new Promised Land of Pennsylvania, seeing as how the old Promised Land of New York did not work out quite so well.

At the window, he asked the agent if the train went to Philadelphia.

"Philadelphia and other places. Would you like a ticket to Philadelphia?"

"Aye."

Devin handed over the five dollars and fifty-three cents requested. With ticket in hand, he asked, "And where might I be finding this train?"

"Right over there, sir. Where those people are standing. The train will be here shortly and departs at exactly 7:05. We have a schedule to maintain."

Devin had never ridden on a train before, although he had seen one once, from afar.

A shrill whistle sounded in the distance, announcing the train's imminent arrival. Minutes later the engine pulled in, hissing and spouting steam from its undercarriage. The massive iron conveyance was a little intimidating. Nevertheless, Devin squared his shoulders and marched up to a man in a blue uniform with matching cap. "Begging yer pardon, sir, but is this the train to Pennsylvania? Philadelphia in particular?"

The conductor inspected his ticket and said, "This is the train you want. Please watch your step as you board."

Devin sat on the edge of his seat, looking out the window. Never had he thought anything or anyone could move at such a speed. The man sitting next to him said they were traveling in excess of twenty miles per hour. The cities and countryside flew by at such an alarming rate, he had no time to take in all the wonders of America. The land rolled on. So much open land!

In what seemed no time at all, the train pulled into Philadelphia Station. Holding his canvas bag, Devin stepped out onto the platform and looked about.

What now? he thought.

He wandered the streets, taking in the sights. One thing he had to admit was that Philadelphia was a much cleaner city than New York. All the streets were paved, and even the footpaths, or sidewalks as they were called in America, were paved with bricks. Devin shook his head in amazement and wondered how many wheelbarrow-loads of bricks it had taken to pave the city.

His first order of business was to find a place to live. Then he'd look for employment. In due course, he came to a large three-story house with a wooden sign affixed to the wrought iron fence that ran along the sidewalk. The sign announced, in bold black letters against a white background, that the building was a boarding house.

Devin looked around and thought the neighborhood would be a nice place to live. Trees lined the street and the people walking by were all well dressed. Better dressed than he, in fact. But as soon as he got himself settled, he'd buy new clothes. And not second-hand clothes either.

He swung the gate inward and walked up the steps. Considering this was a boarding house, Devin walked in without knocking. He stepped into a hallway with a parlor on the right. An elderly woman sat in a high-back chair, doing needlepoint. When she saw Devin, she stopped what she was doing and inquired, "Yes, may I help you with something?"

Devin took a step into the parlor and said, "Good afternoon to ya, mam. Would I be right in thinking 'tis yerself the woman of the house? I'm looking for a room to let, so I am."

The woman had been smiling, but the smile faded. She pressed a hand to her throat and asked, "You're Irish, aren't you?"

"Aye, right enough, and proudly so."

"Well, there's not a room here for you. I think you would be happier with your own kind."

Devin's grin disappeared, and in a puzzled tone, he asked, "My own kind? And what kind would that be, mam?"

The woman's frown deepened. "Irish, of course. You people are not exactly welcomed in this part of the city."

Devin had trouble believing what he was hearing. "Perhaps ya'd be kind enough to enlighten me as to where ya think my kind might be welcome, if ya don't mind me asking?"

To be quickly rid of the papist, she answered his question. "The Kensington District."

Devin knew the woman was ill at ease but did not care. In fact, he enjoyed prolonging her discomfort. "And where might a man such as myself find this Kensington District?"

Another annoyed sigh from the woman. "Down by the river."

Devin was not about to let her off that easily. "The river, mam?"

"Yes, the Delaware River. Now please leave. I have work to do."

Devin bowed deeply, sweeping his hand before him in an exaggerated manner, and walked out. He could not understand why Americans had such a hatred of the Irish. *Well, matters not to me. I'll make my fortune in American dollars and be gone. They'll be rid of me and I'll be rid of them ... and good riddance, I say.*

By asking directions, he found his way to the "Irish" district. The houses were well-kept brick buildings, each two stories high, and the streets were clean. It was nothing like New York. Devin was heartened by the wide Irish smiles that greeted him as he walked the narrow streets.

It was getting late and time to find shelter. On Williams Street, he found what he was looking for. The sign read: Missus O'Rourke's Boarding House.

Again, Devin went in without knocking. The parlor was empty, but he heard voices nearby and walked down the hall until he came to a dining room.

Six people were seated at the table, two women and four men. The conversation fell off when, from the doorway, Devin cleared his throat and said, "Begging yer pardon, all, but I'm looking to know where the man or woman of the house might be, as I'm weary and in need of a warm place to lay my cap for a spell. Would I be right in thinking there'd be a welcome on the mat for a son of Eireann in this here fine establishment?"

A grey-headed woman sitting at the head of the table stood up. She was tall for a woman, five feet, nine inches, and thin as a rail. She looked to be in her fifties. It was hard to judge. Her face was free of wrinkles, but the corners of her eyes were well-lined.

"Enter, young sir. I'm Missus O'Rourke."

Devin took a tentative step into the room. The slightest beginnings of a smile formed on the woman's lips. "Don't be afraid. Come hither, *a leana*. Let me get a good look at y'." Devin walked all the way in, holding the canvas bag to his chest.

With hands on her hips, Missus O'Rourke looked Devin up and down, finally asking, "What is it yer parents christened ya, young fella?"

"Devin Mahoney."

"Might I be so bold as to ask, are y' of good character, young Devin Mahoney? I'll be having no trash in *my* house, I run no kip. 'Tis as clean and proper an establishment as y're likely to find in all of Kensington, sure as my name's Patsy O' Rourke."

"I believe I am of good character. Since y're of a mind to be asking."

Missus O'Rourke removed her hands from her hips and pointed a boney finger in Devin's direction. "Well, y' look like a good boy, but y' also look like yer shoes are still damp after stepping off the

113

boat. Do y' mind me asking, can y' afford a respectable accommodation such as mine? I charge three dollars a week, in advance, and that includes two meals a day, breakfast and supper."

"Aye, mam. 'Tis a fair rent for decent lodgings, sure enough!"

"My place is clean, and I expect my boarders to keep it so. I'll show y' yer room after y've had yerself a bite to eat. Sure yer mother would be praying for me, if I didn't start to fill out yer frame enough to keep yerself upright, young fella. Now take a weight off and introduce yerself to yer new neighbors while I get y' a bowl and a spoon. And for the love of St. Peter and the Apostles, put that bag down. Y're holding it like it's everything y' own in the world, even though 'tis probably so."

Devin took a seat at the end of the table. For a moment there was an embarrassed silence. At last, the sole woman at the table said, "My name is Mary Callahan and I ... I mean we ... welcome you to our little home, Mister Mahoney."

That freed up the men to speak. One at a time, they introduced themselves.

"I'm Edward Lowery."

"William Shannon, but call me Bill."

"Michael Foley from the fair County of Tyrone."

"Glad to meet ya, Mister Mahoney. I'm John Kinney and I hail from County Derry."

Missus O'Rourke returned and admonished her boarders. "Ye men, make yerselves useful and pass the food along to young Mister Mahoney. Look how thin he is."

Foley, from the fair County of Tyrone, was the closest. He reached out and pushed a large bowl containing a thick stew towards Devin's end of the table. There was even meat in it—beef, to Devin's eyes. Bill Shannon handed down a large plate piled high with thick slices of bread. And Edward Lowery passed the butter.

As Devin ladled out the stew, the men started in asking him questions.

Foley wanted to know, "Where are y' from, Mister Mahoney?"

"How long have you been in America?" asked Shannon.

"What are yer plans?" inquired Kinney.

Before Lowery could ask his own question, Missus O'Rourke cut in. "Ye gentlemen be as gracious as Miss Callahan and let Mister

Mahoney get a little stew inside him afore y' start in with yer botherin' ways."

In between mouthfuls, Devin told his story, leaving out the part about Cudahy. He had come to Philadelphia because he wanted to live in a cleaner city, or so he said. As he talked, his eyes kept trailing back to Miss Callahan. She was something to look at. He guessed her age to be about eighteen or nineteen. She wore her long auburn hair down, and when she moved her head, her hair shimmered in the dim light. Her eyes were lovely. Copper-brown in color they were, but two shades lighter, almost golden. The reflecting light of the lantern made them seem even more beautiful. Devin wished that *she* would ask him a question, but she seemed content to let the men and Missus O'Rourke do the talking.

When he had finished with his narrative, he started in on asking the others their stories. He worked his way around the table and saved Miss Callahan for last.

Foley was in his early thirties and had been in America for a little over six months. He had a job working with a crew that was building a new bridge over the Delaware. Lowery worked for the diocese as a carpenter. He had come over in '45, just before the blight hit. He stated his age as thirty-six. Bill Shannon worked as a tutor for two wealthy families. All in all, he had charge of ten children ranging from seven to fifteen years of age. He was in his late fifties with a fine, full head of hair. Very distinguished he looked. Then there was John Kinney. He worked as an assistant clerk for a shipping company. He was twenty-two. All the men, except Shannon who was a widower, were single. Missus O'Rourke was a widow and had been in America for almost two decades. She was originally from County Donegal.

Now it was Mary Callahan's turn. "And y', Miss Callahan? What brought ya to this big, wide country, so far away from yer home?" asked Devin.

She did not answer right away. Instead, she looked down at the lace tablecloth. Just when Devin thought she was going to remain silent, she looked up and said, "My parents, wishful as they were, remained unblessed with a boy. That left me the eldest sibling of four sisters. When The Great Hunger befell us, my father ensured my mother, my sisters, and I had sustenance by taking work on one of those horrible work gangs. As the months wore on, we witnessed him growing thinner and thinner, until at last he died. He had worked himself to death providing for us."

She hesitated for a moment, her eyes darted around the room as though she was unsure what to say next. Then, with a long exhale of breath, she continued. "We decided, my mother and I, that we would use what little money we had to send me off to America so that I could find work and send money back home."

Devin asked, "How long have ya been here and have y' found work as of yet?"

"I've been in America two months now, and I *have* found employment, of a kind. Not, ideally, the sort I'd have wished for, for that I'm still looking. Fortunately, to help ends meet, Missus O'Rourke allows me to lend a hand in her labors in exchange for my board."

Before Devin could ask any further questions, Missus O'Rourke chimed in. "Enough chatter for now. Let ye men retire yerselves to the parlor and smoke yer pipes while Mary and I clear the table and scour the dishes."

The conversation continued in the parlor. Devin was asked about the conditions in Ireland, and he told of all that he had witnessed first-hand. For his part, he wanted to know where he could find employment. "Mister Foley, do y' think there might be work for me on that bridge y're building?"

After a thoughtful pull on his pipe, Foley exhaled a stream of blue-white smoke into the air and said, "Unfortunately, *a chara*, I daren't believe there is such a position available. As far as I know, we have a full crew. But I will enquire for sure, come the morrow."

Missus O'Rourke came in and announced, "Now then, I'm of a mind to be thinking the young Mister Mahoney has had a trying day and would like to rest his head." Turning to Devin, she said, "If you'll be so kind as to follow me, Mister Mahoney, I'll set about showing you to yer lodgings."

Devin bid his goodnights and followed Missus O'Rourke out of the room. She held on tightly to the banister and looked over her shoulder as she led Devin up the stairs. "Yer room's to the back. There's not much of a view, but you'll be spared the street noises.

Y'll find the privy at the rear of the house, and I'll be thanking y' to keep it clean."

The room was small. Nothing more than a bed and a bureau with a mirror on it. Devin thought it the most luxurious accommodation he had ever seen.

The next day was Saturday. After buying a set of new clothes, Devin spent most of the day looking for employment. He was clean-shaven, except for the mustache, and well dressed. He thought he'd have no problem finding a job. However, by late afternoon it had become apparent that there was no work to be had for an unskilled young man. Especially if that young man was of Irish extraction. He returned to Missus O'Rourke's, disillusioned and wondering what his next move should be.

That night at dinner, he was asked about his day, and he told those sitting around the table of the rejection he had experienced wherever he sought work. "All I want is honest employment," he said. "I'm a hard worker, willin' to do any task required of me, but because of the fear and hatred of the Irish, unfathomable to me as it is, no one is willing to hire me."

It was Shannon who asked, "What can you do, my friend?"

"I'll do anything."

Shannon broke out with the slightest of smiles. "That is not what I asked. I asked, what *can* you do?"

Devin put his fork aside, leaned back in his chair, and thought for a moment. At length, he said, "I can farm. I can haul bricks. I can ..."

Shannon interrupted, "There is not much demand for farmers in Philadelphia, and I believe all the bricks that were ever going to be laid in this fair city have already been laid."

Not quite sure what to say next, Devin absentmindedly stabbed at a piece of cabbage lying on his plate. Then his eyes flickered with hope. "Mister Foley, did y' enquire as to the availability of work for me on the bridge?"

Foley forked a potato from the bowl and placed it on his plate. "There was no need to ask. Four men were let go today. And more may lose their jobs in the coming days."

Seeing the concern on the faces of his fellow boarders, he hastily added, "I'm all right. I assist the iron workers and there's plenty of work there."

Missus O'Rourke wanted to change the subject to something a little more pleasant. "Will y' be attending Mass with us in the morning, Mister Mahoney?"

Devin had not been to Mass since before the blight. Somewhere along the way, he had lost his faith. And what little faith he might have had left was surely gone by the second year of *an Gorta Mhór*.

"Mass?" questioned Devin.

"Aye. Mary and I regularly go to the ten o' clock Mass. The men sleep in on Sundays, so they go at twelve. But because y're not yet working, I thought y' might like to accompany us." Missus O'Rourke never imagined for one moment that one of her boarders would not go to church on Sunday and receive the Holy Sacrament.

Devin shot a quick glance at Mary. Her eyes smiled at him while her cheeks took on a rosy blush. "I'd be proud to accompany ye two fine ladies to Sunday Mass," said a hopeful Devin.

The blush deepened on Mary's cheeks.

Later, in the parlor, Shannon took Devin aside. "What I was getting at before Missus O'Rourke intervened was that the only work for such a strapping, young Irish lad as yourself, one without any particular skills, is either building the railroad, working on digging the Mainline Canal, or mining coal. And I would strongly advise against going into a coal mine."

"And why such a worry, sir?"

"They're dangerous. Here's the question that needs answering, young man. Are y' prepared to work on the canal itself or the railroad they're building in the western part of the state?"

"Does it matter one way or the other? I just want to work. To get a foothold in America, to get my start. I know there's opportunity a begging here. And surely I'll find it."

Shannon nodded in agreement. "If I was young and as full of vinegar as you, I'd opt for the railroad. They pay a dollar and twenty-five cents a day. 'Tis not a sum to be sniffed at. They'll feed and house you, and as isolated as you'll surely be, there'll be no spending of your pay. 'Tis a grand way to save yer coins, sure enough, if that be your intention."

Devin was sold, but looking across the room in Mary's direction, he asked, "You said the railroad was being built out West. How far out West?"

Glancing over his shoulder at Mary, Shannon saw the reason for Devin's question. "They're extending the tracks from Harrisburg to Pittsburg. But take heart, *a chara*. Where you'll be working is only a few hours away by train. And once a month, on a rotating basis, the company brings in the workers for two days. From Friday night to Sunday night. Then come Monday morning, it's back to work as if you never left."

"How do y' know all this?"

"I talk to people."

Devin asked where he could find the railroad office.

"The railroad does not do the hiring. They contract the work out. You'll want to see John Kelly & Company. They're over on Front Street. Kelly won't be there, though. He'll be out making sure his men are laying track and blowing holes in mountains. But there'll be someone in the office. Now, if you will excuse me, I must go to my room and prepare my lessons for Monday. Young minds yearning for knowledge, don't you know."

Devin went over to Missus O'Rourke and asked her what time she usually left for church.

"We start out about nine thirty. I like to get there a little early and light a candle for my poor departed husband, Daniel Patrick Allowious O'Rourke. A finer man never did live."

"I'll be right here awaiting ye at nine thirty o'clock, on the button, raring to go," said Devin. And with a goodnight wish to his landlady and a smile in Mary Callahan's direction, he took his leave. He had walked many a mile that day in search of employment and it had taken its toll on him. The soft bed waiting for him upstairs was going to feel mighty fine this evening.

13

The day was sunny and bright as they ambled along the avenue. Always the gentleman, Devin walked on the outside, with Mary on his right and Missus O'Rourke next to her. This way the women would be protected if a carriage splashed by, throwing up mud.

As they passed a woman sweeping the sidewalk in front her house, Missus O'Rourke said, "Excuse me, *a leanai*, but there's Missus Conway. I must have a word with her. Ye children scoot on ahead to church and I'll see ye there."

After a few steps, Mary said, "Subtlety is not one of Missus O'Rourke's stronger points, is it?"

Devin cast a glance in Mary's direction. For a moment, he was distracted by her exquisite, simple beauty. But he quickly recovered. "I'm sorry. Why she did what? Who did what?"

"Missus O'Rourke, of course. Just before we left for church, she'd been telling me what a grand lad you are, and did I think so as well. She held back just now so you and I could be alone for a spell."

Devin saw nothing wrong with that. "Remind me to thank her."

"Well, fret not, Mister Mahoney. There'll be white blackbirds before an unwilling woman ties the knot, in truth! I'm of no mind to be a bride for the foreseeable future, as it's work I'm needing and a regular wage to be sending back home to my family before entertaining the notion of thinking of myself."

Devin did not want to go down that road either. He had his fortune to make and he was determined to do so before he allowed himself any romantic entanglements, although his resolve was temporarily softened by Mary's aurulent eyes, the pert set of her jaw, her trim figure, and the way the morning sun played off her hair.

To change the subject, he said, "Y' mentioned y're working, but it's not the kind of work y' favor. What type of work would y' find suitable if it were to become available, pray tell?"

Mary's pert jaw tightened, her pace slackened. "Well, truthfully, I'm of a mind to become a lady's maid or a house maid. But I've yet to find anyone who would be willing to take me into service. For now, I run errands for a few ladies of means, but the wage is meager, and my time is taken up running twixt houses enquiring as to whether or not there are errands to run, most times for naught. If I could get myself into service, it would provide me with a princely sum of seven dollars a month and a place to lay my head."

"Y' have room and board with Missus O'Rourke, do y' not?"

"Through the kindness and generosity of a giving heart and the motherly nature of Missus O'Rourke, as my funds ran low, I found myself taken under her wing. In return for help around the house, she allows me my room and board. But, in truth, she does not really need me, and I'd rather stand on my own two feet than accept charity. I go out every day looking for work but have yet to find any."

Devin admired the girl's spirit and determination, but one thing did puzzle him. "Y' say y've been in America for only two months?"

"Aye … I mean, yes."

"That is what I'm talking about. Yer speech is more like an American's than any daughter of Erin. How is that?"

Mary stopped in her tracks and eyed Devin. "You may be a good man, Devin Mahoney, but you're slow in understanding the way it is here for us Irish women."

"I think I understand."

"I think not. You men can find work. It's hard work, right enough, but it's work. There is not much a woman can do except go into service." Reaching into her drawstring bag, she pulled out a folded piece of newspaper and handed it to Devin. "Feast your eyes on this, and perhaps it will open them a mite wider to the ways of life in this country. To the way things truly are."

Devin unfolded it and read the words:

Women wanted for general housework.
English, Scotch, Welsh, German, or any
country or color except Irish.
M. Jones Employment Services
101 E. Lehigh Ave.

He carefully refolded the paper and handed it back without saying a word. There was nothing to say. Mary was desperate to find work and she thought the only way to do so would be to sound more like an American. So be it. He was not about to judge a charming and graceful girl such as Mary Callahan. Not in this life.

Bright and early Monday morning, after a breakfast of Missus O'Rourke's special flapjacks, Devin struck out for Front Street, looking for John Kelly & Co. He soon found the desired office sandwiched between a candle maker's shop and a livery stable.

The man inside welcomed him with a wide smile. "And how can I be of service on a grand morning such as this?" he asked.

Devin was heartened to hear a slight Irish inflection within the question.

"Is it from the land of saints and scholars y' hail?"

"Aye, but not for many the day, now. What is it I can do for you, lad?"

"I'm in need of a job, so I am."

"Then opportunity's come a knocking, my young friend. You've come to the right place. Mister Kelly can always use men willing to work, such as yourself. A supply train leaves this very afternoon. If you're on it, then you'll have landed yourself a job. The next train won't leave until the end of the week."

"I'll be on it. But first, what about the pay? I was led to believe it was a dollar and twenty-five cents per day, food included."

While placing a paper onto the desk, the clerk responded. "You'll be paid that amount and fed three times a day. As long as you give Mister Kelly a good day's labor, he'll give you a good day's pay. Now stick your mark on this and be back here by noon."

Missus O'Rourke was busy in the kitchen cutting up vegetables for that evening's meal when Devin burst through the door. "I have myself a job, I have!"

122

"Ah sure, I'd never have doubted you would. When is it you'll be starting?"

"Right away. I mean, I must leave right away. I'm working on the railroad."

"Then it's leaving us, you'll be. And you with four days left on your rent."

Devin held up his last double eagle. "Don't worry about that a'tall. In fact, I was going to pay ya to hold my room. I'll be back two days a month and I'd not wish to stay anywhere else but here."

His landlady wiped her hands on her apron. "Come here, lad."

When he was standing before her, she hugged him and said, "Don't be daft, Devin Mahoney. That's a lot of money to pay for a room you'll not be using. You come here anytime you like. If your room is let, you can sleep in the attic for the day or so you'll be in town, there's a bed up there. You can pay me for that and only that."

He hugged her back and kissed her on the cheek. "I must be off now. Say my good-byes to everyone for me." He slowed at the kitchen door and turned back. "Is Mary in the house?"

≈ ≈ ≈

The cold February air passes through Devin's coat and chills him to the very bone. He sits huddled with two other men on a flat car carrying machinery. They're crouched behind a large slab of metal in an attempt to block the wintry wind, but it does little good. Well, at least it's not snowing. The whipping wind and the clacking of the steel wheels upon the steel tracks preclude conversation.

Devin hugs himself tightly as the countryside slides by. The bare, leafless trees stand as silent sentinels in fields of snow, patiently awaiting spring. Here and there, a lonely cow or horse stares at the train as it passes. But none of that makes the slightest impression on Devin. He's thinking back to the boardinghouse and the last time he spoke with Mary Callahan.

After he'd left the kitchen, he had bounded up the stairs to his room and filled his canvas sack with what little he owned. In the hall, he had hesitated. Should he? Maybe he should just go. Walking a girl to and from church does not mean anything. It does not constitute a courtship. Hell, he'd met her only two days before.

123

Just go and start earning yer fortune. Don't get sidetracked by a pretty face.

Again he hesitated at the top of the stairs. It's those eyes, those golden eyes. And her smile. He had to see her one last time, to say good-bye if nothing else. *It's the gentlemanly thing to do. Is it not?*

Now that the inner debate was over and done with, all that was left to do was knock on her door. So why were his shoes still nailed to the floorboards?

Then Providence stepped in. Mary had come out of her room. Seeing the bag in his hand, she asked, "Is it leaving us, you are, after so short a stay?"

"I found myself a job, but it means I'll be living at the railroad camp, not here. I'll be back once a month, though, and when I am, 'tis here I'll be staying."

Mary held out her hand and said, "It's been a pleasure meeting you, Devin Mahoney. I look forward to seeing you again, soon."

That was all the opening he needed. "Um ... do you ... I mean ... do ya think that maybe ..."

The corners of Mary's mouth turned up in a smile and her eyes flickered with understanding. "Is there something you want to ask me, Mister Mahoney?"

Taking his money back from Cudahy had been a whole lot easier than this.

Y're pitiful, Devin Mahoney. Just ask her!

"Yes, Miss Callahan, there is something I had a mind to ask ya. I was wondering if it might be all right to write y' a letter now and then. I was told the supply train takes mail to and from the camp. You'll need to go by Mister Kelly's office to pick it up. But it's close by, only three blocks from here. The address is 520 Front Street."

From under long, fluttering lashes, her golden eyes had sparkled. "I think that would be very nice. I will look forward to hearing from you. Now, if you will excuse me, I have to be going. I may have found a position. The lady of the house wants her husband to approve of me first. I'm on my way to his office for an interview."

Out on the street, they had shaken hands and wished each other well. Mary then turned and walked north. Devin dallied for a moment, watching her until she rounded the corner. On the way to

Kelly's, he stopped at a bookstore where he bought paper and ink, a pen, and sealing wax.

At Kelly's, he and two other men had been put on a wagon and driven to the train yard. Now here he was, speeding through the Pennsylvanian countryside with the brumal wind embracing his entire being, feeling its uncaring cold right down to the marrow of his Irish bones. And to add insult to injury, his hat had blown off before they were a mile from the city. But Devin felt a confidence deep within himself. A confidence that had not been fully a part of him until now. This time he was going to make it. Something had been added to the mix that wasn't there before. He believed himself to be in love. And a man in love can accomplish anything. At that moment, he felt as though he could build the whole damn railroad single-handedly.

≈ ≈ ≈

The train rolled in about four o'clock. Devin was glad to be off the flatcar and able to walk around and generate a little warmth in his body. He and his two traveling companions were told to go to the large tent in the middle of camp and report to Mister Kelly.

The site was a hive of activity with men bustling this way and that. Seemingly without rhyme or reason. But all the movement was to great purpose. Every man knew his job. A railroad was being torn out of a wilderness, inch by inch, foot by foot.

There was still an hour and a half of daylight left, and Kelly's crews were milking every second of it. The work day extended from first grey light in the morning to the last desperate gasp of twilight in the evening.

The three men were immediately ushered in to meet Kelly. He sat behind a desk stacked high with papers and plans, drawings and designs. A wood stove radiated a glorious warmth, heating the tent.

Kelly leaned back in his chair and spoke softly. Devin had to lean in to hear him above the din drifting in from outside. "So, you're the new men. Well, listen up. I give this speech to all the new men, and you better take it to heart.

"First off, I don't tolerate slackers. You're paid a day's wage for a day's labor. If I find you're not pulling your load, you'll be outta here on the next train. Next, you're no good to me if you're dead or injured. Be careful and keep your eyes open. You three are replacing three men who did not keep their eyes open.

"If at all possible, we work in all weather. We work from morning till night. As long as you can see your hand in front of your face, we're movin' forward. You can bellyache about the hours all you want, just don't let me hear you do it.

"You'll start out clearing land. That's Ed Sisk's bailiwick. He'll be your foreman. He's still out with his crew. But after supper, you go find him, he'll set you up. Now, you boys hightail it over to the supply hut and get yourselves a tent and three cots. You'll be bunking together for as long as you're here. And no fires in the tent. I know it's colder than a witch's tit out there, but you'll have to make do. Take an extra blanket or two when you pick up your tent."

Kelly rose from behind the desk and shook each man's hand. "Welcome to the Philadelphia and Columbia Railroad."

Once outside, after asking directions to the supply hut, Devin introduced himself to his soon-to-be tent mates. "I'm Devin Mahoney."

The man walking closest to him said, "The name's Thady Fleming."

The other man introduced himself as "Bill Shanahan, from County Monaghan."

Fleming was a wiry redhead. On the freezing train ride out to the camp, his smile had never once wavered. He was smiling still. He had been a school teacher in the old country. Shanahan was a big man, broad at the shoulders, standing six feet, four inches tall. His hair was ink black. On that particular day, his eyes were blood-shot red. His ironic grin was the most Irish thing about him. He had been a dock worker in Dublin until one day, on a whim, he decided to go to America.

A cold, black night had fallen by the time their tent was up and their cots in place. Out in the darkness, a steady stream of men were coming in from the surrounding countryside, heading straight for the mess tent. "We better get a get-on before the vittles are all gone," ventured Fleming. There was no argument from either Devin or Bill Shanahan on that point.

As it turned out, they did not have to seek out Sisk. He found them at the table where they sat eating their boiled meat and potatoes.

"You two." Pointing to Devin and Shanahan, "You'll be on the tree-felling line. You, Red," addressing Fleming, "I'm putting you with the oxen brigade, dragging away what these two and others chop down. All three of you report to me in the morning." Having said what he had to say with efficiency and using no extraneous words, Sisk gave a final nod and left.

Devin was roused from a deep sleep while it was still dark out. Men were walking by, talking vociferously about their coming day. Someone stuck his head inside the tent and yelled, "Get a move on, boys. Or you greenhorns will miss out on the food."

After a breakfast of flapjacks and coffee, Devin and his cohorts met up with Sisk. He was standing by a wagon with another man at his side.

He said, "You men come over here."

When they had joined him, Sisk issued his orders. "Red, you go with this man. He'll take you to the oxen corral and show you what to do. You other two, reach into the wagon and get yourselves an axe and one of those iron pry bars. Then follow me."

Sisk led them to a hand-car already sitting on the tracks. "You boys ever seen one of these things before?"

Shanahan said, "The saints be praised. What's that contraption?"

"It's called a hand-car. Lay your tools on it, then get on, one of you on each side of the walking beam. That's the thing that looks like a handle."

They did as instructed and stood by as Sisk climbed up after them. "Now you," speaking to Devin, "push down on the beam, and you ... what's your name?"

"Shanahan."

"And you, Shanahan, you pull up at the same time."

Devin pushed down and Shanahan pulled up, and lo and behold, the thing moved!

"Just keep doing what you're doing, and we'll get to where we're going," directed Sisk.

Nearly a mile later, as they approached the end of track, Sisk applied the brake. "Alright, boys. Follow me and I'll introduce you to your first tree." Other men in the vicinity were already chopping away, two men per tree.

Sisk had them stand on one side of the tree facing each other. "Hold out your axes until they touch. No, hold them at the bottom of the handle. Now, take one step back. That's it. You swing those axes alternately. Like those other men are doing. When the tree starts cracking, move out of the way and yell 'timber!' as loud as you can. After the tree has come to a rest on the ground, get in there and clear the branches. By the time you're done, a team of oxen will be here to help you remove the stump. And one last thing. Here, catch." He tossed an object to Devin. "That's your wet stone, for the two of you. Keep your axes sharp and your work will go a whole lot easier. Any questions?"

Shanahan wanted to know about water and the midday meal.

"A little nigger boy will come around with a bucket of water, and the cook's helpers bring out a pail of something or other around noontime. Eat fast and get right back to work. You better have four large trees to your credit by this evening, or I'll know the reason why."

Devin hefted his axe and let fly. Then it was Shanahan's turn. In short time, they had built up a rhythm of sorts. Swing, strike, pull back, and wait for your partner to do the same, then you swing again. Devin was thinking, *This isn't such hard work.*

But after an hour, his arms ached. His muscles were on fire and blisters were forming on his hands. Still, he sliced and hacked, but it took everything he had in him to keep going. Shanahan attacked the tree as if it were his mortal enemy, his ironic grin never wavering.

At long last, Devin heard the sound he had been praying for, "crack." The first one was soft. Then he heard it again, louder this time, "*crack*." He gratefully stopped swinging his axe. Shanahan did the same. They stood there looking at the tree as though they had never seen one before. Finally, it came. "*CRAACK!*"

"*TIMBER!*" cried Shanahan. And both men jumped out of the way, just in time, as the giant tree came crashing to the ground.

Devin fell to his knees and buried his hands in the light covering of snow. His blisters were bleeding, his palms burned with an intensity he did not think possible. After a moment or two, he looked up. Shanahan was going at the branches with vigor. Devin had to do his part. He raised his hands from the cool and soothing embrace of the snow, leaving behind droplets of crimson on its whiteness. With the heaviest of sighs, he reached for his axe, staggered to his feet, and started in on the branches just as Fleming and another man came up, driving a team of oxen.

When the tree was bare of branches, the real fun began. Shanahan and Devin chopped at the roots of the stump, severing the ones closest to the surface. They then applied their pry bars. The bars were six feet long, two inches square, and made of hardened steel. They weighed twenty-two pounds each. Devin jabbed his into the ground close to the stump. He put his back into it and pushed with all his might. Nothing happened. Shanahan stabbed his bar next to Devin's and together they put their shoulders to the task. The stump barely moved.

"You're gonna have to do better than that," said the man tending to the oxen. "We have to get a length of chain under the roots and then up and around the stump. The oxen will do most of the work from there." Devin was too spent to reply, Shanahan only grunted.

They attacked the stump with renewed vigor, and eventually they were able to secure the chain. With the oxen pulling and Shanahan and Devin pushing on their pry bars, the stump eventually gave way.

That night, Devin was too worn out from the day's work to eat. Instead, he stumbled onto his cot and collapsed. They had made their quota of four trees. It could have been five, but Shanahan had slowed his pace to allow Devin to keep up. Devin had noticed, and on the way back to camp, thanked him for the kindness, and promised that the next day and every day thereafter, he'd do his part.

By Saturday, their fifth day on the clearing crew, Devin's blisters were beginning to heal into callouses. Pain did not shoot through his shoulders with every swing of the axe, and he and Shanahan were clearing five large trees a day. Except the day before when they had cleared six. Shanahan's size and natural strength, combined with Devin's dogged determination to keep up with his partner, made them the best tree-felling team under Sisk's command.

As long as his men pushed forward at the rate predetermined by his contract, Kelly supplied them with liquor on Saturday nights. He knew that after a grueling week of unceasing and rough labor, the men had to cut loose in some fashion or else fights would break out.

Most of the men imbibed their whiskey in the mess tent because of its relative warmth, but a few hardy souls took their liquor to the camp's perimeter and enjoyed it around a roaring fire, where they would tell each other stories of the hardships they endured in Ireland, or on their voyage to America, or perhaps what they had encountered since arriving in the Land of Golden Paved Streets.

The reflected firelight flickered across awestruck faces and mirrored in the eyes of those who listened, as stories were told of yesterday's indignities and tomorrow's aspirations. The look in those yearning eyes spoke of hopes and dreams. The laughter heard around the fire conveyed a sense that somehow it would all work out. For a few short hours, on Saturday nights, in the deep woods of a place none of them had ever heard of before, the constant fear that lived within their hearts was banished from their lives.

In time, they *would* prevail. Their sons and daughters would one day stand straight and tall as proud Americans, as proud as their fathers had been to be Irish.

14

Sundays were a day of rest. A priest would come out from town to say Mass for those who wished to attend. Afterward, Sunday dinner was served. It was no different than the dinners served the rest of the week, but because it was Sunday and they did not have to go back to work immediately thereafter, the men deemed it special.

After dinner, they pursued their own interests. A few nursed hangovers. Some slept, some played vigorous games of horseshoes. Others sat in the mess tent, sipping cups of hot coffee and thanking God that they did not have to work on His day.

Devin used part of his free time that first Sunday—with a little help from Fleming—to write his first letter to Mary.

≈ ≈ ≈

Rail's End
Sunday
17 February 1850

Dear Miss Callahan,

I am writing in the hope that this letter finds you well and in good spirits. I have arrived at the railway camp and have settled in. I'm living in a tent with two of the finest gentlemen that ever hailed from the Emerald Isle, Thad Fleming and Bill Shanahan. Bill and I work together cutting trees to make way for the roadbed.

Besides work, there is not much to do. At night, after dinner, Thad is trying to teach me how to speak proper American. Soon, I'm hoping to be able to speak as proper as you. Ha, ha.

I wonder if you secured the position you were seeking. I cannot see how you could not. I think anyone would want to have you in their employ.

As is plain to see, I am not much at letter writing. Every once in a while, I have to stop and go and find Thad to ask him how to spell a word. I just wanted you to know that I was thinking of you and all the others at Missus O'Rourke's.

If you are not too busy, you might write and let me know if you found employment. I surely hope that you have.

Well, I must go now. The boys are calling to me for a game of horseshoes. When you next see me, I'll be the horseshoe champion of the camp. Ha, ha.

> *Your obedient*
> *servant,*
>
> *Devin Mahoney*

≈ ≈ ≈

Devin blotted the ink, folded the paper, and sealed the epistle with wax. A box had been set up for the men's letters home, but shortly after he had placed his letter within, his doubts and fears started to get the better of him.

What a donkey's ass you are, Devin Mahoney. You call that a letter? All week long as y're swinging that damn axe, ya been thinking of what y'd say to Mary. But when y' finally get the chance, what d'ya up and do? You talk about horseshoes! Y're a pure and utter imbecile, Devin Mahoney! She'll never write back, and no reason that she should. Sure, 'tis only a fool would entertain such foolishness!

Devin was so angry with himself for his inability to put into words what he was feeling, he took it out on the trees the next day. He swung his axe so fast and furiously that Shanahan had a hard time keeping up. Every chop and slice gave vent to his frustration. The mail had gone out on Monday. The next supply train was not due till Friday, but Devin had no illusion that there would be a letter

132

on it for him. And the more he thought of it, the harder and faster he swung his axe.

His hard work was not lost on Sisk.

Come Friday, Devin did not go straight to the mess tent after work as he usually did. "Will ya not be entertaining us with yer presence, then?" asked Shanahan.

"Aye, sure enough, soon as I wash up."

"Wash up?" laughed Shanahan. "The water's nearly frozen. And it's not even a Saturday, ya know."

Devin's real reason for not going to the mess straightaway was that he did not want to be there when they passed out the letters that had come in on the train that day. It was always a joyous occasion. One man would stand on a bench with the letters clutched in his hand. All the men who were anticipating mail would crowd around in eager expectation.

As a name was called out, the lucky man would make his way to the front of the crowd and accept his prize, a letter from his wife or sweetheart. Or, if he did not have a wife or sweetheart, his mother.

When Devin thought it safe, he made his way to the mess tent and stood in the chow line. With a heaping full plate, he joined Fleming and Shanahan, sitting down opposite them.

Slashing at trees all the livelong day tends to work up a man's appetite. Devin dug into his food with enthusiasm and little conversation. On the other side of the table, Fleming wore a sly smile and every now and again, he would nudge Shanahan in the ribs.

Shanahan did not respond. He kept his head down and shoveled in his food, oblivious to Fleming's pestering. When his plate was empty, he pushed it away and rubbed his belly. "Aah! Now that was a feast fit for a king!" he exclaimed. "How ya finding yer food, Devin?"

Devin's mouth was full, so he nodded, signifying he found the food satisfactory.

Fleming could take it no longer. "Quit yer blackguarding and just give the man his letter, Bill Shanahan."

With a devious grin, Shanahan dipped his hand into his coat pocket and came out with a folded paper. "Oh, righty oh! You weren't here, so I took it upon myself to claim this parchment for ya."

Devin stopped in mid-chew, and his eyes widened. He put his spoon down and reached out with an unsteady hand. Could it be true? Or was this a game they were playing? They knew how he had hoped against hope to receive a letter today.

The handwriting was feminine. That's all he had to see. With his mouth still full and his plate half empty, he started to rise. He could not wait to open the letter and read what was inside. But halfway to standing, he hesitated and sat back down. He didn't want to make a fool of himself in front of his friends. Shanahan turned to Fleming and winked. Fleming nodded back with a knowing smile.

"Come on, Bill. Let's leave Devin to finish his meal in peace," said Fleming.

"I'm with you, Thady-boy. When we get back to the tent, I'll tell you about the time, when, by pure chance, I had the Devil's luck in stumbling upon a group of the little people holding one of their ceremonies in a moonlit glen. All dancin' around and laughing, they were. 'Twas a wonder, it was."

The mess tent was now almost empty, and Devin had the table to himself. As soon as his friends were gone, he tore into the letter.

≈ ≈ ≈

Philadelphia
20 February 1850

My Dear Mister Mahoney,

I was very pleased to find your letter waiting for me when I stopped by Mister Kelly's the other day. Thank you for writing. First of all, I must tell you that I have found a position. My interview went well with Mister Alexander and he has hired me as a maidservant. The only condition imposed was that I was not to talk to his children about my religion. They are Quakers, you know. But they are very nice people.

The pay is good, eight dollars a month, most of which I will be sending to my mother.

134

I am no longer living at Missus O'Rourke's. I now live in the Alexander home. Besides Mister and Missus Alexander, there are the three children, two little girls and a boy. I have a very nice room of my own just off the kitchen, so I'm kept warm on these cold nights. The cook does not sleep in. She goes to her own home every night.

How are you faring? Do you find your work enjoyable? How are your American English lessons coming along with Mister Fleming? He must be doing a grand job because your letter was nearly perfect. Please write and let me know these things.

Saturday afternoons are set aside for my time off. Saturday last, I spent my time visiting with Missus O'Rourke. She is really the only friend I have in Philadelphia. She tells me you will be back once a month on Saturdays and Sundays. Perhaps we can see each other on one of those occasions, a Saturday afternoon, of course.

Missus Alexander sends me out on errands on an almost daily basis, and now and then, I pass close by Mister Kelly's office. I will stop in whenever I can to inquire if there is a letter waiting for me. I look forward to hearing from you, Mister Mahoney.

I must go now. Missus Alexander is sending me to the millinery shop to collect the new hat she just had made. I will take a slight detour and leave this letter at Mister Kelly's on my way.

> *Hoping this letter finds you well, your friend,*
>
> *Mary Callahan*

≈ ≈ ≈

The next day, Devin attacked the trees as energetically as he had done the preceding week. "I'd thought now that you'd received word from yer Miss Callahan, it'd put a stop to yer furious pace, just a bit," taunted Shanahan.

"I'll not be making my fortune by slowing down," said Devin as his axe struck the tree, spewing wood chips into the air.

Matching him swing for swing, Shanahan said, "Well, y're making the other cutters nervous. They're grumbling under their breaths that we're making them look bad. Sisk has let it be known that they should be cutting as many trees as we do."

"I can't help that," said Devin as he stood back. "I think she's going to fall, Bill. Y' *might* want to give it a wide berth and yell timber, at yer ease there."

After the tree was horizontal, the two men hefted their axes and advanced on the supine form. There were branches to be removed before they turned their attention to the stump.

Tomorrow was Sunday and Devin would be able to pen his next missive to Mary. It was really the only day he could do so for the simple reason that, after a day of felling trees and removing stumps, he was so exhausted he could barely focus on his dinner, let alone write a letter.

This letter would require all his concentration inasmuch as he wanted to do it right this time. He rewrote it three times in pencil and brought in Fleming to help with the final draft. When he was at last satisfied with what he was going to say and how he was going to say it, he sat down with pen and ink and wrote his second letter to Mary Callahan.

≈ ≈ ≈

Rail's End
Sunday
24 February 1850

Dear Miss Callahan,

I was gratified to hear from you and that you have found a good position.

I am in fine fettle of late and I pray that you are too. I'm enjoying my work. It's hard, but when I think that I'm squaring away thirty dollars a month towards my fortune, it's not so bad. Also, I'm putting on muscles where I never had muscles before.

Yesterday, my boss, Mister Sisk, informed me that soon he would be promoting Mister Shanahan and myself to track bed preparation. The pay's the same, but the work is not as physically demanding as cutting trees. It appears that he is pleased with our work. He said if we continue as we have, there will be other promotions down the road. Some with an increase in our recompense (a word Mister Fleming has taught me). Now I am more determined than ever to work hard and advance myself.

We are out in the wilderness and there is not much to do when not working. I have heard many stories from the men I work with and have pitched many a horseshoe. I reckon when I get back to Philadelphia, I will buy a few books to fill the time when not working, which is not very often. Thad (Mister Fleming) says that reading will broaden my horizons, and improve my mind and my American English.

Besides pitching horseshoes, I have been doing some thinking. I think of you mostly. I am surrounded by a crew of forty-eight men. There is never a time that I am alone, but still I feel lonely. I believe that is because I have met you.

Do you think me saying that is too forward? If so, then I am sorry. I would not have the nerve to say it to your face, looking into your eyes. But I had to let you know how I feel, and the safest way to do so was in a letter. I suppose in some matters I am a coward.

Saturday next, I'll be in Philadelphia. Perchance we can meet at Missus O'Rourke's and have a cup of tea. Then perhaps a walk?

If I have not alarmed you with my impertinence, I hope to see you five days from today on 2 March, sometime in the afternoon.

*I remain your
most obed. servt,*

Devin Mahoney

≈ ≈ ≈

Time dragged on heavily for Devin. More than anything else, he wanted to be in Philadelphia, sitting in Missus O'Rourke's warm parlor, sipping tea with Mary.

When Friday finally arrived and the day's work was finished, he climbed up into an empty boxcar along with ten other men. After a month of hacking and chopping at trees, he was going to enjoy two days without having to pick up an axe.

As the train traveled eastward, Devin patted the bulge in his coat pocket. It felt good. The pocket contained the beginnings of his fortune, two hundred and sixty-three dollars in bank notes and one golden double eagle. All but thirty dollars was what he had taken from Cudahy. But it was those thirty dollars that gave him the most satisfaction. He had earned them by the sweat of his brow. He had earned them in America.

He needed a hat and a new set of clothes if he was to see Mary. And he had to pay Missus O'Rourke for his lodging, but the rest he would save for the estate he would be buying in County Kerry. Even if it was not Lord **Feilding's** estate.

Missus O'Rourke greeted him like a long-lost son. "'Tis good to see you, Devin Mahoney. You're home, safe an' sound!"

"'Tis good to set eyes on ya again, Missus O'Rourke."

"Is it food y'll first be wanting?"

"If only it were. For the last month, it's a hot bath I've been dreaming of most."

"Then come follow me. The tub is off the kitchen and I'll start the water warming if you'll be so kind as to fetch me a stick or two of firewood from the back porch."

After his bath, Devin sat at the dining room table, and, in between mouthfuls of a hot and nourishing Irish stew, answered questions from the other boarders of what life was like at the railroad camp.

His room had not been let, so he would be bedding down in familiar surroundings. Missus O'Rourke accompanied him upstairs to make sure everything was satisfactory. After lighting the candle and ascertaining the pitcher was filled with water and the basin was free of dust, she wished Devin a goodnight and turned to leave.

"A moment of yer time, if y' please, Missus O'Rourke." He pressed his last double eagle into her hand. "Y' take this and I'll not be hearing no argument this time. Put it toward my future rent. I'll be coming by every month, and when that runs low, y' let me know."

She accepted the coin, patted him on the cheek, and again started for the door, but was halted in mid-step by a softly asked question. "Any news of Mary this past week?" He was fearful that she might not have received his letter.

Missus O'Rourke's mouth curved into a smile and she gave a knowing wink. "None of late, no. But she tarries by every Saturday afternoon. Don't be getting yerself in a quandary, young Devin Mahoney, you'll be seeing her pretty face soon enough."

By noon the next day, Devin had bought all the items he needed—a black, dome crown bowler and a complete set of clothes, including boots and an overcoat.

He sat in the parlor, all dressed up in his finery. He was alone. Missus O'Rourke had gone shopping and all the boarders were off working.

When will she get here? Would she even come? What if she didn't come? He had made a fool of himself. He shouldn't have been so forward in his letter. Had she even gotten his letter? What was that? Was that a knock on the door? *Perhaps I should go see. No. Stay where you are, Devin Mahoney. She will either come or not.* The wait was agonizing; the hands of the clock ticked by in increments so slow they seemed to not move at all.

Just as the timepiece chimed one o'clock, he heard the front door open.

He was holding his breath, but immediately jumped to his feet and exhaled as she came into his line of vision.

Mary looked surprised. "Why, Mister Mahoney. It is so nice to see you."

She was radiant. Her eyes sparkled, her smile lit up the room. Devin could only stare at her in wonderment and admiration. Words failed him.

At last he found his voice. "Good afternoon, Miss Callahan. It is good to see y' also. May I take yer coat?" Fleming had given him a lesson on being a gentleman and what to say in certain circumstances.

"Is Missus O'Rourke about?"

"She's gone out."

"Well then, perhaps you'd do me the honor of accompanying me on a short walk? It's not too brisk and I thought I'd show you a little of the city."

Devin welcomed the suggestion.

They strolled the well-kept streets of Philadelphia enjoying each other's company. As they were walking along Chestnut Street, Mary stopped and pointed to a building across the way. "Do you know what that is?"

Short of it being a large building that took up the entire block, Devin had no idea.

"That's where the Americans declared their independence from England. It's called the State House."

"So that's where the dream began."

"Yes, indeed it is."

"*We* ought to declare our independence from England."

Mary took Devin's hand and said, "I brought you here for a reason. I'll have you know that I now consider myself an American. I *have* my independence. Ireland holds no comfort for me anymore."

Devin did not understand what she was getting at and kept his tongue.

Mary released his hand. "Come, it's getting late. I would like to visit with Missus O'Rourke for a spell before I have to return to work."

After a few blocks, Mary elaborated. "I received your letter, and I'm flattered beyond belief that you have chosen to take an interest in me. And I want you to know that the feeling is not just one-sided. But you have told me that you're here in America solely to make your fortune and return to Ireland. Have you not?"

Devin desperately wanted to say, *Yes ... but*. However, there was no "but." He was here to get rich and return to Ireland at the soonest possible moment.

"You know, Devin Mahoney, the Americans call us a strange people with strange voices in a strange land we know nothing about. And yes, our voices are strange to those who were born here.

Perhaps there is little, or nothing, we can do about that. We can try to sound like them so they will not fear us so. But over time, their ways will become our ways. In time, we will get to know this land and our children will know it better still. And their children will be the captains of industry and among the leaders who make the laws. But it has to start somewhere, and as far as I'm concerned, it's going to start with me. My children will be born here and be rightful citizens of this great country known as the United States of America."

Devin was desolate. He felt like he had to say something, but what could he say? She sounded like her mind was made up as to what her future would be. As was his. He could do nothing but agree with her. They had separate dreams and that's all there was to it.

They walked on in silence for a spell. But Mary had not finished. She had one more thing to say and she wanted it said before they got to the house.

"I would ask you a question, Devin Mahoney. Do not answer me now. Listen and take my question with you when you return to your work. Think on it, and then write me a letter with your answer. If it pleases you to do so, you might consent to do that for me?"

"Anything you ask of me, short of staying in America, I will do for you."

Mary turned to Devin. Looking him straight in the eye, she asked, "Is it your wish to return to Ireland and live the life of a lord, the very people you despise? Could you find comfort riding in your fine carriage, passing the hungry and the sick and the dead on the side of the road? Could you do all that and have it not affect your immortal soul?

"This is my question to you, Devin Mahoney: *Why would you return to a land lost in itself ... a land that has lost its soul?*"

15

Rail's End
Sunday
11 March 1850

Dear Miss Callahan,

I am now back in camp. It was most pleasant seeing you during my time off.

Mister Sisk has assigned myself and Mister Shanahan to the leveling crew. It is interesting work. We use scrapers to tear away the land where the rails will be placed. Then we're put to work building drainage canals and viaducts to manage the natural water. When that is done, we start in on the ballasting. That's the laying of the rock, or rip rap as it's called here, for the railway bed. Other men come in after us, as we came in after the tree removers, and those men lay the ties and rails. One thing I must say for the Americans is that they are a well organized people. Each crew here does its job in preparation for the next crew to follow.

I remain in good health, and now that the weather is starting to warm up, the work is a great deal more pleasant. We still work hard, but our fingers and ears are not burning with cold the livelong day as they have been in the recent past.

We're fed mostly beef and potatoes with a little cabbage thrown in now and then. I count the days until I can once again taste Missus O'Rourke's fine Irish stew.

I have been pondering on what you asked me back in Philadelphia and I must admit that you have made some fine points and commenced me to thinking more on what I would do once I set foot back on Irish soil. However, try as I might, I still cannot see myself as an American.

Perhaps we can speak of it further when again I am in Philadelphia. I will be back at the beginning of April. I hope to see you on the 6th, a Saturday. Until then I wish you well in your endeavors and may God in His Heaven look down on you and protect you. You are ever in my prayers.

Please convey my best wishes to Missus O'Rourke when next you see her.

With Sincere Regard,

Devin Mahoney

≈ ≈ ≈

**Philadelphia
18 March 1850**

My Dear Mister Mahoney,

I have a few minutes and so I improve upon this opportunity to write to you. Thank you for your letter of the 11th, and I am sorry it has taken me so long to answer. Lately, I have not been running as many errands for Missus Alexander as before. I was only able to get by Mister Kelly's this morning. I do not have to tell you that I was amply pleased to find your letter awaiting me.

I am gladdened to hear that you are healthy and that you have attained your new position. The work sounds ever so interesting and exciting. When I next see you, you must tell me more about it.

My work also goes well. The family has warmed to me, Irish though I be. I have asked Mister Alexander the requirements of becoming an American citizen. After an inquiry of his own, he has informed me that I must wait five years before I may apply for citizenship. But I remain committed and will happily await my turn.

Well, I must go now. Missus Alexander is receiving guests this evening and I must help her with the place settings and other things pertaining to her soiree.

I look forward to seeing you on the 6th, and Missus O'Rourke has asked me to convey her felicitations.

Faithfully yours,

Mary Callahan

≈ ≈ ≈

Rail's End
Sunday
21 April 1850

Dear Miss Callahan,

It was a grand pleasure to see you again when I was in Philadelphia these two weeks past. I beg your pardon for not having written sooner. There was not much new to say. The job remains the same. We work from sunup to sundown all days, save Sunday.

I am still on the land leveling crew, but there is a strong chance that might change. Mister Sisk has spoken of me to Mister Kelly. He told him I am the hardest working man on his crew, I am proud to say.

Mister Sisk has told me that if I keep up the way I'm going there will doubtless be another promotion for me before too long, accompanied by a raise in pay. Time will tell. But I can tell you, hand on heart, that I will continue to work hard. For it's by hard work that I will get ahead, that I will make good. And now I want to make good as never before. I am steadfast on what I desire.

When I was back in Ireland, I believed all the tall tales about America. That I could come here and pick up the gold off the streets. But now I know it will take much hard work on my part to get what I desire, and doubly so because I'm Irish.

144

You have shown me that my dream, true as it felt, was a false one. I will never make near enough money to buy an estate in Ireland. And now in the thinking of it, what would I do with all that land if I had it anyway? I have come to the conclusion that a small plot of earth with a comfortable house on it, with wooden floors, is all I'll ever need in this life.

After speaking with you on my last trip to town, you have set my mind to thinking that my future, as yours, lies here in America.

I will not be able to get to Philadelphia as frequently as I have in the past. We've pushed too far out and the train ride to and from the city would take too long to make the trip worthwhile. Besides, I was missing one day's work a month. Staying here and working means adding an extra dollar twenty-five to my pay every month.

I heartily thank you for opening my eyes about America and I thank you for being my friend. I cannot write about another subject because what I want to say cannot be said in a letter.

If it pleases you, write and let me know how you are getting along. And tell Missus O'Rourke to be sure to keep the attic warm for me. Ha, ha.

As ever, your friend,

Devin Mahoney

≈ ≈ ≈

Philadelphia
Saturday
18 May 1850

Dear Mister Mahoney,

I had the pleasure of receiving your kind letter a few days since. I am overjoyed to hear that you will be staying in America. In time, I think you will find it best. The way you tell me you are working, you should own that railroad in no time at all. Then you can come by and visit at your heart's desire.

Today is my half-day off, but I'll not be setting foot outside the house, as the Heavens have opened up and it's raining cats and dogs. That is too bad because I so wanted to see Missus O'Rourke and pass on your message about keeping the attic warm for you. Ha, ha.

I've longed to write before now, but was waiting to receive a letter from you first. Is that not silly of me?

It is with much regret I received the news that you will not be coming to Philadelphia any time soon. I have enjoyed our walks and our talks. You and Missus O'Rourke are the only friends I have made since landing in America. Working as I do, I have not had the opportunity to meet very many people of my social standing.

Missus Alexander has informed me that she and Mister Alexander will be taking the children to Europe for an extended stay. He has business interests there. But they won't be leaving until after the new year. She told me that she would talk to her friends and try to find me a suitable position, but she would like me to stay on until after Christmas. It took me so long to find this position and to be told not three months hence that I'll be losing it seems so unfair.

Missus Alexander has a good heart and I have no doubt she will do all in her power to see me right. But, in my heart of hearts, I don't think her friends, from what I have seen of them, have any great love for the Irish.

Hark at me grieving over myself, sounding as though my life is over. A clip on the ear would surely follow if my mother were to hear me. I should be ashamed. It must be the rain. It's casting a gloom over the city, myself included.

I must be about my business. It's getting nigh on time to serve the family their dinner.

I know there is probably little to write about being where you are, but I hope and trust you will write on occasion and let me know how you are doing.

Your sincere friend,

Mary Callahan

≈ ≈ ≈

Rail's End
Sunday
25 August 1850

Dear Miss Callahan,

I did not receive your letter of May 18th until the other day. I have been told it had been misplaced in Mister Kelly's office, but God bless Saint Anthony, it was found and forwarded to me. I thought you— well— I don't know what I thought. Let me just say that, as of now, I am very pleased to have heard from you again. However, I am saddened about the prospect of you losing your position. And you going to such lengths to find it.

Mister Fleming has been schooling me on proper American English and proper writing. I am writing this letter with no help from him at all. The last time I was in town, I did buy three books and they have been a grand help in showing me how proper English should be written.

A lot has happened since I wrote last. And with your permission, I will tell you about it. The first thing is that I was made foreman of the leveling crew back in June. I had the men working so fast, they were about to overtake the tree cutters. So, Mister Sisk and Mister Kelly put me on as foreman of the track layers. But the best part is that my pay is now one dollar and seventy-five cents a day.

Now this is what I could not wait to tell you. When Mister Kelly learned that I could read and write, he offered me a new position. The man who runs his office in town is leaving at the beginning of December and Mister Kelly has offered me his position. It pays two dollars and thirty cents a day. I will have to be there a month beforehand to learn what is expected of me, but I'll be living in town and I will be able to see you more often. That, in truth, means more to me than the pay raise.

So please tell Missus O'Rourke to have a room ready for me on 1 November, it's of a Friday. And on Saturday the

2nd , I hope to be sitting in Missus O'Rourke's parlor, sipping tea with you, looking into your beautiful golden eyes. Perhaps we can put our heads together and come up with a solution to your problem.

I remain yours truly,

Devin Mahoney

≈ ≈ ≈

Philadelphia
Thursday
9 September 1850

Dear Mister Mahoney,

I was so very happy to receive your letter of 25 August. It is grand news indeed that you will soon be living here. When I told Missus O'Rourke, she almost jumped for joy. She told me to tell you that you still have a piece of that double eagle coming to you and that your old room will be waiting for you when you arrive.

Do you really think my eyes are beautiful? It was so nice of you to say so.

I will not take up any more of your time. Just know Missus O'Rourke unites with me in wishing that you were here already.

Your golden-eyed friend,

Mary Callahan

≈ ≈ ≈

Devin jumped off the train and almost sprinted to Missus O'Rourke's. He was home! There'd be no more living out of a tent. He could take a hot bath when he wanted. The food would not be the same old thing day in and day out. And best of all, he would now be able to see Mary at least once a week. *And then after Christmas, who knows?*

A bath was the first order of business. Then he put on his new set of clothes, which he hadn't worn since the last time he was in town. When he was presentable, Missus O'Rourke called him to the dining room and plied him with her cooking. That night it was a large slab of salt pork, roasted potatoes, and boiled carrots. Devin had never eaten so well.

After dinner, he retired to the parlor with the other boarders. Of those who were there eight months previously, only Kinney had left. He was replaced by an aspiring poet who went by the name of Peter Walsh.

It had been a long day. Devin was polite and answered a few questions about the progress of the railroad, but then begged to be excused and took himself off to bed.

As he tried to fall off to sleep, the soft grey light from outside filtered in through the window, throwing ghostly images on the wall. From the shadows, the specters whispered, *"Who are ye, Devin Mahoney? Who are ye to love someone as beautiful as Mary Callahan?"*

"I am no one. But I can love her, and one day I *will* be someone. She needs me as surely as I need her."

"She has been doing just fine these last eighteen winters without yer help, Devin Mahoney."

"But she's about to lose her position. What will become of her?"

"What will become of ye is more to the question."

"What are ye saying?"

"Y're staying in America because of her and y' know it. If y' don't have the courage to ask her to marry y' on the morrow, then go back to yer precious Ireland, lay yerself down on that dirt floor of yer home that no longer exists, and recommence yer dyin', because y'd be a sorry excuse of a man, Devin Mahoney!"

It took a while, but in time, Devin fell into a troubled sleep.

At breakfast the next day, as the other boarders spoke in generalities, Devin sat in silence, eating his eggs and counting the minutes until Mary would walk through the door. Afterward, he offered to help Missus O'Rourke with the cleanup. " 'Tis a good boy, you are. If you would be so kind as to pump me a bucketful of

149

water, I'll get to cleaning the dishes. Y'll remember, the pump is out back."

Devin fetched the water and then spent the remainder of the morning sitting in the kitchen talking with Missus O'Rourke as she went about her work.

In time, he heard the parlor clock chime twelve measures. Mary would soon be there. He went into the parlor and gazed at himself in the mirror. His hair was combed, his mustache neatly trimmed, and his shirt and coat were not too wrinkled. He was far too nervous to sit. He paced the floor, glancing at the clock every few seconds.

Finally, and at long last, she walked into the room. "Hullo, Mister Mahoney," was all she said. But the alluring look in her eyes spoke volumes to Devin Mahoney's tortured soul.

He stopped his pacing, stood tall, and responded to her salutation with a wide smile. It was all that he could muster at the moment. She took his breath away.

My God, she's beautiful.

At length, he found his voice. "Good afternoon, Miss Callahan."

They stood looking at one another. Neither one of them saying anything or making a move. Mary, at length, broke the impasse, "Is Missus O'Rourke about?"

Devin's shoulders sagged. He had hoped to get her alone where they could talk. He should have hustled her out the front door the moment she came in.

"She's in the kitchen."

"Excellent. Let me pay my respects and then we'll go for a walk. It's a lovely fall day. Perhaps a stroll along the river is in order."

Devin brightened and, while Mary was in the kitchen, donned his hat. Tilting it at a rakish angle, he looked in the mirror and nodded. He was ready.

Out on the street, Mary entwined her arm with Devin's, and together they ambled toward the river. The conversation was light. Eventually, Devin asked if Mary had found a new position for when the Alexanders left for Europe.

"Of yet, sadly no. Missus Alexander has not had much luck in that respect. It seems there are no positions open, at least not among her friends. Or maybe it's just because I'm Irish. It's hard to know."

The gentle afternoon sunlight rippled upon the water of the Delaware River as a steamboat fought its way against the fast-flowing current. Puffy white clouds raced across a stark blue November sky.

It had been exactly one year since Devin, sapped of all his strength, had lain on a dirt floor, dying from hunger. Exactly one year since he took that first step on an ancient road that would lead him here, to this land of milk and honey.

He faced Mary and looked directly into her mesmerizing golden-brown eyes. "I love y' dearly, Mary Callahan, and I want y' for my wife, if y'll have me. I'll build y' a house fit for a queen. And in time, we will grow old together, surrounded by our American children and their children. What do y' say, Mary Callahan? Would y' like to change yer name to Mary Mahoney?"

Mary smiled coquettishly. "Missus O'Rourke said you were going to ask me today."

"Did she now? And how could she have known?"

"Women know these things."

"Did y' tell her what yer answer would be?"

Mary kissed Devin for the first time, and with an Irish lilt in her voice, she said, "My answer is yes, Mister Mahoney. I'd realized my heart was smitten for some time now. That's why I wanted you to stay in America. If you stayed, I knew I was going to marry you. I said that to Missus O'Rourke months ago."

Devin hugged her to him. "I'll make y' happy, lass. On that I promise."

Mary, being the practical one, brought up a number of items that had to be considered.

"That may be so, but I still have to stay with the Alexanders until January. I promised them I would.

"And I'll still be needing to send dollars back to my family.

"Where will we live until the house is built?

"I'll need a dress to be married in.

"We should be married in a church.

"If our first child is a boy, I want to name him after my father."

Devin laughed. "Our first child? Is not the cart getting a bit ahead of the horse?"

Mary laughed, too. "I believe you are right, Mister Mahoney ... I mean Devin."

On the way back to the boarding house, Devin stepped into a pub and bought a bottle of good Irish whiskey. He wanted to toast their engagement with Missus O'Rourke.

As they continued on, Devin addressed all of Mary's concerns.

"It's alright that y' stay in yer position until January. Sure enough, a promise is a promise, and the Alexanders have been good to y'.

"Of course we'll send money back to yer family. I'd have it no other way. I'm making enough *and* I have the princely sum of five hundred and twenty-eight dollars saved from my labors!

"We'll board at Missus O'Rourke's until our house is built. She's been dropping the hint that she would like to relocate the bed up in the attic. We can move that into my room.

"I'll find someone to make y' the prettiest dress in the whole of Philadelphia, lass. And we'll get married in the church that yerself and Missus O'Rourke attend.

"What was yer father's name?"

"Dillon."

"Then Dillon it will be for our first born if it's a boy. His middle name will be John for my father. If a girl, we'll name her Hannah for my sister ... and ... for a little friend I met on the ship coming over."

They were in high spirits as they entered the house. Missus O'Rourke took the news in stride. "I knew you two were going to plight yer troth from the first moment I saw ye together, sure 'twas written all over ye, it was."

Devin broke out the whiskey and they had their toast, then Mary had to leave. Devin walked her back to the Alexander house and kissed her outside the gate. "It's only two months, *a chroi*. I'll see y' next Saturday. Until then, rest assured, y'll never leave my thoughts."

That night, Devin polished off the bottle with his fellow boarders as they slapped him on the back and showered him with congratulations.

With Missus O'Rourke in attendance, Devin and Mary were married in the Church of the Sacred Heart, by Father Flannigan, on

152

January 4th in the year 1851. Mary wore a blue gathered skirt with a white chemisette. A white lace veil covered her head and draped down almost to her waist.

Mary looked beautiful and radiant as she quietly said, "I do."

Devin looked like he was going to burst with happiness when Father Flannigan proclaimed, "I now pronounce ye man and wife."

16

Devin's main responsibility was to make sure Kelly's work camp was kept supplied with needed materials. Two supply trains were sent out each week, one on Monday and one on Friday. Most materials were scheduled weeks ahead, but on occasion, Kelly would send word that something special was needed and Devin would have to scurry around town to find it, get it on a train, and send it on its way. After only a few months, Devin excelled at his job.

His home life was also going well. Mary helped out around the boarding house in exchange for a slight reduction in their rent. After dinner, he and Mary would sit in the parlor with the other boarders, and while Devin and the men discussed the goings-on in the newspapers or talked about their jobs, Mary and Missus O'Rourke would speak of things that interested women. It was a good life as far as it went. But the Mahoneys were itching for a home of their own.

One night, Devin came in with good news. He hustled Mary upstairs to their room so he could tell her in private. "'Tis done, *mo chroi!*" he said, proudly. "We'll have no fear of harsh winds from this day forward. I've purchased a lot on which to build our house!"

Mary's face lit up. "That's wonderful news, but are you sure we can afford it? It's a serious undertaking you have in mind."

Devin asked her to have a seat on the bed while he explained.

"All is in hand, Mary. It's called a ground rent. We pay only the interest on the price of the lot for the first year. However, we are responsible for the taxes and any fees the city may impose. Then we're given one year's grace in which to build our home. After it's up, we start paying down the principal."

"And how is it you are so well informed, husband dear?"

"I made it my business to be asking around these last few months. But wait till y' hear the best of it. Our lot is over on Larch Street, not but two blocks from here. If y' get lonely or gossip starved while I'm working, y' can always come here and visit with Missus O'Rourke."

A little concern crept into Mary's voice. "Do we really have enough to build a house?"

Devin sat down next to her and took her hand in his. "We have almost seven hundred dollars saved. It will get us a more than generous start, lass. Besides, I plan on doing most of the work myself. I might ask Ed Lowery to help out with the framing. Him being a carpenter and all."

Mary leaned in and planted a kiss on his willing lips. "Thank you. It's every woman's dream to have her own doorstep, a house of her own that she can make into a warm and comforting home for her husband."

Devin beamed. "God willing, we'll be living under our own roof in the passing of a short year. It would be sooner, but I'll only have Sundays to do the work. Oh, and just one more thing. I'll be putting a pump inside for ya. It'll be right in the kitchen, no less!"

Mary took Devin's face in her hands and gave him another kiss, a longer one this time, full of promise. Devin returned the kiss in like manner.

Before they got carried away, they decided to go downstairs and share their good news with the rest of the house, Missus O'Rourke in particular.

With much hard work on both their parts, the house was far enough along to move into a few weeks before Christmas, 1851. There were still minor things to be done, such as partitioning the rooms. But there were two fireplaces. One in the main room and one in the kitchen. Mary would do her cooking in the kitchen fireplace until they could afford a wood stove.

Things were going well for the Mahoneys. They were very much in love and treasured each and every moment they had together. By 1855, Kelly's work for the Philadelphia and Columbia Railroad was drawing to a close. But Devin had no need to worry. Kelly was now securing contracts from the Pennsylvania Mainline. Many more miles of tracks had to be laid in the state of Pennsylvania before Kelly went out of business. Devin's employment was secure for the time being.

By then his salary had increased to two dollars and sixty-five cents per day. As far as Mary and Devin were concerned, they had the perfect life but for one thing. There were no little Mahoneys running around the house.

As the years passed, they resigned themselves to the fact that, for whatever reason, God was not going to bless them with children.

Devin turned twenty-nine years of age on 20 October 1859. That morning, as he left for work, Mary kissed him at the door, as she usually did. "You hurry yourself home tonight. No dallying nor nonsense at the tavern. We'll celebrate your birthday here, just the two of us. I have a special gift for you and you alone."

Devin leaned over and kissed her on the forehead. "Y'll not be wanting to invite Missus O'Rourke or any of our other friends?"

"No. Only us."

"Then I'll be sure and make it my business to be here exactly at 6:30 o'clock." Devin kissed her again, but on the lips this time. And it was off to work for him. Mary closed the door and leaned against it, smiling and hugging herself. After a moment, and with a deep and contented sigh, she went about her daily chores.

At noon she was off to the butcher shop to buy a Yankee pot roast. By one o'clock, it was slowly cooking on the top of her wood stove, smothered in sliced potatoes, carrots, onions, and its own juices. This meal had to be perfect.

Over dinner, they asked each other about their day. Devin complimented Mary on the meal and how pretty she looked in the candlelight. "Is that a new dress?"

"Why, yes, it is, kind sir. I finished it only yesterday. It had to be done in time for your birthday."

Afterwards, Devin sat in the parlor smoking his pipe. He had picked up the habit while working at the railroad camp.

He looked up to see Mary standing in the doorway. *My, if she isn't a picture worth framing, and I the lucky framer.*

Mary hesitated a moment before entering. She took in Devin's relaxed posture, sitting in his favorite chair, boots off, his feet resting on a foot stool. *He looks satisfied with his life, and as well deserving of it. He's a rare one, Mary Mahoney, and well you know it.*

She came into the room, sat on the arm of his chair, and kissed the top of his head. "Happy Birthday, *gra mo chroi*."

Devin puffed on his pipe in contentment. "Thank you. A man could surely not have wished for a better birthday ever. What more could any Irishman want than sitting in his own home with a full belly, his beautiful wife by his side, and a roaring fire crackling in the fireplace, keeping him warm?"

Mary stirred from her perch. "Aren't you the very beat of my heart, Devin Mahoney. And that reminds me. I have not yet given you your gift."

"Ah but y' have. Sure haven't I been gifted and blessed, more than any one man deserves, since the day y' gave yer hand to me in marriage, Mary Mahoney?"

She kissed him on the cheek, and taking both his hands in hers, she looked directly into his deep blue eyes and forever changed his world. "We are going to have a baby."

Devin stared at her with a bemused look on his face. He *couldn't* have heard correctly. "I'm sorry, Dear, what was that you said?"

Slowly and carefully, she enunciated each and every word. "We are going to have a baby."

This time it got through. Devin's shout of joy shook the rafters and might have been heard over at Missus O'Rourke's, two blocks away. He leapt to his feet and did a reasonable facsimile of an Irish jig.

When he had calmed down a bit, he had a few questions. "Are y' sure? How long? Are y' alright? Shouldn't y' be in bed?"

Mary sat him back down and explained, smiling the whole time. "Yes, I am sure I'm going to have a baby. I have been sure for two months now. And I'm fine, but how are you?"

"I could use a wee dram of whiskey right about now. But why have y' waited so long to tell me?"

"I needed to be sure beyond reasonable doubt before I dared raise your hopes, my heart of hearts."

≈ ≈ ≈

In the early morning hours—seven months later—Mary shook Devin awake. "I believe the time has come, husband."

Devin was instantly and fully awake. "I'll get the doctor and Missus O'Rourke. Y' stay here. I mean, don't go anywhere. That's not what I mean. Just don't move!"

He was dressed and out the door in a moment, his shirttail flapping in the breeze, his hat askew.

Devin paced the parlor. *What is happening? Why can't I be in there with her?* He heard a scream and rushed to the bedroom door, only to be met by a scowling Missus O'Rourke. "And where is it, exactly, y'd be thinkin' y're goin', Devin Mahoney?"

"I want to see my wife!"

She closed the door behind her and led Devin back to the parlor. "Will y' be quitting that mad malarkey and see the sense y' were born with. If not for yerself, then for yer lass' sake. She's got enough on her mind at this moment than to be worrying for the both of ye. Women have been having babies for thousands of years. And for all those thousands of years, you men have been acting as foolish as y're acting now. Let the learned doctor be about his business. Sure aren't I in there to look after and take good care of her? I promise y' no harm will come to her or the baby. Why don't y' go to the tavern around the corner and hoist a few? And when y' come back, y'll have a wee baby to hold in yer manly arms, Devin Mahoney."

At 11:32 am on 9 May 1860, Dillon John Mahoney came into the world, kicking and screaming. It was as though the bright daylight was too much for him and he wanted to go back to the sanctuary of the soft, warm confines he had just vacated.

≈ ≈ ≈

The Mahoney household was a happy household in those days. Devin would rush home from work—bypassing the local tavern—to play with his son. Mary would proudly show Dillon around while shopping. And, of course, to Missus O'Rourke, the honorary grandmother, Dillon was the only child on earth.

Mary and Devin referred to Dillon as their "miracle child." And he grew by leaps and bounds before their very eyes. At nine months, he took his first tentative steps. "He'll be following me to work in no time a'tall," observed a proud Devin.

"As long as it's not into the tavern he be following ya," countered Mary.

They laughed, and Devin patted Mary on her posterior in a playful way. Her eyes widened at such boldness, and they laughed again. With certainty, their blessed life would go on forever.

However, the universe has a way of throwing a monkey wrench into the best laid plans of mice and men, or so say the poets. On the morning of 12 April 1861, General Pierre Gustave Toutant-Beauregard fired the first shot of the Civil War. America had declared war on itself.

The consensus of thought was that the conflict would not last more than a few months, six at the outside. However, when the summer of '62 rolled around and the war looked like it was just getting up a full head of steam, the state of Pennsylvania formed the 116th Pennsylvania Infantry, made up of mostly Irish immigrants.

People from Mister Lincoln on down were saying the war was being fought to preserve The Union. But everyone knew the underlying cause for the war was slavery, one side fighting to keep it, the other to abolish it once and for all.

Devin was dead set against slavery. At the railroad camp, there had been a Negro who worked on his crew. He was a hard worker and never caused any trouble, which was more than could be said for many of the Irish. Then, one day a man rode in claiming the Negro was a runaway slave and that he was there to recover his property. Kelly sent him on his way, but he returned the next day with a federal marshal and an affidavit stating he owned the Negro.

The marshal explained to Kelly. "There's not much I can do. I don't believe in slavery, but the Fugitive Slave Act says that if I don't help this man get his property back, I could be fined a thousand dollars. And you could do six months in jail *plus* fined a thousand dollars for harboring him."

The image of the Negro as he was led away in chains would forever be etched in Devin's mind.

One night on the way home from work, he stopped in at the tavern to gather the latest news of the war. He saw no one he knew, but that day's front page of the *Philadelphia Inquirer* was pinned to the wall. After giving it a quick glance, he started for home. On the way out the door, he ran into Matthew Carey, a man he had shared drinks with in the past.

"Sure if it isn't yerself, Devin Mahoney! Will y' not come and partake of a wee dram with me? I'm celebrating, lad."

"Aye, and what is it y're celebrating, Matt? The days with a 'Y' in them, I'd hazard a wild guess?" quipped Devin.

"I've thrown my lot in with the 116th and, shortly now, I'm off to fight the rebels, I am."

Devin sat down with Carey, and over a glass of whiskey, he learned the particulars.

"We're to report to the Army of the Potomac in Washington City. Once us Irish get in the war, it'll be over in no time a'tall, and those rebels will be put in their place."

Devin was curious. "Why are y' making it your fight, *a chara*? Y're not even a citizen."

Carey brooded on it for a time, then answered honestly. "America has given me so much and I feel I owe Her something. Back home I was starving. Here, I eat every single day. I have work and a place to live. I believe it's my duty to help put this wonderful country back together again. Besides, an Irishman without a cause can hardly be called an Irishman."

"What about the slaves? Do y' think they should be freed?"

"Are y' daft, man? Of course I do. Sure weren't we all slaves to the Crown ourselves for centuries? But they'll not stand a chance at freedom unless we defeat the rebels."

Devin thanked Carey for the drink and took his leave. He had some thinking to do.

A few days later, Kelly walked into the office. "Hullo, Devin. I just came in on the supply train. I've got to meet with the railroad's board of directors and give them a progress report. You would think that all the paper reports I send in every week would be enough."

After a pause to light his pipe, he asked, "Everything squared away and shipshape here?"

"Yes, unless y' have something that y'll be needing that's not scheduled to go out."

"Not this time. The inquisition shouldn't last long. I'll be back here by three and we can go over the list of what I'll be needing next month, just to be reading from the same page. I know we'll have to increase the dynamite shipments for the tunnel. The rock in the mountain is harder than we anticipated."

"There is one thing, Mister Kelly. But it's a matter that can be dealt with when y' get back."

"I have a few minutes. Spit it out."

Devin stood up from his desk so he could look Kelly in the eye. "I'm of a mind to go off and help put down the rebellion and I was wondering what y' thought of that."

Kelly put his hand on Devin's shoulder as a father would, and said, "The decision is yours alone to make, my lad. If you're asking me if I can get along without you, then the answer is yes. But I would ask you to stay a few weeks, three at the most, so I can get a man in here to replace you. Other than that, you have my blessing. And when you return, rest assured, you'll have a job waiting for you."

That was the easy part. Now he had to tell Mary.

It took him a few days to work up the courage. But one night after dinner, and after Dillon had been safely tucked into bed, Devin sat in his chair and Mary in hers, darning a sock. She looked painfully beautiful in the firelight. Wishing he could avoid it, but knowing this was something he had to do, Devin took a deep breath and broached the subject.

"Mary?" he said.

"Yes?" she answered without looking up.

Devin was grateful for that. "I've been thinking …" Then he faltered.

Mary glanced up. "What were you thinking, Devin Mahoney?"

He swallowed hard and said, "I was thinking of signing up and going down to Washington City and help try to put this old country back together again."

Mary put her mending aside. "I don't think I heard you correctly, Mister Mahoney. Would you please say that again?"

"Y' heard me alright, Missus Mahoney."

Devin picked up his foot stool and placed it in front of Mary's chair. He sat down and took both her hands in his. "I've given the matter much thought. I feel in my heart of hearts that I owe this country something. Besides, the evil of slavery must be abolished once and for all. If the war is fought to a draw, and twenty years

161

from now slavery still exists on these shores, how will I explain to Dillon that, when his father had the chance, he stayed home and did nothing?"

Mary leaned away and pulled her hands from Devin's grasp. She was getting angry. "How will you explain anything to him if you go off and get yourself killed?"

This is what Devin had feared. He had to prevail upon her better self. "Sweet Mary, I was a slave all my life. My entire family were slaves. We were bonded to a landlord who took the lion's share of our labors, and in truth, the bread from our mouths. We would work all year just to have a pudding on Christmas. 'Twas a rare week we could afford meat. We lived in a hovel—dirt floors and two rooms for six people—while the landlord had a grand house up on the hill that he used but a few weeks out of the year.

"I feel 'tis only right I should stand shoulder to shoulder with my brothers in slavery, as God would bear witness. It's been weighing heavy on my mind this past year now, ever since the war began. Don't y' understand? I cannot live in this land any longer while other men are held in chains. This is a moment in history that I feel I *must* participate in."

Mary said nothing.

Why doesn't she understand?

At length Mary asked, "And what about Dillon and me? What will we do without you?"

"I've taken steps to assure y'll be fine. I saw Mister Church today, he's the man that holds our ground rent. I paid him all that was owed and now we own this house free and clear. Even after that, we still have a little more than a thousand dollars in savings. That'll hold yerself and young Dillon until I return home. And I'll be paid thirteen dollars a month that I will send to y'."

Is he dead set on going off to this horrible war? What is his truth? And can I live with it?

"Though it grieves my heart to know so, I can see by your eyes you've set yer mind to it and won't be swayed. 'Tis a good heart you have, Devin Mahoney. And a sense of right and justice that I would be wrong to insist applies only to myself and Dillon. 'Tis your way, Mister Mahoney, and I'll not insist otherwise."

162

It was settled. Devin kissed Mary and said, "My heart is yours, Mary Mahoney. Thank y' for understanding."

After checking in on Dillon, they went to their bed and made love as though it was to be the last time.

Going off to war is a grand affair. The regimental band plays martial music as the volunteers march through the city streets. The crowds of onlookers cheer and shout to show their support. Mothers, wives, and sweethearts follow in silent sorrow, farewell kisses lingering on their lips.

Devin's regiment arrived at the Philadelphia, Wilmington, & Baltimore Railroad depot where they were allowed a few minutes with their loved ones for a last good-bye.

Mary hugged Devin tightly. She wanted to hold on to him forever. Tears blurred her vision, her heart ached. Her soul cried out for relief.

Devin wiped the tears from her cheeks and kissed her tenderly. "I'll be back afore y' know I've left," he said, sporting a crooked Irish smile.

Too soon, the men were ordered onto the train.

One last hug, one last kiss, and he was gone.

Mary whispered under her breath as she watched the train recede into the distance. "Farewell and blessings! May God protect you, my darling husband."

17

Washington City, D.C.
Sunday 7 Sept. 1862

My Dear Wife,

I take pen in hand to write you a few words whilst I can. After leaving the depot in Philadelphia, we arrived in Baltimore early the next morning. The good people of that fair city were on hand to feed us a breakfast and wish us well. That being done, we proceeded on to Washington City, arriving at the Baltimore and Ohio depot, which is at the foot of Capitol Hill.

We formed ranks and, with the officers leading the way, we marched down the city's broad avenues, our regimental band playing martial music at its loudest. But it was not like in Philadelphia. No one paid us any mind. Later, we figured that in the last few months, they had seen hundreds of regiments march on the very same streets. Though it be a first for us, we were nothing new to the citizens of Washington City.

As we marched, I stole glances at the capitol dome. It's not yet complete. I'm told there is still a statue to be placed on top. But it makes a fine view with the American flag flying over it. It made me proud to be wearing the blue uniform.

It was a hot, dry day and we kicked up dust as we marched. It then settled on our uniforms, turning the bright blue a dull grey by the time we got to camp. We first made camp at a place called Arlington Heights.

A few days later, we were ordered to Rockville, Maryland. We marched all day only to be told when we

164

arrived that we'd have to return to Washington City. If that sort of thing keeps up, we'll never win the war.

For the last few weeks, we have been making field fortifications which involves shovels and picks and a lot of hard work.

I'll close for now. The chow bell has just rung. Is that not a funny word, chow? It means food. I'm learning how to be a real American. Through my stomach, it seems.

Please write when you can. I do so crave word of how you and Dillon are faring. Just my name and regiment number will insure that I receive your letter. I'm told you need not put a stamp on it.

Your devoted husband,

Devin Mahoney

≈ ≈ ≈

**Harper's Ferry, Virginia
Thursday 9 Oct. 1862**

My Very Dear Mary,

I am sorry I have not written before now, but we have been mightily busy. It would not have done much good anyway. The postmaster who is supposed to follow us got waylaid back in Washington City and we have not seen him until last night when he rode into camp.

I was pleased to receive your letter of 15 Sept. and I am heartened that you and little Dillon are doing well. Please convey my salutations to Missus O'Rourke. I am glad she is there for you when I cannot be.

In late Sept. we were ordered to a place called Harper's Ferry in Virginia. We did not have to march. We were sent by train. When we arrived, we set up camp on a bluff overlooking the Shenandoah River.

The first thing they had us do was target practice. An officer took us on down to the river and had us shoot at trees. We had a good time pretending they were Confederate soldiers.

We are very proud of our regiment. I am on picket duty most days. My part of the picket line runs between two farm houses where two young lovers live. The boy lives within our lines and the girl's house is over the border. They are not allowed to communicate in any way. But they come out during the day and come as close as they are allowed and look forlornly at each other. My heart goes out to them, but we will be moving on soon and then they can resume their courtship.

We are supposed to be paid every two weeks, but the paymaster, like the postmaster, has had trouble keeping up with us. I finally received my pay for the last month and you'll find it enclosed with this letter.

Kiss Dillon for me and mind your worrying. I have not seen hide nor hair of the enemy. But I do hope we see some action soon, so that this war can be finished and I can come home to you. Where my heart beats truest.

Your Loving Husband,

Devin Mahoney

≈ ≈ ≈

**Near Halltown, Virginia
Saturday 25 Oct. 1862**

Dearest Mary,

I have just received your letter of 12 Oct. So, old Bill Shannon is no longer a teacher and is going to New York? It has been nice of him to look in on you now and then. If you happen upon him before he leaves for N.Y., please tell him for me that I wish him well.

So, you've taken up making dresses for the high-end ladies of the town? You know you do not have to do that. We have spare cash, as yet, to carry you until I get home.

But, if, as you said, it keeps you busy and does not give you time to worry, then it serves a noble cause.

The day after I wrote my last letter, we were told we were going to march south to engage the enemy. That night, the faces lit by the firelight, mine too, I'm sure, showed the emotions of each man on the eve of our first battle.

It was a calm, still night and the stars were bright overhead. For the first time since I left you, I thought of my mortality. I am much more aware of the earth, the flowers, the trees. The birds singing in the trees. Leaves floating down a small stream. All of it, when I think I may never see any of it again. I do not want to alarm you. Those are just the thoughts that go through a soldier's mind when he is not kept busy. That is most likely why they keep us busy with inspections, drilling, and marching.

In the morning, we started our march to Charlestown. Within three miles of the city, we encountered the enemy. The cavalry galloped to the front. We in the infantry filed into the fields on either side.

Even though I would soon be trying my best to kill other men, and them trying to kill me, I could not help but notice the beauty of the meadow in which I stood. The goldenrod was in full bloom, late in the year as it was. Its yellow, mixed with the rich green of the clover, reminded me of the old country.

Along our lines, the faces of the men were filled with enthusiasm and courage. Volunteers were called to go ahead and tear down any fences that would impede our progress. The air was clear and bracing. We were ready for battle.

In the end, it was not much of a fight. We had encountered only a single battery of artillery. But we fought as though it was Robert Lee and his whole army out there. The rebels, seeing that they were outnumbered, retreated hastily, and we resumed our march to Charlestown.

We had sustained no casualties, but as we passed the place where the batteries had stood, we saw wounded

167

rebels, bleeding crimson blood onto the white canvas of the stretchers on which they lay. And men were digging shallow graves for those we had killed.

We took Charlestown without incident. The Confederate forces had abandoned the town before our arrival. We did find about one hundred rebels in a church that had been converted into a hospital. They, of course, became prisoners of war.

It rained the whole of that night. But it bothered us little as we were in a festive mood. We had taken Charlestown with none of our number being either killed or wounded. We were now veterans.

I will close for now. I love you very much and miss you and Dillon most deeply. If things keep going as they have, I'll be back home and in your arms within six months. And tell Missus O'Rourke that I miss her fine Irish stew.

Thinking of you always,

Devin Mahoney

≈ ≈ ≈

Near Falmouth, Virginia
Sunday 9 Nov. 1862

Dearest Mary,

I take pen in hand to let you know I have received your latest letter, I live for the day they arrive. It is good to hear that you and little Dillon are doing well and that Missus O'Rourke is in good health. I, myself, am tolerably well at present.

I have met a man in our company who is also from County Kerry. In fact, he lived his whole life not five miles from where I was born, would you believe it? And we never met before coming to America and going off to war. Isn't life strange? His name is Brian Ruddy. He's a little younger than me, about twenty-one, I believe. We have

168

become fast friends in the time we have known each other. As soon as we beat the rebels and this war ends, you'll get to meet him. He's from Harrisburg.

The last I wrote you about, we were at Harper's Ferry after taking Charlestown. From there we crossed the Shenandoah River on what's called a pontoon bridge. They are a marvel of human endeavor. The engineers construct them in no time at all.

We marched three miles before setting up camp. It snowed that night, but it was light, only enough to barely whiten the ground. The next day, the earth was wet and we were knee-deep in mud. A few of the men came down with a sickness.

Three days later, we were at a place called Snicker's Gap in the Blue Ridge Mtns. and observed what looked to be Union cavalry in the distance. Our commander, Major O'Neill, rode out to meet them. But they turned out to be rebels and he was promptly captured. We formed a line of battle, and by the end of the day, we had routed the rebels and captured their cavalry unit, restoring Maj. O'Neill to his command.

Tomorrow we will continue our march into Virginia, deeper into enemy territory. But not to worry. We have not lost a battle yet, and have no intent on doing so.

As I write this letter, I can make out candles flickering in tents all over camp, with men next to them, bent over in the faint light, writing their letters home, as I am.

Well, I had better sign off now. Our company bugler is sounding Extinguish Lights. Some of the men call it Taps. It's new. The army adopted it only a few months ago for telling us when to call it a day. It is a haunting tune.

Kiss Dillon for me, God bless his little soul. I'm sure he's grown a mite since I've seen him last. I miss you, my dearest wife, more than I can ever say in mere words.

Your loving husband always,

Devin Mahoney

≈ ≈ ≈

**Outside Fredericksburg,
Virginia
Fri. 28 Nov. 1862**

Mary Dear,

I once again take pen in hand to write to you on this cold and damp day. We have been bivouacked here for a few weeks now. There is something in the air, a big push is coming, we feel, but we do not know what, as yet. The generals tell us privates very little of their plans until they order us to charge the enemy. Then it's, "Forward march! Keep your lines straight and do not blink in the face of danger."

Every day we form up and parade for a few hours and then it's inspection of our tents and kits. We're living in mud. It's next to impossible to keep everything neat and clean. The officers have taken over nearby farm houses to live in. If their boots get muddy, they have one of us privates clean them. I know I must sound bitter. I assure you I am not. But we signed up to fight, and we've seen very little of that. It's probably boredom more than anything that rankles me.

We've had the first casualty of our regiment last night. But it was not from the enemy. His name was Wm. Tyrrell. He was a private. He took violently ill and died inside an hour. The doctor said he was poisoned. From what, we do not know. The colonel told us to be careful of what we eat if it's not prepared by our cooks.

Because he was of our company, we took it upon ourselves to bury him. We wrapped him in his blanket and then waited for nightfall before bringing him into the woods. We stood over his grave, holding pine torches as the chaplain said a prayer. It was a sad ceremony. One without honor, given the circumstances. We told each other that he would not be the last of our company to be buried a long ways from home.

170

One of the doctors has been dismissed for drunkenness.

When our ceaseless drilling and parading is at an end for the day, we start our camp fires. They are large, fifty-foot-long affairs. Whole trees are piled up and set on fire. We stand around for the warmth and the comradeship until the bugle sounds its sad lament, telling us it's time to go to our tents for the night.

I have not received a letter from you in weeks, but I do not worry. Our postmaster seems to have gotten lost along with our paymaster. But he found his way back into camp today. He carried no mail because he was cut off by rebels and could not make it back to Washington City. The lines are now open, and he'll be taking our letters when he leaves on the morrow. I hope to hear from you on his return.

If you recall, in my last letter I spoke of Brian Ruddy? Well, I've spoken so much about you and Dillon, he feels he practically knows you and has asked me to send along his felicitations the next time I wrote you.

I will end for now so this letter makes it into the mail pouch in plenty of time before the postmaster's departure.

With each passing day I miss you and Dillon more than I did the day before. I'm living for that wonderful moment when I can hold the two of you in my arms. And then, I promise, I will never leave your side again.

> *As ever, your loving*
> *and devoted husband,*
>
> *Devin Mahoney*

≈ ≈ ≈

North of the Rappahannock
Near Fredericksburg, Virginia
Friday 19 December 1862

My Dearly Beloved Wife,

I have just received your last two letters. It does my heart good to know that you and Dillon are faring well. From what you say, your dress making business is doing quite well. Perhaps I will not have to work any longer when I return home. Ha, ha.

I will try to tell you what I've been up to since my last letter. I do not know if I can tell you everything that has transpired because there is much I do not understand, but I will try my best.

I have been shaken to the core of my existence by recent events. I no longer believe war to be a noble venture. Yes, wars must be fought. But I find nothing noble in killing your fellow man or having your fellow man trying to kill you. I sit here assured there are men of like mind on the opposing side, writing their loved ones conveying the same thought.

It has been a busy three weeks since my last letter and a lot has happened. I think some of it has been written about in the newspapers. But of that I am not certain. I want you to know these things so you can tell Dillon if something happens to me and I don't make it home.

It was early on the morning of Dec. 11th, it was still dark. The fog was thick and the air cold. The road was filled with troops. We had been warned not to make a sound. They moved us down to the Rappahannock River and we stayed hidden in the woods while the engineers proceeded to build a pontoon bridge on the bank of the river. They had to be quiet about it because the enemy was on the opposite shore. But because of the fog, the far side was lost from sight. Things were going well. They had three sections braced together, with the planking down, when a single shot rang out. One of the pontoniers dropped what he was holding and fell into the cold dark water. Even in the dim light, I could see his body floating away until it was lost in the fog. That was the first shot of what I think the newspapers are calling the Battle of Fredericksburg.

The shooters on the far bank let loose with more bullets and more men fell into the river, only to be carried away

172

by the current. Now that the element of surprise had been lost, the order was given for our artillery to bombard the town from their position up on a bluff overlooking the river.

For two endless hours, shell after shell passed overhead, lighting up the dark sky with streams of light from their trailing fuses. The booming of the guns reverberated in the dense water-laden air. We could not see the town, but we knew it was burning, the flames reached out for the heavens over the low-hanging fog. We could hear the brick walls crumble as they were hit by our shells. When daylight finally came, all I could see of the town was the top of a church steeple sticking up out of the fog.

But after all that shelling, the sharpshooters were still in place. They couldn't see us any better than we could see them, but still they fired and killed many a brave man. We could not attack the town until the bridge was in place and it would never be in place as long as the sharpshooters were entrenched on the far shore.

At long last, it was decided that men should be sent over in boats to drive the sharpshooters from the shore. Men from the 7th Michigan and the 19th Mass. volunteered. The rebels kept up their fire as our men crossed over and many in the boats were killed. But they got the job done and succeeded in routing the rebels. The riverfront was finally ours.

The bridge was completed and we crossed over. The fighting in Fredericksburg was from street to street. The rebels gave no quarter. We fought like the Devil for every inch gained, and still, as the night fell, we had not captured the entire city.

Just before dark, we happened upon a group of dead rebels. They were all young, barely out of their childhood. It was a frightening sight. There were no bullet wounds on them that we could see. There was no pooling of blood. They looked like they were still alive. Their eyes were open and some of them had smiles frozen on their faces. They were stiff from the freezing cold. They could have been

173

statues. Perhaps the concussion of an exploding shell killed them. I was told that happens sometimes.

That night we bivouacked by the river where two barges had been sunk. Someone discovered that they held tobacco and many of the boys spent their time fishing out enough to hold them for a while.

Sleep was impossible that night. It was too cold, and our artillery was still bombarding the part of the city we did not control. We huddled together for warmth. The morning broke as cold as the night had been.

Our regiment, along with three others, was detailed to take Marye's Heights. It looked to be an impossible task. We would have to cross an open field to get to the base of the heights. But at the base were thousands of rebels, fortified behind a four-foot-high stone wall.

It was plain to see that many a good man was going to die that day. Our commander came to address each company in turn, telling us to uphold the prestige and glory of our Irish ancestry. He wore a sprig of box-wood in his cap. After he rode off, we searched around and soon every cap in the regiment sported a leaf of green denoting our glorious Irish heritage. St. Paddy himself would have been proud.

Soon the bugle sounded, and we formed our lines and advanced on the enemy. Brian was next to me with a smile on his face. I asked him if he was not scared. "As a turkey at a Christmas dinner!" he said. "But I'll be damned if I'll let those rebel bastards know it."

I thought how different battle was from what I had imagined. Men were falling all around me. I had to step over my comrades, my friends, to keep advancing. Some called out in pain, some asked for help or water, but we could not stop. Our major, John O'Neill, fell right before my very eyes and I had to step over his dead body not to break the line. We had to get to that wall.

Our colors often hit the ground, only to be snatched up from dead hands and held high once again.

Shells rained down on us from the hills above, but onward we pushed. One boy had his leg hit by a shell and it tore off most of the flesh, exposing white bone. He did not waver. He marched on until Colonel Mulholland rode up and ordered him to report to the hospital. We were facing a torrent of bullets and tried to make ourselves as small as possible by pulling our heads down into our shoulders.

When we were halfway across the field, the cry, "Faug a ballaugh!" was heard. At first as a soft wind at the rear of our lines, but soon, the yell overtook the entire regiment like a mighty hurricane. Every man in the Irish regiment was shouting "Clear the way!" as we advanced on the rebels.

We had to get to the wall if we were to take the bluff. But it was not to be. We got to within forty yards and the rebels opened up on us. They could scarcely miss. As the bullets whistled by my ears, many more of our boys fell, and I knew then we would never take Marye's Heights. At least not on that day.

Our bugler had been killed, so when the order to retreat was given it took a while for the word to get around. We had to leave our wounded and dead behind or else we would have joined their ranks. We started our assault at noon and were ordered to retreat at one. In that short hour, over a thousand of our brave boys were killed and thousands and thousands more were wounded. Brian and I had moved up to the front line when the order to retreat was given, and I don't know why we weren't killed. There was surely no shortage of bullets aimed at us.

We are now across the river and safe. I do not want to alarm you, but I've been wounded. It's nothing. I have a ball lodged in my left arm. If it was my right arm, I would not be able to write this letter. Ha, ha. I'm waiting my turn to have it removed by a doctor. It's been three days now, but my turn will come. There are so many wounded. Most much more grievously than I. Every day, wheelbarrows pass by filled with arms, legs, hands, and feet that come

175

from the hospital. They are being taken to the woods to be buried. Many of the seriously wounded have died while waiting to be taken care of. I think I have it good compared to them. The arm pains a little, but that is all.

I have told you the worst, dearest, now I will tell you the good news. When the ball is removed, I'll be sent home to convalesce. I shall be seeing you and Dillon soon.

And so I'll end here and now. The postmaster is soon to be departing for Washington City and I need to make sure this is in his pouch.

Though we remain, for now, miles apart, I feel your presence. You are with me always. My love to both you and Dillon, may God look out for you.

Your devoted husband,

Devin Mahoney

≈ ≈ ≈

North of Fredericksburg
Tuesday 23 December 1862

My Dear Missus Mahoney,

My name is Brian Ruddy, I am your husband's friend. I believe he may have mentioned me in his letters to you. It is with trembling hand I write to convey such sad and sorry news. It becomes my painful duty to inform you that your husband Devin has passed on to his reward.

I was with him on his passing and you must know, never have I witnessed such an exhibition of fortitude. In his pain, not once did he cry out, but spoke endearingly of you and little Dillon until the last breath left his lips.

I know that in his last letter to you, he informed you of his wound, but what he did not say was that putrefaction of the flesh had set in. Perhaps, if the ball had been taken out sooner, he might have lived. But the sheer number of wounded from the battle precluded that. There were much more serious cases to be attended to first.

176

I know little of his past life, but I feel from our conversations that you and he must have been very much in love. At any rate, from what I saw of him here, under the most trying of circumstances, I can say that he behaved so brave and so composed, it could not have been surpassed.

And now, like many other noble and good men, after serving his country as a soldier, he has yielded up his young life.

I thought perhaps a few words, though from a stranger, from one who was with him at the last, might be comforting. His character endeared him to his comrades in arms. He was well liked in the regiment, especially by those that knew him best, the men of Company K.

If it is of any consolation, he died trying to eradicate the evil of slavery and to mend his beloved adopted country.

I mourn the loss of a brother. One who, in his dying hours, showed the same courage and heroism as he had on the field of battle.

Sadly, because there are far too many dead, his body cannot be returned home. But I hope you'll find solace in the knowledge that I was with him when he was buried, as were most of the remaining men of our decimated company. It was a grand service. The chaplain spoke most eloquently of Devin. You would have been proud.

I have his possessions and will send them along as soon as I am able. Devin had two months' pay coming. But sadly, you will most likely have to petition the government to receive it.

It is with a heavy heart that I write this letter, but I saw it as my duty to a fallen comrade. I had come to love Devin as a brother. If I may be of service to you at any time in the future, please feel free to write me.

Your obed. servant,
Brian Ruddy, Pvt.
Company K
116th Pennsylvania Infantry
Army of the Potomac

177

Part Two
Dillon

18

My name is Dillon Mahoney. I was born and raised in Philadelphia, Pennsylvania. I never knew my father; he died when I was quite young. My mother raised me with the help of a friend of hers, a Missus O'Rourke. I knew her as Aunt Patsy. She passed on when I was fifteen.

Even though my father was not around, my mother spoke about him on many occasions. She wanted to instill in me a sense of my heritage. She told me about Ireland and her family and the injustices they suffered. She made sure that I knew about my father and how his entire family had died during the potato famine. I learned what he had to go through to get to America, and once here, what his life had been like. I'd heard so many stories about the man, I felt I knew him.

My mother had a dressmaking business and her dresses were in high demand by the wealthy ladies of the town. Though she never once complained, it bothered me to see her working so hard. At twelve years of age, I wanted to leave school and get a job to help out. Rather than allowing me to do so, she sat me down and asked that I promise to continue with my education. At first, I refused. She then threatened to paddle my behind if I ever left school. When that didn't work, she cursed my Irish stubbornness. But when I saw tears forming in her eyes, I relented and gave her my word that I would stay in school.

When I had completed my primary education, my mother wanted me to go on to college, and I might have done so if she had not fallen ill. At first it was only a cough, but then her health deteriorated, and she grew progressively weaker. The doctor said it was consumption and there was very little he could do about it. He suggested the best course of action would be to take her out west to a drier climate. When I brought up the subject, she would not hear of it.

"My dear husband ... *your father*, built this house with his own two hands. It's all I have left of him. I do not even have a photograph of his smiling face. So, no. I will not leave my house."

I could not budge her from her unreasonable stand. After all, it was only a house. We could sell it and, with the proceeds in hand, go out west where she would surely stand a far greater chance at a longer life. But she had an answer for that, too. "When God chooses to take me, it will be from my own home that He'll do so."

By then, I had gotten a job at the *Philadelphia Public Ledger*. I did a little of everything from running copy to helping the typesetters sort their type between editions. I even swept out the newsroom after we had gone to press. I couldn't sweep up beforehand because the place was a madhouse right up until the minute the editor yelled, "That's it, boys. She's gone to bed!" That was the sign for everyone to file out and go downstairs to the local tavern. Everyone, that is, except me. On the way out, the editor would point to the ever-present broom standing in the corner and say, "Hold down the fort, Mahoney." That was his little joke.

I liked the work and thought perhaps someday I might like to become a newspaperman. The editor, Mister Giles, said he would teach me the ropes if I stuck around long enough. But then Fate intervened. My mother passed away. Even though she had been sickly for a while, it still came as a shock. She hadn't even reached her thirty-ninth birthday.

Well, that left me on my own. I stayed with the *Ledger*, but I had lost my enthusiasm for newspaper work. I was at loose ends. I was living in our house, but the memories haunted me. Everywhere I turned reminded me of my mother. If I went into the kitchen, I would see her at the stove, cooking our dinner as I sat at the table doing my school work. Her ghost inhabited the parlor. I saw her sitting in her chair by the fireside, darning my socks or sewing me a new shirt. It was enough to make me cry.

I held on for as long as I could. But right after my twentieth birthday, I decided that the time had come for a new start. Because of my mother's persistence, I had been well educated, and I would have plenty of money when I sold the house. So, I decided to go out west, maybe all the way to California. I would see where the winds of change would take me. I started out on July 10, 1880, on what would ultimately become my life's journey.

If I was going to leave the East, maybe for good, I thought I should perhaps visit my father's grave before departing the vicinity. The only person who knew where he was buried was a man by the name of Brian Ruddy. He was a friend of my father's and had visited us a few times over the years. He once told me that he was there when my father was laid to rest.

I knew he lived in Harrisburg, but not exactly where. I went through my mother's things, found his address, and boarded a train. He invited me into his house and introduced me to his wife. He apologized for his children not being present. His daughter had gotten married a few weeks earlier and his son was in New York looking for a job.

Over dinner, I heard all the old war stories he had told me when I was young. But now that I was older, they meant more to me. They seemed poignant now, whereas before, I had seen only the adventure and heroics of going off to war.

When I broached the subject of visiting my father's grave, Mister Ruddy said, "As I've mentioned, he was buried among a beautiful grove of trees outside of Fredericksburg down in Virginia. But you won't be able to find the grave. Hell, I don't think I could find it now. It's been eighteen years. I did put up a plank with his name on it, but I'm sure it was washed away during the first rain storm."

I must have looked disappointed because he hurried on. "His earthly remains are not what's important. What's important is what he was. He was the finest man I had ever known, and the bravest. But that was only part of him. He was also kind and considerate. He would share whatever he had with anyone in our regiment.

"I'll tell you something that I never told your mother or you. The bullet that struck him in his arm was meant for me. When we got close to that damn wall, I stumbled and fell. Your father thought I'd been hit and leaned over to see if I was all right. That's when the bullet struck. If I hadn't fallen, he might be alive today."

I had to think on that for a minute. Then I said, "From what you told me of that day with the barrage you were under, he might have taken a bullet to the head if he had not leaned over. If that had happened, he would never have written that last letter to my mother. And I can tell you here and now that was her most prized possession. She took it out and read it at least once a week for years. She handled it so much, the paper eventually fell apart. However, by then, she had memorized every word that had been written on those four sheets of tan-colored paper. She kept the tattered pieces in a small wooden box on her bureau after that. Before her coffin was nailed shut, I placed the box in her hands. It was the only thing she took with her."

Mister Ruddy's eyes glistened with tears. He was silent for a moment, then he said, "Thank you for telling me that, Dillon."

I slept in his son's room that night, and in the morning, I took my leave. My next stop would be Washington D.C. There I would change trains for the week-long trip to California. I spent two days in the city taking in the sights, and as I walked the streets, I could not help but wonder if they were the very same streets my father had marched on when he went off to war—when he went off to die.

The train pulled out of the depot bright and early on July 14th, a Wednesday morning as I remember it. A low-hanging fog covered the city, but soon dissipated as we made our way west.

I was fascinated by the scenery. I enjoyed seeing little snippets of peoples' lives as we passed by. In one field, a man behind a plow turning his rows; in the next, a man and his son working on removing a stump; behind a white-painted house, a woman hanging out her laundry; behind another, children playing in the yard.

Of course, I had no idea if the young man with the farmer was his son or a hired hand. And I certainly did not know if the woman with the laundry was the mistress of the house, or a servant. But for the few seconds they were in my range of vision, I wrote their life stories. I never tired of the game. I was sorry when night fell and all I could see in the window was my own visage staring back at me.

The image I beheld wore his black hair almost to his shoulders. In the reflection, his eyes were dark, but I knew them to be blue. His face was clean-shaven—not an altogether unpleasant fellow to look at. But at the same time, I would not have called him ruggedly handsome. My mother had always said I favored my father, and as the train sped through the night, I imagined that the ghostly image floating in the darkness behind the glass was how my father must have looked when he was my age.

The kerosene lamps were kept burning throughout the night, but after a full day of watching the countryside slide by, I had no trouble sleeping. The seats tilted back and were spartanly comfortable.

When we got to the Great Plains, I began to get a sense of how vast this country really was. As mile after mile passed before my eyes, I could not help but think of those who had made the journey in covered wagons. What fortitude it must have taken to travel six months on the trail, fighting Indians, disease, crossing mountains, and enduring any number of other things I could only imagine. As opposed to the seven days it would take me to cross the American Continent in relative comfort.

Mid-morning on the fourth day, the train came to an abrupt and unexpected stop. I craned my head out the window to see what was up, and there, right in front of us, were thousands of longhorn cattle crossing the tracks at the persistent urging of loud, shouting men on horseback. I was seeing my first cowboys! I wanted a better look, so I walked forward through a few cars until my progress was impeded by the locked door of the baggage car.

I started to get off the train but was stopped by the conductor. "Sorry, sir, no one's allowed off. We'll be on our way soon. And you wouldn't want to be left behind out here in the middle of nowhere."

"Does this happen often?"

"Not so much that you'd notice. But if the cowboys get to the tracks before we do, then we wait. If we beat them, then they wait. It's an awful big prairie, but sometimes you have to share the same small space."

I was still enthralled by the spectacle. What a wonderful life it must be, spending your time on the trail, moving great herds of cattle to market to feed a growing nation, sleeping under the stars with your comrades and swapping stories around the campfire. I must admit, I did somewhat romanticize the whole thing. But from where I was standing, it looked exciting.

The tail end of the herd was just coming up. Two cowboys, covered in dust, were driving the last of the cattle over the tracks by waving their hats in the air and hollering their lungs out. One of

185

them, a blond-headed youth who could not have been more than sixteen, looked me straight in the eye and smiled, then went about his work.

The train started to move again, and I went back to my seat. As the prairie rolled on by, I thought back to my younger days. There was a time I could not wait for the latest dime novel to arrive at the general store. They came once a week, bringing me the adventures of Tom Slade and Bill McCrory, among others. Stories of stalwart men who protected the West from Indians and gunfighters filled the pages of those thin, paperbound editions. Virtuous men fought against evil and protected women from ne'er-do-wells. Their deeds of valor never ceased to amaze me. I was spellbound by stories of massive cattle drives and the dangers cowboys faced from Indians, rustlers, and river crossings. I used to fantasize about being a town marshal, or maybe a cowboy, as I lay in bed at night waiting to fall off to sleep.

A few hours later, the train slowed. Up ahead, I got my first view of the Rocky Mountains. We were approaching a small town nestled in their foothills. As we rolled into the depot, the sign suspended from the overhang read:

SLOW WATER–WYO. TERR.

The conductor went through the cars telling us it was only a water and fuel stop and that we would not be there for more than fifteen minutes. We could get off the train if we wanted to stretch our legs, but we were to stay close by; anyone not back onboard when the train pulled out would have to catch the next one, which wasn't due for three days.

As the conductor passed my seat, I asked, "If I got off now, would my ticket still hold good for the next train?"

"It would. But a word of warning, son. Slow Water is a rough town. I would advise you to proceed on with us and not go into town."

I thanked him for his advice but decided to ignore it. I grabbed my bag and stepped off the train. If I had known then what was in store for me, I might have stayed right where I was.

19

I hopped off the platform, made my way through an alley, and came out on a wide, dusty street. A ragged dust devil swirled silently by, but other than that, I saw no life. The sun hung heavy in the western sky, almost touching the mountains. It was late afternoon and the heat was stifling. Beads of sweat dripped into my eyes and I was sweating under my coat. As far as I could see, the place was deserted. Where was everyone? Maybe they were doing the smart thing and keeping out of the oppressive heat, or perhaps they were out on the range herding their cows.

As I was wondering what my next move should be, I heard the shrill cry of a steam whistle. If I ran, I could make it back onboard before being marooned in Slow Water, Wyoming.

After a brief argument with myself, I decided to stay. I would spend two full days in a real Western town. Maybe meet some cowboys, and over drinks in a saloon, they would tell me of their cowboy ways. It would be an adventure, the memory of which I would keep with me the rest of my life.

I mentally flipped a coin to see in which direction I'd go; it came up heads. I turned left and walked down the boardwalk towards the center of town. Eventually, I came across a solitary man sitting in the shade outside the Marble Hall Saloon. He was leaning back in his chair, seemingly enjoying his life.

"Sorry to disturb you, sir. But can you direct me to a hotel?"

"Ain't but one in town, boy. Just keep walkin'. About five doors down and across the street, you'll come to The Alamo Hotel. The finest hotel in all of Slow Water," he said, laughing at his own little joke.

I was standing in front of the slatted swing doors of the saloon, so I took a quick glance inside to see what a real Western saloon looked like. It was smaller than I had envisioned from reading all those dime novels. However, it was busy for being the middle of the afternoon.

My chair-sitting friend stood up and said, "You got tenderfoot written all over you, stranger. What brings you to Slow Water?"

"I was passing through on the train and thought it might be interesting to spend a day or so in your town. I wanted to experience the West."

He laughed. "The name's Yulee Carver, and if you feel like buyin' a shot for the both of us, I'll tell you all I know of this town and any twelve others just like it. I started out for California back in '49 when I was still wet behind the ears. Never did make it. But if there's anything I don't know about this hereabout country, then it ain't worth knowin'."

He was about five feet, six inches tall, bald except for a white fringe circling his head. He had a few pounds on him, but he wasn't fat. On that day, he looked to be old, but now that I think back on it, he was probably no more than fifty-five.

I agreed to buy him a drink. It was a fair trade—a shot of booze for the real lowdown on the West. He pushed open the swing doors, and I followed him into the relatively cool interior of the Marble Hall Saloon.

We had to thread our way through the tables to get to the bar. I placed my bag on the floor and my left foot on the brass rail. I was settled in. On our right, two men were in an animated conversation. To our left, a solitary man, his head hung low, stared into his glass of amber liquid. The barkeep was down at the end with his back to us, talking to a woman. The only woman in the place, by the way.

While waiting to be noticed, I introduced myself, "My name is Dillon Mahoney, and it's a pleasure to meet you."

My new friend, Yulee, yelled down the bar, "Hey, Clyde. You got yourself two thirsty customers who are only getting thirstier by the minute while you're down there jawboning with Elsie."

The woman nodded over the barkeep's shoulder. He swiveled his head and looked at us. With a heavy sigh, he turned and came our way.

Standing before us, the barkeep said, "Yulee, you know Elsie said no more credit until you're all paid up."

Slapping me on the back, Yulee said, "This here fine gentleman is paying. He just stepped off the train and has invited me to have a drink or two with him."

The barkeep looked me over before placing two glasses on the bar. "What's your pleasure, mister?"

I didn't know what to say. I wasn't much of a drinker back in those days. I looked to Yulee for guidance. "Fill those glasses with rye, my good man. And my friend here only drinks the best." Yulee looked to be enjoying himself.

When the rye had been poured, the barkeep said, "That will be twenty cents, friend." He looked surprised when I handed over two bits and told him to keep the change.

With drinks in hand, Yulee clinked my glass and downed his rye in one swallow. After wiping his mouth with the sleeve of his shirt, he said, "That first one is always the best. Now, what is it you want to know about Slow Water?"

Before I could say a word, someone yelled out, "Look at the dude! Ain't he somethin'."

I knew that was directed at me because of the way I was dressed. I was the only one in the place wearing clothes from back East.

I started to turn around, but Yulee grabbed my arm and said, "Just let it be. That's Luke Short and you don't want no truck with him. He's a bad egg. Finish your rye and let's have another."

I downed my liquor as Yulee had, in one gulp. I don't know what he meant by "the best" because it burned all the way down, and when it finally hit bottom, I couldn't help but cough a time or two.

By then, everyone in the saloon was looking at me, including Clyde, the bartender. I held up my glass to indicate I wanted another. While he refilled our glasses, I asked Yulee why the town was called Slow Water.

"This town was settled by folks from Texas back before the war. That's why the hotel is called The Alamo. And that street out yonder is our main street; it's called Texas Street. There's a creek back at the edge of town that flows down from the mountains. In the spring, with the snowmelt, it moves along right nicely. However, the settlers came in late summer, when the creek was barely moving."

"Hey, tenderfoot. What ya got in the bag? You a drummer sellin' foofawraw?"

It was the same loudmouth. Bad egg or not, I had to address the situation. I turned and searched the room. There were eight tables

189

scattered here and there with men sitting at six of them. I had no trouble identifying who I was looking for. He sat slouched in his chair with an unforgiving smirk on his face. With him were two other men who appeared to be enjoying his commentary as much as he was.

When he saw that I was staring at him, he pushed his chair back and stood up. I straightened and waited. Yulee moved off to the side. I wasn't looking for trouble, but I was a Mahoney and I sure as hell wasn't going to duck any that happened to come my way.

He stood in front of me and looked me up and down before reaching out and feeling the lapel of my coat. "Nice material. Know where I can get a coat like this?"

I wanted to brush his hand away, but I thought I'd try the friendly way first. "Let me buy you a drink and I'll give you the name of my tailor."

Instead of accepting my offer as I had hoped he would, he grabbed both my lapels and drew me close. I could smell the whiskey on his breath. "Listen here, Tenderfoot. We don't cotton to no city slickers in Slow Water. So you best be moving on." Then he shoved me backwards into the bar.

No one could say I didn't try. I pushed off and aimed my fist at his jaw. But my feeble punch only grazed him. He came into me lightning fast and landed a solid left. My teeth clicked together and lights exploded in my head. He then moved in with a right and smashed me in the mouth. Blood spurted everywhere. It took only one more well-placed jab to land me on my backside.

I was dazed; my vision hazy. But not so hazy I couldn't see the gun with its large, gaping barrel pointed right at me. I looked into that barrel and saw only Black Death staring back. My assailant's legs were spread wide apart—his feet planted solid on the wooden floor. Shaking with rage, he said, "No man swings at me and lives to tell about it."

So this is it? I'm going to die on a dirty wooden floor in Slow Water, Wyoming, at the age of twenty, without having tasted life hardly at all.

Then, somewhere far off, a leathery voice interposed. "Luke, you pull that trigger and you'll be just as dead as the tenderfoot. I'll shoot afore you can turn your gun on me. That boy ain't even belted.

190

Now if it's gunplay you're looking for, then I'll be more than happy to oblige."

I couldn't see who spoke those words because of my vantage point down on the floor.

The gun wavered for half a moment but was then put back in its holster. My antagonist turned from me and, with his hands held wide, said, "I was just funnin' with the man, Jack. You know me. But any hombre that walks around dressed like he is has to expect some ribbing."

"I can see by all that blood that you were just funnin'. And I suppose the gun was just part of it? Well, you've had your fun. Best be movin' on, Luke, unless you wanna have a little fun with me."

"Not today, Jack. Maybe some other time. Okay?"

He and his two friends pushed through the swing doors and were gone.

Yulee helped me up. Still dazed, I held on tight to the bar so I wouldn't end up back on the floor. During the "fight," the saloon had been deathly quiet. But now that the entertainment was over, the conversations started back up in earnest. From what little I could overhear, Luke Short and I were the main topics of discussion.

A cowboy walked up and looked me over, much as Luke Short had done. With irony dripping from every syllable, he said, "Welcome to Slow Water." It was the man with the leathery voice— the man who had saved my life.

He had no sooner spoken when he was pushed aside by the woman the barkeep had been talking to. In her left hand, she held a basin filled with water; in her right, a small towel. "Jack, get yourself a drink on the house. I think you've earned it. And you too, Yulee … just this once. Now, you boys leave me to tend to this man's wounds."

They moved a piece on down the bar and left me alone with the woman. She took my chin in her hand and turned my face to the left and then to the right, inspecting the damage, tsk-tsking the entire time. "Well, at least he didn't break your nose," she finally said.

I probed a couple of loose teeth with my tongue; my head ached, and I'd most likely have to throw away my coat because of the blood. But other than that, I had come through the calamity in not *too* bad a shape.

"May I ask your name?" I inquired of my ministering angel.

"I'm Elsie Day. I own this place. And don't you dare call me miss or missus. It's just Elsie. Now, hold still while I fix you up." Without further conversation, she dipped the edge of the towel in the basin and went to work.

As she cleaned me up, I looked at her face. It was a pretty face, but one that had grown a little harder than her years. Her eyes were kind, but creased around the edges by worry, or a hard life. She looked to be about forty.

She ran her tongue over her lips as she worked on me, which I found endearing. As she dipped the towel in the basin for the third time, I asked her about Luke Short.

"He's a no-account. Just trouble looking for a place to land, is all. He drifted in about a year ago. Him and a couple of other no-goods took over an abandoned homestead south of town. He runs no cattle and he sure as hell doesn't raise crops. We're all of a mind that he's rustling cattle to the south and east. But no one can prove it. The only thing I can say for him is he's smart enough not to rustle from the Long S outfit."

"The Long S?"

"Bill Slokum's outfit. He's got twenty thousand acres that he's raising beef on. He used to have more, but over the years, he's sold off acreage. This town was once on his land. He figured if he allowed a town to take hold, it would be easier to get supplies. And maybe even the railroad might lay tracks in this direction. As it turned out, he was right on both counts."

By then she was finishing up. But I had one last question. "Who's the man who got Luke Short off my back?"

"That was Jack Bridges. He's *el Segundo* for Bill Slokum."

"Excuse my ignorance, Elsie, but what is an *el Segundo*?"

She rolled her eyes. "You really *are* a tenderfoot, ain't ya? An *el Segundo* is the second in command. Jack answers to no one but Slokum himself."

She picked up her basin and said, "You look halfway decent now. I'm sorry your first impression of Slow Water turned out as it did. Finish the liquor in your glass and I'll buy you a shot. But don't get used to it. I ain't normally so generous."

She left me and went into the kitchen, and that's when Yulee and Jack Bridges came back down to my end of the bar.

Yulee introduced us. "Mister Mahoney, this here is Jack Bridges."

We shook hands and I said, "I do thank you for stepping in. For a moment there, I thought Slow Water was as far west as I'd ever get."

Jack's face was sun-brown and hard from the life he lived, but his eyes were crystal blue and good-humored. He had a ready smile and I think he might have blushed when I thanked him for saving my life.

"You're plumb lucky I walked in when I did. Luke's got the whole town buffaloed. But I know him for what he is, a two-bit gunny and a cow rustler. We're gonna have it out one day, and I thought today would be as good as any. But he's yeller. His way of gettin' at ya is in the back from a dark alleyway. You noticed he had no trouble drawing on you sittin' on the floor. And you with no gun!" Jack just could not believe anyone could be so craven.

I offered to buy a round of drinks and both men accepted.

"So I reckon you'll be leaving on the next train," offered Yulee.

I finished off the rye in my glass and said, "I don't think so. I'm staying in town to prove myself. Then I'll head west."

Jack asked, "What do you have to prove?"

"I just had the tar beat out of me. I don't know when and I don't know how, but I'm going to have a rematch with Luke Short." Maybe it was the liquor talking. I was mad *and* ashamed at the way I had been beaten. I was not leaving Slow Water until I had another shot at *Mister* Short.

Jack put his empty glass down on the bar and said, "While you're waiting to have your rematch with Short, let me ask you something. What do you know about driving cattle?"

I didn't have to think about that one. "Nothing. But I learn quick."

"You can do your learning from the bench of a wagon. My cook needs a helper. We're pulling out the day after tomorrow for Montana Territory. You ride the trail with us and, along the way, when I can, I'll give you a few pointers on the art of fisticuffs. The job pays thirty dollars a month and found."

"Found?"

"That's what we call grub. Pick up your bag and follow me."

I placed a coin on the bar and told Yulee to have another drink on me. As I passed through the swing doors, I looked back to see him holding up his glass in salute. He yelled, "Good luck, boy!" as the swing doors closed behind me.

20

I had the feeling that Jack had offered me the job to get me out of town so I wouldn't get myself killed. But I didn't give it too much thought. I was going on a cattle drive! I'd get back to Slow Water eventually; then I'd see to Luke Short.

Jack had come into town to pick up supplies. He usually had one of the cowhands do it, but seeing as it was a Saturday and they were about to hit the trail for three months, he had told the men that they could go into town for one last hoorah. They were now at the ranch, bathing and putting on their smellum for the ladies—even those men whose only plan was to play cards and get drunk. You never know what the night might bring.

I followed Jack over to the general store, a place impressively named McGuire's Dry Goods Emporium, where he instructed me to buy clothes that would suit me well out on the trail. "And get yourself a pair of good, strong boots," he added as an afterthought.

I pulled two pairs of California pants off the shelf and two cotton shirts. The pants were made of a heavy woolen cloth. To stand up to saddle wear, the seat was reinforced with half-soled soft leather. I picked out a coat for myself and then searched around for a pair of boots. But all I could find were army marching boots. I asked Jack where I could get boots like he was wearing. "You have to have these made to order. The army boots will do you for now. And get a hat, one with a wide brim to keep the sun and rain outta your eyes." He also had me buy a rain slicker, a bandana, a knife, and the makings for a bedroll, including an oilskin. Placed on the ground, under my blanket, the oilskin would prevent the damp earth from seeping through to my blanket. And it was wide enough so I could cover myself with half of it in wet weather.

While we waited for the store clerk to gather together Jack's order, I asked Jack if I should buy a gun. "Not if you're thinking of going up against Short." I assured him I wasn't thinking in that direction. "Then, yes. A gun is as much a part of a cowboy's outfit as his saddle. It's a tool you'll need out on the range. But that's all it is, just a tool. And don't you ever forget it."

Jack was talking to me like he was my father. I didn't mind, having never had a father in my life. He was nearly old enough. I thought him to be about forty-five.

We were looking over the available guns when my eyes were drawn to a Colt Army .45 with a seven-inch barrel and a deer-bone grip. It sure was a beauty. As I reached for it, Jack said, "You don't want that. Barrel's a mite long. You might as well have a rifle sticking outta your holster. If you find yourself in trouble and you need your gun fast, you'll be dead before you clear leather." He handed me a different gun. "Here, look this over." It was also a Colt Army .45, but with a four-inch barrel. The grip was walnut.

As I hefted it to feel its weight, Jack nodded. "That's what you want. It's called The Peace Maker."

I purchased it, along with a holster, and when I strapped it on, I felt a few inches taller. *Now let Luke Short start up with me.* I made sure I left the store with plenty of ammunition. I had to learn how to shoot *and* hit what I aimed at.

The clerk had stacked Jack's supplies outside on the boardwalk, and I helped load them onto the buckboard.

On the ride out to the ranch, Jack asked me a few questions about myself. Not to pry. I think he was genuinely interested in my background. He also informed me about my duties. I was basically to do whatever the cook told me to do. It would be my job to collect firewood each time we stopped. If we were out on the plains and there was no wood about, I'd have to collect buffalo chips. "They make a good fire, but you need a whole heap of 'em for one meal because they burn so damn fast."

"What about a horse?" I asked.

"For you?"

"Yes. Won't I be needing a horse?"

"You got a saddle?"

I didn't answer. After a tick or two, he said, "Cowboys don't own much, but there's one thing they sure can't do without in this country, and that's a saddle. A cowpuncher might not own a horse, but you can bet your bottom dollar he owns a saddle. You see, when a man comes to work on a ranch, the rancher supplies the mounts.

Herding cows is tough on horses. On a typical day during roundup, a man will switch out horses three or four times. We have what's called a remuda. That's a herd of horses handled by our wrangler. When a puncher needs a new mount, the wrangler cuts it out of the herd and brings it to the cowboy. At the beginning of the season, a cowboy will pick out a few horses he's comfortable with and use those until he moves on at wintertime. It's called his string.

"Anyway, I figured you'd be riding in the wagon with Sam. He's our cook."

Nothing else was said until we got to the ranch. Jack pulled the buckboard right into the barn. "I reckon we'll leave things where they are, for now. It'll be your job to load the supplies onto the chuck wagon, but that'll hold 'til tomorrow. Give me a hand unhitching the horses."

When the horses were positioned in their stalls, Jack made sure they had enough water and hay to hold them overnight. Then he pointed to a saddle sitting on a rail. "You see that? It belonged to a cowboy who got dusted. That means he was thrown from his horse. The fall broke his neck and killed him, so he has no further use for it. It's been sitting there for almost a year. The leather's cracked and dry, but a little oil will bring it around.

"I've been thinking. We have a horse in the remuda that no one wants to ride. They think she's crow bait. If you want, you can ride her while we're on the trail. Why you would want to, instead of sitting in a nice comfortable wagon, is your business. But first, do you know how to ride a horse?"

"Of course I do. And I'll be even better at it by the time we get to where we're going."

He clapped me on the back and said, "Alright. Just one last thing." He took down a pair of spurs that were hanging on a post. "A cowboy left these here some years back. You might as well have 'em. They're a little rusted but they'll do. Now I'll take you over to the bunkhouse and introduce you around. But none of those boys is gonna care one way or the other about you joining up. They'll be too busy getting ready to go into town, so don't take no offense by it."

The bunkhouse was a long building, with the entrance at one end. Just inside the door were two large, round tables with chairs scattered around them. Past the tables were the bunks, ten on each side, separated by a wide aisle. In the middle of the room stood a stove. Jack yelled into the mayhem of fifteen men in the middle of getting dressed, combing their hair, and talking up what a highfaluting time they were going to have in town that night. "This here is Dillon Mahoney. He's just signed on. Ya'all can get to know him while nursing your hangovers tomorrow." Most of the men either nodded or raised a hand in welcome. But Jack was right. The only thing on their minds was getting into town and cutting loose.

He did make two individual introductions. First to Sam Hartman. A man of about fifty with world-weary eyes. He was the cook. "Sam, this boy is gonna be your helper. As you can see, he's a greenhorn. So have a little patience with him for a day or two."

He then introduced me to a tall, thin man of indeterminate age. "This is Charlie Bassett. He's got a little Indian blood in him. What he doesn't know about horses doesn't exist.

"Charlie, this here is Dillon. He's making the drive with us. Tomorrow, I want you to cut out that broomtail roan for him. He won't be driving cows, so I reckon that nag will do."

Jack then left me to fend for myself. I found a bunk at the far end that had no blankets on it. I asked a nearby cowboy if it was taken.

"Nope. She's all yours."

In twos and threes, they started to drift out and it wasn't long before I had the bunkhouse to myself. I changed into my new cowboy attire, complete with six-shooter. When I realized how ridiculous that was, I unstrapped and hung the holster on the bunk post.

The bunk looked inviting. I found a stack of blankets over in the corner. I got two of them and laid them out. It had been four days since I last slept in a bed and I was asleep almost before my head hit the thin mattress.

Either the cowboys had come in awful quiet-like when they returned from town, or I was really out of it. The next thing I knew, I was being shaken awake. "Come on, kid. Time to get the coffee on." Sam, the cook, was getting his new helper up and going.

I groggily put on my boots and followed him outside. Sam led me to a log house with a sod roof over it. "This is the eating house," he announced.

It was my job to get the fire going and then get the coffee on while Sam cut the beef and prepared the sourdough bread. "If those boys come in here and there's not hot coffee waiting for 'em, we might git ourselves lynched," Sam joked.

When I had the coffee going in two oversized pots, Sam pointed to a large iron kettle. "Them's the whistle-berries. They've been soaking all night, get 'em on the stove." Whistle-berries, I learned, is what cowboys called beans.

We worked well together. After we had the cowboys fed and I had cleaned the dishes, Sam told me to grab some grub, and then I could have an hour for myself but to get right back. "We have to start in on fixing dinner for the boys."

I used my time to run down Charlie Bassett and ask about my horse. He gave me a tolerant smile. The kind an older, wiser man has for the young and rambunctious. "I'll cut her out after dinner so you two can get acquainted. You can throw your saddle on her and walk her around the yard a time or two, but then she'll have to go back in the remuda until we hit the trail."

After the dinner clean up, I rushed out to the yard and Charlie was waiting for me. And there she stood ... my horse. She was a beautiful strawberry roan with a bushy black tail. She stood sixteen hands high, which was good because I was tall. We would be well-suited for each other. I asked Charlie her name.

"I named this one Betty because, in temperament, she reminds me of a Betty I once knew."

I rubbed her muzzle and told her we were going to get along just fine. She smiled at me, the way horses do, to let me know she was in full agreement with my supposition.

Charlie handed me the reins and said, "The bit and reins are mine, but you can use 'em until you can get your own."

I saddled her while Charlie looked on. His only piece of advice: "She's saddle-broke, but a little contentious. Make sure she knows who's boss."

There was no problem between the two of us, and I was sorry when the time came that I had to take off her saddle and watch Charlie lead her away.

Later, I loaded the chuck wagon under the watchful eye of Sam. The things we were going to need first and use the most went in last. And Sam made sure that I distributed the weight evenly.

After supper, some of the boys played horseshoes, some played cards. A few hit the hay in anticipation of the early start the next morning. I had everything I owned in the world spread out on my bunk trying to figure out what I should bring on the trail when one of the cowboys sauntered over and introduced himself.

"Howdy, the name's Blackie. Hope you don't mind me sticking my nose in your business, but maybe I can be of help. It's plain as the dust on the prairie that this is your first cattle drive."

I said, "It sure is, and I could use a little help. I was thinking of bringing everything. It's only one case."

Blackie laughed. "If all of us brought 'only' one case, then we'd need three wagons to haul all that luggage. Here's what you do. That knife there. Wear it on your belt. That's what the sheath is for. Wrap up the oilskin in your bedroll with your extra shirt and pants. That's all your gonna need on the trail. All those city clothes and such, put in your suitcase and put it under the bunk. It'll be here when we get back."

I thanked him, and as I was slipping the sheath on my belt, he said one last thing. "Wear that bandana. Out on the trail, it might do you better than you think. You can use it as a bandage if you get cut or as a towel when you wash up. When it's raining, tie it tight around your neck. It'll keep the rain water from dripping down your back. And most important of all, you'll use it to cover your nose and mouth in dry weather. You'll find them beef critters kick up a heap of dust. I'm sure they do it just to be ornery, but that's the way it hangs."

I found it strange that no one ever asked me about my past, except for Jack. But he was the boss and he had to know who he was hiring. I later learned it was impolite to ask a man about his past. If a man wanted you to know where he was from and what he had done in his life, he'd tell you without being asked. I never did learn Blackie's last name. Hell, Blackie most likely was not even his real name. But it didn't matter. He became a friend. And what I learned from him and Jack Bridges could fill volumes.

Blackie was only thirty-one, but had been driving cattle since he was fourteen. He was tall and lean. His face was weathered from years spent outdoors. His smile, bright and sincere.

In the morning, I was, once again, unceremoniously hauled out of bed by Sam. "Get a move on, boy. Time for your first cattle drive. We got us a bunch of hungry men to feed. Then we're hittin' the trail."

So it was, on July 20th, 1880, seven days after leaving the secure and safe world of my youth, as the sun struggled to rise up over the eastern prairie, I set out on an adventure that would ultimately make a man of me.

Make no mistake about it. There were costs to be paid, tribute to the gods, if you will, and consequences to be endured, but that's the price one pays to become a man.

21

The trail boss rides point. The chuck wagon trails after in an effort to keep the ever-present dust out of the food stocks. The swing riders are on either side of the herd at the front, with the flank riders farther back. Last of all come the boys riding drag—breathing more dust than a man was ever meant to breathe in one lifetime.

The morning sky was afire by the time Jack started the lead steer on his way with a Texas yell. *"Move 'em on. Head 'em up. Move 'em out!"*

With a little prodding from the drovers, the rest of the cows reluctantly rose from their bed-ground and followed along. The herd was small by Wyoming standards, only a thousand head.

We had seven drovers attending to things, not counting Sam and me. And, of course, there was Jack. The rest of the boys had stayed back on the ranch to look after Mister Slokum's remaining eight thousand head of cattle.

I started out riding Betty, but after a few hours I began to get a mite saddle-sore. So I hitched her to the back of the chuck wagon and rode up on the wagon with Sam. He said it would take a few days for my rear end to get calloused. In the meantime, he had some lotion that might help. "But you'll have to apply it yourself," he laughed.

Even riding point, Sam and I were covered in dust. It was everywhere. It filled my nostrils, which meant I had to breathe through my mouth, which filled my throat with even more of the damnable stuff. My eyes were red and raw from the grit. I had never thought about it before, but prairie dust has its own smell—the smell of dry brown earth mixed with green summer grass.

We came to our first river crossing on the morning of the third day. The cattle were a little skittish about going into the water, but the drovers knew how to handle that and soon all the cows were over on the far side, clambering up the steep embankment.

By the fourth day, my "wounds" had healed enough so that I could get back in the saddle without too much insult to my dignity. I'd spend most of the time riding point with Jack. He was not much of a talker. I guess he looked over and saw in me a snot-nosed kid who was enthralled with the West. A kid who wanted to be a cowboy in the worst way. I reckon he took pity on me because, little by little, he opened up and told me some things about himself and what it meant to live in the West.

He was from Texas and, as he put it, "Born in a saddle." He said he'd been punching cows since he was knee-high to a frog. But when the war came along, he signed up to fight for the Confederacy. He had been wounded once. But it was only a flesh wound. After the war, he went back to Texas. However, punching cows had become too tame for him after four years of fighting the Yankees. When he said that, I couldn't help but wonder if, at some point, he had aimed a rifle at my father. But I kept the thought to myself.

He quit his job as a cowpuncher and took a job as town marshal in a little place called Briscoe, located in Wheeler County, just northeast of Amarillo. Because it was near the border of Indian Territory, what we today call Oklahoma, there was a lot of rustling going on. Once the cattle were over the border and into the Territory, there was not much the Texas lawmen could do about it. That is, not until Jack Bridges came along.

"I got me four good men. Men I could count on. I deputized them and we rode east. We didn't give a hank of hair for the border. Our people were losing cows. Something had to be done about it, and we were the men to do it.

"We had us some good forays. We were all veterans of the war. Fighting didn't bother us none. In the first few months, we rousted five rustling gangs, killing three men in the process. We strung up their leaders and sent the rest riding outta country, telling them if they ever showed their faces again, we'd shoot first and inquire later as to why they came back.

"Then we heard tell of a gang that was hitting one of our larger ranchers really bad. The man was losing a lot of cows. His name was William Petillon, a good man. Treated his help fair, and if one of his waddies took sick or got hurt on the job, he'd keep him at full pay until the man could work again. Everyone thought very highly of him."

"What's a waddy?" I asked.

"It used to mean a low-paid cowhand, but nowadays it's used just the same as cowpuncher."

I nodded thoughtfully and waited for Jack to go on with his story.

"Practically every man in the county wanted to sign on for the posse going after the gang who were thieving from Mister Petillon. But most of 'em were family men, and I reckoned me and my deputies could take care of things. We always had. So just me and my usual deputies lit out one bright, sunny morning aiming to put an end, once and for all, to the rustling going on in Wheeler County.

"It wasn't hard to follow the gang's trail. They weren't exactly trying to hide anything. They thought they'd be safe once they were over in the Territory."

High above, a lone eagle rode the wind currents in lazy circles. A solitary black dot against the biggest, bluest sky I had ever seen. Jack looked up and noticed it, too, then went on with what he was saying.

"We come up over a rise and looked down at an old dilapidated farmhouse. Its wood sides, grey and warped. It held our interest 'cause the tracks we'd been following led right up to the front door. And the cattle we were looking for were in the next field, contently munching on tall summer grass.

"Leaving our horses in a draw, we moved up on foot. Along the way, I told my men to keep spread out.

"When we first spied the house, there was no one about. But as we emerged from a strand of cottonwoods, we got the surprise of our lives. Eleven men were in the yard, talking among themselves. 'Keep walkin', boys,' I encouraged. 'We're gonna take these hombres.'

"We got to within earshot, then the leader called out, 'Who you boys be?' He didn't wait for an answer. Instead, he drew his six-shooter and started firing. His men weren't far behind him in pulling their barking irons, and before we knew it, we were in a gun battle for our lives, with bullets flying every which way.

"We lost one good man, but we laid low three of theirs, including their boss. When he went down, I reckon the rest of 'em lost their taste for battle. They tossed their guns and reached high for some sky.

"We kept 'em covered and told the thievin' bastards to line up. I had no hankerin' to hang 'em all. No sense in that. Better word should get out that if you wanna rustle cows in Wheeler County, then you better be prepared to pay the price.

"I selected one man at random. We tied his hands behind his back and put him on a horse. One of my deputies put a loop around his neck and threw the rope over a branch of a nearby tree. We hung him high and left him swaying in the wind. His body would send a clear message that we Texans meant business when it came to rustlin'.

"I told the others, 'If you want to beat the rope, head out to parts unknown. And along the way, you tell those you meet what happened here today.' We then rounded up the stolen beeves and headed for home.

"A short while after we got back to Briscoe, I turned in my badge. Things were too tame. We had rousted all the rustlers from our neck of the woods. So, I drifted north and ended up working for Mister Slokum. A few years back, he made me foreman and here I am. I figure to ride out my days working for the Long S."

Jack had had a colorful past, alright. They could have written one of those dime novels about his exploits.

Nights, when my work was done, I'd go out a ways to the edge of the firelight and practice my draw. I couldn't shoot because that might have started a stampede. One night, Jack came up and watched me for a spell. At length, he said, "Don't worry about being fast. Be accurate with your first shot. You may not get a chance at another."

"You've been watching me. How am I doing?"

"You've got a long way to go, kid. Let me give you a few tips."

I looked at him expectantly.

"First, don't sight your gun. Point it like you would your finger. Let it be natural, like the gun was an extension of yourself. Next, use your thumb to pull back the hammer as you draw. That way, you'll be ready to fire as soon as the gun is level. And never draw when facing the sun."

I tried drawing my gun a couple of times where I did that thing about pulling the hammer back as it came out of its holster. I was bad at it.

Embarrassed by my ineptness, I said, "I reckon I'll need a little more practice."

"I reckon you will."

"Any other advice you'd give me, Jack?"

"Yeah." He leaned close and, in almost a whisper, he said, "Don't go up against Luke Short. If you must brace him, use your fists. On the way back from Montana, I'll have more time to give you those lessons I promised. And if you do confront him, do it without wearing a shootin' iron. If you're heeled, he'll use it as an excuse to shoot you down. He'll say you were reaching for your gun."

"Jack, I'm not looking to have a shootout with anybody, much less Luke Short. But when I continue on my way to California, I'll need to have my pride intact. And that means I'm gonna have to beat Luke Short into the ground before I get on that train."

Jack's clear blue eyes showed pride in what I had said. "I wouldn't expect anything less from you, Dillon. But I'm gonna tell you so you'll know. As long as you're wearin' that gun, if you put your hand on it, you better draw. If you draw, you better shoot. And if you shoot … shoot to kill. There ain't no bluffin' in gunplay."

When I wasn't riding with Jack or practicing my draw, I was attending to my duties as Sam's helper. One night he let me fix the grits. Usually it was my job to collect the firewood and make sure there was plenty of coffee on the fire. But that night, after I had the fire going and the coffee on, Sam said, " 'Bout time you learned some trail cooking. You're in charge of grits tonight."

I did the best I could, but I overcooked them a bit. I wasn't aware of it until a cowboy with a sour look on his face said, "Them grits was burned." He hesitated a moment, then smiled and hastily added, "But I like 'em that way."

After he had gone, I looked over to Sam and asked, "What was that about?"

"On the trail, cowboys don't complain about the food. Even if there's cause. It's considered bad manners. That waddy just forgot himself for a minute. Don't let it worry you none."

A day or so later, I was riding point with Jack, and he felt like talking. "I reckon it's a good thing you signed up with us when you did. What with the railroad and fences coming into the country, this may be the last time Slokum sends his cows off on a cattle drive."

I hadn't seen a fence since I stepped foot off the train and said so.

"Oh, fences are comin', Dillon. You can bet on that."

Jack moved the wad of tobacco he had been chewing from his right cheek to his left.

"Right now we have fifteen cowboys riding the range of the Long S. Come roundup time, that number will swell to forty or more. That's because the beeves drift south in the winter. When that harsh winter wind blows down from the north, any sane creature would naturally move towards the lee. But the problem is, those cows move onto ranges not owned by Mister Slokum and mix with other ranchers' cattle. That's why there's so much work during roundup time. We have to cut our cows out from the other herds. I wouldn't doubt it if I was told that, some winters, a few of our cows had drifted all the way down to Mexico."

Jack spit the quid from his mouth and retrieved a plug of tobacco from his shirt pocket. He held it in my direction. "Chaw?"

I shook my head. He bit off a piece and worked it around for a while. In due time, he said, "This new-fangled fencing is called bob wire or maybe it's barb wire. Bill told me about it, but I forget what he called it. He has already ordered a trainload of the stuff to fence in his twenty thousand acres. He tells me other ranchers are doing the same. You can't move cows across a prairie if there's a fence every few miles. I'm a tellin' you, Dillon, the days of driving cattle to market are quickly comin' to an end."

I thought on what Jack had said. And the next day I asked him if I could ride with the herd and learn to be a cowpuncher. "If this is going to be my one and only cattle drive, then I'd like to experience it fully."

He let out with a good belly laugh and said, *"Experience it? Sure, you can 'experience' it if you want. But it cain't interfere with your duties."*

I swore that in no way would I let Sam or the boys down. "As soon as it looks like we're going to noon or stop for the night, I'll be at the chuck wagon before Sam can get down from the bench. And in the morning, I won't start herding until Sam gives me leave to do so."

"Alright, Dillon. I've noticed you've been friendly with Blackie. He's riding drag today. It's where you'll breathe and eat more dust than you ever thought possible. You wanna be a cowboy, that's the place to start. Ride with him but keep outta his way. Watch what he does and learn."

"You mean I can start now?"

"We won't be nooning for a few hours yet. So go ahead, but keep your promise, ya hear? Be at the chuck wagon long before we have the cows milling."

I thanked Jack and wheeled my horse. As I galloped off, I heard him yell after me, "Use your bandana to ..." That was all I could make out over the sound of Betty's pounding hooves.

When I got to the tail end of the herd, I knew what Jack had yelled. Blackie and the other drag rider wore large bandanas wrapped around their faces. And for good reason. I could barely see them or their horses through the dust. I pulled my bandana up to cover my nose and mouth and I was ready to ride trail.

I rode drag for three days until I knew the basics, then I was allowed to ride flank. The whole time, Blackie had only one piece of advice and he said it over and over. "Keep 'em bunched, keep 'em movin'."

Betty turned out to be a good cow pony. But it was hard on her—my wheeling her about to get a straggler or spurring her on to chase down a steer trying to make an escape for open range. I needed a second horse from the remuda. Charlie gave me one that he had not named. He said that I could name him, so I called him Sam. He was a good horse but didn't take to driving cattle as well as Betty. Sometimes he was a handful.

It was hard work, harder than I thought it would be. But I kept at it. I was up long before any of the other cowboys, making a fire and starting their coffee to boiling. And I stopped work long after most of them had hit the hay. At the end of my day, I was so worn out, I barely had the strength to unfurl my bedroll.

By the time we hit Miles City, up in Montana Territory, and had delivered the cattle to the buyer, I was a full-fledged cowboy. But it was on the return trip I learned the things that would hold me in good stead with my fellow cowboys and would keep my name alive in that part of the country long after I had departed for greener pastures.

22

Jack had taken payment for the herd with a bank draft and a thousand dollars in gold coin. The cash was needed to resupply for the trek back to Wyoming and to pay us our wages.

There was a small hotel in Miles City, but it had only six rooms available. That meant we had to double up. I bunked with Sam. Out on the trail, I had never noticed his snoring. Must have been because I was too tuckered out at the end of the day to notice anything short of a full-on stampede.

We rested up for three days, during which time we got ourselves scrubbed and shaved. A few of the boys visited the bawdy house. But, back then, I was too shy to attempt such a thing. However, I did do my fair share of drinking at the saloon that had become our headquarters.

The cowboy life was a wandering life, and at the end of trail, there were always a few who had a hankering to move on. Two of our boys figured on going down to Texas and hooking up with an outfit down there for the winter. Jack paid them off and the rest of us hit the trail for home. *Home*? I had spent exactly two nights at the Slokum ranch. How could I think of it as home? But somehow I did.

We, or I should say, Jack, decided we would take it easy on the way back. We were slowed by the chuck wagon and we still had the remuda to herd. We'd make camp one full hour before sunset and wouldn't hit the trail the next morning until the sun was clearly over the horizon. The boys joked about things being so easy-going they were almost embarrassed to take their wages. Still, we were making more than twenty miles a day.

Jack started right in on giving me my boxing lessons. Initially, he did it from the saddle. "The thing you have to know before anything else is that there are no rules out here when it comes to a fist fight. If you can get close enough, bite your opponent's ear off. If you have him down, kick him in the ribs. The only thing you can't

210

do is draw your gun or a knife. You could, but most likely one of his friends would shoot you down to even up the score."

At night, after we had eaten, Jack would teach me a few of the finer points of boxing. Like ducking under a punch and shooting fast jabs when the opportunity presented itself. He showed me how to feint a punch and then go in for the kill with my other hand. He said I should keep moving and not stand in one place like a punching bag. Things like that.

Once I had a few of the basics down, Jack suggested I go a few rounds with one of the boys and he'd shout out what I was doing wrong. Well, everyone except Sam volunteered to "help out."

We started that very night. My first opponent was Blackie. "Now, you men, go easy. Neither one of you are any good to me if you break your hands," decreed Jack. It was still warm, seeing as it was only the beginning of September, so we stripped to our waists and went at it.

Blackie came at me and hooked a left, but I pulled back and it went wide. I tried a few jabs, but Blackie took them in stride. He let go with a haymaker, but I went under it. I was so proud, I looked over to Jack for his approval. That's when Blackie knocked me to my knees with a right to the chin.

"That's a good lesson for ya," said Jack. "Never take your eyes off the man you're fighting."

When I wasn't sparring with one of the boys, I was practicing with my .45. We always camped near trees. Because where there were trees, there was sure to be water. I'd hang a stick from a branch and use that as my target. The stick was only three to four inches long. I figured if I could hit that size target, then I could hit anything.

I sure used up a lot of ammunition before I hit the stick for the first time. But then I got so I could hit it with every tenth shot. After a week—and the firing of a whole lot of bullets—I could hit the stick three times out of ten. I was getting better, but I still had a long way to go before I could face off with a man.

We had been nearly two weeks on the trail when we came upon the wagon. It was sitting out on the lonesome prairie all by itself— its white cotton cover stark against a cloudless blue sky. There were no horses or oxen about and no movement whatsoever. Without saying a word, Jack spurred his horse forward. The rest of us followed.

By the time we caught up, Jack had slipped his horse and was staring down into the tall grass. He was looking at a young blond-headed boy sitting between two corpses, a man and a woman. The woman's clothes were torn and in disarray. To no one in particular, and in a terse voice, Jack said, "Find something to cover them with."

I threw off first. Rummaging around in the wagon, I came up with two blankets.

Jack was sitting on his heels trying to talk to the boy. But the boy was gazing off into a world only he could see and said nothing. Jack nodded at me to cover the corpses.

Gently, but with a firm hand, Jack raised the boy to a standing position, walked him over to the shade of the wagon, and sat him on the ground. By then, Sam had caught up with us in his chuck wagon.

After covering the bodies, I walked around the wagon to where Jack and the boy were. Jack looked up and said, "Make a fire and get some coffee on. And tell the rest of the boys to stay back at the chuck wagon. I don't want to crowd this youngster. It looks like he's been through a pert lot of trouble. And when the coffee's ready, bring a cup of it over here. In the meantime, I'll try to get him to open up a mite."

It took twenty minutes for the fire to get going and the coffee to boil. By the time I brought it over, Jack had the kid talking. He took the cup from me and handed it to the boy. "Drink this. Knowing my friend Dillon here, I'm sure there's lots of sugar in it. So drink it all up. You'll be needing the nourishment."

While the boy sipped at the coffee, Jack told me what he had learned so far. "This young fella's name is Ben Kilpatrick. Him and his folks were headed down to Colorado to homestead with his uncle. Seems Ben's father didn't care much for Montana winters. Right after sunrise this morning, three men came riding out of the east. Ben's father noticed them a far way off and had a bad feeling. Just to be safe, he put Ben off the wagon and told him to run into the grass and lay low and not to come out until he was called for. No matter what."

Jack gave a look to the boy and stood up. "Ben, you drink your coffee. I have to talk to Dillon. We'll be right back." He jerked his head for me to follow. We walked to the front of the wagon where Jack said, "You're closer in age to him than any of us, so I want you there when I start talking to him again. Just before you came back with the coffee, he froze up. I might need your help to get him talking afresh. Before we leave this place, we have to find out what happened here."

We went back to Ben and squatted down to get eye level with the lad. He had drunk the coffee; the cup lay empty on the ground.

"Feel better now?" asked Jack.

Ben was slow in answering, but at length he managed a weak, "Yes, sir."

"That's fine. This here is Dillon Mahoney. He ain't much to look at, but he's a good man. By the way, how old are you?"

Jack was trying to put the boy at ease.

"I'm twelve, sir."

"Are you hungry?"

"I hadn't thought about it … sir."

"Of course you haven't. But when was the last time you ate anything?"

"Last night, at supper. But I don't think I'm hungry."

"I don't reckon you are. Why don't you finish your story? Tell me what happened after you went into the grass?"

A tear trickled down the boy's cheek. He was trying real hard not to cry. I put my arm around him and said, "Let it go, son. There'll be time enough for talking later on." He hugged himself to me and buried his face in my chest.

Jack nodded and walked away.

The kid cried until he had no more tears left to cry. But still he hung on to me as though I were his only hold on reality.

Jack came back with more coffee and tapped Ben on the shoulder. "Here, take this."

Ben let go his grip and accepted the coffee. His hands shook a mite as he drank the warm liquid.

When Ben had drunk his full, Jack asked him if he felt like talking.

"Yes, sir. I'll tell you what happened."

Jack reached out and took the cup from the boy's hands and waited.

213

"I was lying face down in the grass. I was only a few hundred feet away, but I couldn't be seen. I felt, more than heard, their horses' hooves hitting the ground as they came on. Then there was a shot. I raised my head in time to see my father fall from the wagon. The three men were bunched around the front with their backs to me. They didn't see me. I was scared. I laid back down and put my hands over my ears. But it didn't help. I could still hear my mother's screams."

Again, he stopped talking. Jack didn't press him. It took time, but we finally got the whole story. Three men had killed his father, then raped and killed his mother. They ransacked the wagon and took everything of value. After that, they unhitched the team of oxen that had been pulling the wagon, and together with Mister Kilpatrick's horse, they drove the animals westward. All that took place about five hours before we showed up.

Ben felt shame for not running to his mother's rescue. Jack tried to set him straight on that account. He clapped his hands on Ben's shoulders and looked him dead in the eye. One man to another. "You git that notion outta your head. If you *had* gone running up to those men, you'd be lying dead, too, and we wouldn't know who to set out after. Because of what you've told us, those men are gonna hang or be shot down like the dogs they are for what they've done here. That's a promise, son."

While Ben had been crying in my arms, Jack got the other men to start digging two graves. When the graves were deep enough, we wrapped Ben's parents in blankets and laid them to their eternal rest. Sam pulled out his Bible and said a few words that I hope were a comfort to the boy.

When the service was over, Jack said, "Let's see about lining our flues with some of Sam's good cooking. Then I'll fill ya in on what we're gonna do."

It was a silent meal. We sat around the fire, picking at our food. No one seemed very hungry, especially Ben, but we forced the food down because we knew we were going to need the strength for whatever Jack said was coming next.

After we had finished eating, Jack took out a plug and bit off a chaw. He worked it around in his mouth before he said anything, as was his way. "This is how I figure it. We cain't let them long-riders

214

get away with what they've done. True, this is a wild country, but if good men don't stand up to evil, then it's always gonna be a wild country. I'm going after 'em. There's only three, I can take care of 'em myself. I'll need you boys to get Ben back to the ranch and to Mister Slokum. He'll make sure the boy gits to his uncle."

Blackie and a man named Raife Carlson jumped to their feet. Raife spoke first. "You ain't leavin' me outta this. I seen what those bastards did to the woman. I'm going too. I'm the best tracker here. You'll be needing me."

Blackie added, "I respect and like you, Jack, but you're way off your range on this one. I'll be goin' too."

I said nothing.

Jack thoughtfully chewed on his quid before responding to the mutiny. At length, he said, "Alright, you two, pack us some grub and make sure your water bags are full. The rest of you boys start out for the Long S."

I said nothing.

Raife walked around the Kilpatrick wagon until he found the tracks of the oxen and the unridden horse. Those tracks were followed by those of three shod horses carrying men. "I got 'em, Jack!" he hollered.

Jack spit out a stream and replied rather sarcastically, "I can see their trace from here, Raife. A blind man could follow that trail. But if they get into the mountains, I might need you." He said it with a smile, so Raife took no offense.

"Alright. Let's move out," said Jack.

I pulled in behind them as they headed west.

Blackie saw me first and winked. Raife was on point following the murderers' trail. Jack was between Raife and Blackie, so it took him a few ticks to notice me. But when he did, he turned his horse and walked him up to me. "What in blue blazes do you think you're doing?"

I said, "That boy's tears ran down my chest. I'm riding with you."

Jack let fly a stream of tobacco juice before saying, "I'm the ramrod here and you'll do as I say. I'm going out to kill three men. I don't need no greenhorn slowin' me down. You're a good man, Dillon, but let us old-timers handle this."

"Sorry, Jack. I owe you my life, but I'm going. I want to look pure evil in the eye before you send them all to hell."

He shifted in his saddle. He did not look pleased. I could see he wanted to backhand me off my horse and send me on my way. Instead, he let flow a stream that landed between Betty's legs.

"Goddamn you, Dillon Mahoney! I don't have time to deal with you now. Fall in, but keep the hell outta my way."

He angrily wheeled his horse and walked him a few steps before turning back to me. "I'll tell you, and true. Ya got sand, kid. Ain't no doubt about that." He favored me with a slight smile before spurring his horse to catch up with Raife and Blackie.

I'd been out of the respectable and dignified environs of Philadelphia barely three months and here I was on the trail of three men that I had every intention of killing if I got the chance.

You couldn't write a dime novel like that and have anyone believe it.

23

They had a six-hour lead on us. But that didn't worry us none; the oxen would slow them down somewhat. Night was fast approaching, and that *was* a problem. We couldn't track them in the dark. Then again, they wouldn't be traveling in the dark either. We figured we'd catch up with them the next day.

I watched Raife as he followed the tracks of the murderers and was intrigued by his methods. Before we left, he had knelt down on one knee and studied an individual hoof print for a minute or two before moving on to another one. I asked what he was doing. "I'm memorizing each horse's print."

"Why are you doing that? Jack said a blind man could follow their trail."

His answer had been my first lesson in tracking. "You never know what you'll find when tracking a man. Animals are easy; they think only one way. A man, on the other hand, if he knows he's being tracked or he thinks he might be, will take measures to throw you off his trail.

"Those boys up ahead might get spooked and split up. Then I'd have to track 'em one at a time. By the time I ran down the first one, the trace of the others might be impossible to follow because of rain or some such. But because I know their horses' prints, I'll get them eventually. Even if it's months down the road. I'm not gonna stop trailin' them until they're all six feet under. Killing a man is one thing, but raping a woman is something else. I'm gonna see them dead before too long or my name ain't Raife Carlson."

One thing a man never did in the West was harm a woman in any way, by word or deed. Either way, it was a killing offense in most men's minds.

Just before sundown, we crested a rise and saw a stretch of river not too far in the distance. "We'll camp there," said Jack.

That night, sitting by the fire, I asked Raife some more about tracking. I learned that you can determine how fast a man is

217

traveling by the spacing between, and the depth of, hoof prints. A galloping horse has a longer stride and hits the ground harder, making a deeper impression.

Raife taught me how to determine how old a print was. "Look around you. Is the wind blowing? If it is, how long ago did it start up? Then look inside the print. Do you see any dust or pollen? If you do, the layers will determine how many hours ago your quarry passed by. If it's clean, then it was just made and the man you're tracking is right up ahead."

We got an early start in the morning, heading out as soon as it was light enough to see, but well before the sun came up over the horizon. Before hitting the trail, Jack, Blackie, and Raife checked their guns, making sure each chamber held a bullet. Another lesson learned.

We thought we'd catch up with the murderers on the open prairie but were surprised when their trail led into a small town. We rode in four abreast and pulled up in front of the livery stable.

Before we lit out after the killers, Jack had asked Ben about his father's horse. "He's a sorrel, Mister Bridges. His name's Bandit."

Jack told us to stay where we were. "I'll see if the sorrel is here." He went into the barn and came out a few minutes later with a man trailing behind him. "This here is Mister Langston. He owns the stable."

Langston nodded in our direction. He had his hat in one hand and was running his fingers through his hair with the other. He looked a little nervous. Jack filled us in. "The sorrel is in the barn, and the oxen are in Mister Langston's corral out back. I've informed him that they're stolen property."

Langston spoke up. "I didn't know they were stolen. I paid good money for that stock and someone's gonna have to prove to me that they *were* stolen before I'll give 'em up."

Jack didn't say anything right away. He waited a minute, staring at Langston, then asked, "How much you pay for 'em?"

Langston was looking a little sheepish as he said, "Twenty for the horse and ten each for the oxen."

Jack cocked an eyebrow in disbelief. "You didn't reckon anything was wrong? That horse is worth fifty dollars if he's worth a dime. And oxen are going for twenty dollars in big towns. Out here, they gotta be worth at least twenty-five a head."

Langston stuck out his chin. "I'm a business man."

Jack said, "Well, now ya gonna be a talkative business man. I want you to describe the men who sold you the stock and I want you to tell us where they went."

Langston looked at our faces and I guess he decided he wanted to come out on the right end of the stick on this deal. We didn't look like we were fooling around.

"There were three of 'em. Dirty and grungy they were. One had a pockmarked face and mean eyes. Another was wearin' one of them tall hats on his conk, like Abe Lincoln used to wear. But it was kinda crushed up and saggin' a mite. The other one looked like any cowboy passin' through. He was wearin' a high-top Stetson hat. He must have been the leader; he did most of the talkin' and he was the one that took the money when I handed it over."

Jack smiled to show Langston that, so far, he was pleased with what he had heard. "You know where they went?"

"They were talking about getting a drink before moving on."

"Where?"

"Don't know. We've only got two saloons in town. The closest one is the Prairie Palace." As an afterthought, he added, "It's down the street on the left."

"Alright, Mister Langston, we thank you. Now, if you'd be so good as to attend to our horses while we slake our thirst. We'll settle up when we come back. And give the horses a bait of grain. Corn would be better if ya got any. We're good for it."

Langston dutifully took our reins and started to walk the horses towards the barn. Before he made two steps, Jack called out, "Hey, mister, you got a marshal in this town?"

Langston's shoulders sagged. You could tell he just wanted to be rid of us. "We sure do, but it being a Sunday, he's probably home or in church."

"See if you can get word to him that three men have just been shot dead."

"I didn't hear no gunfire."

"You will."

On the way to the saloon, Jack asked me, "You ever kill a man before?"

"Not lately," I replied.

"Okay, Dillon, when we go into the saloon, I want you to hang back with Raife. Me and Blackie can handle things. You take this opportunity to learn. Watch which way the cat jumps. Take everything in. You may have to brace one or two bad hombres at some point in your future. You could live the rest of your life out here and never get the lesson you're about to get in the next few minutes."

With Jack leading the way, we pushed through the swing doors and stood just inside while our eyes adjusted to the dim light. To our left, three men sat at a round table playing cards. But they weren't the men we were looking for. The men we wanted were at the bar. You couldn't miss them. Especially the one with the stovepipe hat.

In a whisper, Jack told me to move to the right and keep back. He told Raife to go to the left and await developments. He and Blackie ambled up to the bar and took a position to the right of the murderers.

The barkeep asked them to name their poison. Jack said whiskey would do. The barkeep poured the liquor into two shot glasses and went back to the end of the bar. He picked up a newspaper he had been reading when we walked in and gave Jack and Blackie no more thought.

Jack downed his whiskey in one shot, Blackie did the same. With a long, exasperated sigh, Jack turned to his left and addressed the three. "You boys new in town? I haven't seen you before."

The man with the pockmarked face said, "We keep to ourselves, mister. It'd do you no harm to do the same."

Jack rapped his glass on the bar to get the barkeep's attention. "Hey, mister. How 'bout another one?"

When their glasses had been replenished, Jack turned back to the man he had been speaking to and said, "Suppose I don't want to keep to myself. Suppose I want to get into you and your partners' business. Are *you* gonna stop me?"

The man farthest down from Jack pushed away from the bar so he could get a good look at who was challenging his partner. His eyes were cold and black as night. He was wearing the Stetson. "We don't want no trouble, mister. Now, why don't you roll your hoop on outta here and we'll all have us a nice quiet Sunday."

Blackie was standing next to Jack, on his right, but well away from Jack's gun hand. The three killers had spread out. They stood stock still, staring across a small space at two men who clearly were looking for trouble. The bartender suddenly remembered something he had to do in the back room. The men at the table stopped their jawing and put down their cards to take in the scene unfolding before them. Time slowed; it got real quiet, real fast. I could hear a solitary horse clopping its way down the street outside. I tensed up. My hand rested on my gun. It took all my willpower not to pull it from its holster, just to have it ready.

With his left hand, Jack picked up his glass. His right was hovering over his gun. Looking into the leader's dead, coal-black eyes, Jack asked, "What be your name? You look mighty familiar."

The man grinned like a weasel in a hen house. "It's Jesse Hibbs, not that it's any of your business. I'm fairly well known hereabouts. You most likely heard of me."

"I've heard of you ... in a way. Aren't you the lowdown son-of-a-bitch that rapes and murders women?"

Hibbs took a step back as though he had been slapped. He reached for his gun, but at the last second, he left it where it was. He wore it border style, on his left hip, butt forward. "Well, you don't leave much chicken on the bone, do you, stranger?" Hibbs' partners were inching sideways, getting in place for what they knew was coming.

Jack downed his booze and put the empty glass on the bar without taking his eyes off Hibbs. He had a sense that, of the three, Hibbs was the most dangerous.

I could tell Jack was burning with white hot rage, but he didn't let it show as he calmly said, "Make your play, Hibbs, because I'm gonna kill you."

The five men at the bar jerked their guns all at the same moment. The guns spoke with rapidity; their barrels spat flames. Jack got a bullet into Hibbs' forehead. Turning his gun on Tall Hat, he fired and hit him in the gut, then put another bullet into the man's head for good measure. Blackie had not been lollygagging; he took down the third outlaw with two bullets to the chest.

Without missing a beat, Jack flipped open the cylinder of his gun and replaced the spent cartridges. Blackie did the same. Then Jack called to Raife and me. "Come up here and get a drink. Those gents are as dead as they're ever gonna be."

After a moment, the barkeep poked his nose out of the back room. Jack waved him over. "Bring us a bottle of your good stuff."

The man did as he was told. He placed the bottle on the bar with a shaking hand. "On the house, mister." Jack tossed him a five-dollar half eagle and said, "Nonsense. You gotta make a living. And I'm sorry for bloodying up your floor. But it had to be done."

The barkeep gave a half-smile and nodded. The other men in the room were gathered around the bodies, speaking in hushed tones. Jack invited them over. "Won't you gents join us? We're celebrating sending three no-good murdering rapists to hell on this fine Sunday morning."

They thought that was a fine idea and crowded us at the bar. Jack even bought the bartender a drink. We were having a good old time. At length, Jack told me to go through the dead men's pockets and collect any bank notes or coins I might find. I did as I was told and put the money on the bar in front of Jack.

"Thank you, Dillon. Ben's gonna be needing this."

The bottle was about halfway to empty when the batwing doors flew open and a tall man purposefully strode into the room. He was wearing a badge. He looked down at the three bodies lying on the sawdust-covered floor. By then, the pools of blood had soaked into the floorboards, staining them forevermore.

"What in Sam Hill happened here?" he asked.

Jack leaned his back against the bar and raised his glass in a kind of salute. "Marshal, we did what we had to do. Why not have a drink with us and I'll explain the situation."

The marshal thought about it for a moment. "Why not?" He had to step over and around the bodies to get up next to Jack.

In due time and after two shots of rye, the marshal had the whole story. By then, he was feeling mighty friendly toward us, but still he said, "They're your responsibility. You're gonna have to pay our undertaker to bury them up at the bone orchard."

Jack counted out ten dollars from the money I had taken off the murderers and handed it to the marshal. "This oughta do it. Now if you'll excuse us, we have to hit the drag. We wanna make some miles afore dark."

The marshal accepted the money with the caveat: "Next time you come into my town, see me first if you're hunting men. I might be able to help out. After all, it's my job."

Jack bought another bottle and paid off the barkeep. He left the bottle on the bar and announced to the house, "This is on Jesse Hibbs. Drink up, boys."

At the stable, Jack flipped a double eagle to Langston and said, "This is what you paid for the sorrel. The oxen you can keep, but we'll be taking the horse with us. He belongs to a friend of ours and we aim to see that he gets him back. You got a problem with that?"

"No, sir. As long as I come out even on the deal, I'm happy."

The setting sun was to our backs; our long shadows preceded us as we rode out of town. After having seen Jack in action, I knew I had a whole lot to learn about gunplay.

24

We caught up with the rest of the boys easily enough. Ben had come out of his shock, but he was still a little shaky. And who could blame him, seeing as what he had gone through. You should have seen the smile on his face when we rode into camp trailing his father's horse. For me, that was the best part of the entire drive. Better than learning to fight or shoot or herd cows.

We all favored on the kid. After stopping for the night, and while Sam and I prepared supper, the boys would teach Ben the cowboy way of life. They taught him how to lasso a steer, taking turns playing the part of the steer by getting down on all fours. They showed him how to throw a houlihan to get a horse out of a corral. And, of course, they had to tell him stories around the fire at night. I reckoned most of the stories were stretching the truth a mite, but they held the boy's interest.

A few days out from the Long S, Jack asked me what my plans were. "Sam doesn't need a helper when we're at the ranch. I hired you for the drive, and that's all."

That threw me. My intention had been to stick around for a while. But I put on a good face. "I reckon after I have it out with Luke Short, I'll continue on my way to California."

With one of his crooked smiles, he said, "I don't need a cook's helper, but I do need a cowhand. How about stayin' on until after roundup? We've miles of fence to lay this winter, so you'll keep busy. Besides, it pays ten dollars more a month than you're getting now."

That son-of-a-bitch! He was just funnin' with me.

As we pulled in, Jack said, "'Bout time you met the boss. He's a tough old bird, but you'll like him. Get Ben and we'll take him to the ranch house."

Jack introduced Ben and filled Mister Slokum in on what had happened. Without saying a word, Mister Slokum took Ben by the hand, led him into the house, and returned a few minutes later. "I put the boy in the capable hands of my wife. We'll see that he gets to where he needs to be."

Slokum was a tall, thin man of about sixty. He stood erect and proud. His hair had gone completely white, but he had a full head of it. He wore a drooping mustache just as white as his hair. His face showed kindness; his brown eyes bespoke courage and fortitude. But there was something else in those eyes that said if you were to cross the man, it would be a Texas-size mistake on your part.

Jack slapped me on the shoulder, saying, "Bill, this here is Dillon Mahoney. He made the drive with us and he's consented to stay on through winter and help out with the roundup."

Slokum eyed me up and down and a broad smile played across his face. "From where I stand, you look kinda young. A little wet behind the ears. But hell, I was about your age when I first came to this country. I was full of piss and vinegar and just as green. Mighty glad to have you on the Long S."

We shook hands, then Jack told me to hit the bunkhouse and relax. "Tomorrow, you and the boys can go into town. But the day after that, we go to work laying fence."

Blackie and I rode into town together. As the buildings of Slow Water came into view, the muscles on my back bunched up. Had the time come to brace Luke Short? If he was in town, it was going to have to be. I made myself relax as we walked our horses down Texas street.

"How about coming over to Missus Peabody's with me?" asked Blackie.

"Who's Missus Peabody?"

"She runs the best whorehouse in town."

"What makes her so special?"

"Well," said Blackie, "there ain't but two whorehouses. The other one is Dolly's over on First Street. Missus Peabody's has a piano player and booze. You can have a reasonably-priced drink and talk to the girls before going upstairs. It cost a little more, a dollar. At Dolly's, it's only four bits, but there's no booze and no talkin'. Just a romp in the hay and then you go and do your drinkin' down to the Marble Hall."

"Sounds like Missus Peabody's is the place to go, alright. But I gotta order me some boots. I'll meet up with you at the Marble Hall."

I turned my horse off the main drag and walked her down a side street until I saw the sign. It was a simple sign, just three words. Daddy Joe Justin. I had been told he was the best boot maker in all the territory.

I tied Betty to a post and went inside where I saw a little old man bent over a patch of leather. At first he paid me no mind, but eventually, in his own sweet time, he said, "What can I do you for, sonny?"

"I want a pair of boots, and they say you're the man to see."

"They do, huh?" He stood up and looked over the counter at the boots I was wearing. "What in darnation are those?"

"They're army boots."

"I know what they are. I mean, what are you doin' wearin' 'em? You look like a cowpoke to me."

I started to say something, but he held up his hand. "Go sit over there in that chair and take 'em off. Let me get a measurement."

When he had my size, he asked me what kind of boots I wanted.

"Cowboy boots."

Shaking his head, Daddy Joe said, "That goes without saying. I mean what color, what kind of leather, how high you want the heel. Things like that."

I didn't know and my confusion must have showed.

Daddy Joe sighed in frustration. "Alright, listen up. I have some Mexican leather, hand-tooled. It's already dyed black. Will that do?"

"I guess so."

"Now stand up and let me see how tall you are so I can get a sense for the heels."

After we had all that out of the way and I had my boots back on, I asked what the cost would be.

"Twelve dollars, sonny."

"Twelve dollars!"

"Yup. My boots are the finest around. And you're in luck. Things are slow right now, so you can have 'em in a week. Will that do ya?"

As I handed over the money, I asked, "Why do cowboy boots have pointed toes?"

He accepted the cash indifferently. "That's so they'll slip into the stirrups easy. And before you ask, the heels are high to catch on the tread of the stirrup. Any more questions?"

I had none. So I said, "I'll see you in a week."

He absentmindedly waved his hand in the air and went back to his work.

I took it slow going to the Marble Hall. I was sure I'd see Luke hanging around and I was figuring on how I'd handle it. Should I walk right up to him and backhand him across the face to get the ball rolling? Or should I wait for him to start something?

As it turned out, he wasn't there. Elsie told me he hadn't been seen in weeks. Well, that was all right. I was bound to run into him sooner or later. It really didn't matter. But when we did face off, he'd remember *this* greenhorn for a long time.

A short while later, Blackie came in looking like the cat who ate the canary. We had a few drinks and then headed back to the ranch.

A week later, I rode into town to get my boots, and still there had been no sign of Luke Short. I decided to put him out of my mind for the time being. He had given me a licking, that was true. But in the long run, it had made a better man of me. If I ran into him, I'd let things slide, *unless* he started something.

Besides, I was going to be busy. We had miles of fencing to put up. We could string wire in most weather, but we couldn't dig post holes if the ground was frozen and covered in snow. The first order of business was to get the posts up.

The plan was to fence the southern border of the ranch first to keep the cattle from migrating south when the storms hit. That border was eight miles long. Jack figured we could cut down on fence posts if we put one every thirty feet and then weaved dead branches and sticks in the wire between posts to keep it from sagging. He said weaving the sticks in every ten feet ought to do it. But that meant we still had to dig fourteen hundred post holes.

I'm proud to say that I dug most of them. I would dig down three feet and then, with compass in hand, I'd pace off thirty feet due east and dig another hole. Two men followed me in a wagon carrying the posts. They would set the posts and fill in the hole. We worked in that manner until we had exactly one thousand, four hundred and eight fence posts strung out for eight miles. While we were doing that, Jack sent out two teams to scour the countryside for dead wood to weave into the wire. Then it was time to do the stringing. That was the hardest part, because by then there was snow on the ground, and it's mighty cold out there on the prairie during the months of January and February. The wind came down from the north and cut through our clothes like a razor.

The only days we had off were Sundays or if there was a blizzard. On those days, most of the men would sit around close to the stove and play cards or sleep the day away in their bunks. There wasn't much else to do. I was lucky. On my few trips into town, I had bought books whenever possible. By the time we got snowed in, I had amassed a small library of ten or so. Those books also made me popular because I'd lend them out to any of the boys who could read.

Come spring, we had a fence running eight straight miles, from west to east. But the rest of the fencing would have to wait until after roundup.

When I first hit Slow Water, I was kind of skinny, but a winter of digging holes and stretching wire, not to mention Sam's good cooking, filled me out. My chest was wide, my arms strong. I turned twenty-one on May 9th, 1881.

May 9th fell on a Monday that year, which meant I would have to wait five days to go into town and celebrate. When Saturday night finally rolled around, we all got gussied up and rode into Slow Water together. I let it slip that I had just turned twenty-one, so Raife and Blackie insisted I let them buy me a romp at Missus Peabody's as a birthday present, signifying that I was now a man. There was no getting out of it. And, to be honest, I didn't want to get out of it.

The girl I chose was a few years older than me, but she was still pretty. Her name was May. When we got upstairs and she realized it was my first time, she was very gentle with me. She told me I was the first man she had ever been with who blushed as he got undressed.

It was dark by the time we left Missus Peabody's, and the lights shining out from the Marble Hall sure looked inviting. We pushed through the doors and entered a world of cigarette smoke, laughter, and lively piano music. It was a typical Saturday night; the place was packed to the rafters.

My elbows were relaxing on the bar and my right foot rested on the brass rail as I enjoyed my booze. At first, I didn't feel like talking. I was thinking about the wonderful experience I'd just had. I was looking in the mirror behind the bar; everyone was having a good time. The place was filled with men, except for the few girls who worked for Elsie. They were going from table to table, flirting and cajoling the men into buying drinks—not exactly the toughest job in the world.

My eyes were sweeping the room for the second time when I saw him. Luke Short! He was sitting at a table with four other men. Two of them I recognized from before. I was feeling good and did not want to get into a fight at that moment, so I didn't turn around.

I was standing between Blackie and Raife. As we talked, I kept glancing in the mirror at Luke. He was busy with his friends and hadn't noticed me. I had grown up some since I had sworn vengeance on him ten months earlier and wasn't itching to start anything. But if Luke felt so inclined, I sure wasn't going to walk away. A small part of me still wanted to beat the hell out of old Luke Short.

Then it happened. Looking in the mirror, I saw the man sitting next to Luke nudge him and point in my direction. He leaned in and said something that made Luke look over, and our eyes met. Things were about to get interesting.

I had kept up with my boxing lessons during the winter on the days we were snowed in. My bunkhouse mates had lined up to be sparring partners, out of boredom if nothing else. I was as ready as I was ever going to be to have it out with Luke Short.

He came up behind me and said, "Well, if it ain't the dandy from back East."

I turned and faced him. "Howdy, Luke."

He looked me over. "What are you doing, playing cowboy?"

"Luke, let's just get this over with. I was enjoying myself and the sooner I send you packing, the better."

229

He turned to his friends back at the table. "You hear that, boys? He's callin' me out. Appears he still ain't got no sense." Turning back to me, he said, "You remember what I did to you last time?"

"I remember."

"So, ya want another beating?"

"I'm willing to let you try, Luke. But we'll take our guns off and leave them on the bar because word is that you're a lily-livered coward who would shoot an unarmed man in the back."

That got to him. I didn't want him thinking. I wanted him angry. "So what's it gonna be, Luke? You got it in you to take me on with your fists or do you need a gun to back up your play? Because I sure as hell don't."

He grinned as he unbuckled his hardware. "This is gonna be fun, Tenderfoot. Everyone heard you call me out, so no one can say squat when I mop the floor with you."

Men started backing up to give us room. This was going to be unexpected entertainment. Even the piano player had stopped his playing and looked on.

We faced off and circled each other. Suddenly, he lunged and hit me with a short left that rang my bell. I had to hand it to him, he did have a punch. But I absorbed it, stabbing with a left as I pivoted away. He thought he'd make short work of me, but when I took the best he had to offer and stayed on my feet, he took a step back to assess the situation. But I didn't give him time to assess anything. I feigned a left and smashed him with a hard right. He rocked on his heels but stayed on his feet.

I thought it a good time to go in for the kill. I gave him a left to the breadbasket that took his wind. Now he was really mad. He came at me swinging and connected with a roundhouse to the jaw that knocked me backwards into a group of spectators. I went down, taking two of them with me.

Luke kicked at my face but missed by a hair. I came up swinging and connected just above his right eye, drawing blood. It flowed crimson-red, blinding him in that eye. I circled to his blind side and hit him with two fast jabs. I was aiming for the cut. I wanted to open it more. But my jabs landed nearer his ear.

He wasn't stupid, he knew what I was going for. He stepped inside and butted me up under the chin. I saw stars. He was tough, but that night I was tougher.

We circled for a minute, both of us trying to catch our breath. He feigned a right, then stiffened a left hook that I easily went under. I stepped in and let go with everything I had. My left fist landed on his jaw and I immediately followed up with a right uppercut to the chin that lifted the son-of-a-bitch off his feet. He hit the floor and didn't move after that. He was out cold. I stood there for a moment, gasping for breath, before I realized the fight was over.

My hands were sore, I could taste blood in my mouth, and I was swaying on my feet. But before I could do anything else, I had to finish what I had started. I called over to his friends, "Get him outta here."

They were trying to decide what course of action to take. Should they gang up on me, or pick Luke up and get him outta there and save the fight for another day? But then Raife and Blackie came up and stood next to me, their gun hands free.

That made up their minds right quick. I reckon they didn't think Luke was worth getting into a gunfight over. Two of them got him to his feet, and half-walked and half-carried him out into the night. The other two followed but hesitated at the door to give me one last dirty look. It was their way of saving face. I allowed them that. At that point, the only thing I wanted was to wash the blood out of my mouth with some good whiskey and maybe have a little more to warm my innards.

Men came up and slapped me on the back. More than one of them said it was about time someone took Luke Short down a peg or two. Raife bought me a whiskey and then Blackie did the same.

I was the man of the moment and I was feeling pretty damn good about myself.

25

Winter, in its own good time, gives way to
spring. The warmth of the sun brings forth new life on the range.
Wild flowers of red, yellow, and lavender bloom amid
immeasurable miles of green prairie grass, their sweet fragrance
filling the air.

Spring for us cowboys meant roundup time. We'd work from
dawn to dark, jerking through brambles and bogs, collecting critters.
As one of the boys exclaimed, *"It's enough to pull the fat off ya!"*
After roundup, we finished fencing in the Long S. By the time we
were done, we had installed over thirty-two miles of barb wire, four
strands high.

All through spring and into summer, the boys and I would go
into town on Saturday nights. I never did come across Luke Short or
any of his friends. I once asked Elsie if she didn't find it queer that
Luke had not been seen for a while.

"That's Luke for you. He's always disappearing. Like I told you
before, we all believe he's cattle rustling. A cowpoke came through
the other day who said he had seen Luke down in New Mexico
Territory, which makes sense. A man can steal cows down there,
drive them across the border into Mexico and sell them, no
questions asked, regardless of brand. But like a bad penny, Luke
Short always turns up back here."

A month later, on another Saturday night, me and the boys were
whooping it up at the Marble Hall. The date was July 2nd. That
meant we were going to have two days off in a row, the fourth being
on a Monday that year. Most of the boys were staying in town for
the celebration, but I thought I'd go out to the ranch and ride back in
on Monday; this way, I would have the bunkhouse practically to
myself. If I stayed in town, I'd have to double up with one of the
boys at the hotel.

I said good night to the men I had been drinking with and waved
to Elsie across the room as I walked out. I forked into the leather and

232

walked my horse down Texas street. I figured I'd take it easy going back. It was a warm night, no use lathering up Betty for no good reason.

I was just getting to the edge of town, when it felt as though someone had hit me from behind with a two-by-four. I felt a burning sensation, followed by a wetness seeping down my back. Then I was hit again. This time, I heard the shot. Before I could think, before I could feel any pain, a third bullet creased my head and knocked me off my horse. I fell into the arms of a bottomless, black abyss.

≈ ≈ ≈

I opened my eyes to see rough-hewed beams supporting a pitched ceiling. I sure as hell wasn't in the bunkhouse. I was lying on my back in a soft bed. I could smell the faint aroma of lilacs. Where was I? I tried to sit up, but an intense pain coursed through my body and I had to lie back down.

"You shouldn't be moving," said a soft feminine voice from about a thousand miles away. I turned my head in the direction I thought it had come from, and there was Elsie, sitting in a chair with knitting on her lap.

She put it aside and came over. Taking a cool damp cloth from the table, she mopped my brow. "So, you've returned to us," she whispered.

'Returned?' Returned from where?

"How are you feeling?" she asked.

I had to think about it. I didn't know how I was feeling. I didn't know where I was, and I sure as hell didn't know how I got there. I reckon I didn't know much of anything.

"Elsie," I rasped, "can you tell me where I am?"

"You're safe, Dillon, that's all that matters. You're in my room. You've been here for three days. Everyone was worried about you. But Doc said if you came out of your coma, you should be alright. He said the bullets didn't do too much damage, considering. It was the head injury he was most concerned about. You've lost a lot of blood, which means you'll be weak for a while. But other than that, you should be back out roping and branding with the other cowboys before too long."

233

I didn't know what she was talking about. I didn't remember being shot. The last thing I remembered, I was in the Marble Hall and thinking about going back to the ranch.

"When was I shot and who shot me?"

"Hush now," she scolded. "Doc said if you woke up, I was to make sure you took things easy."

She lifted my head and held a glass to my mouth. "Here, drink some water," she commanded. "According to Doc, you need to get some liquids into you."

The water was cool and soothed my dry throat. I started to say something, but she cut me off. "You lie there and be a good boy. Jack Bridges has been by every day checking up on you. He'll be here later and he'll answer all your questions. In the meantime, I'll see about getting you something to eat. I figure soup is all that you can handle at the moment."

She tenderly patted my hand and left the room. I tried to think back. Surely I'd recollect having been shot. I lay there, looking up at those rough beams, and gradually it came back to me. I *had* been shot—not once, but three times!

I sipped my soup, drank a little water, and made use of the chamber pot. I then eased myself back down onto the mattress and fell asleep.

The next thing I knew, a man I had never seen before was hovering over me.

"I reckon he'll pull through. There's something to be said about being young and full of piss and vinegar."

"That's good news, Doc."

I knew that voice. "Is that you, Jack?"

Jack's smiling visage replaced the doctor's dour countenance. "You gave us quite a scare, Dillon. It's a damn good thing you're hard-headed."

"Tell me, Jack. What happened to me?"

"We know some of it. Other parts, we surmise. Let me help you sit up and I'll fill you in."

With my back leaning against the headboard, I awaited Jack's elucidation on the matter of my being shot.

"I'll start at the beginning. Someone bushwhacked you at the edge of town. He hit you three times, twice in the back and once in

234

the head. Luckily, the head shot just grazed you. It knocked you out, but it didn't kill ya.

"Raife looked around and found where the bushwhacker waited to ambush you. He trailed the prints to the old homestead where Luke Short was known to hang out. The tracks mixed with four others and then headed south. So, I reckon there's no doubt about it. Luke Short dry-gulched you."

"Why am I in Elsie's bed?"

"A few of the men heard the shots and went out to investigate. They found you, but they didn't know what to do. As you know, Slow Water doesn't have a marshal. While they were arguing if you were dead or not, and where to take your body if you were, Elsie pushed through the crowd and demanded that you be brought to her room."

I was starting to feel weak again, but before I closed my eyes, I said, "Thanks, Jack. And please thank Elsie for me."

"You can thank her yourself," were the last words I heard before revisiting that black abyss.

A while later, I awoke to find Elsie in whispered conversation with May, the whore from Missus Peabody's. Elsie noticed my eyes were open and said, "You have a visitor, Dillon."

May came over to the bed. "How ya doing, my friend?"

I looked up at her. "Can you help me sit up? I'm still a little weak."

She got me situated and then sat down in the chair next to the bed. "I hope you don't mind me coming to see you, unannounced and all."

Elsie, her eyes ablaze with mischief, said, "I'll leave you two alone. I have a saloon to run." Then she was out the door, closing it softly behind her.

May blushed. I think I did too. There was silence between us for a moment. Then I laughed and May smiled. "I reckon we're going to be the talk of the town," she declared.

I reached out for her hand. But I couldn't quite reach it, so she leaned in and took mine. "Dillon, you mean a lot to me. I know I'm but a whore with little or no chance to be anything else, but I consider you a friend and I was worried sick about you."

What could I say? She didn't look anything like a whore. She looked like an older sister filled with love for a younger brother. "May ... I'm glad you're here."

She squeezed my hand tight. "I have only one other thing to say. And that is, you are a good and sweet man, Dillon Mahoney. Women know these things. I was with you only that once, but I saw you for all you are. I'll say it again, you are a good man, and I am glad you were not taken from us."

Abruptly, she pulled her hand from mine and stood up. But not fast enough to hide the tears she did not want me to see. They felt warm on my face as she bent over and kissed me. "God bless you, Dillon," she whispered. Then she was gone.

When Elsie came back, I brought up a touchy subject. "I thank you kindly for everything you've done for me, but I can't be taking your room any longer. I was thinking about going over to the hotel until I'm strong enough to get out to the ranch."

She sat down next to me and looked into my eyes. "How do you intend to get to the hotel? You expect me to carry you? You don't have enough strength to make it to the privy. And even if you could get to the hotel, who would take care of you? Now, don't be silly. I'm staying in the room next door. This whole saloon is my home. It doesn't matter what room I stay in." She said all that in a kind, soft voice as her eyes smiled at me. It seemed I not only had a sister, but Fate had bestowed a mother on me as well.

Days later, Mister Slokum came by. "How you farin', boy?"

"I'm fine, sir. I'm getting stronger every day."

His tall frame loomed over me as he stood holding his hat in his big brown hands. "That's good. Do you mind if I sit for a spell?"

I pointed to the chair. "Please do."

When he was seated, he said, "I want you to know something."

I didn't say anything, so he went on. "When a man rides for my brand, he's family. Me and the boys went out twice to scour the countryside for Luke Short, but he was nowhere to be found."

I was touched. I'd been around for only a year and in that year, I had made some true friends. Jack, Blackie, Raife, May, and Elsie. And now I had a father figure in Mister Slokum. It was gonna be hard to leave them behind.

"Thank you, Mister Slokum, but I'm glad you didn't find him. Luke Short is my problem. I intend to hunt him down myself."

He nodded as though he understood. And I reckon he did. He had come to that country when it was truly wild. He clawed out a piece of land for himself and fought to hold onto it. In those days, there was no railroad and no town. There was no one but him and his wife, alone out on the prairie, surrounded by Indians who burnt him out twice. But he rebuilt each time and stayed right where he was. When rustlers high-jacked his stock, he hunted them down and gave them a taste of Western justice. He had survived and prospered in spite of everything. If anyone could understand my motivation for going after Luke, I knew it would be Mister Slokum.

He was thoughtful for a moment. At length he said, "There are two ways to do what you're setting out to do. You can do it within the law or outside the law. In my day, there was no law. We had to enforce our own self-made laws. But things have changed. You go gunning for a man and kill him, some people might see that as murder. No matter the justification.

"I have some political pull. Why not let me see what I can do? I'll speak with the U.S. Marshal for the territory. If I can get you a commission as a deputy, then you can do your hunting with a badge and under the auspices of the United States Government."

I said, "See what you can do, but I'm going after Luke with or without a badge."

Mister Slokum assured me that he understood.

The days went by fast. Four weeks after having been shot three times, I was up and walking around. I had moved out of Elsie's room and was staying at the Alamo Hotel, waiting for my strength to fully return.

To while away the time, I'd go out back and set up a target on the side of an old ramshackle barn that was out of use. I had to keep my shooting skills up to snuff. I had a feeling I was going to need them before too long.

In mid-August of 1881, Jack Bridges and Mister Slokum came to see me in my room. Jack spoke first. "Good to see you up and around. We brought you a present. She's tied up at the hitching post outside."

I went to the window and looked down onto the street. There was Betty, looking as good as ever.

"She's yours. Mister Slokum is giving her to you."

I turned around. "Thank you, Mister Slokum." He nodded, then drew a paper from his vest pocket and held it out to me. "This is your commission as a Deputy United States Marshal. Your bailiwick is the Southwest District of the Wyoming Territory. However, in pursuit of a criminal, you have leave to follow him anywhere."

I took the paper. It looked official.

"Here's your badge," he added.

Jack suggested we adjourn to the Marble Hall. "It was a dusty ride in. Bill and I would like to clear some of the dust from our throats."

We sat down at a table and Mister Slokum called to the bartender for a bottle of Five Star. After we had tasted our liquor, he said, "There's power in that badge you're gonna be wearin'. I put myself out on a limb by swearin' you are of good moral character. I know you are, but you're gonna have to prove it to others. What I'm sayin' is, you go out there as a gunslinger and you'll end up with the law after you. Your job is to apprehend cattle rustlers and a man that attempted murder on you. You are not to be judge, jury, and executioner. You bring Short and his gang back here to stand trial. Understand?"

I looked into his dark brown eyes as I thought about what I would say next. I wanted to kill Luke Short and that was it. I didn't want to haul him and his gang back for a trial. But this man had gone out of his way for me. I owed him something.

"I understand what you are saying, Mister Slokum. But I don't know if I can get five men back here by myself."

"You have the power to deputize. The pay is two dollars a day. But the government can be slow on payin' its bills. So I'll be responsible for any commitments that you make."

"That's alright, Mister Slokum. You've done enough. I still have the money from the sale of my mother's house. I can foot the bills."

"Well, I'm not gonna argue with you."

"Thanks. I don't think Luke is gonna throw down his guns and let me bring him in willingly. But if he does, I promise you he'll get back here alive."

"Give him the list, Jack."

Jack handed me a list of names:

> Luke Short
> Patrick Hawke
> Chalk Beeson
> Frank McLean
> Pecos Bob Holston

"Hawke and Beeson are the two who were with Luke when he gave you that beating. The other two signed up while you were on the cattle drive. But they were all with him that night you cleaned his clock. They know what you look like, so be careful."

"That makes us even, because I know what they look like."

Mister Slokum paid me no mind and continued on with what he was saying. "According to Raife, they all headed south right after you were shot. They've got a month's lead on you. If I was you, I'd start looking for 'em in the New Mexico Territory. It's a big country down there, but cattle rustlers have a way of standing out. They're always drawing attention to themselves in saloons and dance halls." He turned to Jack and asked, "Anything else?"

"You haven't told him what the job pays."

"You're right." He turned back to me. "The pay is forty-five a month plus expenses. You'll have to keep track of the expenses, so get yourself a notebook before you leave town."

I didn't care about the pay. I only cared about getting Luke. But I'd get a notebook, if for no other reason than to keep a journal of my days as a Deputy U.S. Marshal. I wouldn't be one for very long. As soon as I got Luke and his boys, I was planning on resigning.

Once again Mister Slokum asked Jack if there was anything else I should know.

"No, Bill. I reckon that about covers it."

We had us a few more drinks and then it was time for them to head back to the ranch. I shook both men's hands and thanked them for everything they had done for me. I insisted on paying for the booze and they had no problem with that.

After they left, I sat back down at the table and poured myself a shot. I was twenty-one years old, a Deputy U.S. Marshal, and I was going out to apprehend five desperadoes single-handedly. I shook my head in wonderment. What a difference a year makes.

There was no need to go back to the ranch for my kit. Let the boys have my books, and if any of 'em wanted my eastern clothes, well, they were welcomed to 'em. I outfitted at the general store. I bought myself a long gun, a Winchester Model 73. And I made damn sure I had plenty of ammunition for it and my Colt.

When I was fully outfitted, I went over to Missus Peabody's to say good-bye to May. It was the middle of the afternoon, so she wasn't busy. She wished me well and said that when I came back, we should meet up but not in a professional way. "I like you too much, Dillon. You should do your lovin' with the woman you will marry. You're a good-looking boy. You don't need no whores—even the ones that are kinda sweet on you."

I kissed her on the mouth, lingering for a tender moment. "You know, May, I'm never gonna forget you. You were my first, but that's not the reason. I'm gonna remember you for the sweet little flower that you are, for your kindness toward me, and for not laughing out loud that night. God knows, I was confused."

That put a smile on her face. She looked like a lonesome little girl as I walked out the door. Next, I went to see Elsie. She was sitting at a table in the corner, going over invoices and other paperwork. The saloon was practically empty.

"Howdy, Elsie. I stopped in to say good-bye and to thank you for all you've done for me."

She put her pencil down and told me to sit.

"What am I gonna do with you, Dillon Mahoney? The first time we met, I had to patch up your face from a fight where you got your plow cleaned without getting in a single punch. Then I'm emptying your chamber pot because you got two bullet holes in ya and you're too weak to make it to the outhouse."

I smiled at the saloon keeper—the woman—who had become my friend. "When I get back, I'll make it up to you. I'll buy you a big steak down at the Alamo Hotel. It'll be a lot more tender than the stringy beef you serve here."

We both laughed. From across the table, she took my hand in hers. "You get back here safe and sound, Dillon. And don't think for one minute that I ain't gonna hold you to that steak dinner."

There was nothing else to do now but ride south.

I was two miles out of town when I noticed a dust cloud coming up fast behind me. I reined in and waited. It turned out to be Blackie and Raife.

"You leavin' town without sayin' good-bye, partner?" asked Blackie.

"I didn't want to get into a lot of long good-byes at the ranch. But I'm glad you boys showed up."

Blackie took out the makings and rolled himself a cigarette. When he had her going, he said, "Me and Raife just wanted to send you on your way proper like and let you know we'll be looking for you on the back trail."

We shook hands all around and then I was left on my own. I turned my back on Wyoming Territory and spurred Betty to a slow trot, leaving behind all the friends I had in this here world.

26

I started out taking it slow. Maybe Luke would get himself shot or hanged before I caught up with him. That would save me a lot of trouble. I wasn't looking forward to hauling him and his gang all the way back to Slow Water. Not by a long shot. I was philosophizing that I should never have taken the commission to be a marshal. I should have kept to my original plan to go out and find Luke and just kill him.

At first, I didn't go into the towns I passed along the way unless I needed to resupply. Making camp under the stars and being by myself gave me time to think about things other than Luke Short. What would I do after bringing him to justice? Would I stay in Slow Water and make a life there, or would I go on to California as I had originally planned?

It was in Loveland, Colorado, that I got my first sniff of Luke and his gang. I had gone into town to re-up on coffee and decided to wash some of the dust out of my throat at one of the local saloons. As I was enjoying my whiskey, a man sidled up to me at the bar. "Mind if I ask where you hail from, stranger?"

In truth, I didn't mind. But I did mind the way he had asked. Something about his tone of voice riled me. Without deigning to look in his direction and keeping my eyes focused on a bottle of rotgut on the back bar, I asked, "Who are you? The town census taker?"

"Not likely. But I *am* the town marshal."

I turned my head and saw an older man. I'd say he had about fifty years to his credit. He wore a thick mustache, dark in color even though his hair was mostly grey. He was smiling, but the smile did not extend to his eyes. I noticed that his right hand didn't stray too far from his gun.

"Sorry, Marshal. I wasn't trying to be disputatious. I'm just a little weary from the trail. I must have left my manners back out on the prairie somewhere. My name is Dillon Mahoney and I'm coming in from Wyoming Territory. Let me buy you a drink and I'll tell you my story."

His right hand left the vicinity of his gun and he gave out with a genuine smile that *did* reach his eyes. "The name's Emmett Graff. It's a little early, but I reckon one can't do no harm."

After he had downed his shot, I told him I was a Deputy U.S. Marshal and explained what I was up to.

"You look kinda young to be a U.S. Marshal, and I see you're not wearin' a badge." It was more of a question than a statement.

I took my commission out and showed it to him. The badge stayed where it was, inside my coat pocket. "I don't wear the badge because I feel the kind of men who might know things about the gang I'm trailing would be more open to talkin' to a saddle tramp than a lawman. And as for me being young, I can only say that it pays to have friends in high places."

Graff nodded. "How many men are you trailing? I only ask because our bank was robbed three weeks ago. Five men were involved. One stayed outside with the horses while the others went inside."

He had my attention. "Do you have them in custody?"

"'Fraid not. They got clean away."

"Can you describe them?"

"I didn't see 'em. But the bank manager gave me a good description of the one who did most of the talkin'."

I waited.

The marshal glanced at his empty glass. I got the hint. "Barkeep! Two refills, please."

He drank his whiskey and seemed to savor the taste. At length, he told me what I wanted to hear. "He was a tall man. Almost as tall as you. He wore a mustache, blond like his hair. And, according to the manager, he had small, crazy eyes. Dark brown they were."

That was Luke Short, alright. Somehow, I had gained a week on them. I would have to rethink things. First of all, I'd step up my pace. And I'd have to start going into the towns I came across. I might get further word on Luke or his whereabouts.

"Did you give chase?" I asked.

"We sure did. I formed a posse and we weren't but an hour behind 'em. However, late in the afternoon, we got hit with a deluge that wiped out their trail. The rain looked like it was never gonna let up, and seeing as how no one got hurt, and they made off with less than two hundred dollars, we turned for home."

It was nearing noon as I rode out of Loveland. I gigged Betty to a gallop to let her get some exercise. For all I knew, Luke could be in the next town, sitting in a bar getting drunk or robbing the local bank.

I had no luck in Boulder or Denver. It wasn't until I got to Colorado Springs that I again picked up the gang's trace. I had asked around at a few of the saloons if anyone had seen a tall man with a blond mustache traveling in the company of four other men. No one had. Chances were slim that I'd find Luke or his cohorts that way; however, I had to try. But it was when I was in the general store buying coffee and some canned meat that I had the bright idea to ask the store clerk if he had noticed any strangers passing through town.

"Sure, mister. I remember 'em because they were a mean-looking bunch. They was in here buying supplies and kidding around. They was gettin' kinda rowdy until one of 'em yelled at the others to calm down. He said something about not wanting to bring attention to themselves."

I thought I'd treat myself and placed a can of California pears on the counter with the rest of my goods. "Any idea in which direction they rode after they left here?"

"I watched 'em through the window when they went out onto the street. They got on their horses and rode south."

He cut a length of brown paper from a roll and placed my groceries on it.

"You want anything else, mister?"

"Nope. That'll do it."

He wrapped the items in the paper and secured the package with white string.

"That'll be one dollar and thirty-five cents, please."

"Isn't that kinda costly?"

"It's the pears. They're hard to come by. I gotta charge forty-five cents a can just to make a profit."

I handed over the money and asked one last question. "How long ago were those men here?"

"Hmm ... I'd say about two and a half weeks ago. Something like that."

"Thanks."

I was thoughtful as I rode out of town. No doubt about it. I was closing in on the gang. Perhaps I should start making plans on how I was going to take them down. There were five of them and only one of me. After a few moments, I gave up thinking about it. Maybe I should find them before I worried about the dynamics of how I was going to capture them. Things would work themselves out ... one way or the other.

The terrain gradually changed from high plains to high desert. Late in the afternoon, when the shadows were long, I topped out on a ridge and got my first view of the Sangre de Cristo Mountains, with Blanca Peak off in the distance. Colorful hollyhocks of purple, pink, and red dotted the landscape. At last, I was in New Mexico Territory. I made a dry camp that night and in the morning rode into a small town by the name of Taos.

My first stop was at the marshal's office, but it was locked up tight with no one around. Next, I walked Betty to the livery stable. Tossing two bits to the proprietor, I said, "Give her a wipe down and a bait of grain. I'll be back in an hour or so." I found the nearest saloon and pushed through the doors. Not so much to get a drink, but to get information.

As it turned out, I got more than I had bargained for. Sitting at a corner table, all by himself, was Pecos Bob Holston, one of Luke's gang. He was a big man of brawn and muscle. His long black hair hung past his shoulders. His beard was as black as his hair, his eyes, as blue as the sky. A Mexican sombrero hung down his back, held there by a rawhide chin string. He had a bottle to himself and it looked as though he had already put a good dent in it.

I asked the bartender for a glass and went over and sat down opposite Pecos Bob. "Mind if I join you?"

His eyes widened. "I ... I ... thought you were dead!" he stammered.

"Not nearly, Bob. Wanna buy me a drink?"

He pointed to the bottle without saying a word, his eyes still wide.

I filled my glass and lifted it in his direction. "Here's to reunions. It's good to see you again, Bob."

He downed the contents of his glass in one fast gulp and, with a trembling hand, refilled it, splashing a goodly portion onto the table.

It was time to get down to business. "You do realize I'm not a ghost, don't ya, Bob?"

"I figured that. But you're the last person I thought I'd see down here. Luke told us he had killed you."

There it was! I now had definitive proof that it was Luke Short who'd put those bullets into me.

"Speaking of Luke, you wouldn't know where I could find him and the others? Are they also in town?"

By then, Bob had calmed down some. "Look. I want you to know somethin'. What Luke did, he did on his own. We were makin' plans to come down here and do a little rustling, but the night before we was to leave, he said he had some business in town and rode off. When he came back, he was tight-lipped, not sayin' a word. It wasn't until we were well out on the trail that he opened up and told us what he had done."

I was unmoved. "So where's Luke now?"

"Him and the rest are probably down near Las Cruces. Luke said he knew of some big spreads down that way. We figured no one would miss a few hundred beeves outta thousands. We planned to take 'em over the border and sell 'em in Mexico."

"Mind if I have another shot, Bob? Listening to all yer talkin' has kinda parched my throat."

Staring at the bottle so he wouldn't have to look at me, he said, "Help yourself, mister."

I studied him for a moment. He was an outlaw alright, but his bright blue eyes did not seem to be the eyes of a killer. "So why aren't you with the others?" I asked.

For the first time since I sat down, he relaxed. "Rustling's one thing. But when it comes to murder, I gotta draw the line."

"What about bank robbery?"

"So you know about that, do ya? Okay, I'll tell you how it was, but I don't know why I should."

I took out my badge and showed it to him. "This is why. I'm a Deputy U.S. Marshal, duly appointed by the President of the United

States. I've come to arrest you and the other members of Luke's gang. But you were saying …?"

That let the wind out of his sails. He looked tired. "Okay, Mahoney … I mean, Marshal, this is the way it is. I had run into Luke from time to time in my travels. So when the opportunity presented itself, I joined up with him to rustle cattle and that's all.

"We had good luck rustling up around Slow Water. Never got caught in the act, and after changing the brands, we sold the beeves off to unsuspecting nesters. All the same, we didn't wanna press our luck, so we made plans to come down here. However, after you gave Luke that beating, he said he wouldn't leave until he settled up with you. But I swear, I thought he meant settling things by returning the beating.

"Anyway, once on the trail, we needed money. Luke said we should rob that one-horse town's bank. I was against it, but there wasn't much I could do. So I did lookout while the others went inside. Afterwards, while he was feeling good about the robbery, Luke opened up and told us he had killed you. That's when I decided to go my own way. I waited until we made camp outside of Boulder and then stole off in the night, while the others were asleep."

"Why did you come here?"

"I needed to get out of Colorado because of the bank thing. I reckoned I'd be safe here. Safe from the law and safe from Luke. He's gone a little crazy, or I should say more crazy, since you gave him that beating. I knew he wouldn't take kindly to my leaving."

Now that I had learned where Luke was, what was I going do with Pecos Bob? I was thinking I could deposit him in the local hoosegow and collect him on the way back. But I really didn't want to do that. I had no beef with the man, and now that he had quit Luke's outfit, he was no threat to me. Sure, I was a lawman and he had robbed a bank, but, somehow, I couldn't get all that worked up over it.

The bottle was getting low and the day was moving on. I had to hit the trail. In a flash, I made up my mind. "Bob, I'm not gonna arrest you. But I need you out of the territory. You can go east or west, but if I see you again, I'm gonna haul you in for bank robbery."

"I promise, you ain't gonna see me for my dust."

"One last thing, Bob. How do I get to Las Cruces and how far is it?"

"It's due south. You got some riding ahead of ya. I'd say it's about three hundred miles, maybe three-fifty. The trail's marked. Just follow the wagon ruts."

I nodded and stood to leave, but three steps from the table, a little man wearing an ill-fitting grey suit and a top hat blocked my way. "Mind if I talk to you, Marshal?"

I looked behind me to make sure he wasn't addressing someone else. There was no one there. "What makes you think I'm a marshal?"

"I'm sorry. Your conversation with that man over there," he was pointing at Bob, "was overheard and reported to me. I'm the mayor of this town. The name's Jim Greathouse. May I ask your name?"

"My name ain't important because I'm shuckin' outta here and ya not gonna have time to get to know me." I stepped around him and was almost to the swing doors when he yelled out, "Are you a lawman or not?"

I'm sure my shoulders must have sagged at that point. I turned around, and even as I was doing so, I was telling myself, *Don't do it. Go through the swing doors, get on your horse and ride.* But I didn't listen to that sage advice. No, that would have been way too easy.

"Okay, mister. What's on your mind?"

The frown on the little man's face reversed itself into a smile. "Why not let me buy you a drink and we'll palaver for a spell?"

I walked up to him and said, "I got places I gotta be. Speak your piece, mister."

He looked around and eyed an empty table next to where Bob was sitting. "Alright. Grab a chair and I'll be brief. But if you don't mind, I'm getting some whiskey for myself."

In a resigned, defeated voice I said, "Get one for me too."

While we waited for our booze, he asked, "To whom do I have the honor of speaking?"

"My name is Dillon Mahoney. And yes, I'm a Deputy U.S. Marshal. But I'm on the trail of some bad men and I don't have time to get to know you or your town. So let's get this out of the way. What do you want?"

The bartender put a bottle down on the table, along with two glasses. Greathouse did the honors and poured us each a healthy shot. I picked up my glass and took a sip. *Hmm ... not bad.*

Greathouse sampled the liquor and nodded his satisfaction. "Marshal Mahoney, this town needs your help."

I must have had a sour look on my face because he quickly declared, "Now, don't look at me that way. Please hear me out."

I nodded and took a sip of that good-tasting whiskey. It sure was smooth. *Maybe I should get a bottle of this stuff to have on the trail.*

"We've got us a bunch of outlaws that need to go," said the mayor, bringing me in from my thoughts. "They're robbing stages and rustling cows, committing all sorts of nefarious acts, including murder. We've kind of tolerated 'em up 'til now because there wasn't much else we could do. And to be completely honest with you, we were afraid of them. Besides, most of their criminal activity took place over the line in Arizona."

"What has changed?"

Greathouse took a slug of whiskey before answering.

"Whenever they came into town, they were more or less law-abiding. You know, on their good behavior. But a few days ago, they were here, got drunk, and shot up the town. A bullet went through a wall and killed a woman. When our marshal tried to disarm them, he got a bullet in one of his lungs for his trouble. He's home now, flat on his back."

"I don't see how any of that concerns me."

"Look, Marshal. The honest citizens of Taos have decided to roust out these evil-doers once and for all. But we want to do it under the authority of the law. We're a growing town and it wouldn't look good if word got out that we had to resort to vigilante justice. We're trying to attract good, God-fearin' people. If we do this thing right, we'll make Taos a byword in civilized communities."

"And you want me to ...?"

"I want you to lead us. I've got twelve men who know how to use a gun. All of 'em ready to follow you. And there's only six of them outlaws. You deputize us legal-like and we'll go get 'em, give 'em a quick and fair trial, and then we'll hang 'em. We can have this wrapped up by suppertime."

There was no way I was signing on to lead vigilantes on a lynching party. But the booze had been good, so I thought I'd let the little mayor down easy. "You can appoint a new or temporary marshal. You don't need me."

"Our town marshal has legal power only to the edge of town. The desperadoes are out in the county."

"Then ride with the county sheriff."

"There is no county sheriff."

"Where's the U.S. Marshal for this area?"

"He works outta El Paso, four hundred miles to the south."

"Well, send for him. I'm sure you have a telegraph."

"He's a political appointee. He's worthless."

He hastily added, "No offense. I'm not sayin' all U.S. Marshals are worthless, but in the three years he's been marshal, he's never once been up here. Claims he has a bad back. I hear he stays drunk most of the time."

I noticed Bob had been leaning in, listening. And right about then, he thought he'd throw in his two cents' worth. With a devious sparkle in his eyes, but a serious look on his face, he said, "Marshal, I think you oughta help these good people. I, for one, would be honored to ride with your posse."

The mayor beamed at the unexpected support for his cause. He had found an ally. "Why, that's right friendly of you, stranger. Please, won't you join us?" And just to make sure of Bob's continued support, he added, "We're drinking my private stock. I think you'll find it some of the smoothest whiskey you've ever had."

Bob settled in, poured himself a shot. I should have arrested him right then and there. Instead, I said, "Mister Greathouse, this man is a cattle rustler and a bank robber. The only reason he's not down at your jail this very moment is because, stupid me, I had a momentary lapse of judgment."

It did no good. Greathouse slapped Bob on the back with enthusiasm. "As long as he didn't rob *our* bank or rustle cattle in Taos County, he's welcome to ride with us." His smile quickly faded as a thought entered his head. "You didn't do your rustling in Taos County, did you?"

Bob assured him that he did not steal any cows in or around Taos. "And besides, Mister Mayor, I'm a reformed man. Those days are long behind me. Just ask the marshal, he'll vouch for my current uprightness."

He was pushing it.

I ignored Bob and his malarkey and gave Greathouse my full attention. "I cannot—and will not—lead a lynch mob."

You would have thought I had slapped the man across the face. His head jerked back and his eyes widened. His mouth was moving but no words were forthcoming. Finally, he found his voice.

"Those are harsh words, Marshal. Didn't I tell you we were gonna give 'em a trial before we hanged them?"

I looked him in the eye and held his gaze until he looked away, seeking solace in the doings of a fly walking along the edge of the table. He knew what he was saying was bullshit, and so did I.

As far as I was concerned, the conversation was over and I stood to leave. But he stopped me with a plaintive entreaty before I could take a step. "Please, Marshal, sit back down. A few more minutes can't make a difference to you, and I have something I wanna say."

Pecos Bob said nothing. His smirk had vanished.

I sat down.

"Marshal, I didn't tell you everything. I was afraid that you might not sign on if you knew how dangerous that gang is. It's led by a man by the name of Heck Thomas. He's a curly dog and crooked as a Virginia fence. He's a mean, cruel sonavabitch. He'd just as soon kill you as look at you. We've been spared most of his and his gang's barbaric atrocities because they need a town to buy supplies in and do their drinking, not to mention their whorin'. Lately, they've gotten more brazen and it's affecting us. I'm ashamed to say that, as long as we were making money off them and were left alone, we had no problem with what they were doing across the border in Arizona. But now that they've killed one of our own, a woman, nonetheless, we have to do something."

He gabbed for the bottle and filled all our glasses. To be polite, I drank his liquor. Bob was also being polite.

I waited for Greathouse to get to it. So far, nothing he had said made any difference in my thinking. I still wasn't going to lead the town's lynching party. If anything, what I heard got me to wondering if Taos wasn't getting exactly what it deserved. After all, it had made a deal with the Devil.

"I'll tell you this, Marshal. If you lead us, everything will be done according to Hoyle. All legal and above board. We'll bring 'em back alive and hold 'em until the circuit judge comes by. I know they can afford lawyers, so they'll be well represented. But we will prosecute them with vigor.

"We'll have to hire a prosecuting attorney because we don't have one here in town. And I assure you we'll get the best. We don't want those sons-of-bitches to go free. But in the end, they'll have had a fair trial. I promise you that." I saw why he was the mayor. He made a damn good speech.

His plea did bring one thing to mind. Something that Jack Bridges had once said to me. *"If good men don't stand up to evil, the bad men will win, and this land will never be tamed."*

It might have been Jack's words or it might have been the whiskey. Either way, I figured if I could help clear up Greathouse's mess and everything was done legal-like, and I could be on my way in the morning, why not? Luke would just have to keep for a day or two.

"Alright, Mister Greathouse. You go round up your men. I'll swear them in and we'll ride. If they're not here and ready to hit the trail within the hour, then you can have Pecos Bob over there lead you, 'cause I'll be hightailin' it south."

Greathouse jumped to his feet and started for the door, but after a step or two, he stopped and came back to the table. "Sorry. I was in such a rush to get things moving before you changed your mind that I forgot to say thank you. Please enjoy the rest of my whiskey. It's the best in town." Then he was gone.

I looked across the table at Bob. He shrugged and hefted the bottle and poured us each a healthy shot, smiling the whole time. He seemed to be enjoying himself.

"Hey, Bob. You got any of that stolen bank money on ya?"

All of a sudden, he got real cagey. Looking at me sideways, with hooded eyes, he asked, "Why do you wanna know?"

"Because if you do, I want you to go up to the bar and order us two steak dinners with all the trimmings. If I'm gonna lead a posse, my first posse, come to think of it, I don't wanna do it on an empty stomach. And get me some coffee. I gotta sober up."

27

As we were finishing our steaks, Greathouse returned. "The boys are outside and ready to go. We got ourselves a posse of fifteen, including you two."

While we were eating, Bob told me he had been serious about riding with the posse, as long as I had no objections. I tried to think of a few, but couldn't come up with anything that would hold water.

I pushed the now empty plate away and leaned back in my chair. It had been an exceptionally good steak.

"Okay, Mister Greathouse, let's get this over with."

The inside of the saloon had been dark and cool. Outside was the exact opposite, hot and bright. I pulled my hat down low to shield my eyes. The men of the posse sat their horses in the middle of the street. There were no cowboys among them; they all wore city clothes. Two of the men had some years on them. The rest were considerably younger, but still, they were all older than I was. Betty was there waiting. "I hope you don't mind, Marshal," said Greathouse. "To save time, I took the liberty of having her saddled and brought here."

Being a politician, he had to make a speech. He stood on the boardwalk in the shade of a ramada and started in. "I told you boys we had us a U.S. Marshal who was offering to help us root out the Thomas Gang. Well, here he is." He pointed to me, making me feel like I was in a circus or something.

He went on. "His name is Dillon Mahoney and we're damn lucky he happened along just when he did. And I gotta tell you, this is gonna be done by the book. We're gonna round up Thomas and his gang and bring 'em back for a fair trial. And any man who wants to do things different or take the law into his own hands can just stay here in town."

One of the men, he looked to be about thirty-five, took off his hat and wiped his brow with the sleeve of his shirt. He cleared his

253

throat to get Greathouse's attention. The mayor noticed and said, "What is it, Abe?"

The man walked his horse to the boardwalk and addressed me directly.

"My name is Abe Styles. It was my wife who was killed. I want you to know that I appreciate your help. If there was any man in this posse who would want to string Thomas up, that would be me. But we have to do things by the law. Without the law, we're no better than a pack of coyotes fighting over the choicest piece of meat. We'd be no better than Heck Thomas. I'm proud to ride with you, Marshal."

Greathouse started to say something, but a voice rang out. "Cut the speechifyin', Jim. Let's ride."

I climbed into the leather. Greathouse and Bob did the same. We took our place at the head of the posse, and with twelve men behind us and under a blistering hot sun, we rode out of Taos, trailing southwest. Off in the distance, shimmering heat waves rose from the desert floor.

"It's a two-hour ride if we don't push the horses. And in this heat, I'd advise against that," said Greathouse who rode to my right.

"That's fine, Jim. You mind if I call you Jim?"

He pulled a white handkerchief from his coat pocket and wiped the sweat from his face. "Not at all. Everyone does."

Bob was on my left. Now I saw why he wore a sombrero. It afforded him a heap of shade. "What do you think, Bob? Glad you came along?"

"Dillon … you mind if I call you Dillon?" he said with a grin and a touch of sarcasm.

I ignored the sarcasm but allowed that he may address me as Dillon if he wished.

"Well, *Dillon*, the way I see it, I'd rather be back in Taos sippin' on a beer, but I knew you'd need my help, so here I am."

I gave a quick glance at the twelve men who made up the posse and said, "I'm sure they appreciate your help as much as I do."

"Anytime, Marshal."

Turned out Bob could also ignore sarcasm.

The sun had inched over a mite, and we were throwing off slight shadows that trailed behind us by the time we saw the smoke.

254

Greathouse pointed and said, "That would be coming from their cabin. It's about two miles on."

I figured we had five hours of sunlight left. If Thomas and his gang surrendered immediately, we could be back in Taos by nightfall. But I had a feeling things wouldn't play out that easily.

I reached into my shirt pocket and pulled out my badge. I held it in my hand as the desert sunlight reflected off the highly polished tin. I looked at it for a long moment before sighing and pinning it on.

I asked Greathouse if there was any cover where we could observe their cabin unseen.

"Up ahead a little ways there's an arroyo that meanders close to the cabin. The closest point is about fifty yards from their front door. And the best part is, there's no back door."

"You're kinda knowledgeable about the gang's hideout," I observed.

"Taos County ain't that big. And I've lived here near on ten years. I know my way around."

I acted like I was impressed. "Alright, Jim. Now tell me about the layout."

"There's the main cabin, an outhouse, and a small barn with a corral next to it."

A plan was beginning to form in my mind.

Back when I was on the cattle drive and still a greenhorn, I'd listen intently as Jack Bridges told me of his lawman days. Jack had a few tales to tell, and I learned a thing or two from a man who rode with a star pinned to his chest when the West was significantly wilder than the West in which I now found myself.

One of the things that had struck me regarding Jack Bridges was that he had no fear about confronting a dangerous outlaw. He once told me, "You gotta make 'em think that you're as crazy as they are. That you can't wait to pull your gun and kill them, but the only thing holding you back is the star you're wearin'. At heart, most of 'em were cowards and they'd back down. A few didn't, but I'm here and they ain't, so you know how that worked out."

Well, Jack ol' friend, let's put your theory to a test.

"Mister Mayor, have you any objections to riding into the yard with me when I ask them to surrender?"

255

"I thought that was the idea. We all ride right up to 'em and tell 'em we're taking 'em in. You know, a show of force. Fifteen against six."

Another thing Jack had told me was never bunch up your men. *"Keep 'em spread out. Makes 'em harder to hit."*

"This is the way we'll do it, Jim. You, me, and my main deputy here, Pecos Bob, will ride into the yard and state our case. The rest of the men will be in the arroyo, covering us with their long guns."

I could see that both Bob and the mayor might have had a problem with that idea. The mayor was the first to speak. "You think just the three of us are gonna talk Heck Thomas and his gang into surrendering?"

"Probably not. But we have to give them the chance."

Greathouse took off his hat and squinted at the smoke rising from the cabin, thinking hard. Off to the south, a lone buzzard made slow circles in the sky.

At length, the mayor said, "But why don't we all ride in together?"

"Because if the ball goes up, they'll thin out our ranks with the first salvo. I need you there because he knows you, and, as the mayor of Taos, you represent the town's authority. And I need the men in the arroyo to give us cover if a hasty retreat is called for."

Bob had a question of his own, which he was not too shy to ask. "And what authority do I represent, Marshal? If you don't mind me inquirin'."

I wanted Bob with me because I figured he could handle a gun better than any of the store clerks that made up the posse.

"What? You don't wanna be my main deputy?"

Bob shook his head. It wasn't a negative shake, just his way of saying that I had outfoxed him. "It will be my pleasure and honor to act as your *main* deputy, Marshal."

We split up at the arroyo. The posse rode down into the wash, single file.

Bob, Jim, and I wide-circled the cabin and came in from the west. I wanted the sun at our backs—a trick that Jack Bridges had taught me.

The first thing I noticed was a windmill.

"You never told me about that, Jim."

"I didn't think it mattered. That's what we were gonna hang 'em from before we decided to do everything legal-like."

The three of us rode in under a cloudless, blue vaulted sky that seemed to go on forever. I glanced toward the arroyo. Sunlight glistened off a dozen rifle barrels. The sight of those guns gave me hope. Maybe I'd live long enough to see Luke Short in prison. I'd sure hate to die in this scrub patch while Luke was down in Las Cruces drinking and whoring it up.

The place was quiet. But we knew they were in there because of the horses in the corral and the chimney smoke. Pointing out the obvious, I said, "If any shooting starts, get to cover real fast." Bob and Greathouse said that would not be a problem.

We pulled up well before the cabin, so as not to be in the line of fire from the posse, and waited. After what seemed like a long time but couldn't have been more than a minute or so, the door creaked open. At the same time, I saw a rifle barrel edge out from an open window.

A man stepped out of the cabin. He looked to be in his forties, or else he'd led a rough life. His chin sported a few days' worth of dark stubble. His right eye drooped unnaturally. A wine-red scar ran down his left cheek, indicating a recent wound. His tan duster was open to show a pearl-handled Colt sticking in his belt. He wore no hat.

He used his left hand to shield his eyes from the sun. His right hand stayed near his gun. His eyes darted from me to Bob to Greathouse and then back to me. "Whatcha men lookin' for? This here is private land and we don't 'preciate no trespassers."

I turned my horse so that I was facing him dead on. I wanted him to see my badge.

"I'm Deputy U.S. Marshal Dillon Mahoney. May I ask who you are?"

He did a quick glance toward the cabin. Most likely to make sure he was still covered. He was.

"The name's Heck Thomas."

The sun felt hot on the back of my neck. There was not a wisp of wind in the air. The world had suddenly gone silent and it seemed like everyone in it was waiting for me to say something.

So, I did.

"I want you to know, Mister Thomas, we are not here about any of your doings over in Arizona Territory. We're here because of an unfortunate incident that occurred in the town of Taos last week. It seems that you and your boys got a little rambunctious and the end result was a women's death. Then you made matters worse, if that were possible, by shooting the town marshal. I'm sure you'll be happy to know that he's still alive. But he is feeling a mite peaked. Probably from that bullet you boys put into his lung.

"Now, to answer your question as to why we're here. We're here, Mister Thomas, to arrest you and your men."

He stared at me like I was a two-headed calf. Then he laughed. The man was starting to annoy me. I told Bob and Greathouse to spread out.

Thomas took a step forward and said, "Do you three piss ants think you're gonna take me and my boys in?"

He hadn't seen the rifles pointed at him from the arroyo.

"Are you saying you won't go peacefully?"

He yelled over his shoulder, "Boys, come on out here. Ya gotta hear this."

One by one, his gang sauntered out. Four of them. Two were holding Winchesters loosely in their hands, the barrels pointed to the ground. The other two were belted with the holsters tied down. Someone was missing.

"I thought you rode with five men."

Thomas took a quick look behind him. More for show than to see who was standing there. He was enjoying himself. Things must have been real boring before we showed up.

"You mean Totillo? That Mex took up with a Navajo squaw and they're livin' with her people. Don't reckon we'll be seeing him anytime soon. But don't worry, we can accommodate ya, even without him around."

The ball was about to go up. However, I thought I'd give it one more try.

"You know, if you kill a United States Marshal, the Army will come looking for you. So, unless you wanna relocate to Mexico, best not start anything the Army's gonna have to finish."

"I reckon I'll have to worry about that after we get you all planted six feet down."

258

I had arranged a signal with the rest of the posse for when they were to open up with everything they had. It was when I took my hat off. I looked over at Bob. He was sitting his horse with his arms folded like he didn't have a care in the world. Greathouse, on the other hand, looked a little nervous, and I couldn't blame him.

"Alright, Thomas. You got us outnumbered, but it sure is hot out here. Reckon we could get some water for us and our horses before we discuss this any further?" I raised my hat and wiped my brow.

The initial volley took down two of the gang. Unfortunately, Thomas wasn't one of them. I tried for him, but the noise from the guns spooked my horse and she moved sideways, spoiling my shot.

The outlaws backed up toward the cabin, firing the whole time. Thomas was the last one through the door, slamming it shut behind him.

"Time to find cover!" I yelled.

We made for the barn. When we were safely on the far side, I ordered Greathouse to the arroyo to tell the posse to stop shooting and conserve their ammunition. "Take a roundabout route so the outlaws can't get a bead on you. But before you go, leave me your handkerchief."

He looked at me funny but placed the linen in my hand without comment.

When Greathouse had gone, Bob exhaled a long breath and said, "Kinda lively being your special deputy."

"That's *main* deputy, Deputy."

"My mistake."

I discarded the spent cartridges from my Colt and slid .45 bullets into the empty chambers of the cylinder. Bob did the same with his gun.

As I was sliding my Colt back into its holster, Bob broke out with a wide grin.

"What do you find so amusing, if I may ask?"

"I was just thinking how surprised ol' Heck Thomas must have been when twelve rifles he didn't even know were there opened up on him."

"I find that rather amusing myself."

"So, what are we 'piss ants' gonna do now?" asked Bob.

I had a question of my own. "You know anything about Thomas?"

"Sure. Everyone does. He's a big bug in these here parts."

"Tell me, is he fast on the draw?"

"He's still alive and kickin'. That says something. I can tell you this much. I wouldn't go up against him."

Bob took the canvas water bag hanging from his saddle horn and took a long pull before handing it to me. As I drank the tepid water, he said, "We got 'em penned up for now, but unless you wanna starve them out, which might take a while, we should do something before it gets dark."

I handed him back his water bag. "My thinking exactly. You go to the arroyo and tell Greathouse and the rest of 'em to keep me covered. I'm going to try to get Thomas out of the cabin by challenging him to a draw. I'm hoping his pride will make him do it. That and the fact I'm going to tell him if he wins, he and his men will go free."

"Are you crazy? Thomas will have you biting dust before you can clear leather."

"Listen, Bob. I've been practicing my draw for almost a year now. I've gone through boxes and boxes of ammunition getting so that I can hit what I aim at ten times outta ten. I think I can take Thomas."

"You *think*!" shouted a very incredulous main deputy. "How many of those bottles or targets you were shooting at were shooting back at you? And another thing. I've never rode with a posse before—been chased by a few—but I don't think those men over there are gonna let Thomas go anywhere. *Especially* if you're dead."

"I don't want them to. Tell them to let me have my play, but if he kills me, then I want them to open up with everything they've got before he can get back into the cabin. However, if the other two surrender, tell Jim it was my dying wish that they be taken in and tried in a court of law. The man who gave me this badge would want it that way."

Bob flapped his arms in frustration. "I left Luke because I thought *he* was crazy. Talk about jumping out of the frying pan and into the fire."

I held out my hand and said, "Thanks, Pecos Bob. You're the best main deputy I've ever had."

We shook hands.

"I kinda think I'm the only main deputy you've ever had."

I couldn't argue with him on that point. I pulled out Greathouse's handkerchief and went to the corner of the barn and yelled, "Thomas, can you hear me?"

It took a few moments, but at length he answered. "I can hear you just fine."

"Good. I want to parley. Maybe you can get outta this with your skin intact. You *and* your men."

There was a long lapse before he finally answered. "Alright, talk."

"No. Not like this. Face to face. I'm walking out with a white flag in my right hand. If you come out and meet me, I give you my word that I will not go for my gun."

He laughed. "You think I'm afraid of a snot-nosed kid like you? It's those goddamn rifles that you got down there in the wash that have my attention."

"Those men will not shoot. They are under my orders and I've ordered them not to shoot at you if you come out. If you don't come out, we'll shoot up the place until the roof falls in on you."

I waited while he thought it over.

"Okay, Marshal. But any funny business and you'll be the first to die. My boys will have you in their sights the whole time. And make sure you're holding that flag in your right hand like you said."

Feeling vulnerable, I stepped out into the open.

28

A little wind must have come up from somewhere. I could hear the faint squeaking of the windmill's blades as they laboriously turned in the hot desert air.

Off to my left, the men of the posse had climbed out of the arroyo and were standing on its lip, their rifles pointed downward. I didn't see Bob among them.

I walked up to within a few feet of the two dead men and waited. I held the handkerchief in my right hand, which was nowhere near my gun. If Thomas planned on pulling any funny business, now would be the time to do it.

The cabin door opened with a wary ease, but no one stepped out. I waited.

From inside, a voice shouted, "How do I know those men over there at the wash won't open up the minute I walk out?"

"You have the word of a Deputy U.S. Marshal. And the mayor of Taos will back it up." Without taking my eyes from the cabin door, I yelled, "Mister Greathouse, I've given Mister Thomas my word that you will not shoot at him or his men if they come outside, is that not true?"

"Sure is, Marshal. You're in charge."

"And if Mister Thomas beats me in a fair fight, he and his men will be allowed to ride out of here unmolested?"

"That's right," he lied. "As long as they ride out of Taos County and do not return."

I waited.

Nothing.

Jack had been right, most of them are cowards at heart.

Time to move the ball along.

"It's the best deal you're gonna get, Thomas. Even without me, there are fourteen armed men over there with plenty of food, water, and ammunition. What do you have?"

I waited a tick, but no answer was forthcoming. I hadn't really expected one, so I went on.

"They won't wait you out. They'll burn you out."

That did it. Thomas stepped through the door. He was now wearing a holster, tied down, that held his pearl-handled Colt. The duster was gone. He was wearing his hat.

Now to get the other two out in the open.

"Let's get your men out here, too. I want 'em where I can see 'em. I don't fancy being shot in the back if I win."

Thomas knew he had this. "Come on out, boys. This won't take long and then we'll be on our way."

His men exited the cabin and stood off to the side, out of the line of fire.

I dropped the handkerchief and lowered my hand.

Thomas looked almost bored as he said, "Anytime you're ready, Marshal."

I slapped leather and put a bullet dead center into his smirking, unpleasant face before he had time to level his gun.

Bob appeared out of nowhere and stood at my side, his gun pointed at the two remaining outlaws. He had them covered before they could cause any mischief.

Without taking his eyes off them, he said, "Nice shooting, Marshal."

I looked down at my still-smoking gun as if I had never seen it before. "Keep 'em covered, Bob. I'll be right back."

Still holding my gun, on unsteady legs, I walked to the back of the barn and emptied my gut, splashing my boots in the process. I heaved everything I had in me and then some. When I was done, I wiped my mouth with the sleeve of my coat. On that fiery-hot day, in the middle of nowhere, in a godforsaken patch of desert, I learned that it is not easy to kill a man. It's not easy at all, even if the man needed killing.

When I got back to the cabin, the whole damn posse was there and had taken what remained of the gang into custody. They were slapping each other on the back and congratulating themselves on how well everything had gone.

Bob was nowhere to be seen.

I found him where we had left our horses. He had a whiskey bottle in his hand, which he held out in my direction. "Figured you might be needing this about now."

I gratefully accepted the bottle and downed a respectable portion of its contents. Bob was right. I did need it. I needed it badly.

"Your first?" he asked.

"Yup."

And that was all that was said on the subject.

We buried the dead outlaws and got our prisoners back to Taos without further incident, just as the sun was setting behind the taller peaks of the Sangre de Cristo Mountains. The mayor thanked me for my help and asked if I'd like to join him for a drink. I shook my head. "I'm gonna see to my horse, get something to eat, and then get a room at the hotel. It's been a long day."

"Well, thanks again, Marshal Mahoney. This town is in your debt."

That was the last I saw of the little mayor.

Bob waylaid me at the stable. He stuck out his hand and said, "It's been a pleasure, Marshal."

I shook his hand and said, "You stay outta trouble. I'd sure hate to have to arrest my main deputy a ways on down the line."

He gave me a wink and said, "Don't you worry none about that. I plan on stayin' within the law from now on."

We parted company at the hotel after one final handshake.

The next morning, I headed south. A few miles on, I came around a dogleg in the trail and there was Pecos Bob sitting his horse. With a twinkle in his eye, he said, " 'Bout time you showed up. I was beginning to think I'd have to go back to town and drag ya out. Let's get goin', time's a wastin'."

I rode up to him and said, "What are you doing here?"

He took out the makings and started to build himself a smoke. "I thought I better ride with you for a spell. You might have need of an ex-outlaw down trail."

"It's not that I don't appreciate your intentions, Bob, but I don't know if a U.S. Marshal should be seen in the company of a cattle rustler."

"I'm no longer a cattle rustler."

"Sorry, my mistake."

He flared a match and lit his cigarette. "You know, Dillon, I think you're gonna need my help taking down Luke and his boys. I admit you're fast, but there's four of 'em. No one is that fast."

"You'd go up against your old gang?"

"Hell, Dillon, it wasn't exactly a gang. Except for Luke, we were just a few cowboys that got together and rustled a cow or two because we didn't want to work for forty and found. And it's not so much I'd be going against 'em; it's more like I'd be helping you."

I was going to have to hire a deputy sooner or later to help get Luke and the others back to Slow Water. At least I knew I could count on Bob in a pinch.

"Let's ride," I said.

The day slowly fell behind us, and when it started to get dark, we made camp by a small river under a strand of cottonwoods. We ground hitched the horses and rubbed them down. With that out of the way, we got outside of some salt pork and pan biscuits. A slight wind had come up while we were eating, and the cool air was a welcome relief from the heat of the day. While Bob did cleanup, I pulled out the notebook to make a few entries for the government.

"Whatcha doin'?" asked Bob.

"Keeping track of expenses so I can get reimbursed for what I'm plunkin' down."

"Am I one of them expenses?"

"I reckon you are now."

Bob snaked an ember out of the fire and used it to light a smoke. "That's good because I'm down to the blanket."

"You're broke? What about the bank money?"

"We didn't get all that much. Luke got the lion's share because he was the boss and it was his idea. The others split the rest. They gave me only twenty dollars because all I did was hold the horses."

"I'll advance you a dollar a day for your booze and tobacco until we get back."

"That's right friendly of you, and I appreciate it."

A strong, sudden gust of wind blew through the camp, rustling the cottonwood leaves and bending the flame of the fire almost flat. I put the notebook away and asked Bob if he had thought to bring any booze along.

He reached into his saddlebag and pulled out a bottle. "Here ya go, Marshal. Compliments of His Honor the Mayor."

I pulled the cork and took a modest slug. It felt good going down and spread through my being like a jolt of warm spring sunshine. I handed the bottle back to Bob and leaned against my saddle. Bob tossed a stick onto the crackling fire, sending ocher-colored sparks swirling into the dark night air. A few more pulls from the bottle and I was feeling downright friendly. "So, Bob. Howcha get the handle Pecos Bob?"

He took a swig before answering. "I spent some time down in Val Verde County, near the Pecos River. Got myself into a little trouble here and there, which brought me to the attention of the authorities. It was a sheriff down in West Texas that gave me the name, and it just kinda stuck."

"So, you're from Texas?"

"Nope. Paterson, New Jersey. The garden spot of the earth."

He held the bottle out towards me.

I shook my head and yawned.

"Where are you from?" he asked.

"I'm from back East, too. Philadelphia, to be specific."

"Ain't that somethin'. We were practically neighbors!"

We chewed the fat for a few minutes more, then turned in. We were anticipating a hard ride the next day and every day thereafter until we caught up with Luke Short and his gang.

Six days hence, after passing through Santa Fe and Albuquerque, we rode into Las Cruces, tired, dirty, and hungry. The first order of business was to take care of the horses. We found a livery stable adjacent to the local hotel and made a deal with the owner to board both horses for a dollar a day.

I procured two rooms at the hotel, one for each of us. After that, the only thing I wanted was a thick steak. The only thing my main deputy wanted was to wash the dust from his throat. "Alright, Bob. But if you walk into a saloon and you see any of your old friends, especially Luke, you turn around and come right back here and tell me. If you *don't* see anyone we might be interested in, ask around. See what you can find out. But don't be obvious about it."

I was sitting in the hotel restaurant putting the finishing touches on an exceptionally tender piece of beef when a tall man walked through the door. He sported a thick, dark handlebar mustache. The ends were finely waxed; it was a work of art. He looked to be about twice my age. On his vest, he wore a star. He scouted the room and his gaze eventually landed on me. Nodding to himself, he made a beeline for my table.

He took off his hat and asked in a friendly manner, "Would you be Dillon Mahoney?"

"That would be me."

He stuck out his hand. "It's truly a pleasure to meet you, Marshal Mahoney."

Out of politeness, I laid down my fork and shook his hand. "Please have a seat," I said.

He nodded and pulled out a chair.

"You want coffee?" I offered.

He placed his hat on the table, off to the side, and said, "Don't mind if I do."

While we waited for the girl to bring his coffee, I asked if he cared if I finished my dinner while we talked.

"Not at all! Dig in."

With a mouth full of longhorn beef, I said, "Mind if I ask your name?"

"I'm Jesse Evans, sheriff of Doña Ana County."

When his coffee came, he spooned a generous amount of sugar into the cup and blew on the surface to cool it down before taking a sip.

"Sheriff Evans ..."

"You can call me Jesse."

"Jesse, how is it that you know my name and the fact that I'm a marshal? I just got into town. I haven't even had time to finish my steak yet."

"Your deeds have preceded you, Marshal. Three days ago, two freighters on their way down to El Paso spread the word that some kid up in Taos outdrew Heck Thomas and laid him low. Most of us didn't believe it. It was just too fantastic. Heck Thomas was way too fast to be beaten by anyone, let alone some kid. But then, the next day, a cowboy passing through told the same story. And he supplied a name. He said the kid's name was Dillon Mahoney and that he was a Deputy U.S. Marshal."

I swallowed the last of my steak. "Okay, fair enough. But how did you figure out that *I'm* Dillon Mahoney?"

"A fella over at the Green Cactus Saloon is letting it be known that he's riding with the hombre who killed Heck Thomas. And, at the moment, you're the only other stranger in town."

"That fella would be my deputy. Deputy Big Mouth."

Sheriff Evans laughed.

"By the way, Jesse. Did word also reach you about me throwing up after I shot Thomas?"

Before he could answer, the girl came over and refilled our coffee. When she was gone, he reached for the sugar and said, "Nope. Can't rightly say that part of the story made it this far."

I nodded and sipped at my coffee. "So, let's not make a big deal of me killing Heck Thomas. I assure you, I took no pleasure in it. It was just something that had to be done."

"It don't work that way, Marshal. Heck Thomas was a famous gunman, almost as well known as Billy the Kid. By now, in people's minds, you're ten feet tall and chew nails 'stead of tobacco. And the worst part is the young gunnies. They'll be looking to brace you to make their reputation. They'll want to be the one who out-drew the man who out-drew Heck Thomas."

"That's not gonna happen. I'm gonna get the outlaw I came down here after and take him back to my home range. Then I'm gonna hang up my badge and go back to being a cowpuncher or maybe head out to California. Either way, I do not intend on becoming the stuff of dime novels, as much as I liked reading them in my youth."

He drank the last of his coffee and put on his hat, tilting it down over his eyes. "Why don't we go to my office and talk further. You can tell me who you're after and perhaps I can be of some help."

Sounded good to me. I left a silver dollar on the table, and together we walked out onto the boardwalk.

His office was small and sparse, a desk and chair against the far wall, a stove in the corner, and a divan off to one side. He sat down behind the desk and, from a drawer, pulled out a bottle of Irish whiskey and two small glasses. After filling them half-full, he leaned back, put his feet up on the desk, and pointed to the glasses. "Help yourself."

I picked up a glass, sat down on the divan, and took a sip of his booze.

Sheriff Evans opened the conversation. "Now, who are you after and what is the poor bastard charged with?"

"Before we get into that, let me ask *you* something. Why a divan? I mean, it's comfortable and all, but I wouldn't think it's something you'd usually find in a town jail."

Sheriff Evans jerked his thumb behind him. "The cells are back there. Most of the time my customers are drunks or cowboys I had to arrest for fighting. I let them go as soon as they sober up and calm down. But now and then I get a bad actor—a killer or a cattle rustler. Then I have to stay here at night to make sure their friends don't bust them out. And given the choice of sitting up all night in a hard wooden chair or reclining on a nice soft divan …"

"Makes sense. Now to your question. I'm after an outlaw that goes by the name Luke Short. He's wanted for shooting a man in the back and leaving him for dead. Have you heard of him or seen him?" I failed to mention that I was the man who had been shot.

Evans let out with a low, long whistle. "You don't fool around, do you? First Heck Thomas and now Luke Short."

I finished my whiskey and placed the empty glass on the desk. Jesse pointed to the bottle. I shook my head. "So, you *do* know him?"

"He's been coming and going through Las Cruces for a few years now. I saw him not two weeks ago."

"*How* do you know him?"

"Everyone in these parts knows Luke Short. And most are afraid of him. Hell, he's killed three men in Doña Ana County that we know of, just in the last two years alone!"

"That being the case, and if you don't mind me asking, why is he still running around loose?"

The sheriff poured himself a little whiskey and, without asking my permission, put a healthy splash into my glass.

"Because in every instance it was self-defense. There were witnesses who swore that Luke drew only after the man went for his gun. I *know* Luke egged 'em on until they had no choice but to take a stand. I also know that Luke Short is a murdering, lowdown, son-

of-a-bitch cattle rustler, but I can't arrest a man for what I know …
only for what I can prove."

I shrugged. I wasn't judging him. I hadn't been a lawman long
enough to judge him or any other lawman.

He asked if I had a warrant for Luke's arrest.

"There wasn't a judge to issue one. But there is circumstantial
evidence, and a witness to Luke admitting to the shooting."

"Doesn't matter about the warrant. You want help bringing him
in?"

"I'll need help finding him first. They told me over at the hotel
that there's about thirty-eight hundred square miles to Doña Ana
County."

"There is, but I can narrow it down for you. If I had to take a
guess, I'd guess that right about now ol' Luke Short is somewhere
down near the border, hazing stolen cows over into Mexico."

Maybe a little more booze *was* in order. I took a sip before
asking what I figured would be a highly insulting question. "If you
know where he is and what he's doing, why are you not down there
arresting him?"

He didn't seem to take offense.

"It's a big county, and we have a lengthy border with Mexico.
Luke can cross over anywhere along that border that he pleases. The
ranchers have their own riders looking out for cattle thieves and they
know that country better than I do. If they can't stop him or even
find him, then what chance would I have?"

This was getting me nowhere. It was time to thank him for his
information, little as it was, collect my deputy, and head south
where I'd be more likely to run into Luke Short. But, before I could
say anything, he went on.

"I can see it in your eyes. You're gonna saddle up and take off
after him. If you hold on a minute, I'll tell you something you may
not know. Luke is coming back here. Within a week, he'll be sitting
in one of our saloons with a pocketful of gold coins, talking trash to
the whores and getting drunk. This is the only town of any size
where he can spend his ill-gotten gains after one of his rustling
ventures. In just a few short days, Luke Short will come riding right
up our main street and into your waiting hands. That is, if you're
still here."

"Sheriff ... I mean Jesse ... may I have another shot of that fine Irish whiskey? All of a sudden, I got no place I gotta be, 'ceptin' this fine, hospitable town of yours."

29

While we waited for Luke and his boys to show, Bob and I took it easy. After breakfast, we'd sit outside the hotel, leaning back in our chairs with our feet up on the rail, enjoying the coolness of the morning. Around noon, we'd amble over to The Green Cactus for a drink or two before lunch. After eating, we'd doze in the same chairs we had occupied that morning. In the evenings, after supper, we'd play cards and do a little more drinking. Bob said it was the best job he had ever had.

Perhaps Bob was enjoying himself, but I wanted to get it over with and get back to Slow Water. I was itching to see Luke sent off to prison for what he had done to me.

One morning, while digesting a breakfast of bacon, eggs, and biscuits, I said to Bob, "Tell me about those other three."

"What other three?" the big oaf wanted to know.

I looked over and shook my head. It was a good thing he was a lousy poker player. I held twelve of his markers to the tune of thirteen dollars and fifty-five cents. So, I had to keep him around at least until he paid off his gambling debt.

"Bob, I'm talking about your ex-saddle partners, Chalk Beeson, Frank McLean, and Patrick Hawke. What I want to know is what we can expect from them. Will they back Luke or will they fold without a fight? You once told me they were just cowboys, not killers like Luke. You still hold with that?"

"Well, it's like I told you, Marshal. Hawke and Beeson have been with Luke for a while now, long before I hooked up. Me and McLean joined up a few months after Luke gave you that beating last year."

"You know about that?"

"I know about it because Luke spoke of it all the time. He was right proud of what he had done. He said you were a greenhorn, still wearin' city clothes, and he reckoned he had chased you clear back

East, back to wherever you came from. He sure was surprised that night when he saw you in the saloon, I can tell you that."

"I can tell *you*, he'll be even more surprised when he sees me this time. He thinks I'm dead, just like you did."

"Ah, come on, Dillon. You know I had nothing to do with that."

"I know."

A freight wagon, carrying a load of lumber, came up the street, kicking up a little dust on its journey. The grizzled teamster driving the team nodded in our direction as he passed by.

I had to know about the men riding with Luke. Bob had been right when he said I could not take all four of them alone, but maybe Luke was the only one who would put up a fight.

"So, tell me, Bob, who do I have to worry about, besides Luke?"

He leaned back in his chair and pulled the makings from his shirt pocket. I had noticed that Bob would always build himself a smoke when he wanted a moment to think things over. Finally, with the unlit cigarette dangling from his mouth, he said, "Don't forget, I'll be there with you. And I'm sure the sheriff is gonna lend us a hand."

"I want to take Luke myself. You and the sheriff are gonna be off to the side, ready to help if need be, but I gotta do this alone. I wanna look him in the eye as he backs down. I want him to know that I know he's a coward. This is between Luke and me and I don't want you to interfere unless the others pull their shooting irons."

Bob scratched a match on his britches and lit his cigarette. "Luke might not back down, especially if he's got three men standing with him. But I'll tell you what I think. Chalk and Frank will not want to shoot it out. It's like I told you, they're just cowboys who went wrong, like me. But I don't know about Hawke. He's ridden with Luke the longest. He's mean enough to give a rattler the first bite. So, if I was a betting man, which I am, I'd give odds that Patrick Hawke will stand with Luke when the ball goes up, and the other two will stay out of it."

Having offered his advice, Bob tipped his sombrero down low, tilted his chair back against the wall, and put his boots on the rail. It looked like he was thinking of taking his siesta a little early.

I was just getting up to go into the hotel for a drink of water when I looked down the street, and there, big as life, was Luke

Short. He was riding in with his gang. I sat back down and nudged Bob. "Take a gander at this," I said.

He peered out from under his hat in the direction I was looking. Luke and his boys turned into the corral next to the Cactus and were out of sight for a few minutes. Soon, they came around the corner and went into the saloon. They hadn't seen us.

I stood up, and after checking my Colt to make sure all the chambers housed bullets, I said to Bob, "Let's go get Jesse and get this over with."

Bob got to his feet. "I'm with you, Marshal."

At the sheriff's office, I informed Jesse of Luke's arrival and asked if he had a shotgun.

"Sure, I got one in the closet over there."

"Mind if Bob borrows it? I'm gonna try to convince the men riding with Luke to stay out of it. I figure a shotgun speaks loudly when it's aimed in your general direction."

Jesse pointed to the closet and told Bob to help himself.

It was a double barrel ten gauge. Bob broke it open to see if it was loaded. It was not. Jesse reached in the desk draw, brought out a box of shells, and tossed it to Bob. "I don't keep it loaded. You never know what damn fool might get his hands on it."

Bob caught the box and took out two shells. "This oughta do me. If I can't hit what I'm after with a ten gauge, then no amount of shells is gonna help me."

I asked Jesse if he minded me running the show, it being his town and all.

"I might have had a problem. But you handled Heck Thomas readily enough, so I reckon you can take care of yourself. And you being a U.S. Marshal, I know things will be done all legal-like and above-board. So, no, I have no problem with you arresting Luke and his boys in my town."

"Thank you, Jesse."

He was strapping on his gun belt as he said, "But are you sure you wanna do it this way? I mean, face him head on? We could sidle up to him unawares while he's drinking, arrest him, and throw him in the hoosegow without any gunplay."

"Jesse, I've been shot and I didn't like it. So, given the chance, I'm not gonna allow myself to get shot again. But Luke Short is a

274

coward and I aim to show the whole territory just what a coward he is. If he was liquored up, he might go for his gun, but he hasn't been in town long enough to work up his bottle courage."

"Fair enough. It's your play."

I looked over to Bob. "You ready?"

"Yup."

"Alright. I've noticed it's Luke's usual habit to take a table on the far left as you walk in. But regardless of where he is, I'll go in first. Jesse, you come in after me and spread out. Try to blend in if you can. Bob, you come in last. Stay by the door. Anyone wants to leave, let 'em go. But don't let anyone in."

I adjusted my gun in its holster, making sure it was loose. "You boys ready?"

They both nodded.

It was like I thought. Luke and his men were sitting at a table on the left, all the way in the corner. When I walked in, one of the whores was leaning over Luke, her bosom in his face, whispering something in his ear. Whatever it was must have been good; Luke was wearing a three-by-nine grin.

I stood where he would be sure to see me, once the whore got her tits outta his face.

She finished what she had to say and kissed him on the cheek, then left to go to another table. Much like a honey bee flitting from flower to flower.

Luke lifted his glass to take a drink, but it never reached his mouth. It was halfway there when he saw me. He slammed it back down on the table and yelled, "*YOU!*"

Tilting my hat back with my left hand, I nodded but said nothing.

He pushed himself up with such force that his chair fell backwards. He pointed at me and shouted, "You're supposed to be dead!"

I was almost enjoying this. "Not hardly, you back-shootin' son-of-a-bitch."

By now, his friends were also standing. The one called Hawke stood by his side. The other two were a little farther out. Those two didn't look any too happy with the sudden turn of events. I figured they were out of it, and even if they weren't, I had Bob and Jesse backing me.

I gave my full attention to Luke and Hawke. "I'm here to arrest you boys for cattle rustlin', and you, Luke, for attempted murder."

Luke let out with a shrill laugh. "*You*? You're gonna arrest *me*? By what authority?"

I pointed to my badge. "By this authority."

Beeson and McLean put a little more distance between themselves and Luke. Hawke stayed where he was.

By now the saloon was dead quiet. Time started to slow down. I reckon it always does in situations like this. The same thing had happened when I faced off against Heck Thomas.

Luke looked around the room at the faces of the men, and I don't think he liked what he saw. They were looking at him in a different way. He was used to being feared and he took that fear as respect. But now, here was a young kid standing up to him and he had not yet drawn his gun.

I thought for sure he'd back down. But I was wrong, Luke was going to draw no matter what, and so was Hawke. I saw it in their eyes. Beeson and McLean were out of it. They had seen Bob holding the shotgun. Seconds ticked by. The only sound was the shuffling of boots against the wooden floor as the men in the room inched out of the line of fire.

Luke would go for his gun first. Hawke, a split-second later. *Someone* was going to die in the next few minutes. I had the feeling most of the men in that room thought it was going to be me. And that was fine, as long as one of the men thinking that was Luke Short. I wanted him to be as overconfident as Heck Thomas had been.

Jack Bridges had advised me to stay away from gunplay if I could help it. But if I couldn't, then always look into a man's eyes. *"That will tell you, without fail, when he's going to go for his gun."*

I stood wide-legged and waited.

I was calm. The only thing that existed for me at that moment were the dark eyes of Luke Short.

He blinked.

His gun cleared leather a fraction of a second before mine, but he fired wild. The bullet missed my head by the width of a pencil.

276

He had not taken the time to aim. I did not make that mistake. I killed Luke and dropped Hawke, firing so fast it sounded like one shot.

I wasn't sure if Hawke was alive or dead, but I knew he was out of it. Beeson and McLean were standing with their hands held high in the air.

I emptied the two spent cartridges from the cylinder of my Colt and replaced them with two .45 bullets, just like Jack Bridges had taught me. *"You never want to get caught with an empty chamber."*

Bob came up. "I'm sure glad I'm on your side, Marshal."

Jesse had gone over to check on Luke and Hawke. He knelt down and was hidden by the table for a moment. When he stood up, he said, "They're both dead."

Bob leaned in and whispered, "You wanna vomit now?"

I didn't feel the need, but I didn't feel any too good either. I had now killed three men. True, they were bad men and they would have killed me if they had been a little faster. I was glad it was them and not me, but still, the taking of a life is an unpleasant sensation. Besides, it cut a little that I had broken my word to Bill Slokum. I had promised to bring Luke Short back alive and now that was not going to happen because I wanted to show Luke up for the coward I thought he was. But I had been wrong. Luke did face me.

The undertaker took care of Luke and Hawke. We took Beeson and McLean to the jailhouse. After they were safely in their cells, Jesse asked me when I'd be leaving with my prisoners.

"I've been thinking about that. If I had gone along with your suggestion to take them unawares, there wouldn't have been any need for gunplay and I wouldn't have had to kill two men. I don't believe I have the right to wear a badge. I realize now I was out for vengeance, not justice. So, I'm going to resign my commission. As to those men back there, I won't be taking them back. If you have something on them, then they're all yours. If not, I reckon you can let them go."

Jesse and I were standing by the desk. Bob was sitting on the divan with the stock of the shotgun resting on his knee. He broke it open and took out the shells, one at a time. "Dillon, you know I rode with Luke. I never saw him kill a man, but there were many a time I had to listen to him talk about killing this one and that one. At first I thought that's all it was. Talk. Him trying to be a big man and all. At least his version of what a big man should be. Then he told me he had killed you. That I believed. His gun is over there on the desk. Take a look at those notches on the handle. I don't know how many there are, but far too many from my way of thinking.

"Now, this is what I wanna tell you. There are farmers and cowboys and maybe even a few bank clerks who will live to see their children grow up because of what you did today. Luke Short would not have ceased his murdering ways until someone stopped him, permanently. So, I wouldn't feel too bad about killing him if I was you. He was a killer, plain and simple. The world is better off without him."

Those were the most words I had ever heard Bob speak at one time.

Jesse echoed Bob's thoughts. "You've done yourself and New Mexico Territory proud, Marshal Mahoney. You have nothing to reproach yourself for."

I appreciated what they were trying to do and understood what they were saying. But I had made up my mind. I was getting out of the law business. I changed the subject by saying, "It's almost dinnertime. Let's head for the hotel."

Jesse said he had to make his rounds, but he'd see us later when he came to get the prisoners' supper.

Before leaving, I asked him, "What are you gonna do with those two?"

"I've got nothing on 'em. So, if you don't want 'em, I'll let 'em cool their heels for a day or two and then run 'em outta the county."

At the hotel, I asked the clerk if the town had a telegraph and was told the closest telegraph office was up in Albuquerque.

I had two telegrams I needed to send. One to the U.S. Marshal in Cheyanne, to tender my resignation. He did not need to know the reason why, just that I was turning in my commission. The other telegram would go to Mister Slokum. I owed it to him to tell him what had happened and why I was resigning. And I would ask him to convey my thanks to Jack for all he had taught me and to Elsie for being my friend.

At dinner, I asked Bob what he was going to do now that his lawman days were over. He looked a little surprised at the question. "I thought I'd stick with you for a spell."

I had planned on trailing alone. It wasn't that I didn't like Bob. I did. But I didn't want to be responsible for him or anyone else. Jack Bridges once told me saddle partners had to look out for one another. The trouble was, at the moment, I didn't think I could look out for myself. I was filled with self-doubt.

"Bob, I'm drifting on to California, but first I have to go through Albuquerque. You're welcome to trail with me that far. But that's where we split up."

He shrugged and threw a wink my way. "I'm gonna miss lookin' out after you." He paused for a moment to take a sip of coffee. "Maybe I'll go back East. My father's a brewer. Actually, he's the biggest brewer in the state of New Jersey. He's selling barrels of Holston's Original Ale all over the place. He wanted me to go in with him, seeing as I was his only son. Said he'd change the name to Holston and Son's Brewery if I stuck around. But I had a wandering eye. I wanted to see the real West and experience a little adventure before I got old."

He grew quiet and reflective. Looking down at his plate, he absently played with his food. At length, he said, "Maybe it's time I became a respectable citizen."

The Government owed Bob some wages, but Cheyanne was a long ways off. I figured he'd need money to get back to New Jersey, and I didn't want him rustling cows or robbing banks to come up with it. I dipped into my poke and paid him what he was owed, forgiving any advances he had received. It wasn't much, but it was more than he got for robbing that bank up in Loveland. I also tore up his markers from our poker games.

That night, we went over to the Cactus and had a few farewell drinks with Jesse. The next morning, we collected our horses from the hostler at the livery stable and hit the drag just as the sun crept up over the eastern horizon.

30

The Chihuahuan Desert spread out before us.
The cholla cactus cast long shadows across the ivory-colored sand,
their white spines shimmering in the early morning light. Green
creosote bushes dotted the hills. Yellow flowers—reflecting the
yellow light of the sun—basked in a golden-colored radiance. Long
stretches of blue grama grass and green tobosa grass rippled in the
wind. The blue and purple of the magenta flowers spoke of a Divine
presence. Bob and I rode through all that beauty in quiet reverence.

That night we dined on a jack rabbit Bob had shot with his long
gun. The flame from our fire illuminated his smiling face as he
spoke enthusiastically of his future. "It's gonna be a whole lot
different from the life I've been living these last few years. Boy, will
my father be surprised when I show up."

He went on in that vein for a while as I inwardly smiled at the
big man's excitement at going home to become a beer baron. I said
very little about my plans. I knew where I was going, but not what
would be waiting for me when I got there.

Four days later, we rode into the town of Albuquerque.

We corralled our horses and set out for the closest saloon. As we
were walking by a barber shop, Bob stopped to look at his reflection
in the window. He stroked his beard a few times, then said, "I think
I'll get a haircut and have my beard trimmed. Looking wild may be
okay for out here, but back East, people might look at me askance."

I looked at him askance and asked, "Askance? Where did you
learn a word like that?"

"This might surprise you, Dillon, but I went to college and even
graduated."

"That does surprise me. Imagine that. Pecos Bob Holston, rustler
and bank robber, a college man."

"Yeah, my father wanted me educated, so he sent me off to The
College of New Jersey at Princeton. It wasn't so bad. I enjoyed it.
But I don't let on about my education. In fact, I went outta my way

to speak the vernacular of this part of the country so I could blend in."

"Vernacular? Now you're showing off. Let's go into the barber shop. I could use a shave. I think it's about time I got rid of this beard."

Bob insisted I take the chair first. When the barber had done his best and my face was clean-shaven, I told Bob I'd go and get us rooms at the hotel. "If I'm not there, you'll find me at the nearest saloon."

After I secured our rooms, I went to the train depot to send off those telegrams to Cheyanne and Slow Water. As the operator was keying in my message to Bill Slokum, an idea struck me.

The way things stood, it was going to take Bob about two months to get to New Jersey riding his horse. By train, he could be there in a week.

Why not?

With my telegrams on their way, I went to the ticket window and purchased a ticket for as far east as the Atchison, Topeka and Santa Fe Railroad could get him, which was someplace in Kansas. From there, I was told, he could connect with another train that would take him the rest of the way.

Bob and I met up at a place called the Buckhorn Saloon. He looked downright dapper with a haircut and his beard trimmed. There was even a whiff of smellum about him.

"You smell real pretty, Bob. You plan on hittin' a whorehouse or two while we're in town?" I teased.

He looked uncomfortable. "Ah, come on, Dillon. The man put that stuff on me before I could say anything."

I gave him a look of disbelief, and then we laughed.

The Buckhorn served food, but we decided to eat at the hotel. We were both itching to hit the hay. It had been a long and dusty four days on the trail up from Las Cruces.

It was over supper that I laid Bob's train ticket down on the table.

"What's that?" he wanted to know.

"It's your ticket home."

He picked up the collection of tickets that would get him to Kansas and looked them over. Back in those days, people were

281

issued a separate ticket for each leg of their journey, and the conductor would collect them, one at a time, as their trip progressed.

"I can't let you do that," he said.

"I've already done it. Now put those in your pocket and take this." I held out a stack of banknotes and he accepted them with a questioning look on his face. "That's for buying your train ticket for the rest of the way, once you get to Kansas," I explained.

He fanned the bills, not counting them, just playing with them. "I've known you but a short while and, in that time, you've become a true friend. Thank you, Dillon."

"Bob, you were there when I faced off with Thomas. He hadn't even hit the ground before you were standing by my side to keep those other two outlaws from opening up on me. And you backed me when I went against Luke and his men, even though you knew there was a good chance of gunplay. That's what I consider a true friend."

The next morning, I went with Bob to the depot and saw him off. As he stepped onto the train, he took off his sombrero and handed it to me. "I won't be needing this in New Jersey."

I accepted his hat and said, "It has been a pleasure to have known you, Bob."

As the train started to move, he shouted over the blast of the whistle, "You're one to ride the river with, Dillon Mahoney. If you're ever near Paterson, stop in for an ale." He gave me one last smile and one last wave and then he was gone.

I stayed on that platform until the train had shrunk to nothing more than a black dot in the far distance. I was going to miss ol' Pecos Bob Holston.

≈ ≈ ≈

I had no schedule to keep, so I thought I'd stay in Albuquerque for a while. Bob had given me his horse and saddle. The saddle I sold, but I kept the horse because I was going to need a good, strong pack horse. And any horse that could carry Bob's bulk could handle anything I put on its back. I spent my days getting my kit together for the trek to California and spent my nights at the Buckhorn, playing cards and doing a little drinking.

On my third day in town, just before noon, I was sitting in the Buckhorn, looking out the window, enjoying a beer, and thinking that maybe it was time to pull up stakes and head for California. I had asked around about the best route and was told that following the railroad tracks would lead me straight into Los Angeles.

At first, I didn't notice when the saloon started to fill up. And when I did notice, I thought nothing of it. It was noontime, after all. I reckoned the men were coming in for their mid-day meal. It wasn't until I stood up to get a refill on my beer that I realized things weren't exactly as they should be.

There were a lot more men in the room than I had thought. When I started for the bar, the crowd parted as the Red Sea must have parted for Moses way back when. Still, I had no clue as to what was going on. It wasn't until I stood waiting for the barkeep to fill my glass that it started to dawn on me: *I* was the subject of everyone's interest. What had I done? While in town, I'd kept to myself. I hadn't caused any trouble that I knew of. What was going on?

I soon found out. I was making my way back to my table when a loud voice stopped me in mid-stride.

"Hey, Mahoney. I hear you're yellow."

What?

I turned to see a young cowboy.

"Were you speaking to me?" I inquired.

"Damn right I was. I called you yellow. Whatcha gonna do about it?"

"How did you know my name?"

"You're registered over at the hotel. Everyone in town knows who you are. You beat Heck Thomas and Luke Short. But I'm here to say you shot 'em both in the back when they wasn't looking."

Here it was. Just what Jesse had warned me about. Here was some young kid trying to make a reputation for himself by killing the man who had outgunned Heck Thomas and Luke Short.

By now, the men closest to us were discreetly moving away. No one wanted to be hit by a stray bullet. But no one was leaving the place either; no one wanted to miss out on the action.

Holding the beer in my right hand, I said, "May I ask your name? I think it's only fitting that a man knows the name of the man who's gonna kill him."

"The name's Bill Haney, and you best put down that beer and get ready to draw. Besides you being a coward, I just don't like your face. Get ready to go for your gun, mister!"

I had to hold in the laugher. He was trying too hard.

"Look, I'm not gonna draw on you. I don't want to kill you. And I don't think you want to kill me. You just want to get a name for yourself. Well, you got it. I'm backing down."

He stood wide-legged, his hand hovering over his gun. He didn't know what to do. You can't shoot a man who's holding a glass of beer with his gun hand and who refuses to draw on you. You'd get no reputation that way. Might even get yourself hung.

Time to end it. "If you don't mind, I'd sure appreciate it if you waited until I finished my beer before you kill me. I'm a mite thirsty." A few men chuckled. The would-be gunny looked both confused and relieved.

That did it. The tension fled the room and the boys went back to their drinking. I went back to my table and sat down. Bill Haney pushed through the swing doors in a huff, climbed his horse, and rode on down the street and out of town.

I figured it was time to leave Albuquerque. Head off to parts where my name was not so well known. I finished my beer and walked over to the hotel. My kit was ready to go and so was I. One hour later, I was riding Betty and leading the pack horse out of town. Bob's horse's name was Jack, by the way.

It was the beginning of October, so things had cooled down a mite. It was pleasant sleeping out under the stars. There's a sense of freedom in being surrounded by all of nature's majesty that I would be hard-pressed to put into words.

A few days later, running low on coffee and sugar and a few other necessities, I pulled up in the small town of Holbrook. It was a Saturday morning. The people of Holbrook were going about their business and took no notice of a lone saddle tramp riding into their town.

I figured since it had been a week since my last bath, I might as well get one whilst the getting's good. And I'd get a hotel room so I could sleep in a bed for a change. First thing in the morning, I'd be on my way, clean and refreshed. That was my plan.

As it turned out, I hit town on a momentous day. The hotel clerk asked if I were going to the big dance that night.

"What dance would that be?" I asked.

"The one celebrating the railroad tracks being laid down and the station being built. We're a growing town, mister. All the freight supplies going south to Fort Apache will now be going through Holbrook. It's gonna mean a lot of business for us."

"Where is this dance?"

"Over at Brown's barn. It's located just behind Front Street at Third Avenue."

"Thanks. I may just mosey on over there."

As the sun was going down, I made my way to Mister Brown's barn. It was a festive affair. Men shook my hand as I entered and invited me to have some punch. Holbrook was a cow town, and the city fathers who were hosting the shindig assumed I was a cowpuncher from one of the surrounding ranches.

I got myself a cup of punch so I'd have something to do with my hands and took it and myself over to a far wall where I settled in to watch the festivities.

A short while later, a cowboy came by and noticed the cup in my hands. It was empty by then. He winked, pulled a bottle of rye from his pants' pocket, and poured a generous portion into the cup. He winked again and ambled off without having said a word.

I was having a good time. The music was pleasant and watching people dance reminded me of back home in Philadelphia. I hadn't seen people dressed up in their finest for a long time. And here I was, seeing it in a one-horse town in the middle of a desert.

After a while, I decided to call it a night. I was placing my empty cup on a table by the door when a girl of about my age walked up and said, "It's awful warm in here. Would you mind escorting me outside for a breath of fresh air?"

She was beautiful. She wore her hair long, almost down to her waist. It was reddish-brown in color; her eyes were green, sparkling green. Her smile lit up the room.

"I … I … would … I would …" I gave up trying to say something elegant and simply said, "No, I don't mind."

She wrapped her arm around mine and nodded towards the door. "Shall we?" she said.

Once outside, she walked me around the building where we stood in the light emanating from a side window. "My name is Katie Murray. And whom do I have the honor of addressing?"

"My name is Dillon Mahoney."

We were quiet for a moment. I think she was waiting for me to say something else, but for the life of me, I couldn't think of anything to say. At length, she asked, "Do you work for the Hashknife outfit?"

"No. I'm just passing through on my way to California. What is the Hashknife outfit?"

"They're the biggest outfit around. They have fifty thousand head of cattle spread out over two million acres. The million that they own outright and the million they lease from the government."

I was duly impressed and ready to say so when a man walked up. He was about forty years of age and well dressed in a city sort of way. He wore no hat, but he was heeled. He wore two six-guns, cross-belted, and he looked angry.

"What are you doing to this woman?" he demanded.

Before I could say anything, Miss Murray said, "Tom, I asked this gentleman to escort me outside because you were too busy with all your cowboy friends to even notice me. You haven't danced with me once."

So that was it. I tipped my hat to the lady and was about to leave when the man grabbed my arm. "Not so fast, mister. You left the barn with my intended. I don't think I like that."

I didn't care what he liked or didn't like, but I thought I'd be civil. "I'm sorry, mister, I didn't know the wind blew in that direction. But I assure you, it won't happen again."

That wasn't good enough for him. "Do you know who I am?"

"I don't. Now, if you'll excuse me, I've got a nice soft bed waiting for me."

"I'm Tom Hardy. Head ramrod for the Hashknife. That mean anything to you?"

His hands were near his guns. He was itching for a fight.

"I'm sorry, Mister Hardy. I've never heard of you. My name is Dillon Mahoney. You ever hear of me?"

A slant of yellow light from the window played across his eyes as they widened in fear. He *had* heard of me.

I didn't want to draw on him, I didn't want to kill him, and I surely didn't want him to lose face in front of his woman. All I wanted was to go to bed. I'd give him a way out of the mess he had started and hope he had the smarts to take it.

"Look, Mister Hardy, I am truly sorry for leaving the barn with Miss Murray. I didn't know she was someone's intended. But can you really blame me? She is beautiful." I threw that last part in so she wouldn't egg him on any more than she already had. She was trouble waiting to happen.

He took the life-line. "Okay, Mahoney. No harm done."

I winked at him so the girl couldn't see and went out onto the street.

In the morning, I would resupply with enough to get me into California without having to go into another town. Towns meant trouble for me.

31

Two days out from Holbrook, I camped in a
dry wash. The horses were ground-hitched with enough tether to
reach the scrub. They had drunk their fill at a watering hole we
passed a few miles back. I was tired and decided not to cook that
night. I had some jerked beef and that would do me fine.

I was staring into the fire, trying to get up the gumption to root
around in my pack and find the jerky, when an Indian appeared out
of the darkness. He wasn't painted for war, but his attitude sure said
he was leaning in that direction. He held a large Bowie knife in his
right hand, the business end pointed my way.

He started towards me, the metal of the knife glittering in the
firelight. I didn't give him a chance to use it. I sprung and hit him
with a right jab that rang his bell, immediately followed by an upper
cut. I ended it with a roundhouse to his chin.

He lay sprawled in the sand, the knife three feet away and out of
reach. He wasn't out, but he was groggy. I walked over and put my
foot on the knife, then pulled my gun.

He started to get up, but I put a bullet into the sand next to him
and he sat back down.

"Do you speak English?"

He spat on the ground and said, "I speak the White Man's
tongue."

"Why did you attack me?"

"You are white."

We stared at each other for what seemed like a long time, the
only sound—the crackling and popping of the fire. I was trying to
figure out what to do with him. The easiest thing would be to shoot
him. I didn't think he'd let me tie him up without a fight. I could
keep my gun on him all night. But I was already tired, I wanted to
get to sleep. Besides, if I kept my gun on him all night, in the
morning I'd be right back to where I started.

Before I could come up with a suitable solution to my dilemma, he spoke.

"I do not want to die in the sand, like a dog. Allow me to stand, so I may die like a man."

I made a motion with the gun for him to stand up. He stood ramrod straight and looked me dead in the eye, his chest puffed out, ready to die. There was no fear in his eyes, only hate. I pulled back the hammer of my Colt. The click sounded loud in the still desert air. I hesitated. But I had to get it over with. Having him stand there waiting for me to fire the bullet that would end his life was tantamount to torture.

I pointed the gun in the air and fired a single shot. "There, you're dead. Are you happy now?" I kicked his knife over to him. He looked down at it but did not move to pick it up.

I pointed to the coffee pot hanging over the fire. "You want some coffee?"

He looked to where I was pointing, then back at me. "Coffee?"

I nodded.

"With sugar in it?"

I nodded again.

He bent down, picked up the knife, and slid it into his rawhide belt.

"Come," I said, "sit down by the fire. We will drink coffee with sugar in it and we will talk."

He sat cross-legged as Indians do, while I knelt on one knee and poured the coffee. I handed him the cup along with the bag of sugar so he could sweeten it to his taste.

I think he liked it sweet. He put a whole handful of sugar into the cup.

We sat and silently drank our coffee. As far as he was concerned, we could have done that all night. But me being a White Man, I had to fill the silence with words.

"What is your name?"

"Dasoda-hae. In your tongue, it is He Just Sits There. It was my father's name."

"My name is Dillon Mahoney. Mahoney was my father's name."

He nodded but said nothing.

"How is it that you speak English so well?"

"I was taken from my mother at an early age and sent to the missionary school. There, they tried to beat the Apache out of me, but they failed."

I studied him as he sat sipping his coffee. He wore leggings and a white cotton shirt. His buckskin moccasins came up to mid-calf. A red headband covered his forehead. His long black hair hung past his shoulders. He looked to be about forty years of age, but it's hard to tell with Indians. He was a mite on the thin side and looked like he hadn't had a square meal in quite a while.

"Do you want something to eat?" I asked.

"Why would you feed a man who tried to kill you?"

"I'm hungry, and in the White Man's world, it is rude to eat in front of someone without offering them to join in. I was going to chow down on some jerky before you came along. But now, I think I'll fry up some bacon and make us some pan biscuits. How does that sound?"

He startled me by suddenly standing up and placing his cup on a rock. "My pony is down the draw," he said. "I will bring him closer to your camp for safety. There are many pumas in this country."

I got out the bacon and flour and went to work. I had made plenty of coffee, so that was no problem. But I didn't know how long the sugar would hold out.

His horse must have been a ways off because it took him a long while to get back. By the time his horse was safely tethered with mine, the food was ready.

We sat down to a meal fit for a king. At least, that's the way my stomach felt about it. We each sat with a tin plate in one hand and shoveled food into our mouths with the other, grunting and smiling now and then at how good the food tasted. When we were done, we wiped the grease from our hands onto our pant legs. It had been a satisfying meal.

I pulled a bottle from my saddlebag and offered it to Dasoda-hae.

"If that is the White Man's whiskey, I do not drink it. It is bad for my people."

"Then pour yourself some more coffee. And help yourself to the sugar … whatever's left."

He didn't catch on to the sarcasm.

With full stomachs, me holding a brown whiskey bottle and him holding a tin cup of coffee that was mostly sugar, I decided it was time to pow-wow. I threw a few sticks on the fire to build it up, and to give me time to marshal my thoughts. At length, I said, "I never met an Indian before. I've been in the West for over a year now and you're the first one I've come across."

His words cut like a knife. "That is because the White Man has taken our land and put us on reservations."

I said, "So, why are you here and not on the reservation?"

"I escaped with Goyahkl to fight the Whites."

"Just you two are at war with America?"

"There are many of us. Goyahkl is known by his Mexican name. Have you not heard of Geronimo?"

I had heard of Geronimo. Most people had. And here I was sitting and talking with one of his warriors.

"Where is Geronimo now?"

"He is in Mexico, in the mountains of Sierra Madre. Your soldiers know where he is, but they cannot find him, or they are not looking very hard. I came over the border to steal cows with others from our band. We have many warriors who came to us with their wives and children. We must feed them."

"Where are the others you came with?"

"We were raiding a ranch when a group of White Men came upon us and we scattered. The White Men gave chase, but I have lost the ones that came after me."

"What about your friends?"

"We have a place to meet. I will see them tomorrow. I could not go there while the White Men were chasing me."

I took a pull from the bottle and said, "Help yourself to the coffee. Drink up whatever's left. I'll make some more in the morning."

As he poured coffee into his cup, I asked him to tell me a little bit about himself. It wasn't likely that I'd sit down with an Apache warrior again any time soon. His story, I thought, would have to be far more interesting than anything I would find in a dime novel.

"As I have told you, my name is Dasoda-hae. And, as I have told you, I have taken my father's name. The Whites knew him as Magnus Coloradas. He was of the Mimbreño Apaches, as I am. He was the greatest of our war chiefs. Geronimo fought under my father and learned the strategies of war from him."

"My sister, Dos-The-Seh, married Cheis, a great war chief. He was known as Cochise to the Mexicans and Whites. He was of the Chiricahua Apache. He is now dead. But the Whites did not kill him. He died of a sickness. Another of my sisters married Bidu-ya, or Victorio, as the Mexicans called him. He was Mimbreño Apache. The Mexicans killed him last year."

Dasoda-hae went on to tell me about life on the reservation and how hard it was. Of the constant hunger because the Indian agents did not supply enough beef to feed everyone. How the U.S. Government was trying to make farmers out of his people in a place where no food would grow. He was silent for a moment, then told me of his father.

"My father was killed many years ago. I was of eighteen summers at the time. He fought the Whites and Mexicans for many years. As he grew older, he wearied of war and sent word to the Whites that he was ready to talk peace. They invited him to come in and parley. They said he would be safe. He went to them under a flag of truce. Instead of honoring their word, they took him prisoner and tortured him. Then they shot him and cut off his head. The Loafs-Around-The-Forts brought us word of how he had died."

"The Loafs-Around-The-Forts?" I asked.

"The Apaches who live outside the soldier forts. They have no honor. They beg for whiskey and handouts from the Whites."

Dasoda-hae was proud of his family and his heritage. I came to understand why the Apaches were at war with America.

I felt uncomfortable. After all, I was a member of the race that was oppressing Dasoda-hae and his people. It was time to change the subject. I leaned back on my saddle, looked up at the stars, and pointed. "Look at that. What a wondrous sight. I'd never seen anything like it until I came out West. Back East, we light our streets and pour black smoke from our factories into the air. We find many ways to diminish the beauty of the night sky."

"I have seen pictures of your cities in the books I was forced to read at missionary school. I do not know how a human being can live like that."

"We've grown accustomed to it."

Dasoda-hae handed me his empty cup and what was left of the sugar. "I thank you, Dillon Mahoney. I will make camp farther down the wash."

"No need to do that. You are welcomed to share my fire, and in the morning, there will be hot coffee." At the mention of coffee, Dasoda-hae sat back down.

I put away the booze and was just emptying the dregs from the coffee pot when the sound of horses' hooves came at us from out of the night. We both stood up. Dasoda-hae had his hand resting on the hilt of his knife. My right hand hovered over my gun. I was afraid Indians were descending upon us. Dasoda-hae looked as worried as I was. He was fearful the men riding in were White Men.

They rode into the camp, six of them.

Their leader was a rough-looking man. He walked his horse right up to me and said, "Good. You caught him."

I needed more light, so I threw some wood onto the fire. When the flames had come back up, I said, "May I ask who you are and why you rode into my camp unannounced?"

He let fly a stream of tobacco juice that landed at my feet. "The name's Ike Bowdre. I'm the foreman for the Circle T. These boys," he jerked his thumb behind him, "work for me."

I didn't think I was going to like the man, but I was willing to give him a chance. "My name is Dillon Mahoney. This here is my friend, Dasoda-hae."

Bowdre rubbed the stubble on his chin and said, "Since when did a White Man ever have an Injun for a friend?" It was definite. I was not going to like the man.

One of the cowboys behind him spoke up. "Ike, you know who that is?"

Bowdre turned and looked at the cowboy. "What are you talking about?"

"He's the fella that killed Heck Thomas and now they're sayin' he got Luke Short, too."

Dasoda-hae hadn't moved a muscle since they rode in.

Bowdre turned back to me. "Is that true?"

"If you don't mind, let me ask *you* a question."

"Sure."

"What did you mean when you said I 'caught him'? Caught *who*?"

"Why, that stinkin', thievin' Injun standing right next to you. That's who."

I adjusted my gun in its holster and made sure they all saw me do it. "I don't take kindly to you insulting a friend of mine. You best have some proof of what you're saying."

Bowdre exploded. "'*PROOF*'?" he yelled. "We caught him and his thievin' friends stealing our cattle. Caught them red-handed, we did. We've been tracking him all day."

"Couldn't have been him. He's been with me for two days now. We're out here hunting big cats. He's my guide."

"I don't see any skins or meat."

"We've been having bad luck. But we almost got us a puma this afternoon."

"I told you, we've been tracking him. And he's the only Injun around."

"It's been dark going on four hours now. You track in the dark, do you?"

He squirmed in his saddle. "Enough of this!" he shouted. "We're taking the Injun and we're gonna hang him from the first tree we come across."

What's the use of having a reputation if you don't use it to your advantage every now and then? "Mister Bowdre, you lay one hand on my friend, and I will kill you."

He let go with another stream of tobacco juice, but this time it didn't land anywhere near me.

"Look here, Mister … what did you say your name was?" He knew full well what my name was.

"It's Mahoney."

"Look here, Mister Mahoney. We don't have no fight with you. But we can't let you interfere with a duly sworn posse going about its lawful business. Any way you slice it, there are six of us and only one of you."

"If you're duly sworn, where's the sheriff?"

"He's out chasin' the rest of the band of thievin' Redskins. We had to split up when they split up."

294

I was beginning to wonder if Dasoda-hae had turned to stone. He still hadn't moved.

I looked behind Bowdre at the rest of the duly sworn posse. Not one of them seemed as eager to make an arrest as he was. It was time to send them on their way.

"Mister Bowdre, I've had a tiring day. I suggest you leave my camp before there's any trouble."

He took off his hat and waved away a fly that had been buzzing him.

"The only trouble there's gonna be is if you continue interfering in our business."

He yelled over his shoulder, "Jim … Boone, get the Injun and tie his hands."

It was my turn.

"Jim … Boone, if you make a move to get off those horses, I'll kill you both."

Bowdre was feeling confident. "That still leaves the rest of us."

"Won't matter to you, you'll be dead. Before Boone and Jim hit the ground, I'll have a bullet in you."

Bowdre's men, all of them, backed their horses a few steps. Bowdre stayed where he was.

I had to hand it to him, he had sand. Or maybe he'd rather die than lose face in front of his men. I wasn't looking to kill him, but it's like Jack Bridges had said, "It ain't a game, boy. If you draw your gun, shoot to kill."

I couldn't let them take Dasoda-hae. Not after the things he had told me. What the soldiers had done to his father and what the White culture had done to his people. I was determined to show him that not all White Men were alike.

I took my badge out of my pocket and tossed it up to Bowdre. "I'm a Deputy U.S. Marshal, duly commissioned," I lied. "I could kill you right now with no repercussions. And any of you other men who would take part in harming a U.S. Marshal will either hang or spend many, many years in prison. Now be on your way. If you have any complaints, you can lodge them with my boss up in Cheyanne."

Bowdre was beaten and he knew it. But now he had an excuse for backing down. He tossed back my badge and said, "Damn right we're gonna make a complaint."

After giving one last, hateful look in Dasoda-hae's direction, he turned his horse and rode off into the darkness, followed by his men.

I gave a sigh of relief. I had been serious about not letting Dasoda-hae be taken prisoner. To do that, I probably would have had to kill Bowdre or at least wound him. I was certain if Bowdre went down, the rest would have folded.

Dasoda-hae came over and shook my hand. "I never shook a White Man's hand before. I will tell Geronimo what you have done for me."

"That's fine, Dasoda-hae. But right now you better be on your way, just in case those men have a change of heart and creep back here in the middle of the night."

"I will not leave! I will fight them by your side."

"They don't want me, and they certainly don't want any trouble with the U.S. Marshal's Service. If you're not here, they'll leave me be. Then they'll go out and try to pick up your trail, so be careful."

Dasoda-hae clapped me on the shoulder and looked me in the eye. The hate I had seen earlier had been replaced by something else, something softer.

He started for his horse, but I yelled out, "Hold on a minute."

I reached into my saddlebag and came out with the bag of sugar. "Here, take this. You can never have enough of this stuff."

He smiled as though I had given him a bag of gold.

As the posse had done, Dasoda-hae rode into the night, but he went in the opposite direction.

The next morning, I continued on my way.

After going over a few mountains, through a few gorges, and trampling through a desert or two, I arrived on the outskirts of Los Angeles, California, on November 15th, 1881.

32

It was early morning. The sun was edging its way up over the horizon as I made my way towards the center of town. I rode in from the south, passing through miles and miles of orange and lemon groves, a tomato field or two, and many vineyards. To the west, the last lonely star of the night hung suspended in a dull grey sky. But to the east, out over the Los Angeles River, the heavens glowed with a golden splendor. Pewter-colored clouds, changing to white, dotted the skyline.

My first order of business was to secure accommodations for Betty and Jack. I found a livery stable on Olvera Street and paid the hostler to rub them down and give them both a bait of grain along with their hay. He was kind enough to allow me to store my kit in his barn until I got my bearings.

Once the horses had been taken care of, I asked where I could find the finest hotel in town.

"Just down the street, next to The Plaza."

"The Plaza?"

"That's the center of town. Across the way stands the Pico House. You can't do any better than that. They have gas lighting and bathrooms on every floor, one for men and one for the ladies. They even have bathtubs with running water."

I thanked the gentleman and turned to leave.

"Excuse me for mentioning it, but is it your intention to go into the Pico House wearing that gun?"

I instinctively looked down at my holster.

"Why? What's wrong with it?"

"Nothing, mister. However, you did ask me for the *best* hotel in town. That place even has a fancy French restaurant. They might look past you being all dusty and dirty and such. A person gets that way while traveling. But you go in there carrying a gun out in the open …"

He was right. I was no longer in *the* West. I unbuckled my holster and put it and the gun away with my kit. It was a strange feeling walking around without a gun strapped to my hip.

The desk clerk at the hotel did look at me a bit funny but said nothing. I had tried my best to shake off the dust clinging to my clothes, but there was still a fair amount left. I hadn't shaved for a month, and my hair was a little too long. Nonetheless, the clerk handed me a key. "You're in room 202. The bellboy will show you the way. Enjoy your stay with us, Mister Mahoney."

When we were in the room and after he had opened the window, the bellboy, in his own casual way, taught me the ins-and-outs of tipping. He hung around until I finally had to ask him what he was waiting for.

"I can see you're in from the country, so you probably don't know this, but it's customary to tip the bellboy. That's how we make our living."

"Tip?"

"Yes, you give us a dime, or better yet, two bits, for carrying your bag and opening the window. Then we ask if there is anything else we can do for you. That's the part where we're hinting for a tip."

"Even though I carried my own saddlebags up the stairs?"

"I tried to take them from you, sir. However, if you remember, you said you would carry them yourself."

I liked him. He was honest.

"What's your name?"

He fidgeted before answering. "It's Johnny … John Elroy, but if you're gonna report me downstairs, I'd like to ask you not to do so. We ain't … I mean … we aren't supposed to ask for tips. It will get me in hot water with the boss."

I flipped a coin in his direction, which he caught in midair. I had to smile at the look of astonishment on his face when he saw the denomination. It was a five dollar half eagle.

"Don't worry, Johnny. I like your style and I figure you know your way around. You might be able to help me get settled here. Right now, I need to know where I can buy some city clothes and where I can find the nearest barbershop."

By sundown, I was clean-shaven and my hair was considerably shorter. I stood nervously in the doorway of the Pico House's French restaurant, wearing my new set of city clothes, and clutching my new hat in my gun– … I mean … my right hand.

The food was good, although a mite costly. Can you believe it? I paid three dollars for a small piece of chicken swimming in some sort of brown sauce with a few green peas on the side. I'd have to give that place a wide berth if I was going to get established in Los Angeles. The money I carried with me was for investment, not for fancy meals. Which meant I would have to find employment of one sort or another for my day-to-day needs.

At that time, there were still a few *ranchos* around, mostly out in the valley. I could have found work as a cowboy, or as a *vaquero*, as cowboys were called in that part of the country. But I didn't want to make my living on a horse. I figured those days were behind me.

As luck would have it, there was a new enterprise in town called *The Los Angeles Daily Times*. It opened for business a few weeks after I hit town. I went to see the managing editor and told him I had experience working on a newspaper, which was true. But I didn't inform him of my lowly position. I intimated that I had been a star reporter.

He was doubtful. "You look kinda young to have had so much experience."

After a few more questions concerning my newspaper work, or lack thereof, he got around to asking me what I had been up to since leaving the paper.

"I traveled out west. I reckon that would be east to you. I spent some time in Wyoming Territory working on a cattle ranch, and I went on a cattle drive. Then I spent a little time down in New Mexico Territory." I neglected to tell him I had been a marshal.

His eyes brightened. "Did you ever witness a gunfight?"

"One or two."

Up until then, I had been standing, hat in hand, in front of his desk. He graced me with a smile and pointed to the only chair in the immediate vicinity. "Take the weight off," he said.

I sat down, placed my hat on my lap, and waited.

He leaned back in his chair and asked my name.

"Dillon Mahoney, sir."

"My name's Nathan Cole and I just might have a job for you."

He hesitated as if he expected me to say something. Did he want me to plead for a job? I just wished he'd get on with it. The new celluloid collar I was wearing was awfully uncomfortable. Wearing city clothes again was going to take some getting used to.

After a tick or two, he came to the realization that I was not going to say anything. So he continued: "I need a weekly column for our Sunday edition. And I was thinking, if you could write about your experiences in the West, then I could justify putting you on the payroll. Everyone's interested in the Wild West these days, what with all those dime novels floating about."

I didn't want to write about myself and get the label of an ex-gunman. I had come to Los Angeles to escape my reputation. I had to think for a moment. Finally, I knew what to say.

"My personal experiences were not all that exciting. But I did witness a few things and heard a whole lot about other things. I reckon I could come up with something that will intrigue your readers and hold their interest."

He leaned forward. "Write me five thousand words on the Wild West. If it's any good, you got yourself a job."

"Five thousand words?"

"I told you I needed a column, not a three-hundred-word essay on the fire department's new pumping engine. Don't worry. I'll edit it down some. But I need something to work with."

"When do you want it?"

He looked at me as though I were crazy. "When? I want it now, goddamn it! Go sit at that empty desk over there. You'll find pencils and paper in the drawer. Now leave me alone. I got a deadline to meet."

Well, I did ask for the job.

I wrote about me getting off the train in Slow Water, getting beaten up by Luke Short, and being hired on as an assistant cook for a cattle drive. But I changed things around a bit. First of all, I changed the names of all the people involved. Then I had the main character winning the fight. And he didn't just get hired on as a lowly cook, no sir. They needed him to *lead* the cattle drive. It was a wonderful work of fiction but based on some truth. At least it was authentic sounding.

I handed Mister Cole my story and sat down in the chair, anxiously awaiting his praise. As he read, he scowled, he frowned, he made queer noises with his teeth. I was ready to skulk out of the newsroom when he looked up. "This ain't too bad. Of course, I'll have to fix it up some, but still, it's not half-bad. However, for the next one, I'm gonna want some bloodshed."

I was given my own desk and a supply of pencils and paper. Mister Cole didn't care if I came or went as long as my story was on his desk by noon Thursday, so he'd have time to edit it for the Sunday paper.

The newsroom was made up entirely of men, except for a solitary young woman who sat in the far corner of the office. She wrote the society column. Whenever there was a party thrown by the well-to-dos, she would attend and write about it the next day. Who was wearing what, who was back from the East, or back from the Continent, that kind of thing. Her department was called the "Ladies Section." The things only women would be interested in, she wrote about. Her name was Emily Johansson.

She was tall for a woman, about five feet, nine inches. Her hair was blonde, and she wore it up, as was the fashion in those days. I'd take a side-long glance in her direction now and then. But I never had the nerve to go over and talk to her.

It was shortly after I had written about my encounter with Heck Thomas that she came up to me and asked, "Did you actually see that gunfight you wrote about?"

I had written about it in the third person, as though I were one of the onlookers.

"Yes, ma'am. I was there, sure enough. I was riding with the posse." Which was not a lie.

She clasped her hands together. "How exciting! What ever happened to Mister Butler?"

Jed Butler was my alter ego.

"I don't know what became of him. He's probably dead. That's where all those gunslingers end up. They die an early death."

"You didn't call him a gunslinger in your story. You said he was a lawman."

"I heard he went bad, took off his badge, and started having gunfights in every town he rode into. I'll most likely be writing about his downfall in some future column."

"Well, I wish *I* could see a gunfight. It would be so thrilling."

I was sitting at my desk and she was standing. I looked up at her and, for the first time, I noticed that her eyes were light blue in color, almost grey. They were full of life and amazingly innocent. Sparkling sapphires came to mind.

Those eyes mesmerized me for a moment, but I shook it off and said, "I don't think you'd like to see a man shot to death. There's something about it, something not right. I mean, even if the man is trying to kill you and you have no choice but to defend yourself, it's still a horrible experience.

"At first you're glad that it's him lying on the floor and not you. Then you look down into his face, his half-closed vacant eyes, his slack mouth. You think how, just a moment ago, he was a living, breathing human being. Maybe he had a mother who loved him or a sweetheart who would cry over his grave.

"They usually urinate themselves, sometimes worse. Their blood pools and glistens in the light before seeping between the cracks of the floorboards.

"And all the while you're thinking that the taking of a human life could have easily been avoided if you had just walked away. They say it steals a man's soul to end the life of another. The more you kill, the more soulless you become."

I was speaking mostly to myself. I was a thousand miles away, looking down on the dead bodies of Luke Short and Patrick Hawke.

Her voice brought me back to Los Angeles. "You sound like you've been in a gunfight or two yourself."

"No, Miss Johansson. That was just me repeating something I heard a long time ago. Now, if you'll please excuse me, I have to get back to writing next week's column."

"Well, Mr. Mahoney, I, for one, can't wait to read it." She turned and walked back to her desk. The scent of sweet-smelling perfume lingered in the air.

I wrote that week's column and the next. I had a new story on Mister Cole's desk every Thursday by twelve noon without fail. When I ran out of stories about myself, I started writing about things

Jack Bridges had told me. Always changing the names, of course. Then I started making things up, writing pure fiction. But it didn't matter. No one knew the difference, and by then my column was one of the most popular features running in the *Daily Times*. People need heroes, or so it seems.

However, after eight months, the well had run dry. When I told Mister Cole I would be leaving, he tried to talk me into staying. He even offered me a raise, but it was of no use. I had no stories left in me.

I made the rounds, saying goodbye to the men in the newsroom. They all wished me well. Then someone came up with the bright idea that I should be given a proper send-off at the local watering hole, a place called Connie Doolan's. I agreed to meet them there after the paper had been put to bed.

On my way out, I stopped by Miss Johansson's desk. We really hadn't spoken since that first encounter when she complimented me on my Heck Thomas column. We nodded to one another now and then from across the room. And we would always exchange courtesies wishing one another good morning or good afternoon if we passed each other in the hall, but that was about it.

"I just stopped by to say it's been a pleasure working with you, Miss Johansson."

She put down her pencil and steepled her fingers under her chin. "Why, Mister Mahoney, I am honored that you have stopped by to speak with me. We've worked together for eight months and this is the first time that you have come over to my desk."

I didn't know what to say. Thankfully, she went on.

"You men are going down to Doolan's, and, as you know, women are not allowed through the door. So, I'll say my goodbyes now."

I shook her hand when it was offered. It was soft and smooth to the touch. I didn't want to let go. There was nothing else for me to say, so I grinned like the idiot I was and walked away. But halfway to the door, I abruptly turned around and marched right back up to Emily Johansson's desk.

I waited a moment for her to finish the sentence she was working on. After she placed the period, she looked up and asked, "Did you forget something, Mister Mahoney?"

303

"Yes, I did. I forgot to tell you that I think you are the most beautiful woman I have ever seen. There were many a day that I wanted to come over and ask you to step out one night and have dinner with me. But I didn't have the nerve. I just wanted you to know that."

I did not wait for her response. I shoved my hat down onto my head—a little too forcefully—and stormed out of the room.

≈ ≈ ≈

I had moved out of the Pico House shortly after getting hired on at the *Daily Times*. With help from my bellhop friend, Johnny Elroy, I found an old adobe that was a little worse for wear. It stood on two acres of land on Sunset Boulevard, on the south side of the street, just west of La Cienega. In those days, it was far from the center of town. It had a kitchen, a large front room, two bedrooms, and a small enclosure built onto the side, containing a washtub and a long-handled pump that actually worked. The privy, of course, was out back. The roof needed repair, and Johnny offered to help out with that. The property also included a small barn that would be perfect for Betty. I had sold Jack, my old pack horse, because my days of needing a pack horse were over.

It was not easy finding the owner of the property. That's where Johnny came in. He seemed to know everyone in town. And if, by chance, there were a few he didn't know personally, he knew people who knew people.

We eventually located the owner and I asked him if he'd be interested in selling. He readily said yes. I paid the asking price with no dickering and became a California landowner. My plan was to eventually tear down the old house and build a new one.

The only furniture that came with the place was a scarred table and three chairs. I bought a bed and a few pots and pans and that was it. I was all set.

I still had a few thousand dollars left, so that went into a bank until I could find somewhere to invest it.

≈ ≈ ≈

At the time I quit working for the newspaper, I was only twenty-two years old and still a mite restless. I thought I'd take a trip and asked Johnny to keep an eye on the house while I was away.

"Where ya going?"

"Not far. Just up the coast to San Francisco. Maybe go inland a little. I wanna see what the rest of California looks like."

"How long are you gonna be gone?"

"I don't know. But I would appreciate it if you'd come by every once in a while and make sure there are no squatters. If there are, run 'em out. Here's fifty dollars for your trouble."

He didn't want to take the money, because by then we had become friends.

"Consider it a *tip*," I said with a smile.

He accepted the money with a smile of his own.

I had been told that in the latter half of the 18th century and the beginning of the 19th, Franciscan monks and priests built a string of missions along the coast of California. Each mission was intentionally built to be only a day's ride apart. Those missions eventually became towns and cities. I would have no trouble buying supplies or finding lodging on my way up the coast if I followed the old mission trail, so that was my plan.

I saddled Betty and started out on a crisp September morning. I brought along two hundred dollars for pocket money, leaving the rest in the bank for when I returned.

33

Five and a half years later, I returned to Los Angeles. I was twenty-eight years old. By then I had enough miles under my belt to call myself a full-fledged man. I had spent long stretches of time alone. I had also been pressed so close together with my fellow men that I thought I'd go crazy for lack of solitude. I'd seen humanity at its best and at its worst.

After leaving Los Angeles, I had made it halfway up the coast before I decided I'd like to try my hand at panning for gold. I yanked the reins, turning Betty's head eastward, and we headed for the mountains. My endeavors provided me with just enough of the yellow metal to keep me going. But not much more than that. I loved living in the mountains, though. I loved the stark loneliness. Being my own man, not having to answer to anyone. The only time I saw another human being was when I went into a little town down in the foothills to buy supplies. A man can get to know his own soul if he has no one to talk to except himself and his horse.

After almost a year of that, I started to yearn for a modicum of human companionship. And seeing how San Francisco wasn't that far off, I packed up my things and rode down into that fair city.

I thought Los Angeles was populous. Well, San Francisco had it beat by a country mile.

I worked as a bartender in the Barbary Coast at various buckets-of-blood saloons. That's where I saw humanity at its worst. I found employment in a rolling mill as an iron moulder's assistant. That was hot, sweltering, dangerous work.

I did any number of jobs around the city before I took on the last job I'd have before going back to Los Angeles. I signed on to a small whaling schooner as a foremast hand. Not just any foremast hand, I was a "green" foremast hand. I was the lowest of the low. The lowest paid, the last to eat, and the first to be given the most disagreeable jobs.

Before shipping out, I had to find a place to board Betty. A widow woman living on a farm outside of town agreed to look after her until I got back. She had a kind demeanor, and I could tell she took to Betty right away. I gave her eighty dollars and told her I'd pay her anything else that was owed when I returned. She assured me that was enough and not to worry. "Betty and I will get along just fine."

When I signed on, I was told the voyage would take six months. However, the night before pulling up anchor, I was informed it might take longer. "We will not return," said the captain, "until the hold is filled to the brim with casks of whale oil, no matter how long that takes."

If I had known what was in store for me, I would have gone ashore right then and there, even if I had to swim.

The work was unremitting, the food horrible and bug infested. I had never thought about how whale oil was collected. It tore me apart to see those beautiful creatures harpooned, dragged to the side of the ship, their flesh then cut up and boiled in iron cauldrons. I swore I'd never use whale oil again. Even if I had to spend all my remaining nights in darkness.

After eleven months of that hell, we sailed into San Francisco Bay. Our pay was a percentage of the haul. My end came to only sixty dollars. But I didn't care. I was happy to be on dry land once again and away from that damnable ship.

Betty was well and fit when I went to collect her. She was as happy to see me as I was to see her. I gave the woman an extra twenty dollars for taking such good care of her.

Los Angeles had grown while I was away. I found no squatters in my house, but it was filled with dust. Other than that, it was in good repair. Johnny had done a fine job of looking after it. I went in search of him; however, he was no longer employed at the Pico House and no one there could tell me where he was working. I knew where he lived and assumed I'd find him there, but it was the same story. He was gone and no one in the neighborhood knew where he had gone to.

I had plans and they included Johnny. I was sure if he was still in Los Angeles, he would eventually come by to check on the house. But until then, there were things I could do to get the ball rolling.

For the next two weeks, I left the house early in the morning and did not return until long after dark. Soon, I had the first phase of my plan in place.

≈ ≈ ≈

I was cooking breakfast in the fireplace one morning when the door burst open. "What are you doing here?" a loud voice demanded.

I turned and beheld my friend Johnny standing in the doorway, silhouetted by the bright morning sun. I can't tell you how happy I was to see him. We met in the middle of the room and enthusiastically shook hands.

"I knew you'd be back some day," he said.

I invited him to have a seat at the table while I got my food off the fire.

"I saw smoke coming from the chimney and thought you were a squatter."

"Not hardly."

"When did you get back?"

"A few weeks ago. Speaking of squatters, any trouble?"

"Just one fella. He said he was only staying the night, that he was just passing through. He looked kinda down and out, so I let him stay. I came by the next morning and, true to his word, he was gone."

I offered to share my breakfast, but Johnny said he had already eaten.

"By the way," I asked, "where are you living? I went looking for you."

"I'm living *and* working a little north of here, in the foothills near the Cahuenga Pass. It's a new town some lady and her husband are trying to get started. They call it Hollywood. I'm selling city lots and I live in the back room of their sales shack. At least I don't have to pay rent."

"You making any money?"

"Not much, to be honest. I get paid only when I make a sale. But they make sure I don't starve. The lady advances me a few dollars now and then when my poke gets empty. I'm their only salesman, so they try to keep me happy, to a certain extent."

308

I looked at him across the table as I sipped my coffee. Johnny was three years younger than me. His sandy blond hair suited him well. It fit with his boyish good looks and his ever-present smile. He wasn't as tall as I was, missing the mark by two inches—topping off at six feet even. But at the age of twenty-five, he exuded an air of natural confidence, far more than I was ever able to muster.

"I'm glad you came by. I have a business proposition that might interest you."

He perked up. Johnny always did like to make a dollar.

"What do you have in mind?" he asked.

"Let me ask you a question. What do you know about the oil business?"

"The oil business?"

"That's what I said. Do you know anything at all about it?"

"Just that they make kerosene from the stuff."

I finished eating and pushed the plate off to the side. "That's a start, I guess. I don't suppose you have a horse."

"You suppose right."

"Okay, let's go for a walk. I want to show you something."

At the door, he asked me where we were going. "We're going downtown."

"That's some walk. I'm supposed to be at the shack, smiling and selling real estate, by nine o'clock. If I go with you, I'll be late."

"If you don't go with me, you may regret it the rest of your life."

"Okay. Let's go."

As we walked, I told him what I had in mind.

"When I was up in San Francisco, I worked as a bartender in a section of town that sailors like to frequent. And, they being a loquacious lot, I learned a few things."

"What kind of things?"

"Hear me out, Johnny. Then you can ask all the questions you want."

He bowed in an exaggerated manner. "You have the floor, Mister Mahoney."

"Good. Now listen carefully. There are men in San Francisco who are buying all the oil that they can get their hands on. Right now, crude is selling for ninety-four cents a barrel."

"I do have to ask one question," said Johnny.

"And that would be?"

"How many gallons to a barrel?"

"Good question. The answer is forty-two. Now may I continue?"

"By all means, do continue."

"Thank you. That information got me thinking. You've seen the oil seeps all over town. That means there's gotta be oil under those seeps just waiting for two enterprising fellas to pump it outta the ground and sell it to some gents who just happen to own an oil refinery.

"So, this is what I did. I went up to Pico and Wiley Canyons to where they're bringing up oil as fast as they can. I watched as they drilled new wells and talked to the men doing the drilling. I asked questions. And I got answers.

"I then went to the refinery in Newhall, in the Santa Clara Valley, and talked to the gent running it. He didn't think much of me, he could tell I wasn't an oil man. But I told him that if he didn't want my crude, I'd sell it to the fellas up in San Francisco. I knew from what I'd heard while bartending that the refinery up there is sending ships down here to buy all the crude they can from any and all wildcatters.

"He was skeptical that I could supply him with anything; however, he did commit to buy all the crude that I could deliver. Or as he put it, '*if*' I could deliver."

Johnny couldn't help himself. He said, "I'm sorry, Dillon, but I do have a few questions."

"Ask away."

"First: What is a wildcatter?"

"Men who go out on their own to find oil. Men like you and me."

"Okay. Second: You don't have any oil, crude or otherwise. So, what are you gonna sell? Third: If you did have oil, how would you get it to the refinery? And fourth: Just for the hell of it, how much does a barrel of oil weigh?"

They were all good questions and right on the money. Johnny had been paying attention. But by then, we had arrived at our destination. "I'll answer your last question first. A barrel of oil weighs about three hundred pounds. Now, if you will just bear with me, I think all your questions will be answered before too long."

"It's your show. Please proceed."

"Thank you, Johnny. Now, look around. What do you see?"

"What do I see?"

"Yes. What do you see?"

"I see the same thing you do. I see empty land and a few buildings scattered here and there."

"Johnny, I see opportunity. It's not empty land. What you see are city lots that people have bought for investments or to build on. They all want to make money off their investment. Now, follow me."

For the next two hours, I walked Johnny around, pointing out oil seeps on twenty different parcels of land. At the end of the tour, he said, "That's very interesting. Too bad you don't own all that land."

"But I do, Johnny, in a way."

"What do you mean?"

"There's a bar down the street. I'll buy you a beer and tell you all about it."

With beers in hand, we made ourselves comfortable at a table in the back so we could have a little privacy. While I waited for the foam in my glass to subside, I said, "Do you know what an oil lease is?"

Johnny took a heathy sip of his beer. After wiping off the foam mustache, he said, "Not really."

"An oil lease gives the person who owns it the exclusive right to drill for oil on a particular piece of property. They're usually for a duration of fifteen years. The property owner gets a one eighth royalty of whatever the leaseholder finds. If anything."

I took a sip of my beer and went on.

"I secured oil leases on all that property I just showed you. You and I, my friend, are going to start drilling for oil. Then we'll probably have no choice but to become filthy rich."

"So, how is all this gonna work?"

"We're gonna finance the drilling with the money I have left over after buying the leases. And I've arranged with the refinery to pick up our oil so we don't have to deliver it. They already have the tank wagons to do the job. They're gonna charge a small fee, but that's okay because it'll be cheaper than us hauling it up there."

"Okay, what's the deal? What's the partnership? What do you need me for?" he asked in rapid succession.

"I'm advancing the money, so the deal is sixty-forty. I need you because it's back-breaking work, drilling for oil is. We might drill a dry well or two before we get lucky. The days will be long and hard, and there'll be nothing coming in until we do hit. I can't afford to hire men who would expect to get paid every day or once a week. The money would run out real fast. I need a partner that's in it for the long haul. We'll be living in a tent at our drilling sites and it probably won't be pleasant."

Johnny held out his hand. "You got yourself a deal, partner."

We decided to call the company Alta Oil because California was originally called Alta California when it was under Spain's control. Alta means upper and we figured that name was as good as any.

While Johnny went north to quit his job and collect his things, I went to the bank and drew out the last of my money, a little over twenty-seven hundred dollars. It wasn't much to start an oil company with, but it was going to have to do.

Johnny spent that night at my house, and the next morning we set out to get everything we were going to need, including a drill bit, iron pipes, tools, lumber and nails, a small steam engine, a water pump, a tent, and a portable stove.

We picked the lot with the largest seep to drill our first well, Alta #1. In the meantime, we had to wait for the supplies to be delivered. I asked Johnny if he wanted to go out for one last hurrah before we got down to business. "I think we can afford a good meal and a few drinks. God knows, it's gonna be a long time before we sit down at a table again."

"I'm beat," replied Johnny. "I'm gonna hit the hay, but you go if you want to."

All the running around had tired Johnny out, but I was bursting with nervous energy.

I took a bath, put on my best clothes, saddled Betty, and went in search of a good restaurant. Eventually, I came to that section of town lit by gas lamps, and where carriages abounded. I tethered Betty outside a place called Rosie's Steakhouse and went inside, anticipating nothing more than a steak and a few whiskeys.

As I walked through the restaurant, heading for a small table in the back, someone called my name. I turned to see Emily Johansson sitting with two older gentlemen. At first, I didn't know what to do. Should I just wave and continue on my way, or should I go over and say hello? If only I hadn't made such a fool of myself the last time I saw her. But that was five years ago, maybe she's forgotten. Not to go over would be rude.

"Miss Johansson, it's so nice to see you again."

"And you as well, Mister Mahoney." She turned to the man seated next to her. "I'd like to introduce you to my father, David Johansson." Looking across the table, she said, "And this is my uncle, Harrison Otis. He's the publisher of the *Daily Times*."

Without missing a beat, she went on. "Gentlemen, may I present Dillon Mahoney, late of the *Daily Times*. You must remember him, Uncle. He wrote that column on the West that was so popular."

I shook her father's hand, and as I turned to her uncle, he said, "Of course, I remember you. We received quite a few letters to the editor demanding that your column be reinstated. A few people even threatened to cancel their subscriptions if you weren't brought back."

I told both men that, likewise, it was a pleasure meeting them and was about to take my leave, when Miss Johansson said, "Why don't you join us? We haven't ordered yet."

Before I could respond, Mister Johansson said, "Yes, do. Please sit down, Mister Mahoney."

I was no sooner seated when Mister Otis asked if I'd like a drink. I hadn't noticed, but there was a bottle of very expensive whiskey on the table. "They don't sell that brand here, but they stock it for me. It's one of the perks of owning a newspaper, my boy," he said with a wink. He then poured a healthy shot into an empty water glass. "Here, this will get you started."

They were genuine people and I was enjoying myself. They asked what I had been up to since leaving the paper, and I told them about my recent travels. They all seemed interested, especially Miss Johansson. I was glad that I was sitting opposite her. She sure was a delight to look at.

At one point, she asked what I had been doing since my return.

"I've started an oil company with a friend of mine."

"You have?" asked Mister Johansson.

I told them about Alta Oil, and finished my recitation around the time the men were lighting their cigars. They offered me one, but being a non-smoker, I politely declined the offer.

While her father and uncle were busy getting their cigars burning just right, Emily asked me where I'd be drilling my first well.

"Over at Cotton and Patton Streets."

"You mean here in town? Not up where everyone else is drilling, in the canyons?"

"No. We thought we'd try our luck right here in the city."

Mister Otis, having gotten his cigar burning to his satisfaction, said, "You know, drilling for oil is an expensive proposition. I assume that you're properly financed."

"Alta Oil is financed to the hilt," I fibbed.

I tried to pay for my share of the meal, but they wouldn't hear of it.

Outside, on the sidewalk, we said our goodbyes. And as I was putting my foot in the stirrup, Emily said, "Maybe I'll come by and visit the Alta Oil Enterprises sometime. Unless I'd be imposing?"

In the glow of the streetlight, I could clearly see her sparkling blue-grey eyes. They were smiling.

"That would be an imposition that Alta Oil and I would be more than happy to endure, Miss Johansson."

34

Once we had the derrick built and in place, we started drilling. That first week, we drilled only fifty feet, an average of seven feet per day. But after we got to know what we were doing, things started to fall into place, and at three hundred and ten feet, we hit oil. It wasn't a gusher like you hear about. Once we punched through, the crude quietly bubbled to the surface and the Alta Oil Company was in business!

Alta #1 wasn't what you'd call a rich find, but it did supply us with enough income so we could get to sinking our second well. Unfortunately, at five hundred feet we still hadn't hit oil, so we moved on to another seep and started building the derrick for Alta #3.

Johnny was at the general store replenishing our food supply, and I was sawing wood for #3's derrick when Emily Johansson rode up. I stopped what I was doing and looked at her in wonder. She was beautiful; an absolute vision. Her smile dazzled and enchanted me.

She waved and said, "I thought I'd come for a visit. Is this a bad time?"

I laid down the saw and went to her. "As far as I'm concerned, this is the perfect time. May I help you off your horse?"

I showed her around and explained the drilling process. She asked intelligent questions and seemed genuinely interested in what Johnny and I were doing. When Johnny returned with our supplies, she said, "I'm keeping you from your work, so I'll be on my way. But if you don't mind, I'd like to come back sometime."

"Anytime at all, Miss Johansson."

Alta #3 came in much like #1 had. We still hadn't hit a large reserve. But the oil from #3 did allow us to hire two experienced oil men, which meant that Johnny and I could take turns going to the house once in a while and sleep in a bed.

During this time, Emily would come by every so often. And as I got to know her a little better, my confidence grew. It grew to the point where I had the nerve to ask her to have dinner with me one night.

"Why, Dillon, it sure took you long enough."

While we were eating, I finally got to know the real Emily Johansson. I let her do most of the talking and when she'd run down, I'd ask a question to get her going again.

She was an only child, doted on by her father. Her mother had died when she was a young girl. She got the job at the *Daily Times* because her uncle was the publisher. But she had tired of covering parties thrown by the rich and resigned. Her only job now was looking after her father's household.

Emily did not tell me her age, but I reckoned she was about twenty-seven. I was wondering why she hadn't married, so I decided to ask her. "How come an attractive and intelligent girl like yourself is not married?"

"I could ask you the same thing," she said with a sly smile. "But to answer *your* question, I'm not married because I have not met a man I was interested in marrying, or who I would even consider marrying. Until now." The look she gave me left no doubt of whom she was speaking.

I could hardly believe it. Subsequent to that night, we saw each other as often as possible, which still was not enough for me.

Johnny and I had been wildcatting for a little over a year and we had sunk a total of seven wells, five of them pumping oil every single day of the year. Two had come up dry. We had not gotten filthy rich. But we had a steady source of income and ten employees. Johnny took over the running of the oil field, and I devoted myself to the business end of our venture. I was trying to find financing for a pipeline, so we could send our oil directly to the refinery without the delay and cost of having it carted there.

One of the men I spoke with was Edward Doherty. He had been a wildcatter up at Pico Canyon and had gotten lucky. Now he was looking for a place to invest some of his oil money. He came down to look over our field.

"It looks promising," he said, "but you're not pumping enough oil to justify the expense of a pipeline."

I couldn't argue with that. He was right. We needed to bring in a gusher.

My thirtieth birthday was fast approaching, and I decided to give myself a present. I asked Emily to marry me, and she said yes. Now all I had to do was ask her father for his one and only daughter's hand in marriage.

I pulled up to the house driving a rented buggy, wearing my Sunday best. Emily answered my knock and escorted me into her father's study, where she gave me a quick peck on the cheek. "You look so handsome! And don't be afraid. He knows how I feel about you. This is just a formality."

I wasn't so sure about that. "What if he says no?"

"Then I'll marry you anyway!"

I caressed her cheek and kissed her tenderly. "Thank you. That's all I needed to hear."

After having a little fun with me and making me squirm for a few minutes, her father happily gave his consent and Emily and I were married soon thereafter.

Emily moved into the adobe and set up housekeeping. I told her to buy any furniture she thought we may need. A few days later, I came home to find curtains on all the windows, rugs on all the floors, a table and chairs set, and a new bed in our bedroom. She had turned the house into a home.

That was in the summer of '88. For the next two and a half years, Alta Oil supplied us with a modest income. By then, we had drilled ten wells, eight of which were pumping oil. We did not drill on the other ten leases because it was our belief that all the leases were sitting over the same limited reservoir.

Late in the fall of 1891, our wells started to go dry, one by one. Our income dropped proportionally, and we had to let our employees go. Soon we were back to where we had started. It was just Johnny and me. No ... that's not right. I had Emily.

Johnny came by to discuss our future. We had enough money to drill *maybe* two wells, and we debated if it would be worth the effort. If the field had gone dry, we'd be throwing the last of our money into dry holes. It was Emily who set us straight.

"If you men believe in Alta Oil, go and drill those wells. If they come up dusters, then so be it. If that happens, you'll just go into another business."

317

She was right. Johnny and I decided to go for broke. He stayed for dinner, and afterward, I said to Emily, "I'm sorry, Sweetheart, but after tonight, I won't be home for a while. I'll be living on site with Johnny until we either run out of money or hit oil."

Johnny and I were sitting at the table, and Emily was clearing the dishes. She stopped what she was doing and cupped my face in her hands. Looking into my eyes, she said, "You better have two tents, Dillon Mahoney. One for Johnny and one for us. I'm your wife. I am not going to sit here and do nothing while you and your partner live out of a tent on a dusty lot, drilling for our future."

"But …"

"But nothing! I can help out. Three sets of hands are better than two. If nothing else, I can do the cooking."

She turned to Johnny. "Do you have anything to say about it?"

Translation: *You better not say anything unless you agree with me.*

Johnny was no fool. "I reckon I'd be a mug to turn down your cooking for Dillon's … or mine, come to think of it!"

The die was cast. We started with enough piping to go down fifteen hundred feet. We had never drilled that deep; our deepest well to date had been six hundred and seventy-five feet. But we were gambling that there was a larger reservoir of oil under the pool we had been tapping.

To save money, Johnny gave up his hotel room and moved his belongings into our house.

Johnny and I, without consulting Emily, named the new well Emily #1.

Emily kept up. She was with us every step of the way. From fetching tools to tending the steam engine we used to pound the drill into the ground to buying supplies to doing all the cooking.

We drilled Emily #1 to almost fifteen hundred feet … and nothing. I was for giving up and moving to another lease. Try our luck somewhere else. It would have to be our last well. We were pretty near scraping the bottom of the barrel, where money was concerned. Maybe Emily #2 would be lucky for us.

That night after work, while eating flapjacks that Emily had made, she suggested we keep at it. "Buy additional piping and go deeper," she urged. "I have a feeling about Emily #1."

I looked at Johnny. He shrugged. That was his vote. So I voted with a half-hearted shrug of my own. We would keep drilling at Emily #1.

We bought five hundred feet of additional piping, all that we could afford, and went to work. Inch by inch, foot by foot, day after relentless day, our drill penetrated deeper and deeper into the earth. It was hard going. Our biggest fear was that the bit would break. We couldn't afford to buy another one.

When we reached two thousand feet, we had only forty feet of pipe left. We were out of business. It had been a grand dream, and it sure was heady while the oil was flowing. But we had no money left in which to build another derrick. Not even enough to buy kerosene for our stove. Johnny and I talked it over. We could sell the equipment and the nine remaining leases. At least we would walk away with something.

While we were discussing what we could sell and how much we might be able to get for each item, Emily said nothing. She waited for me and Johnny to finish our conversation before she spoke up.

"It's three o'clock in the afternoon. We have hours of sunlight left. May I ask what you boys plan on doing for the rest of the day?"

I knew her well enough; she had a point to make.

"Okay, Emily. What's on your mind?"

She stood up and held out her hands, palms down. "Look at my fingernails, look at my hair. I'm a mess! I wouldn't mind any of that if we had given it our best shot and then lost out. But there's pipe lying right over there, waiting to be put to use. What if there's a giant reservoir just a few feet farther down? What then? How are we going to feel if someone comes along next week or next year and finds one hundred thousand barrels of oil just inches from where we stopped drilling? It's one thing to run out of pipe, but to walk away when there's still a chance ..."

Damn it! She was right. Johnny looked embarrassed and I'm sure I did, too.

I went to her, moved a wayward strand of hair from her face, and kissed her on the forehead. "Your hair looks beautiful. You are my pride, my joy, and my heart of hearts. Now, if you will excuse me, Johnny and I have some drilling to do."

319

It took us two days to go another twenty feet. The drill was getting hung up on something. In desperation, we cut down an oak tree, stripped it of its branches, and ended up with a log ten feet long and three feet in diameter. It weighed a ton if it weighed an ounce. Using Emily's horse and Betty to haul it up to the top of the derrick, we positioned it and let it go.

The weight came crashing down onto the pipe. Whatever the obstruction had been, the drill was now free. It had punched through. But before we could get back to drilling, a chunk of mud spurted out of the hole.

"That's strange," said Johnny.

I was about to agree but never got the chance. There was a rumbling sound and the earth tremored, ever so slightly. Then it came. Fwoosh! The sun was blotted out by teeming black crude. We were covered in oil. Dark, greasy-smelling, wonderful oil. We had hit a gusher!

Emily ran out of the tent and joined us, her hair forgotten. We danced and frolicked in the black rain until our senses returned. We had to cap the well! We were losing money with every drop that soaked back into the ground. Covered in crude, we went to work and had her capped in no time at all.

We were rich, Emily, Johnny, and I. *Rich!* What to do now?

All three of us agreed that the oil business was a little too volatile for us. We kept Emily #1, but made a deal with Edward Doherty to work her for an eighty/twenty split, eighty to us.

Of course, our find inevitably brought in others—wildcatters and established oil companies alike. Before too long, where once empty lots pervaded the landscape, a forest of wooden derricks had grown, seemingly overnight. That location turned out to be the richest oil field in California.

≈ ≈ ≈

We all moved into the Pico House. Emily and I, temporarily, Johnny on a more permanent basis.

I had the old adobe demolished and hired a contractor to build Emily her dream house. She was thrilled and oversaw all aspects of the design and construction. In fact, I think she would have carried the bricks and mortar herself, if it would have made the build go any more quickly. After seven months, when the last nail had been hammered, she rejoiced in decorating the interior.

While she was busy with the house, I would take Betty for long rides up into the hills. I liked to get above it all and look out at the Pacific Ocean. It had been named well: *Peaceful Sea*. I'd spend hours up there contemplating my future. I had more money than I could spend in three lifetimes, and more coming in every day.

During those forays into the hills, I'd sometimes think about my mother and father. They had come over from Ireland for a better life. From what my mother had told me, it was not easy getting to America in those days, especially for my father. I thought back to the things she had told me about him. How all his family had died during the Great Famine. His journey to America on a coffin ship. How he had watched half the passengers die: men, women, and children. How he was chased out of New York by gangsters. The hard, physical labor of working for the railroad. His going to war to free the slaves, and his love for my mother. I wished I could have known him.

I swore that I'd honor my parents' memory by never forgetting who I was and where I came from. To never believe that my wealth made me, in any way, better than other people who were less fortunate.

≈ ≈ ≈

We had designed the house with children in mind, lots of children. It was time to get started filling up those rooms. But, as usual, Emily was ahead of me. When, one day, I suggested we might want to think about starting a family, she informed me that it had already been taken care of.

"In eight months, you'll be a proud father, running up and down Sunset Boulevard, handing out cigars."

The astonishment I felt must have shown on my face. She said, "I'm sorry for not telling you sooner. I wanted to prepare a special dinner and tell you then. But now that you know, what do you think?"

I let out with a cowboy whoop and said, "I think it's wonderful, Missus Mahoney!" I took her in my arms and kissed her long and hard until she had to push me away.

She was blushing. "Not now, Dillon. Let's save it for after dinner."

As the months rushed by, Emily blossomed, growing bigger and bigger, and more beautiful, with each passing month. Johnny was as excited as we were. After all, he was to be the godfather *and* honorary uncle. If it turned out to be a girl, we would call her Mary, after my mother. If a boy, David, after her father.

Finally, the day arrived. Emily woke me early, while it was still dark out.

"I think it's time," she said.

I bounded out of bed, got dressed, and went to fetch the doctor. For the last few nights, I had kept Betty saddled for just this kind of emergency. I pulled the doctor out of his house half dressed. *He* had not had the foresight to keep his buggy hitched up. I told him to take Betty and get to the damn house. I would follow on foot.

I ran most of the way, but still it took me a half hour to get there.

I burst through the door to see the doctor seated in the parlor. "Shouldn't you be in with Emily?" I asked.

"I just left her. She's fine."

"But shouldn't you be in there? The baby could come at any minute."

"The baby has already come. It came right after I got here."

"What is it? A boy or a girl?"

The doctor pointed to a chair. "Sit with me for a moment. I have something to tell you. Then you can go in and see your wife."

My heart sank. I didn't know what he wanted to say, but, somehow, I knew it couldn't be good. I fell into the chair, not because he had asked me to, but because my legs had failed me.

I was afraid to say anything, afraid to ask anything, I was just plain afraid. He wore a heavy look on his face. "Mister Mahoney, there's no other way to say it, but your baby came to us still-born. I'm sorry."

"What? Where? Where is the baby? Was it a boy or a girl?" I didn't know what I was saying. Then it dawned on me. Why was I talking to this man? I should be in there with Emily. How she must be feeling! I bolted from the chair and ran to her side. She was sitting up in bed, quietly crying. I sat down beside her and hugged her with all the love I had in me.

322

"Where's the baby?" I asked. She pointed to the crib I had recently bought. In it lay a swaddled little bundle. "Boy or girl?" I asked.

"Girl," she whispered through her tears.

I walked over and lifted a corner of the blanket. I *had* to see my daughter. She looked so beautiful and so tiny. After what seemed like a long time, and perhaps it was, I laid the blanket back over her little face.

We buried her in Rosedale Cemetery. I had a stone carved for the grave. It reads simply:

Little Mary Mahoney
Born June 15 1893
Died June 15 1893

35

It took me a while to come to terms with our loss, but it was harder for Emily. Even though she presented a brave face as she went about her day, I had the feeling she had not fully recovered from our tragedy. She was not the same woman who had stood shoulder to shoulder with me as we drilled Emily #1.

Her father came to visit more frequently than he had before. He, too, could tell there was something sadly amiss. He suggested I take her to San Francisco to get her mind off things. "You can sail up there, and without a doubt, the sea air will do her good. San Francisco has more of a cultural life than we do here. Take her to the theater. She was always interested in that sort of thing when she was a little girl."

"If you think that will help," I said. "I'll book passage first thing tomorrow morning."

It was indeed a wonderful experience. We attended the theatre and dined in fine restaurants. Emily was delighted with the dress shops, especially the ones carrying the latest Paris fashions. After three weeks, we returned home invigorated. But most importantly, the trip had put the bloom back in her cheeks. The healing process had begun.

≈ ≈ ≈

By January of 1894, Johnny and I were raking in close to eighty-five thousand dollars a year on our oil leases. My share came to fifty-one thousand a year. *And* I had over one hundred thousand dollars sitting in the bank. That made David Johansson, my father-in-law, a little nervous.

"You must let your money work for you," he advised. "One day those wells are going to run dry. Then what will you do?"

I'll still be rich, I thought. But aloud, I said, "What do you suggest?"

"Why not meet with my stock broker? He's good at what he does, and he can tell you where to place your money so you'll get a better return on it than any bank will ever give you."

"Sure, David, I'll meet with your man. What's his name and how do I find him?"

"His name is Jeremiah Healy. I'll arrange a meeting between you two."

I rode up to Prospect Avenue in the town of Hollywood, where Johnny had built himself a house. I wanted to see if he would like to take advantage of Mister Healy's counsel.

"I don't think so, Dillon. I've got close to ninety thousand dollars, and more coming in every day. That oughta last me."

We were standing in Johnny's kitchen, as he busied himself making his famous stew. Back at the beginning, when we were living at the drill site and it was his turn to do the cooking, that's what he always made, *Johnny's Famous Irish Stew*.

Continuing with our conversation, I said, "If I didn't have Emily, I might think along similar lines. But I have to plan for her and any children that might come along."

Johnny was busy cutting vegetables and only partially focused on the discussion at hand.

"You seem preoccupied. Want me to go?"

"Of course not. It's just that I have a lady friend coming by for dinner and this meal has to be perfect. Tonight I'm going to ask her to marry me."

I was flabbergasted. I had always thought of Johnny as a confirmed bachelor.

"Congratulations! What's her name? Have I met her?"

"Her name is Virginia. And no, you have not met her."

"You must bring her over sometime. Emily and I would be honored to meet her. I'll tell you what. I'm sure Emily would love to throw a dinner party for the two of you, so why don't you talk to your lady friend and we'll set about arranging things."

≈ ≈ ≈

I eventually met with Jeremiah Healy and he advised me to invest in banks and insurance companies. "They're both rock-solid

325

investments and will provide for you and your family long after your oil wells have run dry," he counseled.

I told him I didn't know anything about investing or which banks and insurance companies, in particular, to invest in.

"If you authorize me to act as your agent, I'll do the legwork and deliver the stock certificates to your office."

I had to explain to him that I did not have an office. But once we got that straightened out, I authorized him to buy thirty thousand dollars' worth of bank and insurance stocks in my name. And just like that, I was diversified, a man of means in a rapidly changing world.

$$\approx \approx \approx$$

Emily's duties in running the house did not take up much of her time. And I had absolutely nothing to do most days. Being rich was turning out to be kind of boring. But we had each other, and with the grace of God, we would soon have children to occupy our days.

I started taking Emily with me on my rides up into the hills, and like me, she loved to look out at the endless blue ocean. Sometimes, we would pack a picnic lunch and stay up there all day. I must confess that, on occasion, right there on the picnic blanket, we gave it our best effort to conceive another child. Those were the days that we fell in love all over again. But now it was a deeper love because of our shared sorrow at little Mary's stillbirth.

It was the beginning of February, a cool, pleasant evening, when Johnny brought his lady love to dinner. Her full name was Virginia Howell, a stately raven-haired beauty, with almond-colored eyes. She was from New York and had come to Los Angeles to be a schoolteacher. One look at her and the way she looked at Johnny, you could tell she was in love. As for Johnny, there was no doubt that he was in love.

We had also invited Emily's father. It was to be a special night for many reasons.

Virginia and Emily hit it off right away. They disappeared into the kitchen and us men were left to our own devices, which meant bringing out a bottle of the "good stuff" and seeing how much of it we could drink before the women returned.

Emily had outdone herself. The meal was superb. Halfway through, she caught my eye and nodded. That was my cue.

I tapped my fork to my water glass to get everyone's attention.

I addressed the newly-engaged couple first. "Virginia, Johnny is an old and dear friend of ours. If you're with him, then you are also our friend. We are so happy to finally meet you and wish you and Johnny endless happiness together." Then, turning to Emily's father, I continued: "We have yet another good cause to celebrate."

Emily was sitting at the other end of the table. I would have preferred having her next to me when I gave my little speech. But I had already started the ball rolling, so on I went.

"Emily is going to have a baby, and we wanted you, our dear friends, to be the first to know."

Virginia squealed with delight. Johnny slapped me on the back and David shook my hand.

David asked Emily, "When's the baby due?"

With the candlelight reflecting in her silver-blue eyes and an angelic smile playing across her face, she had never looked more beautiful.

"The beginning of August," she responded.

After dinner, while the women were at the table talking of womanly things, us men withdrew to the parlor. David took out a cigar and did the usual rigamarole. When at last he had it lit, he said, "I think you should look into hiring a housekeeper to help Emily around the house. She's got to take it easy this time."

"It hadn't occurred to me. But you're right. However, it might take some doing to sell Emily on the idea."

David chewed on his cigar for a moment. "It doesn't matter what she wants. I admit, she can be a bit headstrong, but you're the man of the house. Put your foot down."

Easier said than done.

"I don't know. I'll bring it up after you leave. If she's receptive to the idea, I'll find someone. If not, I can't force a housekeeper on her. I only wish I could."

That's when Johnny spoke up. "I know of a Mexican woman that would be perfect for what you want. She's about thirty years old, a widow. She worked for a family I knew, but they went back East. Magdalena, that's her name, is very efficient and she's a sweetheart. And the best thing for your purpose is the fact that she's also a midwife. That might prove useful if things start to happen before the doctor can get here."

I said to David, "She sounds ideal. What do you think?"

"I think you better hire her before someone else snaps her up."

Johnny had another thought, and it was a good one. "I wouldn't tell Emily about hiring a housekeeper tonight if you think she might be opposed to the idea. Let her meet Magdalena first. She won't be able to help but like her. I'll bring her by in the morning, sometime before noon."

A moment later, Emily and Virginia came into the room and we three conspirators ceased our conspiratorial conversation and stood up out of respect for the fairer sex.

"Would anyone like a brandy?" I inquired, innocently.

≈ ≈ ≈

I need not have worried. Emily took to Magdalena immediately, and it appeared the feeling was mutual. When I said I was thinking of hiring her to help out around the house, Emily put up no fight at all. In fact, she was all for it.

Magdalena was a first-class cook, an excellent housekeeper, and more importantly, a good friend to Emily—in short, she was a godsend.

One day, soon after Magdalena had come to live with us, Emily told me her story. We were out in our yard, sitting in the shade of an old oak tree. "It's so tragic. Her husband and their only child, a boy, were drowned in a flash flood. Their bodies were never found. That was ten years ago. She was just a child of eighteen."

I was watching a flock of birds flying overhead, which held my interest for a moment. When they had passed, I said, "You'd never know it from her demeanor. She's always smiling and cheerful—always the first one with an encouraging word when it's needed."

≈ ≈ ≈

There was no question about it. Emily would no longer be riding with me into the hills. In fact, we had decided she would not ride her

328

horse again until after the baby was born. If she had to get around town, there were plenty of street cars available.

As the pregnancy progressed, I was loathe to leave Emily alone. True, Magdalena was in the house; however, I wanted to be close by in the event something happened. The baby was not due for months, but I was taking no chances this time.

It finally became too much for her. "Dillon, you're underfoot. Magdalena and I are trying to do our spring cleaning and you're in the way. I promise, when the time gets close, you can be underfoot all you want. But for now, please go and visit Johnny, or go see Mister Healy and catch up on how much money you're making."

I loved her so much. We kissed, and then she shooed me from the room.

In late May, Johnny informed me that he and Virginia would be going back East to get married.

"Shucks, Johnny. That means Emily and I won't be able to attend the wedding!"

"I'm sorry, Dillon, and I'd love to have you there. But Virginia is set on being married by her father. He's a preacher and she promised him when the time came, he would be the one performing the ceremony."

"So, you're going to New York."

"I've never been there. It might be interesting."

"Is it New York City that you'll be going?"

"Someplace north of there, someplace in the country. But we'll be honeymooning in New York City."

"Not Niagara Falls?"

"No. Virginia's already been there many times as a tourist. She has her heart set on going to the big city."

"Well, you can't leave without us giving you a send-off. How about Rosie's Steakhouse? It's where Emily and I got reacquainted. It's kinda sentimental for us."

A few days later, I was at the train depot, standing on the platform with Johnny. Emily was at home and Virginia had already boarded the train. Johnny stuck out his hand and said, "Well, amigo, it sure was my lucky day the day I ran into you."

I shook his hand and said, "Likewise, partner." He gave me a brisk nod and got on the train. We had already said our goodbyes at Rosie's the night before; there was nothing left to say.

≈ ≈ ≈

As the morning sunlight slanted in through the windows and danced playfully across our bed, Emily opened her eyes. "Good morning, Dillon, my love." Her eyes held me, her smile owned me.

I had been lying there, looking at her as she slept. "Good morning, Beautiful. And how are you this fine morning?"

She moved closer and we kissed. "I'm famished. But let's stay in bed for a little while longer."

I agreed. Entwined in each other's arms, we listened as the birds sang their morning songs. We believed they were singing for us alone, in celebration of our happiness.

At length, we pulled ourselves out of bed and went downstairs.

"Buenos días, Señor y Señora."

"Good morning, Magdalena," said Emily.

"What's for breakfast?" I asked.

"You sit yourself down and you will find out, *Señor*," was Magdalena's playful reply.

In the late afternoon when things had cooled down, Emily and I would take long walks in an adjacent orange grove. The sunlight filtering through the trees dappled the dry, brown earth; the scent of orange blossoms filled the air. We would hold hands and talk about our future and what a wonderful future it would be with a house full of children.

In the evenings, after dinner, we would sit in the parlor, happy, contented, and satisfied with our lives. Emily knitting a baby blanket, me reading the newspapers. At times, Emily would ask me to come to her. And without saying a word, she would place my hand on her swollen belly, so I might feel the baby move.

≈ ≈ ≈

The day started out like any other. We went down to breakfast, sausage and egg tortillas. Magdalena was slowly introducing us to food with more of a Mexican flavor, but we didn't mind. Everything she prepared was delicious.

We had just finished eating when Emily bent over in pain. "The contractions are starting," she gasped. By then we had a telephone and so did our doctor. I ran to the parlor and rang him up, but the fool was out on a call. I left word with his wife that he was to come to our house directly upon his return. "My wife is having her baby!" I yelled into the contraption's mouthpiece. I dropped the receiver without replacing it on its hook and ran out of the room.

When I got back to the dining room, Magdalena was standing next to Emily, who wore a chagrined look on her face. "I'm sorry, Dillon. That was just the first one. It may be a while before the baby comes. That's what Magdalena says."

I decided to take charge until the doctor came. "Magdalena! Take Emily upstairs and get her into bed, right now!" The women exchanged a look, but they obeyed. As Emily passed me, she said, "Listen to me, Dillon Mahoney, this baby will be born healthy. It will be a boy and his name will be David ... David John Mahoney."

The doctor finally arrived and consulted with Emily and Magdalena. I was not allowed in the room. When he came out, he said, "She's doing fine, Mister Mahoney. Her contractions are far enough apart that I don't expect the baby until later this evening. Magdalena will know when it's time."

"But what if something happens before then?"

"Like I said, Magdalena will know what to do. When the time comes, your job will be to call me. I can be here in a few minutes."

"But ..."

"Mister Mahoney, do you have any liquor in the house?"

"Yes, but ..."

"I want you to pour yourself a stiff shot. No, upon further reflection, make that two stiff shots. Drink 'em both down to calm your nerves and call me when Magdalena tells you to."

Instead of following his advice, I went right upstairs to Emily.

"How are you feeling?"

"I'm fine."

"The last time, you gave birth less than an hour after your first contraction."

"That was not ordinary. Both Magdalena and the doctor have said so. This will be a normal birth. I know it for certain."

"What can I do?"

"You can do what expectant fathers have done since the beginning of time."

"What's that?"

Laughing, she said, "You can pace back and forth and worry."

I leaned over and kissed her. "Alright, if you say so. The doctor prescribed something to relax me. It's in the parlor. And as soon as I've taken my medicine, as prescribed, I'll come right back. Perhaps I can read the *Daily Times* to you, so you'll be up on all the latest news, including the gossip."

"That will be fine, Dillon. And don't worry. This baby *is* healthy. I can feel him, and he's ready to come into the world. This time tomorrow, we'll be a family of three."

I sat with Emily most of the day. I wouldn't let her go downstairs for lunch. I had Magdalena bring it up and we ate in our bedroom. The contractions increased in frequency as the day wore on. Still, neither Emily nor Magdalena seemed the least bit concerned, unlike me. Along about sunset, I had to go downstairs and partake of another healthy shot of "medicine." I was a nervous wreck.

About nine that night, Emily asked me to get Magdalena. The women conferred in hushed tones, then informed me it was time to call the doctor.

When the doctor entered the bedroom, the first thing he did was ask me to leave the room. I looked at Emily and she said, "Magdalena is in the kitchen boiling water, you can carry it up here for her."

Upon completing my chore, I went to Emily and took her hand. She had just had a contraction and sweat beaded her brow. She gave me a weak smile and said, "I'm in good hands. You go downstairs and wait. Your son will be here soon."

I started to lean over to give her a kiss, but just then another contraction hit. I squeezed her hand instead and went down to the parlor. I tried sitting in my chair, but I couldn't. I had to pace. When I couldn't take the strain any longer, I took a slug of rye right from the bottle. That didn't help. At one point, I even prayed.

After what seemed an eternity, I heard a baby's cry. I ran upstairs and burst into the room. Magdalena was at the basin washing the baby. Emily was lying on the bed, she looked to be asleep.

The doctor took me by the arm and led me from the room. "Congratulations, you have a healthy baby boy. Now, give us a minute to clean things up and for Emily to recover. She's a little worn out, but other than that, she appears to be fine."

A short while later, I was allowed in. Emily was sitting up, holding our son. She looked angelic. For a moment, I thought I saw a halo around her head. I sat in a chair that had been pulled up next to the bed. "How are you feeling?" I asked.

"I'm a little weak, but that's to be expected. Would you like to meet your son?"

I leaned in and took a good look. "He sure is a handsome boy."

"Of course he is. He takes after you."

She was awful pale.

"Doctor. Can you come here for a moment?"

He was in the midst of rolling down his shirt sleeves, but he came over.

"Look how pale she is."

He asked me to get up from the chair and he took my place. The first thing he did was tell Magdalena to take the baby. I took a step back as he started to examine her.

"DOCTOR, LOOK!" I was pointing to a crimson stain forming on the top sheet.

He looked back, then jumped to his feet and pulled the sheet away to reveal a steadily increasing pool of blood between Emily's legs.

"What is it, doctor? What's wrong?" I demanded.

"She's hemorrhaging."

I was frantic. "What the hell is that?"

"She's bleeding on the inside."

"DO SOMETHING!" I shouted.

He turned on me and practically pushed me from the room. Before slamming the door, he said, "I can't do anything with you hovering over me and yelling in my ear."

It was probably the only thing he could have said that would have kept me from barging right back in. What was important was Emily. I couldn't help her, only the doctor could. I'd do my part by staying out of his way. But I did not budge from that hallway.

Many, many years later, the doctor opened the door. His expression said it all. I looked past him and saw Emily. A sheet covered her body.

The doctor put his hand on my shoulder. "I'm sorry, son, but there was nothing I could do."

I was numb. I went to Emily and knelt down and cried. Through my tears, I asked out loud how God could let a woman—a new mother—die like that.

The doctor stood next to me. "I want you to know she did not suffer. She went into shock because of the loss of blood and then she was gone."

"Please, doctor. I want to be alone with my wife. You, too, Magdalena. Take the baby. I'll be down presently."

When they had gone, I asked Emily why she had to leave me. *How am I supposed to raise a child without you? How am I expected to live without you?* If she answered from The Great Beyond, I did not hear her.

By the time I'd gone downstairs, the doctor had left.

"He has gone to make arrangements with the undertaker," Magdalena informed me.

"Fine!" I seethed, and brushed past her, headed for the parlor.

"Don't you want to hold your baby?" she called out after me.

"Not right now."

I came out of the parlor wearing my old six-shooter.

Magdalena was still where I had left her and she was still holding the baby. "What are you doing?" she asked.

"I don't know, Magdalena. I don't know what I'm doing, but I have to do something."

I started for the door, but she blocked the way. "*Señor* Dillon, you listen to me. You think you're the only one who has ever lost a loved one? The only one who ever felt the pain that you're feeling now? I lost my man *and* my baby. I wanted to die, but I went on because that's the way the world works. You have a baby that needs you ..."

"I also had a wife that *I* needed."

"Be quiet. I needed my husband and child. If I could only have them back." At that point, a tear trickled down her cheek and her voice wavered. "But I can't have them back. I'll *never* have them back. I'll never be whole again. But I go on because that is all I can do.

"If you go out and get yourself shot up, or worse yet, kill someone, what will become of David? Look at him. There's a part of Emily inside this beautiful little baby. If you loved her, then for her sake, you must be here to raise her child. And you can't do that if you're dead or in prison."

Filled with rage and indecision, I glowered at the woman tenderly holding my son. She unflinchingly stared right back at me until finally, overcome with emotion, I hung my head, unstrapped the gun belt, and let it fall to the floor. "Get rid of that, Magdalena. I never want to see it again. Now, hand me my baby."

I took David into the parlor and sat down in Emily's chair. Soon we were both crying. He for his own reasons, and I for mine.

36

On a rainy day, two days after David's birth, August 7, 1895, to be exact, we buried Emily. She now sleeps in eternal peace in Rosedale Cemetery, next to Mary, our little girl. Magdalena became David's wet nurse. And I, his father, was at a loss on how to raise my son. However, with Magdalena's help, patience, and perseverance, I soon grew into a reasonable approximation of what a father should be.

David took his first step at nine months, and Magdalena and I were as proud as could be. However, the joy I felt at seeing my son take his first step was bittersweet. Emily should have been there to see it. Once David started walking, he was a handful. But I loved playing with him, even though it was tiring at times. I never knew children had such unlimited energy.

When David turned three, I started taking him for long walks around the city, or we would ride streetcars to the end of the line and then walk back home. In this way, David discovered a whole new world outside his house.

In our travels, we had seen a few "horseless carriages" on the streets. And whenever I had the chance to talk to an owner of one of those things, I did so. They were always proud of their machines and would go on at length telling me of their many attributes. One man even took us for a ride. David was thrilled and so was I.

I bought my first automobile in 1898, a Duryea. The old girl ran well on her one-cylinder, four-horsepower engine, but Magdalena refused to get in it. She believed the noise it made and the smoke it expelled was the Devil's work.

In the fall of 1902, David started school. By then, I owned a Haynes-Apperson Runabout. David was the only child driven to school in an automobile. On the first day, all the children and some of the adults crowded around us as we pulled up and I switched off the magneto. David beamed with pride at being the center of attention.

When he was eight years old, David came to me and asked, "Father, why don't I have a mother?"

A few years earlier, when he was old enough to understand, I had told him that his mother had died when he was a baby.

"Hasn't Magdalena been like a mother to you?"

He fidgeted for a moment before saying, "But I want a *real* mother."

"What is this about, David?"

He averted his eyes. I waited. At length, he said, "All my friends have mothers, and I want one, too."

It was that simple for him. He wanted what everyone else had, something I had hoped he'd outgrow. Well, it was my own doing, I had spoiled him. Magdalena had too, but not to the same extent. I gave him everything he ever asked for. Not once did I deny him anything. Now the chickens were coming home to roost. However, some things were beyond my power to provide. I explained that I had loved his mother very much and I had no intention of remarrying. That was probably the only time in his entire life I did not give him something he had asked for.

It was not only Magdalena and I who spoiled him; his grandfather outdid us both. In 1904, for David's ninth birthday, his grandfather took him to the Louisiana Purchase Exposition in St. Louis.

David returned with stories of wonder. "Father, we saw an airship contest! Giant dirigibles raced overhead. And there were so many people. I have never seen so many people! And guess what? There was an old Indian sitting in a teepee and he would let people take his picture for ten cents. His name was Geronimo. Grandfather told me he had been a great warrior in his day, and that he had killed many white men."

At the mention of Geronimo, I could not help but think of Dasoda-hae and wonder what had become of him.

When David enrolled at the Los Angeles High School, I gave him my 1908 Model T Ford and bought a new one for myself. David was the only pupil in the entire student body with his own car. He was only fifteen years old, and perhaps I should have waited a year or two before giving him an automobile, but he did want one so badly.

337

Money was never a problem. Mister Healy had invested my money wisely. My net worth was now close to two hundred and fifty thousand dollars. And what good is money if you can't use it to make your son happy?

The year David graduated from high school, 1914, his grandfather died, leaving him a trust fund of one hundred thousand dollars that he would have access to on his twenty-first birthday.

We talked, David and I, about what he would do after high school. I asked him if there was a particular profession or trade he might like to go into. He looked at me, horrified. "Work? Why should I work, Father? To what end? We have plenty of money. I thought I'd go to college, just for the fun of it."

"What would you study?"

"I don't know. Something will come to me."

Well, I couldn't fault him on that. It's hard to know what you want to do with the rest of your life when you're only eighteen. I was twenty when I got off that train in Slow Water, and I surely had no idea what I wanted in life.

I suggested he attend Stanford College. "It's a little south of San Francisco, which means you can come home more often than if you were at a college farther away."

Magdalena agreed. "That is an excellent idea. This house will be lonely without you. I think you should be close by and come home as often as possible."

David wasn't having any of that. "I want to go to a school back East. It's too primitive out here. I want to experience a little sophistication. You know, rub shoulders with the upper crust, people of my own class. I do sincerely feel I'd fit in better."

Magdalena and I exchanged looks. Had we raised a snob?

I could have sent David to just about any school in the country. Money was not an issue, but David's grades might be. He had not exactly buckled down and studied while in high school. He skated through and graduated only by the skin of his teeth.

I thought of Pecos Bob Holston's old school, The College of New Jersey. Once he dropped the ignorant cowboy act, he turned out to be a right smart fellow, and he sure had an impressive vocabulary. I figured he had to have learned something while there. By 1914, the school had changed its name to Princeton College.

338

I sent off a telegram to Bob in care of Holston's Original Ale Company in Paterson, New Jersey, asking if he could help me get my son into Princeton. I thought he, being an alumnus, might have some pull. It had been many years since we had parted ways. He might not live in New Jersey any longer, or his company could be out of business, or he could be dead. If he were still alive, he would be about my age, fifty-four.

The next day, I received a reply to my telegram. He was surprised and pleased to have heard from me after all these years. He included his address and asked me to correspond so we could catch up on each other's lives and reminisce about old times. But in the meantime, he advised that David, or I on his behalf, should apply for admission to Princeton. The good news was that the president, John Hibben, was an old family friend. Bob told me not to worry about a thing and to put pen to paper as soon as I could.

That was in early June. By late August, David had been accepted to Princeton.

I accompanied him on the train to New Jersey. After I had him safely enrolled in college, I planned on spending a few days with Bob and his wife. Then I'd go up to New York City and see Johnny. He never did make it back to California. Well, he did, but only long enough to sell his house and say goodbye. He and Virginia had fallen in love with the city and bought a house there. Johnny had gotten into buying and selling real estate, and he was doing quite well at it. Most likely because of his training in selling those lots in Hollywood. Whatever it was, he knew what he was doing and he had made a bundle.

Bob picked me up at the depot, and on the way to his house, he asked me not to bring up any of the old stories from our time out west. "My family doesn't know about my misspent youth. If they ever found out, I'd never hear the end of it. I'm supposed to be a well-respected citizen, if you can believe that."

I believed it. He looked prosperous driving his shiny new Dodge Coupe. "Don't worry, Bob. Your secret is safe with me. Besides, I owe you. I want to thank you for your help in getting my boy into Princeton."

"Think nothing of it, *Marshal*."

I spent two days with Bob and met his family, his very nice wife and his two children, a boy of fifteen and a girl, seventeen. Then it was off to New York.

Johnny was there waiting for me when my train pulled into the station. We slapped each other on the back, shook hands, and asked rapid-fire questions of each other, smiling the whole time. It was good to see him again.

Johnny also drove a Model T. On the way to his house, I remarked, "I have the same kind of automobile. And what a coincidence, mine is also black." We laughed. Black was the only color old Henry Ford painted his cars. He used to say, "You can have any color you want. As long as it's black."

Johnny and Virginia owned a four-story house at the corner of 51st Street and 5th Avenue. I reckoned they needed a large place to hang their hats. They had five children, four of whom lived at home. Their oldest boy, who was the same age as David, was off attending Cornell College. I stayed with them an entire week and enjoyed every moment of it. They showed me around town and we did it up right.

It was with a heavy heart that I boarded the train that would carry me back to Los Angeles. I knew Johnny wasn't much on writing, so I asked Virginia to keep me posted on how things were going. She promised to do so and kissed me on the cheek. Johnny shook my hand, and I was off.

Magdalena was happy to have me back home again. "It has been lonely with both you and David away, *Señor* Mahoney."

"Magdalena, you've lived here almost twenty years. I think it's high time you started calling me Dillon."

Under her olive-dark skin, I think she was blushing. "You are the *jefe*, I must show respect."

"Okay, Magdalena, if you insist."

It turned out David was not much of a letter writer, either. The only time I ever heard from him was when he needed money. I always sent whatever he asked for. Mostly because I harbored a secret guilt. I was trying to make up for the fact that he did not have a mother. Although, God knows, Magdalena was as close to a mother as any woman could be.

Our lives went on. My oil revenues had dropped significantly over the years. The oil was running down. When my leases came up for renewal, I assigned the rights to all of them, except Emily #1, to Edward Doherty for a nominal fee. I kept Emily #1 for sentimental reasons.

Jeremiah Healy came to me on a warm summer day in 1916, carrying a thick portfolio. "In here are all your records, Mister Mahoney. I'll be retiring in a few weeks and I wanted to set everything straight.

"As you know, well over ninety percent of your income is derived from the stocks we've bought over the years. I think I've done well by you, if I say so myself."

"On that we are in total agreement, my good friend."

He accepted the compliment with a smile.

"If you'd like, I can recommend a stock broker or you can find one on your own."

I accepted the bulging portfolio from Healy's thin hands. "I don't think I'll be diversifying any further. You've made a lot of money for me, Jeremiah, and I want to thank you."

"Just doing my job, Mister Mahoney."

"Can you stay for lunch?"

"Thank you, no. I have other calls to make. I just want you to know that it's been a pleasure working for you."

We shook hands and I watched him shuffle on out to his horse and buggy. He knew the stock market inside out, but automobiles were a little too complicated for Jeremiah Healy.

I missed David. In the few letters he did send our way, he told me about his new friends, many of whom had invited him home for various holidays. I saw less and less of him as his schooling progressed. I couldn't blame him for not coming home. It was a three-day train trip as opposed to a quick jaunt by automobile to a palatial estate in Newport or out on Long Island.

Just before David turned twenty-one, President Wilson signed into law the Selective Service Act of 1917. That meant David would have to register for the draft. And in all likelihood, he would be sent overseas to France. The United States had finally entered the Great War.

David wrote, beseeching me to do something. But there wasn't anything I could do. Deferments were limited and did not include students. He took the news badly and accused me of not *wanting* to help him.

He stated emphatically that he was not going to register. "Let them find me! *And*, in four months, when I come into grandfather's inheritance, I plan on quitting school." I wrote back, trying to explain why I couldn't do anything about the draft and how foolish it would be to leave college one year shy of graduating. But I received no answering letter from my son. That's when I lost touch with him. It would be six long years before I heard from him again.

By 1923, transcontinental telephone service had finally come to Los Angeles. I was sitting in the parlor after one of Magdalena's delightful dinners, about to delve into the afternoon papers, when the phone rang.

"Hello. Father, can you hear me?"

My heart skipped a beat.

"Yes, David, I can hear you. How are you?"

"I'm fine. I'm just calling to let you know that I'm alive and well. I have a flat in New York City and I'm enjoying life."

He sounded a little drunk, but I wasn't going to say anything and spoil the moment.

"What's all that noise?" I asked.

"Those are some friends of mine. We're on our way to a speakeasy. You know, twenty-three skidoo and all that."

He was starting to sound distracted, and I was desperate not to lose touch with him.

"Will you give me your address so that I can write you?"

"My friends are calling. I have to go. Give my best to Magdalena."

Then all I heard was the sound of a dial tone.

I looked at the clock on the mantel. It was nearing seven o'clock. That meant it was ten o'clock in New York. Too late to call Johnny. But first thing in the morning, I'd call him and see if he could help me find David. I wasn't about to let him disappear for another six years. I was sixty-three years old. I doubted I had another six years left in me.

342

I must not have been thinking straight because Johnny got right to it.

"He should be easy to find. He has to have electricity; the Edison Company will have his address."

"How do I approach them? I wouldn't know where to start."

"You don't have to do anything. I'll hire a Pinkerton. This kind of thing is right up their alley."

"A Pinkerton?"

"A detective. Leave everything to me. I'll have his address in twenty-four hours."

It was more like forty-eight hours. But now that I knew where to find David, I boarded an eastbound train and headed for New York.

Rolling across The Great Plains, I thought back to my one and only cattle drive for Bill Slokum. I remembered Jack Bridges and all that he had taught me. Which got me to thinking of the hot-headed kid I was in those days. Imagine! Strapping on a six-shooter and going on the trail of a known killer. Was that really me?

I wasn't going to New York to drag David home. He was twenty-seven years old. He knew his own mind. I was going to New York to see my son because I missed him and I loved him.

I hailed a Checker cab outside Pennsylvania Station and gave the driver David's address. It was a short ride. As I exited the cab, I was having second thoughts. But I had come three thousand miles for this, so I squared my shoulders and went inside.

On the ride up in the elevator, I asked the operator if he knew Mister Mahoney.

"Yes, sir. He's a wild one, but very generous. You know, he gave me a twenty-dollar tip for Christmas last year."

When the operator opened the elevator door, I hesitated. I was actually afraid. Would David slam the door in my face? Would he not even open it when he knew it was me?

"Just to your right, sir. Down the hall. Number 1026," said the helpful elevator operator.

"Thank you," I said and stepped into the hallway.

Taking a deep breath, I proceeded to apartment 1026 and knocked. There was no answer. I knocked again. Still no answer. I noticed the doorbell button for the first time and gave it a vigorous ring. From inside, I heard, "Alright, already! I'm coming."

The door flew open and there stood David. Even though it was one o'clock in the afternoon, I could tell he had just roused himself from sleep. He was wearing a wrinkled tuxedo and only one shoe. It must have been some party.

He blinked a time or two. When his vision cleared, he said, "Father?"

"May I come in, David?"

He took a step back and waved me inside with a pretentious flourish.

The apartment was a mess. Ashtrays overflowed, empty gin bottles littered the floor. You'd never know there was a prohibition against alcohol. On the couch, a diminutive blonde snored softly.

"A friend of yours?" I asked.

"That's Jenny. She can't hold her booze."

I stood there a moment, not knowing what to say. David swayed on his feet, looking like The Wreck of the Hesperus. At length he said, "Find a seat, have a drink if you want, if there's any left. I'll be right back."

He returned a few minutes later, minus the tuxedo jacket and wearing a dressing gown. He had found his other shoe and he had combed his hair.

I was still standing. He brushed debris from a chair and said, "Please have a seat. If you don't mind, I'll help myself to a little hair of the dog that bit me. Are you sure you won't join me?"

"No, thank you. It's a little early for me." I didn't mean for it to sound judgmental, but that's the way it came out. I'd have to watch myself. I had not traveled three thousand miles to start a fight.

David had caught the inflection in my voice. "That's all right, Father. I can drink enough for the two of us."

"Is there a place where we can talk without disturbing your friend Jenny?"

"I have a sitting room and I believe it's relatively free of snoring damsels. As soon as I get the fizz in this gin, we'll repair to that sanctuary and you can tell me what you're doing here in New York."

Sitting across from David, with his bloodshot eyes and a drink in his hand, I said, "It's been a long time. I've missed you, and so has Magdalena. You could have enlightened us occasionally on how you

344

were doing. At the very least, you could have let us know that you were still alive."

He looked hungover and bored. I was beginning to think my cross-country trip had been in vain.

"Look, David, I am not judging you. You're a grown man, entitled to do as you please. I would just like you in my life. Is that asking too much?"

He took a gulp of his drink and said, "No, Father. That is not too much to ask. But you have to understand that I have my own life now. However, in the future, I'll be in touch more than I have been. I promise."

I reckoned that was the best I could hope for and thought it wise not to press my luck. But there was one thing I was curious about. "What are you going to do when your money runs out? This apartment looks like it costs a pretty penny, and I'm sure you have other expenses. One hundred thousand dollars won't last you for the rest of your life. Not at the rate you're spending it."

He stared into his glass and said nothing. It took a few ticks, but at last it dawned on me. "You expect to inherit my money when I die."

"Who else you gonna leave it to?"

I had to admit, he had all his bases covered.

"You're right, David. Everything I have will be yours. I just want you to know I love you. I daresay if your mother had lived, you wouldn't be as spoiled as you are. She would have seen to that. Neither the world nor I owe you a living, Son, but perhaps I raised you to think otherwise. If there's any fault, it is my own. I'll go now, but before I do, can you give your old man a hug to send him on his way?"

He stood up, came over, put one arm around me, and gave me a half-hearted squeeze.

I saw Johnny before I left New York and thanked him for his help. And that's the way my life stood for the next seven years. David kept his promise and called occasionally, usually around Christmas time. That was it. Still, it was better than nothing.

In March of '27, Magdalena passed away in her sleep. She now resides in Rosedale, next to Mary and Emily. There's one plot left next to them and that will be mine before too long.

345

In 1928, my bank stocks doubled in value. I was close to being a millionaire. But shortly thereafter, on that fateful Tuesday in 1929, a black day for everyone, I lost everything. I was seventy years old and didn't mind all that much. I owned the house and still had a small income from Emily #1.

I sat back and waited for the inevitable phone call. It was not long in coming.

"Hello, Father. Can you hear me?"

"Yes, David, I can hear you."

"Good. You know, I've missed you, and I was thinking of coming home for a visit."

"I would love to see you. When are you coming?"

"Why wait? I'll buy my tickets today."

"That's fine. I assume you can find your way to the house. I'd come to meet you, but I'm not getting around like I used to. Old age, ya know."

It was good to see David. It took him a few days to work up the nerve to broach the subject he had traveled so far to discuss. It was after dinner. We were sitting in the parlor, glasses of brandy in hand. I still had access to good liquor. It came up through Mexico.

David remarked how well I looked for my age. Then he dove into it.

"This Wall Street crash has really played havoc with my finances. How are you faring?"

"Much like the rest of the country."

He looked a little green around the gills. "You can't be. People are always going to need oil."

I asked him if he would like some more brandy.

"I think I could use it," he said, honestly.

"Please help yourself."

Once settled back in his chair, he said, "What do you mean, you're doing like the rest of the country?"

"I mean, I'm broke."

"*YOU CAN'T BE!*"

"No need to shout. I can hear you."

"I'm sorry. It just came as a shock."

Up until then, I had been playing a little cat-and-mouse with him. But I didn't have it in me to take it any further.

346

"David, I know you only came here because you need money. I wish I could help you. But all I own is this house. It will be yours when I pass, but until then, I need a place to live. And I'd never give it up while I'm alive because this is your mother's house. She planned every part of it. It's all that remains of her. It's all I have."

He stood abruptly, sloshing a little brandy onto the rug, and started to pace the width of the room. I didn't say anything. I knew he'd get to it in a moment or two.

"You sit there with that smug look on your face. You're old, what have you ever done with your life except drill an oil well? You've told me time and time again about my Grandfather Mahoney and how he came to this country. And how hard he had it, and compared to him, how easy I have it. Well, I'm tired of hearing about Devin Mahoney. What about *David* Mahoney?

"How could you do this to me, Father? How am I supposed to live? You owed it to me not to lose my inheritance … my birthright."

"Have you gone through one hundred thousand dollars in … what … thirteen years?"

He turned and looked directly at me for the first time since he'd come home. "It's really not that much money. It goes fast."

I sipped my brandy and smiled inwardly. This might be a blessing in disguise. Perhaps our reduced circumstances would force David, at thirty-five years of age, into becoming a productive member of society. Perhaps it would make a man of him.

It was a short-lived hope.

"Okay for you. I have many friends in New York and when I ask for their help, they'll help me, unlike you. I don't even know why I came here."

He sat back down and finished off his brandy.

"Help yourself to some more," I offered.

We did not speak for the rest of the evening.

He left in the morning and I haven't heard from him since. I could have told him about the cancer that is eating me from the inside out. I could have told him I had only a few months left and then the house would be his. But I didn't. He'll find out soon enough.

Part Three
David

37

The rhythmic rolling of the steel wheels, combined with the swaying of the coach, lulled the passengers to sleep as the train sped through the night. But not so for David Mahoney; he was a worried man.

His world had suddenly been transformed from one of leisure to one of vexation. He'd spent his entire life in pampered splendor. First his father had indulged his every whim, and then, when he reached his majority, one hundred thousand dollars had been handed to him on a silver platter. It had been liberating to be able to gratify one's desires with no thought to necessity and no matter how extravagant.

Having read that both Al Capone and Greta Garbo drove a Duesenberg Model J, David also sported around town in one. His was the same color as Miss Garbo's, burgundy. It had set him back some. But what was money for, if not to make one's life more pleasurable?

His flat was located in the sharpest part of town where swank speakeasies abounded. Where a man could eat at the best restaurants without being accosted by the lower classes. And when he brought women back to his apartment after an evening of making the rounds, they were always impressed that he lived on Park Avenue, a locale nearly as fashionable as 5th Avenue.

The thought of his apartment, with its lovely view of the city, further creased his brow and deepened the dread in his heart. He was two months behind in his rent. There would be a confrontation with the manager. There was no doubt about that. However, the showdown might be averted or at least delayed if, upon his return, he entered through the rear of the building.

No. I will not sneak, skulk, or slip in surreptitiously like a thief in the night!

He had lived at the Carlton Arms for nearly six years and had always paid his rent on time—until now. He would tell the manager that he would just have to wait an additional day or two and that the rent would be paid before the end of the week.

But where would he get the dough? If only the old man had not lost all his money. Well, no use thinking about that. He could sell his car, though he would hate to do so. She sure was a beauty. Or he could ask a friend for a loan. Yes! That's it. On a nightly basis, his apartment was lousy with friends. Any one of them would gladly float a small loan in his direction.

David Mahoney leaned back and relaxed for the first time since leaving Los Angeles. The crease lines on his forehead smoothed and the dread in his heart dissipated. Perhaps now he could get a little sleep. With a contented sigh, he closed his eyes.

$$\approx \approx \approx$$

As David entered the lobby of his apartment building, the day manager approached in an obsequious manner. "Excuse me, Mister Mahoney. May I have a word with you?"

David displayed his most winning smile. "Not now, Mister Pembroke. I'm just coming from the train station and I'm rather fatigued."

The obsequiousness vanished quite suddenly. "I'm dreadfully sorry, *sir*. But I must insist. It will take but a moment."

David looked around the lobby, not for an avenue of escape, just as an instinctive response. "Very well, Mister Pembroke, what do you want?"

Pembroke's demeanor softened. "Perhaps, Mister Mahoney, you would prefer to have this conversation in my office?"

David gave a curt nod and said, "Lead on."

Once seated, Pembroke behind the desk, David in front, they got down to business.

"Mister Mahoney, your rent is three months in arrears. We'll need payment today or else we'll have to ask you to vacate the premises."

David shifted uncomfortably and ran his fingers through his hair. Trying for a lifeline, *any* lifeline, he said, "Surely, it's only been two months."

"I'm sorry, Mister Mahoney, as of five days ago, it's three."

352

A soft sepulchral smile played across David's face. "Well, I was in California on business. Time slips away. You know how it is."

He went on: "This Wall Street mess has wreaked havoc with my finances. That's why I was in California, endeavoring to straighten things out."

"I understand, Mister Mahoney. Would you like to write a check now?"

This was the moment of truth, so David lied. "My bank in California is wiring me money. You'll have a check on your desk tomorrow, at the latest."

The manager seemed relieved. These types of situations always distressed him. Thank God they were few and far between.

The first thing David did upon entering his apartment was pick up the phone. There was no dial tone. *Damn! I should have paid the bill before leaving. But I couldn't, could I? I needed all the cash I was capable of scraping together for that fruitless trip out to California. At least the electricity is still on. I made sure* that *bill was paid.*

He had had the foresight to have a bottle of gin on hand for his return. He needed a drink and he needed it strong. He had some thinking to do.

Sitting on the couch, holding a large glass of gin mixed with very little tonic and no ice, David contemplated his options.

How much ready cash did he have on hand? He went through his pockets and came up with two hundred fourteen dollars and fifty-seven cents. That was it. There was nothing in the bank. Hell, there wasn't even a bank any more.

David could not blame his predicament on The Crash. He had pretty well gone through his inheritance by the time the bottom fell out. His car alone had cost him thirteen thousand dollars. What was he thinking? Just because that bitch Garbo drove a Duesenberg didn't mean he had to run out and buy one. That was one hell of an extravagant expense.

And his apartment! Five hundred dollars a month! He had been happy at his old digs, but he had relocated uptown because his friends lived uptown. Another foolish move on his part, no pun intended.

First things first. He would approach Blake Sheldon for a loan. Blake was young and rich. A man about town as David was ... or had been. Good ol' Blake. He can always be counted on in times of trouble. Next, David would have to sell his car. The proceeds from that should hold him for a while. By then, hopefully, the old man will have gone on to his Great Reward and he could get his hands on the house and sell it.

All in all, there wasn't that much to worry about. It looked as though he was good for a year. By then things should have rebounded and he'd figure out some way to make a living. How hard could it be? This was a big, rich country. His friends who came from Old Money would help him find something. He'd call Blake from the phone booth at the corner.

$$\approx \approx \approx$$

"Hello, Blake? This is David Mahoney."

"Hello, Old Sport. When did you get back in town?"

"Just now."

"How about we meet at Maxie's for a drink and you can tell me all about California?"

David had told his friends he was going to California to visit his father, nothing more than that.

"That sounds good, Blake. I gotta talk to you about something anyway."

"I'll leave the office early and see you there about four."

Asking for a loan was going to be embarrassing, but it beat the alternative. He would also have to ask Blake to keep it under his hat. He did not want word getting around about his being insolvent.

Maxie's was located downtown, and Blake was already sitting at a table when David walked in. The darkened room and its welcoming atmosphere of good comradeship instantly lifted his spirits.

"Sorry I'm late. The battery on my car was dead. It took me a while to find a cab."

"That's alright, David. Would you like some 'tea'?"

At Maxie's, the booze was served in tea pots and everyone had their individual tea cup.

"Sure. Make mine the usual."

354

"Way ahead of you, old buddy," said Blake as he poured *tea* into David's cup.

After some small talk, David eased into telling Blake about his trip to California and its utter futility.

"I didn't know," said Blake, "that you were in such dire straits."

"Well, I am. What I need now, until I can sell my car, is a short-term loan to enable me to pay my back rent."

"You're gonna sell your car?"

"I don't want to, but I have to."

"She sure is a beauty."

"That she is. But what else can I do?"

Blake Sheldon's eyes gleamed with longing for the Duesenberg. He could easily afford to buy one. However, he had been taught two precepts on his father's knee: You never delve into your principal and you never pay more for anything than you absolutely had to. The Sheldon family had done quite well by adhering to those two simple tenets since the first Sheldon landed on the shores of the New World way back sometime in the mid-1600s. The family had amassed more New York real estate than even the Astors.

David had not noticed the gleam in Blake's eyes and pressed ahead.

"So, I was thinking I'd hit you up for a small loan. Say about five thousand dollars. Just to tide me over this unforeseen little setback."

Blake thought back to something else his father had instilled in him. *"Neither a borrower nor a lender be; / for loan oft loses both itself and friend."* Blake poured more tea into David's cup, stalling for time. At long length, he said, "That's quite a lot of money, David. Haven't you heard there's a depression on?"

David, not getting the direction the conversation was headed, said, "That's not a lot of money to us."

"It seems, at the moment, to be a lot of money to *you*."

It then dawned on David. His good friend was not going to loan him five thousand dollars. He thought for a moment of asking for a lesser amount, but the look on Blake's face told him he'd be lucky if Blake picked up the tab for the afternoon's refreshments. What a fool he had been to think of Blake as a friend in any way, shape, or form.

This was more embarrassing than he had imagined, but he was determined to keep his dignity. David downed what was left in his cup and said, "Thanks anyway, Blake."

After being rebuffed in such a fashion, David could not sit there and make small talk with the man. He was looking for a good exit line when Blake unexpectedly said, "You know, I was thinking. I might be able to see my way clear to helping a friend out, after all. You mentioned something about selling your car. I'll take it off your hands for four."

David blinked and looked confused. "Four? Four what?"

Blake laughed, showing his pearly whites. "Four thousand dollars, of course."

David thought of sharks. If their teeth were as white as Blake's, that would be two things they had in common. "Four thousand dollars! I paid thirteen for it less than a year ago. I can get ten for it anywhere in town, just like that," he said, and snapped his fingers for emphasis.

Blake held up the tea pot, silently asking David if he would like a refill. David shook his head. Blake shrugged and poured what remained in the pot into his own cup while saying, "You don't seem to realize that times are tough, and money is tight."

David shot back. "It seems money's not tight for *you*." He was getting angry. Before Blake could say anything else, David stood up, and without offering to cover his end of the check, stormed out onto the street and into the bright sunlight.

The nerve of that son-of-a-bitch! It just goes to show you never know who your real friends are. That's alright. I'll sell the car first thing in the morning. I should have done that instead of wasting my time going to Blake for help. However, it wasn't a total loss. At least now I know Blake Sheldon for what he is. Well, I have other friends. I've hosted far too many parties where everyone drank my booze and told me what a grand fellow I am. There's Percy Taylor and Philip Pyne. They're two stalwart gentlemen if ever there were stalwart gentlemen. They'll stand by me in my hour of need.

In the morning, after getting the battery charged, David drove to the Duesenberg dealership.

"What! Five thousand dollars? Do you know what that car's worth?"

The owner of the dealership sighed. This was the third Model J someone had tried to sell him in as many weeks. He had bought the other two. Granted, at a good price, but that's what he was in business for, to make money. Why couldn't people understand that? He would have to explain the facts of life to this desperate man standing before him.

"Mister Mahoney, I agree with you. That automobile is worth ten thousand dollars if it's worth a dime. But only if someone comes along and wants to buy it at that price. I'm willing to take a chance that things will get better before too long and I'll be able to sell the car. But that could take months. And there *is* the cost of inventorying it, insurance, and all that.

"If you think you can get a better price elsewhere, then, by all means, do so. Put an ad in the paper and see who responds. I sell Duesenbergs for a living and, believe me, business is way down. Five thousand is my best and final offer. Take it or leave it."

David took it and paid off his back rent. He could not help but smirk as he counted out the cash and placed it on Pembroke's desk. He didn't come right out and say so, but his attitude bespoke: *Never doubt your betters again, my good man.* Afterwards, he was left with close to thirty-five hundred dollars. That should do him until the old man passed on.

Word had gotten around, thanks to Blake, that he was down on his heels. David had spent his life cultivating the rich. Now he was learning that the rich were indeed a fickle and shallow lot.

As the months crept by, he had less and less contact with his friends. Even Percy Taylor and Philip Pyne failed to return his calls. He had stopped throwing parties. What was the use? Few people showed up. Girlfriends suddenly remembered they had to wash their hair when he called for a date. Male friends couldn't break away from work when he called to see if they'd like to have lunch, and their dinner plans had already been made. He was truly persona non grata among his old friends.

By July, two weeks before his thirty-sixth birthday, his money had dwindled to less than five hundred dollars. And his rent was due on the first, ten days away. David Mahoney seemed to be at the end of his tether.

He had given up on his father. The old bird would probably outlive him and everyone else on the planet. What the hell was he going to do? If he paid the upcoming month's rent, he'd be completely broke. And what would that accomplish other than buy him a month's reprieve from total disaster?

He was thinking those thoughts on the day the letter arrived.

≈ ≈ ≈

Peabody, Doyle, and Lane
9 Main Street
Los Angeles, California

July 18, 1930

Mr. David Mahoney
3812 Park Avenue
New York, New York

Dear Mr. Mahoney,

It is my sad duty to inform you of your father's passing. He died the morning of July 10th of this year. The cause of death was cancer of the stomach. I spoke with him a few days before he died and it was then that he gave me his last instructions regarding his estate.

His only asset at the time of his death was the house in which he lived. There had been an oil lease, but that was recently sold and the funds used to pay off his few remaining debts. He was most adamant that the house be free and clear for you. He wanted no liens against it.

I have filed our petition, along with a copy of the will, with the probate court. Now we'll just have to wait. These things usually take three to four months to be resolved. When the probate process is complete, I will forward the deed to you.

If I may be of any further service, or if you have any questions, please contact me at the above address.

Very truly yours,

William F. Lane, Esq.
Peabody, Doyle, and Lane

≈ ≈ ≈

Three or four months! David could not wait that long. He needed money. He needed to sell the house immediately or he was going to be out on the street. The phone had been turned back on; little good it did him, though. No one ever called anymore.

≈ ≈ ≈

"Hello. Long Distance?"
    "Yes, sir. How may I help you?"
    "I need to make a long-distance call to Los Angeles, California."
    "Yes, sir. May I have the number please?"
    "I don't have a number. But I want to talk to William Lane. He's an attorney and his address is 9 Main Street."
    "Very well, sir. I'll call you when the connection goes through."
    "Yeah, thanks."
    David hung up and made himself a stiff drink. He had worked halfway through it when the phone rang.
    "Your call is ready, sir. Please go ahead."
    "Hello?"
    "Hello. This is David Mahoney. I'd like to speak with Mister Lane."
    "This is Lane. I assume you've received my letter."
    "That's why I'm calling. I can't wait three months for this probate thing to go through. It's essential that I sell the house now!"
    "I'm sorry, Mister Mahoney. It's out of my hands."
    "Goddamn it! That house is mine and I want to sell it … now!"

"Calm down, Mister Mahoney. You do not own the house until the probate court says you do. Now if you'll …"

CLICK.

David had slammed the receiver back onto its cradle and reached for the bottle of gin.

Things were getting desperate. He *could* stall Pembroke for a month … maybe two. But then what? Hell! There was no getting around it. He was going to have to relocate to cheaper digs and hunker down until he could get his hands on the house. What was it worth? He should have asked Lane before hanging up on him.

He delayed his departure for as long as possible. But it was stressful. He had to come and go through the back entrance. He did not answer his phone because he was sure it was Pembroke calling. When there was a knock on the door, he stayed quiet until he heard the receding footfalls in the hallway. Finally, he could take it no longer. He had to leave.

He found a small flat in Greenwich Village. Not all his furniture would fit in the new place, so he had to pick and choose what he'd take with him. Certain pieces—the bed, the kitchen table and chairs—definitely. The couch would not fit through the door, and even if he had somehow gotten it inside, the cramped living area was just too small to accommodate its size.

As he walked through his beloved apartment with its magnificent view, trying to decide which items he would leave behind, David came to the realization that most of his possessions were just useless things.

He hired a man with a horse-cart to move him and his belongings to his new home: a third-floor apartment at 259 Bleecker Street, up over Zito's Bakery. Very few young ladies would be impressed with *this* address, and certainly not after having to walk up two flights of stairs.

Okay. He had a roof over his head and a few hundred dollars in his pocket. If he was careful with his spending, he could stretch his remaining funds for a few months. Then what? No sweat. He'd have the house by then. He'd sell it cheap. Well, not that cheap. He figured it was worth fifteen thousand. He'd direct the lawyer to put it on the market for twelve. That should move it.

Not having a car and unable to afford cabs, he now walked everywhere he went. He roamed the streets taking in the sights, the sounds, the smells. It was a new experience for him.

The proprietors of the various shops had placed selected items outside on the sidewalk to stimulate sales. Aproned women perused the wares and, on occasion, bought something. Men paused their sidewalk strolls to engage in conversations with one another, their arms and hands gesturing wildly. The streets were too congested for the boys to play stickball, so they dispersed their youthful energy by loudly running up and down in front of the shops, chasing one another. The little girls clung to their mothers' aprons, wishing they could join in the fun. The aroma of a thousand simmering stews wafted down onto the street and filled David with a longing for a good home-cooked meal.

All this conspired to change David Mahoney's perception of the lower classes. It took a while, but over time, he came to see these people as human beings, not the rabble he had once believed them to be. True, they were roughly hewed and uncouth, but they did possess a small spark of humanity. He'd still rather be back on Park Avenue, among his own kind, but his banishment had not turned out to be the hell he had once envisioned it to be.

After a month of living on Bleecker Street, David called the lawyer in California and was told to be patient, that the probate would not be completed for another two months, maybe three. This time he did not hang up on the lawyer, but rang off in a civilized manner. What a waste of a dollar twenty. Long distance calls were not cheap.

He was doing everything possible to conserve his remaining funds. He switched from gin to nickel beers, which he drank in a low-rent speakeasy. His meals consisted mostly of ten-cent hamburgers, consumed at a greasy spoon located around the corner from where he lived. How he wished he could once again walk into Delmonico's, where the maître d' knew him by name, and be seated at his usual table. The service and the food had been excellent. His mouth watered at the very thought of their Lobster Newburg. And what a wine selection! However, everything changes. It's inherent with life. It's intrinsic with being. It's how things are.

After one hundred years, Delmonico's had gone out of business. The location was now a high-class speakeasy. And after thirty-five years, David Mahoney had also gone out of business, so to speak. He was no longer the young man-about-town, the gay bon vivant. He was now a middle-aged failure facing oblivion.

38

The incessant knocking roused David from a troubled sleep. He had been dreaming he was being chased by a tiger. The ravenous beast pursued him hither and yon. Worse still, he was running as though his feet were trapped in molasses; he could not shake the monster. Just as the soulless creature sprung for the kill, its body hovering in mid-air, David sat bolt upright and opened his eyes to find he was safe and sound and in his own familiar room. The only sound other than the thunderous beating of his heart, he now realized, was coming from the front door.

The knocking continued, but David waited for the last vestige of the nightmare to dissolve into an aerial mist and fade from his mind. As his pulse steadied, he pulled himself out of bed, shambled to the front of the apartment, and opened the door to reveal Mister Lombardi, the landlord.

He took one look at his tenant's disheveled, half-asleep appearance, still wearing his pajamas at eleven o'clock in the morning, and said, "Mister Mahoney, may I ask what you are doing sleeping in the middle of the day when you are behind in your rent? Shouldn't you be out working or at least looking for work?"

"I'm only ten days behind. You'll get your money, Mister Lombardi. I'm good for it."

Lombardi was having none of it. "I'll have you know, Mister Mahoney, that I have seven children depending on me for their daily bread *and* I have a wife who buys hats like they were going out of style. But that's neither here nor there. I've come to collect my rent, or out you go."

David tried to keep the panic from his voice as he said, "You can't do that. Where will I go? What will I do?"

"That's none of my concern. Now, do I get my rent?"

"What if I refuse to leave?"

With a world-weary sigh, Lombardi said, "Do you think you're the first bum I've had to throw out in the twelve years I've owned this building?"

The word "bum" stung David to his soul.

Lombardi continued. "My two oldest sons, together, outweigh you by a hundred pounds. They could pick you up and throw you out onto the street like you were a sack of potatoes. But I'd rather not go through that unpleasantness."

David's body sagged, he felt utterly defeated. He was now officially a bum.

How the mighty have fallen.

"What about my furniture?" he asked.

"Take it with you. If you leave it, you'll find it out on the street in the morning."

In his walks around the neighborhood, David had seen furniture piled up on the sidewalk. Sometimes an entire family had been sitting around their dining room table, in a state of shock. *Now that we're here on the street, what will we do? Where will we go?*

David had no desire to fall that low. He was going to have to do something. At the moment, he didn't know what, but there was one thing he was certain of. He was not going to be sitting in the middle of the goddamn street surrounded by all his belongings.

"You can keep the furniture, Mister Lombardi. All I ask is that you give me an hour to get myself together, and then I'll be more than happy to vacate your premises."

"Not an unreasonable request, Mister Mahoney. I'm just sorry things had to get to this point. Up until now you've been a good tenant." The hardness around Lombardi's mouth softened. "And I'm sorry I called you a bum."

David favored Lombardi with a genial smile. "If the shoe fits, Mister Lombardi. If the shoe fits."

After a quick wash, David packed his solitary suitcase with a few clothes and toiletries, and within the allotted hour, he was down on the street, looking at his reflection in the front window of Mister Zito's bakery.

What he saw dismayed him—a thirty-six-year-old man who had never worked a day in his life, and who had never really cared about anyone but himself. His current predicament was all his own doing.

364

One hundred thousand dollars was enough to last anyone a lifetime. But not him. He went through it like a kid in a candy store. He had to have everything, and he had to have it instantly.

He hadn't been thinking straight since his money ran out. It was time to calmly take stock of his situation and make the appropriate plans. He was a Mahoney after all. According to his father, his grandfather endured much worse and came out on top.

David squared his shoulders, nodded at himself in the window, and headed down Bleecker Street. As he walked, he tried to come to grips with his situation. *My mistake, up to this point—other than blowing through my inheritance—had been thinking that I'd soon have the house. It's been almost three months and it could be another two for all I know. And then what? It's got to be sold. And how long will that take? And who's going to sell it for me? Most likely Lane, the attorney. But he'll need signed papers to give him authorization. I should have thought of that before. I'll have to take care of that as soon as possible. But in the meantime, I need a place to stay. It's October and it's getting chilly. And, of course, I have to eat.*

David had no idea where he was going. He was walking just to be moving while he thought about his circumstances. He was not fully cognizant of his surroundings. The people and shops he passed along the way were not registering on a conscious level. However, as he turned a corner, he did notice a line of men in front of a shop with a large sign painted on its plate-glass window. It read:

Free
For the Unemployed
Soup Coffee & Donuts

All of a sudden, David realized he was hungry; he had not eaten since the night before. He had a few dollars in his pocket, but why spend them if he didn't have to? And he sure as hell was unemployed. He took his place at the end of the line. Ten minutes later, when the line had not moved, David asked the guy standing in front of him what the holdup was.

The man spoke over his shoulder, not looking at David. "They're not open, mac. They don't open 'til five."

"Then why are we standing here almost two hours beforehand?"

The fellow turned around and gave David the once-over, taking in the suitcase and David's clean-shaven face.

Shaking his head, he said, "Your first time, huh?"

"Yes, it is."

"Don't let it worry you none. My name's Joe, by the way."

"I'm David. So tell me, Joe, why are we standing in line two hours before they open?"

"Sometimes they run outta soup." Joe pointed to the end of the line, which had grown considerably since David had joined it. "Most likely those gents back there will be going to bed hungry tonight. Besides, what else you gotta do? Standin' here is just as good as standin' anywhere else."

Just to kill time, the two men continued their conversation. Joe was happy to tell the tenderfoot the ins and outs of surviving on the streets.

"Where do you sleep at night?" asked David.

"Depends on the weather and what you got in your pocket."

David gave him a questioning look.

Feigning exasperation, Joe, quietly and distinctly, as though speaking to a child, said, "When it's warm, you got yourself the park. Don't go to sleeping on benches, though, because the police will make you leave. What you do is, find a nice shrub you can crawl behind. But in the winter, you go to a flophouse. If you can't afford a flophouse, you can go to an all-night mission. Kneel in one of their pews, place your folded arms on the back of the pew in front of you, and lay your head down. It looks like you're praying. You can catch a few winks that way. Thems that run the missions know what we're up to, but they're mostly good people and leave us be."

The doors eventually opened and the line shuffled forward. Sitting at a long wooden table with a spoon in his right hand, a bowl of soup in front of him, and a rather large chunk of bread in his left hand, David asked about bathing. "Can you get a bath at a flophouse?"

Joe, whose mouth was filled with bread, held up an index finger. David hungrily slurped his soup while waiting for an answer. Finally, Joe said, "No, you cannot get a bath at a flophouse. And before you ask, you get clean any way you can. I personally prefer fountains. But you gotta do it late at night when there's no one around."

"You take a bath in a *fountain*?"

Joe was amazed at the naïveté of his protégé. "You don't jump in. You wash your face and hands. If it's warm enough and there's no one around, you take off your shirt and splash a little water under your arms and onto your chest."

With their bowls empty and their stomachs a little fuller than they had been when they walked in, David and Joe took their leave, freeing up two seats that were quickly taken.

Out on the street, Joe said, "You're welcome to come along with me to the park. I'm sure we can find you a spot where the police won't bother you none."

David was not quite ready to sleep under a bush. Not yet, anyway. "No, thank you. I think I'll try a flophouse tonight. Can you tell me where I might find one?"

Joe pointed down the street. "That way. Two blocks, then turn right. It will be on your right, halfway up the block. And I'd advise that you get there early 'cause they fill up fast."

David thanked him for his help.

"Think nothing of it. Didn't cost me nothin' but time, friend, and that I got plenty of," said Joe before turning away and walking up the block as though he hadn't a care in the world.

I hope I never get that complacent about living on the streets, thought David.

He made one stop on the way to the flophouse, a telephone booth at the corner of Hudson and King Streets. It was still early enough to call California.

≈ ≈ ≈

"I have a person to person collect call for Mister William Lane from David Mahoney. Will you accept the charges?"

A female voice said, "One moment, please."

A moment later, a male voice came on the line. "This is Lane and I'll accept the charges."

"Thank you, sir. Please go ahead."

"Mister Lane, this is David Mahoney. I'm sorry I had to call you collect, but my situation has changed considerably."

"Think nothing of it. How may I help you?" Before David could answer, Lane went on. "If you're calling about the probate, I still haven't heard anything."

"No, that's not it, sir. I was wondering if, when the house is finally out of probate, you could find your way to selling it for me, taking a commission, of course."

There was silence for a moment. David thought the connection had been broken and shouted into the phone, "Mister Lane? Mister Lane, are you still there?"

"I'm here, David. I was just thinking. I can sell the house, but I'll need a signed contract to do so. Nothing elaborate. Just something authorizing me to act on your behalf."

"I figured that, too. That's why I'm calling. As you probably have already surmised, I need the money from the sale, and I need it as soon as possible. If you could send me the papers, I'll sign 'em and send them back right away."

"I'll send the contract today. Are you still at the same address?"

"No. Please send it in care of General Delivery, New York City."

"Will do. Have you a phone number where you can be reached?"

"No, I don't. I'll call you, but don't worry. I won't be pestering you. I know it's going to take time to find a buyer."

"That will be fine, David. Is there anything else I can do for you? If a small loan would tide you over ..."

David interrupted. "No, thank you. I've gone through enough money that people have given me. I want to try and see if I can provide for myself for a change. And Mister Lane ..."

"Yes?"

"I want to apologize for my rudeness when we first met."

"I hadn't noticed," said Lane, lying through his teeth.

≈ ≈ ≈

In his wildest dreams, David could never have imagined such a place. The sign outside read:

U.S. Hotel
Beds 25 Cents

Beyond the front door, a flight of dreary stairs led to a realm of dismal gloominess. At the portal, a short, rotund creature sat behind a desk, the unlit stub of a cigar crammed into the corner of its wide mouth. Its garments dirty, its manner, uncouth.

"That will be two bits, bub," barked the troll.

David felt the urge to run … run all the way back to Park Avenue. But no one there would have him. He didn't have to check his pockets to ascertain his net worth. He knew it down to the penny: five dollars and thirteen cents.

David fumbled in his pocket, came out with a crumpled five dollar bill, and handed it to the odious gatekeeper.

"I see we have J.D. Rockefeller himself staying with us tonight."

After making a big show of counting out the change, the troll jerked his thumb in the direction of an open door. "In there, Mister Rockefeller. Choose your bed and be out of here by six or you'll be thrown out."

David walked into a dormitory-like room and beheld the splendor of the U.S. Hotel in all its soul-crushing glory. His nose wrinkled at the overpowering stench of urine and body odor. He also discerned an almost tangible whiff of deep despair.

Three rows of beds stretched out from the door to the far back wall, fifteen per row. Most of the beds had a man either lying on them or sitting on them. For a room so big, housing so many men, things were eerily quiet. These men were mostly loners and did not engage in idle chit chat.

David made his way forward and found an empty bunk in the middle row, about three quarters of the way in. The blanket covering its surface was worn and sported multiple holes. Its color was once blue, but was now more of a slate-grey. The pillow case looked moderately clean, except for a smudge here and there. He wasn't even going to look at the sheets. He would sleep on top of the blanket; that would be bad enough.

He threw his suitcase and hat on one end of the bed and sat down on the other. What a day. Thrown out onto the street, his first soup kitchen, and now this. Could tomorrow be any worse? And what about employment? It was a horrible thing to contemplate, but he was going to have to get a job. He couldn't afford twenty-five cents a day for a dirty bed in a Dantean version of hell unless he replenished his resources. Well, he would worry about that tomorrow. He'd be out and on the streets early enough to be first in line for any available jobs. He was willing to take anything. He had to hold on at any cost until the house was sold. Even if it meant going to work.

An old man lay on the bed next to him, propped up on one elbow, reading a book. He paid no mind to David until David took off his shoes and placed them under the bed. "I wouldn't do that if I were you," he said.

"Excuse me?"

The gentleman, who had clearly seen better days but still had a quiet dignity about him, dog-eared the page he had been reading and sat up. "My name's Nate Wilson, and I didn't mean to jump into your business; however, I couldn't help but notice that you need a little advice."

"I'm David Mahoney. Forgive me, but I didn't catch what you said before."

"When you sleep in a place like this, and if you have shoes such as yours, meaning no holes in the leather, keep them on or you won't have them come morning."

David looked down at his stocking feet and reached under the bed for his shoes. As he was tying the laces, he said, "Thank you, Mister … ah, what was your name again?"

"Just call me Nate."

David extended his hand. Nate grabbed it and pumped it twice. "Welcome to the U.S. Hotel. You ever thought you'd be staying in such a high-class establishment?"

David laughed, his first laugh in many a day, a welcome relief of sorts. "Can't say that I have. Let me ask you, Nate. What about my suitcase? Do you think it will be safe?"

"Probably not. My advice would be to carry on your person anything you don't want to lose or that you can't live without. Get used to the idea that, at some point, someone is going to steal that case from you. It could happen here or somewhere else. Once you understand that, you won't mind so much when it does go missing. Now, if you'll excuse me. I want to get a little more reading in before they shut off the lights."

David thanked his grizzled mentor for the tutelage and started pulling items out of the suitcase, shoving them into his pockets. At least he'd have his razor, a half a bar of soap, a comb, and an extra pair of socks and underwear.

The case was now half-empty, holding the few remaining pieces of David's clothing. He slid it under the bed, hoping for the best. But truth be told, he wouldn't mind losing it. It had been a pain in the neck, carrying it around all day. He lay down, staring at the ceiling, thinking he would never be able to get to sleep in such a godforsaken place.

The next thing he knew, someone was yelling, "All you bums, get on your feet. Time to go out and conquer the world." Whoever it was must have thought it was funny because he kept repeating it.

It was 5:30 in the morning and they were being asked to leave the U.S. Hotel in a not-so-gentle way. Nate's bed was empty, but the suitcase was right where he had left it. As David pulled it out from under the bed, he realized that it felt lighter than it had the night before. He opened it to find that it was empty. With a sigh, he slid it back under the bed and left it there.

David's first full day of being a "forgotten man" was disheartening. He had never noticed before, but almost every business establishment had a sign hanging in their front window or taped to their door, stating they were not hiring.

The only positive thing to come out of his wanderings that day was his discovery of other soup kitchens. Some served only in the morning, others at noon, and still others, only in the evening. At least he was assured of eating once or twice a day, as long as he got there before the soup ran out. That night, he went back to the U.S. Hotel a dejected man, but he did have a full belly. He looked for Nate Wilson, but he was not among the "guests" that evening.

After a few days, he gave up looking for a job. It was plain to see there were none to be had. He spent his days walking the streets or sitting in the park. He knew the hours of all the soup kitchens in that part of town and made sure he was one of the first to line up, thus assuring himself three meals a day. Nights, he would spend at the flophouse, but he was down to his last couple of dollars. What would he do when they were gone? It was mid-November and too cold to sleep in the park. He reckoned he'd soon have to go to an all-night mission and sleep in a kneeling position. He could hardly wait for that.

One thing he made sure to do was go to the main branch of the Post Office on a daily basis until the letter from Lane arrived. When it did, he signed where instructed and invested in a stamp and envelope to send the paperwork back to Lane.

Things were getting desperate. He needed the money from the sale of the house. Then a thought struck him. Could he live in the house until it was sold? At least California was warm, and he could probably find work picking fruit. He would have to call Lane to find out about that, because in eight days he would no longer be able to afford the luxury of staying at the "ritzy" U.S. Hotel.

He called the next day, but was told Lane was out of town and not due back until the beginning of the following week.

Maybe I should just go out there. It's my house, after all.

At the soup kitchens, he had met numerous men who were veterans at riding the rails, so he knew he could get out to California without the cost of buying a ticket. However, he had heard that it was a week's journey, if you were not arrested along the way. How would he eat? How did those men do it? He resolved to take a day or two to ask around and learn what he could. Maybe he could find a traveling companion. Someone who knew the ropes.

The next day, he was back in line at the Hudson Street soup kitchen, waiting for the doors to open. The line was long and David was about a third of the way back. It was a cold autumn day. He stood with his hands in his pockets, his cap pulled down low. No one was talking; the chill in the air restrained the desire for communal discourse.

He was hopping from foot to foot and occasionally blowing his warm breath into his cold, cupped hands as he looked down the line to see if the doors were open. So far, not yet, but he did see a fellow walking the line, stopping now and then to say a few words to one man or another. *One of them damn line-cutters*, thought David. *Well, he'll hear from me if someone lets him in.*

When the guy came abreast of David, he said, "Not working, huh?"

"I wouldn't be in this line if I had a job."

"Any prospects?"

Before deciding whether or not to answer the question, David made a quick assessment of his interrogator. He was not a forgotten man or a bum, as some people called those out of work because of the Depression. He was in his mid-thirties, clean-shaven; his clothes were clean and neatly pressed. He had an honest look in his eye and a ready smile, so David decided to be civil and answer the question. Perhaps it might lead to a job.

"I have no prospects. None whatsoever. In fact, I was thinking of going to California to look for work out there."

"I might have a job for you, right here. You interested?"

At the word "job," the other men in line, the ones nearby, jostled to get closer to the action and to the angel who was offering what they had all prayed for, until they had given up hope of ever again doing an honest day's labor.

The angel held up his hand. "Sorry, boys. I have only one job to offer and I think I found my man." The disappointment in the air was palpable. He nodded to David. "What do you say? Do you want to talk about it?"

"I say yes, but can I get my soup first? I haven't eaten yet today."

"I'm Ben Shahn. There's a coffee shop around the corner. Lunch is on me if you take the job or not."

David stepped out of line and introduced himself. "I'm David Mahoney."

They shook hands and David followed his benefactor around the corner to what he hoped would be an opportunity to escape the veritable hell he had been living for the last few months.

39

The old Tin Lizzie chugged down the dark two-lane, the glow from its headlights splayed out to the edges of the asphalt but no farther. At that hour, it was the only car on the road. The sound of its engine and the rattling of its fenders drowned out the music of a thousand crickets as it made its way down the lonely country road. Above, billions of silent stars set the clear night sky ablaze with their brilliance.

The passenger leaned his head out the side window and asked, "Have you ever seen so many stars in all your life?"

The driver answered: "I've been concentrating on keeping this old rust bucket of yours on this poor excuse for a road, so I have not had the opportunity to do any stargazing."

David Mahoney was in a foul mood and didn't give a flying fig if it was his boss he was speaking to or not. It was nearing midnight. They had been on the road since early that morning, and David had done most of the driving.

Ben Shahn pulled his head back inside. "Okay, just a few more miles and then we'll pull over and make camp, I promise. I'm sorry I'm pushing so hard, but I can't wait to get started. We should be there tomorrow."

In a resigned voice, David said, "I'd just like to know where we are now."

"We're in the Great State of Georgia."

"I know that. But where exactly in the Great State of Georgia are we?"

"The last town we passed was Baxley," said Ben.

"That does me a lot of good. Look, Ben. I need sleep, so I'm gonna pull over at the next clearing I see."

"Fine by me, David. I could use a little shuteye myself. But we have to get an early start in the morning. That should put us well into Florida by lunchtime."

David stared out the windshield into the darkness and thought back to how he had ended up in the backwoods of Georgia, in the middle of the night, sitting next to an energetic do-gooder. A man who had a need to set the record straight.

$$\approx \approx \approx$$

They had been sitting at a table across from one another, and Ben asked, "Hamburger and fries okay with you, David?"

"Sure."

Ben called to the girl behind the counter. "Two hamburgers, with fries, and two coffees, if you please."

The coffee was served immediately. And while they waited for their food, Ben laid out his proposition. "You ever hear of Rosewood, Florida?"

"I don't believe I have," said David as he sweetened his coffee.

"About eight years ago, it seems there was a race riot down there. According to the papers, six Negroes and two Whites were killed. I read about it at the time, but didn't think much of it. But then, a few weeks ago, I ran into this guy from that neck of the woods and we got to talking. One thing led to another and before I knew it, he was telling me about mass murder and an entire town being burnt down right to the ground."

David put down his coffee cup. "What do you mean by 'mass murder'?"

"That's what I asked. But the guy didn't know the numbers for sure. He said there are whispers here and there that one hundred and fifty Negroes were killed. No one knows exactly how many whites were killed because no one down there is talking about that aspect of it. And by no one, he meant *no one*. Not the whites and certainly not the Negroes. He says the whites don't want it to get around that they committed out-and-out murder. And the Negroes in the surrounding towns are afraid to open their mouths for fear of inciting another mob and possibly having fire set to *their* houses."

"So, you're telling me that over one hundred and fifty people were killed and an entire town wiped off the map and there wasn't a peep about it in the papers?"

"That's not what I'm saying at all. The story *was* in the papers, but what was reported was only a small part of what actually happened. The rest of the story, as per my contact, never came out. The officials in Florida hushed it up as best they could because they were afraid the whole sordid mess would adversely affect their tourism."

The waitress placed the hamburgers on the table, refilled their cups, and left. David hungrily eyed his burger. "It's been a long time since I've eaten any meat."

"Dig in," said Ben. "And while you're at it, I'll tell you what little I know and what we're gonna do."

David picked up the Heinz ketchup bottle and smacked the bottom a few times, splashing a goodly portion of the red sauce onto his hamburger and fries.

Ben popped a French fry into his mouth and started his story. "This is the tale of two towns, three miles apart. Rosewood and Sumner. Rosewood was made up of Negroes and Sumner was an all-white town. According to the 1920 census, their populations were three hundred and fifty-five and two hundred and ninety-four, respectively. I know because I checked. Then I looked up the census numbers for 1930. And what do you think I found?"

David was chewing on a mouthful of hamburger and could only shrug.

"In 1930, Sumner had about the same population, but Rosewood was not listed at all." Ben paused in his narrative to take a bite of his hamburger and a sip of coffee. After patting his lips with a paper napkin, he continued. "There's a story here and I intend to dig up the truth. If something so vile did take place, I think people have a right to know about it."

David slowed down his eating long enough to ask, "What do you need me for?"

"I need a photographer to document my investigation. And I need someone to help out with the driving."

"I'm not a photographer."

Ben was about to put another French fry into his mouth, but put it back on the plate instead. "Anyone can be a photographer if he can point a camera and press a button. But that's not all I'll need you for. Your main job will be to drive, but I'll expect you to help out in any way you can. I'm going down there with you or with someone else. And I'm coming back with one humdinger of a story. So, what do you say? Are you in or out?"

"What's the pay?"

"Well, that's the thing," said Ben. "That's why I was looking for a man standing in a soup line."

"What do you mean?"

Ben took a deep breath and blurted it out. "I can't afford to pay anything up front. But wait! hear me out. I'm doing this on my own. I'm what's called a stringer. I don't work for any one newspaper. If I get a good story, I sell it to the highest bidder. If they syndicate my story, I get a cut of that, too. And I can tell you right now, this story is big enough for syndication.

"So, here's my deal. You'll eat three meals a day, guaranteed. You'll have a place to sleep, although it will be in a lean-to on the side of the road. And when I sell my story, you'll be in for thirty percent of whatever I get. I'm hoping, if we get some good pictures, we'll be able to sell them to *Life Magazine*. They pay top dollar. And if we do connect with *Life*, it'll be a fifty-fifty split on the pictures. What do you say?"

David pretended to think it over. But there really wasn't anything to think over. In a few days, he'd be reduced to sleeping while in a kneeling position. And he was so damn sick and tired of soup.

"Will you be serving soup in that lean-to of yours? The one on the side of the road?"

"Nope. I'm more of a meat and potatoes man myself."

≈ ≈ ≈

David nearly missed it. But there it was—caught in the wash of the headlights—a small clearing off to the right. He pulled the ancient Model T onto the hard-packed dirt and turned off the ignition. There was instant and total silence. Not even the crickets chirped their welcome.

David was bone-weary, but they had to set up camp. This would be the second time since they left New York, so they knew what they were doing, more or less. Despite an absent moon, the stars provided enough light to allow David to find the lantern and get it lit.

By then, Ben had the canvas unfolded and one end attached to the roof of the car. David rooted around in the back seat and came up with two pegs and a hammer. The pegs went into the ground and the corners of the unattached end of the canvas were tied to them. Voila! Instant lean-to. Being early December, and the weather cool, mosquitoes were not much of a problem.

There was no discussion of eating. They were both too tired. In silence, they laid out their blankets and were soon lulled to sleep by the sound of crickets resuming their mellifluous mating sounds after having been so rudely interrupted.

In the morning, Ben prepared a breakfast of scrambled eggs, toast, and coffee on the small portable stove they carried with them. There was no cleaning up afterwards. Each man had his own plate and eating utensils. They didn't carry enough water to wash dishes after every meal.

When they were ready to continue on their way, David took down the canvas and pulled the stakes out of the ground. Ben folded up the stove and gathered whatever else was lying around and stored it all in the backseat. Everything the two men owned in the world was jumbled into that backseat, with the overflow stuffed into the small trunk alongside the gas tank. Long before the sun made its appearance, the vintage '23 flivver was once again headed south, with David at the wheel.

Ben had a Rand McNally automobile road map of Florida unfolded on his lap. "According to this and my best estimate, we should roll into Cedar Key around one o'clock this afternoon."

David looked over at Ben. "Where's Cedar Key? I thought we were going to Sumner."

"Cedar Key is in upper Florida, on the west coast, about ten miles from Sumner. I'm hoping the people there will be more open to talking to us. I don't think anyone in Sumner will give us the time of day. From what I was told, they're pretty close-mouthed about what happened. That's where the mob that attacked Rosewood first formed up. I think most of the guilty parties still live there."

"Whatever you say, Ben. You're the boss. I'm just along to take pictures and to drive this decrepit vehicle."

Ben, taking no offense at the aspersions cast on his fine automobile, folded the map and put it away. "We have five hours to kill before we pull into Cedar Key. What do you want to talk about?"

"I'm driving, I'm not killing time."

Ben laughed. "Okay, I'll do the talking."

"Whatever suits you."

"Tell me about yourself."

"I thought you said you were going to do the talking."

"So, I lied. Where are you from, originally?"

With a sigh, David gave a brief outline of his life to date.

The reporter in Ben asked, "You went to Princeton? How'd you ever end up in a soup line?"

David wasn't quite sure if he wanted to go into all the details of what an over-spoiled idiot he had been. But then he thought, *What the hell. Perhaps laying it all out will get it straight in my own mind why I ended as I did.* So David gave a more detailed account of his life.

When he had finished, Ben said, "You didn't get along with your father?"

David took his time in answering. He wanted to get it right. "I did get along with him when I was young, but somewhere along the way, the relationship changed. I now know it was all my fault. I thought he was weak, and subconsciously, I hated him for it."

"Why did you think he was weak?"

"He gave me everything I ever wanted. Everything I asked for. He never said no, even when he should have. And on some level, I resented him for it."

"What was your father's name? I mean his first name."

"His name was Dillon."

Ben had been slumped in his seat, but now he rocketed upright. "Are you telling me your father was Dillon Mahoney?"

David, not hearing the urgency in Ben's voice, simply said, "Yeah. That was his name."

"HOLD YOUR HORSES! PULL OVER ... PULL OVER!"

"Why?"

"Pull the goddamn car over to the side of the road. Right now!"

David had no idea what was going on, but did as he was told. "Okay, Ben, I'm pulled over. Now, what is this all about?"

Ben was already half into the backseat, pushing things this way and that. "I know it's here. Give me a second," he said over his shoulder.

David was willing to give him all day if need be.

"Here it is!" said a triumphant Ben. He sat back down and held out a slim volume in David's direction. "Take a gander at this."

David accepted the proffered publication. It was what was called a dime novel. The paper had yellowed with age and felt brittle in his hands. Blazoned across the front, in faded red ink, the banner read:

Wild West Weekly

But it was the subtitle that caught David's eye.

Dillon Mahoney, U.S. Marshal, Conquers the Luke Short Gang

"Where did you get this?"

"I collect them," said Ben, proudly.

David held the magazine gingerly in his hands. His mind could not comprehend what he was seeing. In due time, he said, "There has to be some mistake. It can't be my father. It has to be some other Dillon Mahoney."

"Did your father ever talk about being out West?"

"No. I mean yes. Once, when I was little, he told me about a cattle drive he had been on. But he never said anything about being a marshal."

Ben got out of the car and walked around to the driver's side. "I'll drive for a while. Why don't you read that and tell me what you think."

David stayed right where he was. "I don't have to read it. It's not my father. And I've heard about these dime novels. There's no truth in them. They're just sensationalized rubbish."

"Granted. The stories are undoubtedly wild exaggerations or out-and-out fabrications. But sometimes they *are* based on real characters. I got a whole slew of 'em about Wild Bill Cody and Buffalo Bill and they were real.

"How many Dillon Mahoneys do you suppose were in the Old West? Come on, get out. I'll drive, you read. And I suggest that you read the introduction carefully."

David settled into the passenger seat, opened the thin publication, and read the first page.

> Who was Dillon Mahoney and where did he hail from? No one seems to know for sure. Some say he came from way back East. Still others say he was reared in Texas, down Galveston way, or perhaps in the panhandle. As to who he was ... there is no doubt about that: He was the man who put an end to the outlaw Luke Short and his ruthless gang of cattle rustlers and murderers.
>
> As lawlessness ran amuck in the territory of New Mexico, Dillon Mahoney burst forth onto the scene, his six guns blazing justice, eventually making the territory safe for decent men and women to go about their business without fear of being murdered in their sleep.
>
> As mysteriously as he had appeared ... he disappeared. It is believed the remnants of the Short gang exacted their revenge. After shooting him down in cold blood from ambush, the cowards buried him in a lonely grave out in the New Mexican desert.
>
> What follows, kind reader, is the story of the stalwart and true Deputy U.S. Marshal, Dillon Mahoney, and how he bested one of the most feared gangs ever to roam and terrorize the Old West.

David laughed and said, "This is unmitigated tripe."

"Of course it is," laughed Ben. "Us aficionados know that. That's the point. It's so bad, it's good. But what about your father?"

"Whoever *this* Dillon Mahoney was, if he even existed, was *not* my father."

"Maybe there was more to your old man than you thought."

"I doubt it."

"Okay, have it your way. But if it were me, I'd want to know if my father had been a famous lawman."

"If he were around, I'd ask him. But seeing as he's not, there's not much I can do about it."

"Well, if you ever find yourself in Las Cruces, New Mexico, you should check out the local newspaper. Maybe you would find something of interest about your old man."

David looked over to Ben. "Why Las Cruces?"

Ben took his eyes off the road for a moment and said, "That's where the story takes place. Many of the stories found in the dime novels were taken from newspaper accounts written at the time."

David offered to get back behind the wheel.

"I'll drive for a while. Just for the hell of it, why don't you read the story?"

David tried to get comfortable in the cramped seat and opened the flimsy periodical. He read a few pages and shook his head. "It's still tripe," he muttered under his breath.

"What was that?" asked Ben.

"Nothing."

They rolled over the last bridge into Cedar Key at 2:05 that afternoon and landed on D Street. Their first order of business was to get something to eat, and while they were at it, maybe get a little information. They were in luck. Right there in front of them, on the corner, stood a small wooden building with a white sign hanging in the front window that read: "Mama's Home Cooking." Ben parked the car on the street, a few doors down.

As they approached the restaurant, Ben said, "Let me do the talking. I have a way of getting people to open up."

"Whatever you say. You're the boss, Boss."

They sat down at the counter. Soon a rotund, matronly-looking woman came out from the back and asked them what they'd like.

Ben put on his best New York smile and said, "You must be Mama. We've heard the food here is the best in the South. We've driven many a mile to taste your fine cuisine."

The woman smiled a thousand-watt smile. "I've heard about you smooth-talking Yankees. And I gotta say, *you* must be the smoothest of 'em all."

"How'd you know we were Yankees?" questioned Ben.

The woman placed a motherly hand over Ben's and said, "Honey, you're not only dressed like a couple of Yankees, you *talk*

382

like a Yankee. I reckon I know a couple of city slickers when I see 'em."

The woman and Ben laughed. David was wishing they could get down to ordering some food.

"Okay," said Ben, "you caught on to us. Now, what do you recommend? What's good?"

"You leave it to Mama. I'll fix you fellas up fine. You want some coffee?"

Ben informed Mama that, indeed, they would love a cup of coffee. She poured out two large mugs, and then, with a final smile and a wink in Ben's direction, she retreated into the kitchen.

"See how easy that was?" said Ben. "I'll have the whole story of Rosewood before we leave here."

David sipped his coffee, and looking around the small restaurant, he spied a phone booth in the back corner.

"Excuse me, Ben. I gotta make a phone call. You got a nickel? I'll give it right back."

David pulled the folding door shut behind him and dropped the nickel into the slot.

≈ ≈ ≈

"Long distance, please."

"Yes, sir," said a pleasant-sounding disembodied female voice.

A moment later, a different but just as pleasant female voice asked, "How may I help you?"

David went through the rigamarole for placing a long distance collect call and said he'd hold on while the call went through. In a very few minutes, he was speaking to William Lane

"Hello, David. I'm glad you called. I have good news. The house is out of probate and I have someone who's interested in buying it."

"That's wonderful!" exclaimed David.

"I just need to know what's the lowest you'll go. He offered thirteen thousand. And I countered with fourteen. Right now I'm waiting to hear back from him."

"Take whatever you can get. If it's thirteen, that's okay with me."

"I'll call him right away, but I'll still try for fourteen. If things can be worked out, the money should be in escrow in a day or so, and the closing soon thereafter."

"That's great, Mister Lane. I'll call tomorrow to see if the offer was accepted."

"That's fine, David. Is there anything else?"

"No ... wait a minute. You knew my father for a long time. Is that not correct?"

"I was his lawyer for close on to forty years. He retained my services right after he hit it big in the oil business."

"Did he ever mention anything about being in the West? Anything like that?"

Lane had to think for a moment, and then said, "When I was setting up the corporation to administer his oil interests, I asked him if he had any liabilities. Or if he knew of anyone who might come along and try to lay claim to his assets. He told me that he'd had some dealings with unscrupulous men back in New Mexico, but they weren't around anymore. He then asked if perhaps their next of kin might cause trouble. I told him I'd have to know more details, but then he changed course and said the past was dead and gone and that, no, no one would be coming after him or his assets. I let the matter drop after that."

David was astonished. Could it be possible that his father had been a gun-slinging marshal in the Old West?

"Thank you, Mister Lane. I'll call you tomorrow."

He made sure to retrieve the nickel from the coin return before leaving the booth.

≈ ≈ ≈

David got back to the counter just as Mama came out of the kitchen carrying two large, fully loaded, oval-shaped plates. She placed one in front of Ben and one in front of David. "What is this ambrosia that you put before us?" asked Ben in a flirtatious manner.

"That ain't no *brosa*," said an indignant Mama. "That's chicken fried steak and gravy, along with my mouth-waterin' biscuits. That green stuff is okra, in case you Yankee boys ain't never seen okra before."

384

Duly chastised, Ben said, "My mistake. Anyone could tell at a glance it's chicken fried steak. And not just any chicken fried steak, but Mama's *special* chicken fried steak. The best in the South."

Mama, satisfied with Ben's sufficiently semi-contrite apology, went back to her kitchen.

Under his breath, David said, "What the hell is chicken fried steak?"

Ben whispered, "I don't know. Let's dig in and find out."

It did turn out to be steak, or at least some kind of meat. However, David would be damned if he could find any chicken in the thing. The biscuits were great, and the okra was different, but good.

They finished everything on their plates and mopped up the last of the gravy with the last of the biscuits.

"That wasn't bad," observed Ben.

David concurred. "I've got no complaints."

Ben caught Mama's eye and asked for a refill on the coffee. Mama complied and went about her business.

When she was safely out of earshot, down at the other end of the counter, talking to a man wearing a blue-grey mailman's uniform, Ben whispered, "When she gives me the check, I'll start our investigation into the Rosewood Affair."

"The Rosewood Affair?"

"That's what I'm calling it until I can come up with a better title."

Mama wandered over. "You boys want dessert? I got fresh peach pie."

"I don't think we have room right now. But you can bet your life we'll be back," said Ben.

"So, you boys liked my cooking?"

"It was the best chicken fried steak we've ever had. Isn't that right, David?"

"Sure was," said David, eyeing the peach pie sitting under a plastic cover a little ways down the counter.

Ben asked for the check, paid it, and left a healthy tip. He stood as if to leave, but at the last moment, turned to Mama and said, "We heard there was a little ruckus over at Rosewood a few years back. You hear anything about that?"

Mama, who had been lazily leaning against a cooler, happy with the entire world, her eyes shining love for all of God's creatures, suddenly stood erect and placed her hands on her broad hips. In a flash, her eyes grew dark and her manner threatening. "You damn meddling Yankees!" she screamed. "Get out of my restaurant. And don't you ever come back. If you do, I'll have the law on you."

Ben and David beat a hasty retreat. They were out on the street and walking fast. "Well, you really got her to open up. That's some knack you have," said David.

Ben was smiling from ear to ear as though he had just won the Irish Sweepstakes. He felt like jumping into the air and clicking his heels. Instead, he said, "I think we got ourselves a story, partner."

40

Back at the car, David asked, "What now?"

Ben leaned against the right front fender and, looking thoughtful, took his time in answering. "We probably need gas. Let's find a station. Gas jockeys are usually a talkative lot. Let's see what we can find out."

Two blocks down and one block over, they came to a Standard station. "Pull in here," said Ben. "Ask the attendant to check the air and oil to give me time to talk with him."

David had no sooner shut off the engine when a man wearing a white long-sleeve shirt, blue bow tie, and a blue cap appeared at the driver-side window. The patch on his shirt identified him as Sam. He greeted David with a touch to the brim of his cap. "How may I help you, sir?"

"Fill 'er up, please, and while you're at it, check the tires and oil."

"Yes, sir."

Ben got out of the car and opened the trunk so the attendant could access the gas tank. "It should take about six or seven gallons," he advised.

As they waited for the tank to fill, Ben casually said, "Nice town you have here. You lived here long?"

"All my life."

"It's Sam, isn't it?"

"That's what it says on the shirt," said Sam with a friendly southern drawl.

"Well, Sam. My friend and I are thinking of doing a little fishing. Can you recommend a place where we might have some luck?"

"You can drop a line off any bridge in town and you'll be eating fresh fish tonight."

When the tank was full, Sam looked over at the pump. "Six gallons exactly."

387

Ben followed the attendant around the car, making small talk as Sam checked the tires' air pressure. By the time Sam flopped open the hood to check the oil, Ben thought he had sufficiently ingratiated himself to ask the big question. But before he could do so, another car pulled up to the island and stopped opposite the Model T.

With his hand hovering over the dipstick, Sam said, "Be right with you, Mister Brady."

Ben had dallied long enough. "Say, Sam, can you direct us to Rosewood? It's on the map, but my friend and I can't find it. The map says it should be on Highway 24, but coming into town, we saw neither hide nor hair of it."

Sam had the dipstick pulled halfway out but shoved it back down into the dipstick tube without checking the oil and closed the hood. The friendliness was gone from his voice. "That'll be one dollar and thirty-eight cents you owe me."

Ben had not anticipated such an abrupt change in the man's manner, but he should have, given Mama's reaction just a few minutes earlier. He thought of saying something to put Sam at ease, but couldn't think of anything. He noticed that the guy in the other car was taking it all in, but when Ben made eye contact, the man quickly looked away.

Ben paid for the gas, climbed into the Model T, and with a weary sigh, said, "Let's go."

David pulled out onto the street and asked, "Where to now?"

"Just drive. I gotta think."

After a few minutes, Ben said, "Did you hear that guy's reaction to my question about Rosewood?"

"I heard it. And that jasper in the car next to us heard it too. I was watching him. He was very interested in what you were saying."

"I noticed that, too, but I don't care about him."

"You should. Counting him, that makes three people who know we're interested in what happened at Rosewood. This is a small town. Come sundown, everyone's gonna know why we're here. And based on the reactions of Mama and that gas jockey, we're gonna be in big trouble."

Ben slumped in his seat. "I'm going to get to the bottom of this, come hell or high water. But maybe you're right, David. Perhaps we should circle the wagons and assess the situation. Let's get some groceries while someone will still do business with us. Then we'll make camp outside of town. We passed miles and miles of wooded country coming in. We should be able to find a spot conducive to our needs."

They stocked up on food supplies and rode the highway out of town. About five miles out, they came across an overgrown rutted trail that led into a dense pine forest. "Turn here," said Ben. "We'll go in a little ways and make camp. It doesn't look like this road's been used in a while. We should have a little privacy while we figure out what to do next."

It was nearing on dark by the time they had set up camp. "Why don't we make a fire tonight?" suggested Ben.

"That might not be a bad idea," said David. "It's getting a little chilly."

"Then let's collect the wood before it gets too dark. And while you're getting the fire going, I'll crank up the stove and get dinner going."

An hour later, they were sitting around a warm fire, eating "homemade" beef stew, straight from the can.

Between mouthfuls, Ben did most of the talking. "There has to be someone in that town who will speak to us. What's going on, anyway? You'd think they had a part in what happened at Rosewood."

David had his own thoughts on the matter and was about to articulate them when, through the pine trees, he glimpsed a set of headlights coming their way. "Looks like we're gonna have company," he said.

They put their plates aside and stood up, waiting.

The car pulled up behind the Model T. Its headlights went dark, its motor died. With the firelight reflecting off its windows, they could not see who was inside. Except for the crackling of the fire, all was quiet.

Was this the land owner, here to tell them to get off his land? Or the sheriff, come to arrest them for disturbing the peace of Cedar Key? Perhaps a few of the town people come to run them out of the county on a rail, after a tar and feathering ceremony? Whoever it was could not be bringing good news. Not the way their day had gone.

They heard the door open and the dark figure of a man stepped out. "Mind if I join you at your fire?" he asked in a not unfriendly manner.

David called out, "Please do. It would be a pleasure to have your company."

The man stepped between the cars and walked into the light of the fire. It was the man from the gas station. The one who had overheard Ben ask the gas jockey about Rosewood.

"I'm Chet Brady," he said as he approached their campsite. He was holding a glass jar containing a clear liquid. "I brought something to warm you up on this cold night."

Ben took charge. "Come sit down, Mister Brady. I'm Ben Shahn and this is my friend, David Mahoney."

When the three men were comfortably seated around the fire, Brady held the jar out to Ben. "Here. Try some of this and then pass it on to your friend. After you boys have partaken of its sweetness, I'll tell you why I came out here tonight."

Ben was a bit leery. "What is it?"

"It's good old mountain dew. You know, moonshine. I make it myself. A man's got to do something to combat prohibition."

Ben was hesitant. He had never drunk moonshine before. Is it supposed to be clear? Could this be a trick to poison them in an effort to keep the secret of Rosewood buried forever?

David reached out and gently took the jar from Ben's hand, saying. "If you don't mind, Ben. I've never declined an offer of booze in my life, and believe me, it's been a long, long time since I've tasted the sweet distilled nectar of the gods. I thank you, Mister Brady."

Brady nodded and David took a long, satisfying pull. As the one hundred ninety proof liquid hit his stomach, he scrunched up his face, demonstrating that it was, indeed, the good stuff. He held out the jar in Ben's direction. "Here, Ben, this will put hair on your chest."

Ben took a sniff, then a sip. "Hmm … not bad." But he drank no more.

Brady accepted the jar from Ben and took a good swallow.

Now that the formalities were out of the way, Brady got down to business.

"I came to tell you boys something."

Ben and David leaned in a little and waited.

"Here's the deal. No one is gonna talk to you. Not in Cedar Key and probably not anywhere in the state of Florida."

"What do you mean?" asked Ben.

"Let me ask you," said Brady, "what do you know about Rosewood?"

"Not much. That's why we're down here. To investigate it. The papers up North called it a race riot where six Negroes and two Whites were killed."

Brady took another swig of his liquor and said, "What happened was a lot worse than that."

"Please go on, Mister Brady," implored Ben.

"I'm not sure if I should. I came out here with the intention of warning ya'all that you stirred up quite a hornet's nest back in town. And if I were you boys, I'd head back to wherever you came from, lickety-split."

Ben expressed his frustration by raising his voice. "We came a long way to find out the truth of what happened at Rosewood. And I don't think we'll be leaving until we've uncovered that truth."

Brady said, "You don't seem to understand that you're in danger. Most of the men in Cedar Key took part in what happened over at Rosewood. Hell, men came in from all over the state, and from out of state, too. We all just want it to go away. Some men are remorseful, right enough, and others are fearful. But any way you slice it, people in these here parts are not gonna talk to you about Rosewood. And if you go into town again, or any other town, asking about Rosewood, you'll be taking your life in your hands. There are a lot of swamps hereabouts and they've been hiding people's secrets for near on forever."

The talk had been between Brady and Ben, but at the mention of swamps, David chimed in. "That sounds awfully like a threat to me, Mister Brady."

Brady laughed. "Far from it. I'm actually here trying to save your lives."

David glanced over at Ben. It was his show and David didn't want to horn in. But he had a few questions of his own. Ben nodded, silently giving him permission to plow ahead.

"Okay, Mister Brady. I guess we're indebted to you for your efforts. But may I ask how you found us out here?"

Brady unscrewed the cap on his jar and took a pull before handing the jar to David. "I can see that this is gonna take longer than I anticipated. Drink up. It'll make you impervious to the cold. As to how I found you and your friend, your fire can be seen from the road. After you left town, word spread like wildfire regarding the two Yankees asking about Rosewood. People are nervous. Some talk went around about how maybe it wouldn't be such a bad idea if you two weren't around any longer to ask no damn fool questions."

David extended the jar to Ben. "No, thanks. I'm not much of a drinker."

Brady went on with what he was saying: "I figured ya'all had either left the area or were camping out somewhere nearby. So I grabbed myself a jar and decided to go for a ride. If I found you, I'd warn you. If not, I'd take me a couple of swigs of moonshine and go home."

Ben cleared his throat to get Brady's attention. "I need to ask you, did you participate in what happened at Rosewood?"

"I'm the town barber. When they came to me and asked if I wanted to do some coon hunting, I knew what they meant. By then the town was abuzz with what had happened to Fannie Taylor, and everyone was determined to avenge her. Most of the men had been drinking. I knew some niggers were gonna die and I wanted no part of it. When they asked if they could borrow my shotgun, I told them I would not loan it out for murder. Does that answer your question, *Mister* Shahn?"

"I'm sorry. I didn't mean anything. I'm just trying to get things straight in my head."

Brady nodded, but his feathers were still a bit ruffled.

David threw a few sticks on the dying fire, sending up sparks. In a few seconds, the flames grew higher.

"I told you boys that your fire could be seen from the road. If I were you, I'd move farther back into the woods. A few hundred yards on, the trail we came in on ends at a swamp. You'll be safe enough there for the night and then tomorrow you should hit the road north."

"Sure," said Ben impatiently. "We'll move our camp. But first, can you tell us what you know about Rosewood? We came a long way for the story and we just can't tuck our tails between our legs and run outta here at the first sign of trouble."

Brady handed the jar to David and stood up to stretch his legs. "You get kinda kinked up sitting like that. I'm on my feet most of the day."

Ben said nothing. David took a pull from the jar. They both waited. Brady sat back down. "Let's get one thing straight. These are good people. They just lost their minds for a little while. I won't mention the names of those involved, but I'll tell you what happened and why, so you'll get your story and get your butts outta here before you're the cause of more trouble."

David handed the jar back to Brady. Ben got out his notebook and a pencil.

After taking a long, slow swallow and wiping his mouth with the back of his hand, Brady began his story.

"It all started with Fannie Taylor. Her husband, Jim, he's a salesman and is on the road more often than not. She was seeing John Bradley, who works for the Seaboard Railroad, when Jim was away. Well, one day ..."

Ben held up his hand with the pencil in it and said, "I'm sorry to interrupt you so soon into your story. But I need all the facts. Was it common knowledge that Fannie was having an affair?"

"Not likely."

"Then how did you know?"

Brady sighed and looked over to David. In response, David shrugged.

"I know because Aunt Sarah told me."

"Who's Aunt Sarah?"

"She was the Taylors' nigger wash woman. And before you ask, Aunt Sarah's name was Sarah Carrier. I've always been friendly with the colored folks around here, and one day she told me about Fannie and Bradley. All the blacks knew, but they also knew enough to keep their mouths shut around white folks. All white folks except me, that is."

393

"Did you tell anyone else?"

"Nope. That's why the niggers tell me things. Because they know I can be trusted to keep my mouth shut."

David had to ask, "It sounds like you like the Negroes, so why do you call them 'niggers'?"

"It's just the way we talk. It don't mean nothing. Now, if you boys will let me get on with my story, I'd be mighty obliged. I've got a wife waiting for me at home and I'll catch hell if I'm out late."

"Please continue," said Ben. "We'll hold our questions until you finish."

"Alright. And I'll try to remember that you boys ain't from around here and put in as much detail as I can.

"So, Aunt Sarah had been seeing Bradley come and go while Jim was away. Then, on New Year's Day, a neighbor heard Fannie scream, and after getting his gun, he ran next door to find her with a bloody lip and lookin' like she'd been punched around some. She claimed that a nigger broke in and assaulted her. At the time, she said nothing about being raped.

"On the second of January, when things were really heating up, Aunt Sarah whispered to me that, on the previous morning, she saw John Bradley leaving the house just before the neighbor went running over. But by the time she told me, it was too late to stop what was about to happen.

"Word went around that Fannie had been raped by a nigger. And as it so happened, a nigger had escaped from a chain gang just the day before. So Sheriff Walker raised a posse to look for him and find out if he was the culprit. But in a very short while, he lost control of the posse. It wasn't a posse anymore, it was a mob. Men were coming in from all over. From Chiefland, from Bronson and Otter Creek. That was just the second day. As word spread, more men showed up from as far away as Jacksonville. Then the Klan got involved. By the third day, men were coming in from out of state.

"You gotta understand how we feel down here. Folks don't tolerate miscegenation. And when it comes to our women folk being assaulted by black men, that we just can't abide. I might have joined the posse myself if Aunt Sarah had not told me about John Bradley. I tried to tell the sheriff what I knew about Bradley and Fannie, but he thought Aunt Sarah was just making it up to protect the nigger convict. He said Fannie Taylor wouldn't lie about a thing like that. So what could I do? I closed up shop and went home to the missus. There was no business anyway. What with all the men running around looking for an escaped convict who was by then up in Georgia, if he had any sense at all.

"By the next day, there were maybe four hundred men roaming the countryside looking for that nigger. When they couldn't find him, they had to turn their anger and their lust for vengeance somewhere. And that somewhere turned out to be Rosewood.

"A group of them vigilantes came across Sam Carter walking down the road, minding his own business. They figured him being colored, he'd have to know where the escaped nigger was hiding. They tortured him until he said he was hiding the nigger out in the woods and he would lead them to him. Of course, he wasn't hiding anyone. He just wanted to put an end to the pain. When they got to the place in the woods, there wasn't anyone there. So they shot Sam and hung his body from a tree as a message to other niggers that they better watch their step. Then things got worse."

"Things got 'worse'?" exclaimed Ben, wide-eyed.

Brady used the interruption to wet his whistle. Afterward, he handed the jar to David who did the same, even though his whistle needed no wetting.

"Yes, things got progressively worse," said Brady. "And I'm gonna tell you how."

Ben nodded. David sat upright. He could not believe what he was hearing.

"So," continued Brady, "you got four hundred men who have been hunting one nigger for four days, all over the county. And by now, they're kinda irritable. Most of them have been away from their homes and families, sleeping out. They haven't been eating too good either, but they've been drinking a lot. I didn't sell 'em any of my 'shine, but I know others who did.

"A mob is a living organism. No one's in charge. It moves on its own. It has no head, just a body. On the fourth night, the mob went to Rosewood, figuring the people there had to be hiding the escaped nigger. Where else could he be?

"I don't think they went there with the intention of killing anyone or burning the town. They just wanted to force the people there to turn over that nigger.

"Now, before I go any further, I gotta tell you how it is in the South. Our niggers never give white people no lip. They're respectful. They step aside if they meet you coming down the sidewalk. A black man will always divert his eyes to the ground if he passes a white woman in the street. That's just the way things are and how they've always been. So, the mob was anticipating no trouble from the niggers of Rosewood that January night eight years ago. Boy, were they ever mistaken.

"They went to Sylvester Carrier's house first, Aunt Sarah's husband. Now, if you knew Sylvester, you knew he didn't take no guff from nobody, black or white. He was the exception among niggers. I respected the man.

"The mob surrounded Sylvester's house and demanded that he come out and tell them where the nigger was hiding. There had to be over two hundred liquored-up white men outside that house, some of them holding torches, all of 'em holding guns. No way was Sylvester going out to talk to that mob.

"What they didn't know was that there were twenty people inside Sylvester's house, hiding out. He was not only protecting himself and Sarah, he had a lot of people depending on him. Some of those people were women and children and some of them were men with guns. It was known that Sylvester's twelve gauge was his pride and joy. He always kept it well-oiled and clean.

"When he didn't come out as ordered, two men went up onto the porch and kicked in the front door. That's when Sylvester let 'em have it with both barrels. Knocked them clean outta their shoes. Then all hell broke loose. When the shooting stopped and the smoke cleared, there were dead lying everywhere. Everyone who had been in the house was dead, except for a few of the children who had made it out the back door and into the woods.

"If the mob wasn't crazy before, it sure as hell was now. They went from house to house pouring kerosene on them and setting them on fire. Then they shot the people as they ran outside, trying to escape the flames. A lot of the nigger men didn't want to go down peacefully and turned their guns on the whites. Some of the women and children made it into the woods.

"There was only one white couple who lived in Rosewood, the Wrights, John and Mary Jo. They were sheltering a whole slew of scared people in their house after the other houses were set on fire. When a group of men demanded that they turn over the niggers hiding in their house, John and Mary Jo stood side by side at their front door and told those men to go to hell. Their house was the only house not burned that night."

Brady reached out for the jar; David handed it to him. "That was mighty thirsty work, tellin' all that," said Brady.

Ben looked up from his notes and rubbed his eyes. The fire was dying and he needed more light. "David, will you please throw a few sticks on the fire?" He turned back to Brady and said, "Thank you for telling us that. If you don't mind, I have just a few questions."

"I'm sorry, Mister Shahn, but I have to be getting on home. I've said all that I have to say. It was pleasant out here under the stars and the company was good. But now that you have your story, you can go back up North and do with it what you will. Just don't use my name. I gotta live here, still."

Ben looked stricken. "Is there anyone else in Cedar Key who will talk to us?"

"I can't think of anyone, unless it's someone who will talk to you while you're dancing from the end of a rope. This is still lynching country around here. You just don't seem to understand how serious this is. I can't be responsible for you after this."

"How about the Wrights? They were heroes. They did the right thing. They should want to talk about it."

Brady ignored Ben and stood up. He offered the jar to David. "Here, take one last pull and make it a good one. It warms my heart to see people enjoying my liquor."

Ben was frantic. "What about the Negroes, the survivors. How can we find them?"

Brady thought for a moment. "As soon as it was safe, the ones hiding in the woods scattered like leaves in the wind. But I heard most of 'em ended up in Gainesville. And good luck finding 'em.

You boys should be packed up and out of here by morning. And don't go into town again."

David was about to say goodnight and thank Brady for the hooch. But instead, he said, "What's that?"

Ben and Brady looked to where David was pointing. Through the trees, they saw a line of five sets of automobile headlights heading their way.

"Sweet Jesus!" cried Brady. "You boys hightail it down the road as fast as you can. There's a swamp at the end. Stay there until they're gone. If you see lights coming your way, go into the water, it's not deep, and hide behind a cypress tree. They won't go in looking for you."

"I'm not leaving," said Ben. "And I'm certainly not going into any swamp!"

"Oh, yes, you are," said David, pulling on Ben's arm. "And so am I. Now, come on. You heard what they did to those Negroes. Do you think they'll treat us any differently?"

Brady slid the jar of moonshine into his side coat pocket and said, "You boys skedaddle. I'll handle things here. They'll go looking for you, but I don't think they'll look for long. Now get going."

"Let me get a few things out of the car," said Ben.

David, his hand shaking, grabbed Ben's arm and pulled him away from the car. "Goddamn it! Do you want to get us killed?"

Ben, seeing the fear in David's eyes, allowed himself to be pulled out of the comforting firelight and into the cold darkness of the pine forest. They made it around a curve in the trail just as the headlights of the first automobile in the procession played across the trees and lit up Brady, standing next to his car.

The men got out of their cars, leaving their headlights on. Two or three men emerged from each vehicle. Some held rifles, some did not. The driver of the first car, Pete Lee, came up to Brady and asked what he was doing there.

"I wanted to avoid trouble, Pete, so I came out here to tell those Yankees to pack up and get out first thing in the morning. I didn't know you boys were so anxious. I figured you would wait and see if they went back into town before you took action."

Lee laughed. "Always the peacemaker, huh, Chet? Well, we can take it from here."

"That's good. My wife's waiting for me anyway. You think you boys could move your cars outta the way so I can get out of here?"

"You know the road's too narrow to turn around. Wait until we take care of our business, then we'll all leave together."

"What are you planning on doing?"

"We just want to put the fear of God in 'em and send them on their way."

"Is that why you're carrying that rope, and the other men, those guns?"

Before Lee could answer, there was a shout. "They're not here, Pete!"

Lee held up the hand holding the rope and shook it in Brady's face. Between clenched teeth, he said, "Where are they, Chet?" His voice barely containing his fury.

"Don't take that tone with me, Pete Lee. And don't you try to threaten me, either. I remember when you was still wearin' short pants."

Lee eased up a bit. In a calmer voice, he said, "I'm sorry for getting excited, Chet. But I still gotta ask you to tell me where the Yankees have gone to."

"I don't know, Pete. When I got here, all I found was their car and a dying fire. I built it up some and waited for them to come back. After about ten minutes, I got tired of waiting. I figured they went out to collect firewood and got lost. I was just about to leave when you pulled in."

Lee went over to the fire and called his men to gather around. "We got us some Yankees to find. Any of you men with flashlights or lanterns in your cars, go get 'em."

Three hundred yards away, standing at the edge of a swamp, Ben asked, "What do you think? You think it's safe to go back?"

Hugging himself to keep warm, David answered, "Let's give it a few more minutes."

They gave it more than a few more minutes and it was a good thing they did. Down the road, heading in their direction, a parade of flashlight beams cut through the night.

"Come on," said David. "Let's ease into the water. That looks like a good old-fashioned lynch mob coming our way."

41

David flinched as he stepped into the dark, knee-deep water. But it wasn't as cold as he had expected. Ben, right behind him, asked, "Do you think there's alligators in here?"

"Don't think about that. Let's just make our way to the trees before those yahoos get here."

They had just secured themselves behind two thick-bodied cypress trees when the men from Cedar Key showed up. They milled around shining their lights out onto the water and into the adjacent woods.

One of the men said, "You reckon they went into the swamp?"

"Not them Yankee boys. They wouldn't have the gumption. Hell, I wouldn't go in there without a boat. If the quicksand don't git ya, the water moccasins will. Them boys gotta be hiding in the woods. They probably saw us comin'."

At the word "quicksand," Ben and David, from behind the relative safety of their respective cypress trees, glanced at one another. Ben was about to whisper something, but David silenced him with a quick shake of his head.

Someone shouted, "Let's go find 'em."

Someone else said, "They'll see us coming from a mile off, us with these lights. They'll just move deeper into the woods."

Pete Lee took charge. "We can't stay out here jawing all night. We'll leave 'em be for now. If we run into them tomorrow, well, we'll just have a little *talk* with 'em then. You boys agree?"

One of the vigilantes, a man by the name of Will, spoke up. "Sounds good to me, Pete. My old lady said I had to be home by nine to tuck the kids into bed. Thinks I don't spend enough time with 'em."

There were a few snickers and a laugh or two at Will's expense.

"Okay," said Lee. "Let's head back to town. And any of you men who *don't* have to run home to your wives, I'm buyin' the first round at Charlie's Bar."

A murmur of approbation arose from the group before the men turned away from the swamp and headed back the way they had come.

Ben and David waited a full five minutes before splashing their way back onto dry land.

"That was close," said Ben.

"Yes, it was," agreed David.

While they waited for the vigilantes to get back to their cars and leave, David asked Ben what they were going to do now.

"I hadn't thought about it. I first wanted to see if we were going to live through the night."

"We sure as hell can't stay around Cedar Key."

Ben thought for a moment. "Okay. This is what we'll do. I have Brady's version of events. So, we'll go to Gainesville and see if we can run down any of the Negro survivors and get their stories."

As Ben was talking, David noticed a yellowish-orange glow reflecting off the treetops, back near their camp.

"What do you think that is?" he asked.

Ben looked to where David was pointing. "Looks like a fire to me."

They looked at one another and then started running. As they neared their camp, they could see that, indeed, it was a fire, a large one. They hesitated, hanging back in the shadows, making sure the Cedar Key men had left. When satisfied on that count, they warily approached their camp, or what was left of it. The vigilantes had set fire to Ben's car. The Model T was completely enveloped in flames. Thick acrid black smoke rose into the air and disappeared as it mingled with the black of the night sky.

Ben dropped to his knees and mouthed *No*, over and over.

David stood next to him with an unfathomable look on his face. At length, he said, "We better go. The gas tank might explode. Besides, we don't want to be here if the cops or the fire department show up."

Ben got to his feet and shouted, "Go? Go where? Everything I owned was in that car. I don't have enough money to buy another one. Things were tight enough before we started out. I barely had enough to make this trip. Now I'll never get the story. And how are we gonna get back to New York? And …"

402

He was beginning to get a bit hysterical. David grabbed him by the shoulders and gave him a good shake. "Calm down, Ben. I have a plan."

"You have a plan? That's rich. Mind telling me what it is?"

"I'd be happy to if you'll come with me. We have to get away from here."

Ben looked over at his burning automobile and then back at David. "You know, my dime novel collection was in there."

After taking one last, loving look at his old Ford Model T, he squared his shoulders in resignation and said, "She wasn't much, but she got me around."

Once out on the highway, they walked in silence, Ben thinking that even if David didn't have more of a plan than walking back to New York, he had been right. They did have to get away from there.

His thoughts turned to his lost cause.

What a shame. It would have made one hell of a story. It would have made my name in the newspaper business. I could have had my pick of jobs.

David's thinking was not so fatalistic. In fact, just the opposite. He knew they were not beaten, not yet ... and not by a longshot.

They were walking in the middle of the highway. No traffic came from either direction; they had the road to themselves. After a mile or so, Ben said, "Just to while away the time, you wanna fill me in on your plan?"

David's thoughts had been a thousand miles away. Ben's voice brought him back to the here and now.

"Sorry, Ben. What did you say?"

"I said, except for the crickets, it's awful quiet out here. I thought we could talk just to pass the time. Maybe you could fill me in on your plan. But before you do, I want you to know that I'm okay now. I got a little crazy back there. But I've come to terms with the situation. And I realize that you can't win 'em all."

In the darkness, Ben could not see the smile that played across David's face.

"Alright, Ben. But we're gonna win this one. This is what I propose. We walk until daylight. If we see headlights headed our way—from either direction—we hide in the brush and let them pass. We don't know who it might be. But once it's light out, we should

403

be safe. Then we'll start hitchhiking. We gotta get to Gainesville, like you said, and get the Negroes' version of events."

Ben admired David's tenacity, but it wasn't practical. "How are we gonna get around? And don't forget the Model T was also our hotel. I've less than fifty dollars left."

"Let me ask you something, Ben. Do you believe in this story? I mean, does it make you angry what was done to those poor people? Or are you out just to get a byline and make some money?"

Ben did not answer right away, and David didn't press it. After a few minutes, Ben said, "Up until a moment ago, it's been about getting a good story and making a buck. But you're right. What was done to those people and the horror they suffered through *should* be told, no matter what the cost. I say let's get the rest of the story, even if we have to walk to Gainesville and sleep out in the rain to do so."

David slapped him on the back. "That's the way to talk. But we won't be sleeping in the rain or doing much walking once we get to Gainesville. I may have a little surprise for you when we get there."

"What do you mean?"

"I don't want to talk about it just yet. Wait until we get to Gainesville."

They walked on. Each man lost in his own thoughts. There was nothing else to do but put one foot in front of the other and keep walking.

After a while, Ben asked, "What time do you think it is?"

"I don't know. You're the one with the watch."

"It's too dark. I can't read it."

"I figure it's about ten, maybe eleven. Why, what difference does it make?"

"None. Just making conversation, is all."

Behind them, to the west, stars were slowly dropping below the horizon. To the east, other stars rose into the velvety black sky to take their place. And all the while, David and Ben trudged on.

Around three in the morning, Ben asked David, "Why don't you tell me why you're sticking it out? When I was ready to give up, you egged me on to persevere. And you were right. But what are you getting out of it? I know all you had going for you back in New York was a soup line. But it beats the hell outta being lynched."

"First of all, Ben, we're not going to see any more lynch mobs. Not in Gainesville. We may or may not find any Negro survivors. And we may have to go back to New York City with only Brady's version of events. But it shouldn't be too hard to imagine the fear those Negroes went through that night. We lived it in a small way when those men were hunting us. But can you envision how much more horrible it was for the people of Rosewood, as they cowered in their homes while hundreds of enraged white men went house to house pouring kerosene on front porches, then lighting their houses on fire?

"I can see it all in my mind's eye. A father, the man tasked with protecting his family, he's looking down at his little children huddled on the floor, shivering and crying in fear. His wife is trying to calm them, but she too is crying. What is he to do? Surrender? But he can hear the gunshots. He hears the laughter as someone shouts, 'Just got me another nigger!' And someone else shouts, 'That ain't nothing. I got me two piccaninnies running for the woods!'

"He knows that those outside are shooting anyone who runs from a burning building, including women and children. If they were killing only men, he'd gladly give up his life to save his family. What is he to do?"

David stopped walking and turned to Ben. "We gotta tell this story. If we can't find any of the Negroes from Rosewood, then we'll just have to write that part ourselves. People have to know about it. Now, come on. We have some miles to cover."

David purposefully strode off, walking at a faster pace. It was as though his little speech had made him even angrier and spurred him on to getting to Gainesville all that much sooner. Ben stood in the middle of the road for a moment, watching the dark form of his "assistant" fade into the night. Then he hurried to catch up.

They were lucky. Just after sunrise, they caught a ride from a man going all the way to Jacksonville. He let them out in downtown Gainesville just as the town was coming to life.

"Well, we're here," said Ben. "What's your plan?"

"The first thing we're gonna do is get something to eat."

They found a little place on Main Street and ordered bacon and eggs and lots of coffee. They were too hungry to do much talking

405

while they ate, but after their empty plates had been pushed to the side and their coffee cups refilled, David told Ben what he had in mind.

"I got a surprise for you, Ben. I'm coming into a little money. For all I know, I may already have it. I'll have to make a phone call in a little while and then I'll know for certain."

It took a tick or two for Ben to digest what he had just heard. "Of course, I'm happy for you, David, but what does that have to do with us getting the story?"

David sat back in his chair and sipped his coffee. He didn't say a word. He wanted Ben to figure it out for himself.

Finally, Ben's eyes grew wide. He leaned forward, elbows on the table. "Are you saying that you're gonna finance the rest of our little excursion?"

David nodded.

"If that's the case, then we're equal partners."

"We can talk about that later. We have a couple of hours to kill before I can make my call. Why don't we walk around town and get our bearings. I have to get the name of a bank to have the money sent to and maybe we can find out where the colored folks live in this town."

By noon, both objectives had been achieved and they were back in the small café where they had eaten breakfast.

"It's now nine o'clock out in California," said David. "It should be safe to call."

$$\approx \approx \approx$$

"Hello? Mister Lane?"

"Hello, David."

"Did the house sell?"

"Yes. The final offer was thirteen-five, and I accepted on your behalf. The buyer was anxious to take possession and plunked down cold hard cash. There was no escrow."

"That's great! When can I have access to the money?"

"Anytime. After my commission and fees, your net is twelve thousand."

"Can you wire me two thousand dollars and hold on to the rest of it for me?"

"That would not be a problem. Where do you want the money sent?"

"To me, in care of The First National Bank of Gainesville, Florida."

"Are you sure they're stable? I mean, with the condition some banks are in today."

"They were established in 1885 and look to be going strong. I went by there this morning and spoke with the manager. He's expecting the wire transfer."

"I'll have to send it through Wells Fargo. It should be there by tomorrow. I can't leave the office right now, but it will be taken care of today."

"Thank you, Mister Lane."

"There's just one more thing."

"Yes?"

"The furniture."

"The furniture?"

"The furniture in the house. I had an inventory taken. Do you want any of it? Or should I sell it?"

"That's not important. Let the buyer have it or throw it away. Whatever you want to do with it is fine with me."

"There was one item I thought you might want. It was found in the bottom drawer of a bureau in the maid's room. I met her a few times, but I can't remember her name."

"It was Magdalena."

"That's right."

"So, what's the item?"

"It's an old six-shooter. A Colt .45. You had asked me about your father and the Old West, so I thought you might be interested in keeping it."

"I sure am. Can you hold on to it for me? I plan on being out that way in the not-too-distant future. I'll pick it up then."

"I look forward to meeting you."

"Same here. And thanks, Mister Lane."

"You're welcome, David."

≈ ≈ ≈

"We got the money, Ben. It should be here tomorrow."

407

"Great!"

"That's what I said."

"Whereas you're putting up the money, David, I'll defer to you. What do we do now?"

"Don't be silly. You started this thing. You know what you're doing. I'm just along for the ride. You pulled me out of a soup line when I was at my lowest. For all I know, you may have saved my life. I don't think I could have lived like that much longer. Besides, last night when I heard Brady's story, something snapped inside of me. I swore I was gonna see this thing through to the end. We just got lucky that the money came along when it did."

"Okay, David. I still have close to fifty bucks. Let's buy some clothes, shaving gear, and toothbrushes. Then we'll find us a hotel room. I think we both could use some sleep."

"Sounds good. Tomorrow we'll buy a car and then go over to the colored part of town to see if we can find any of the survivors from Rosewood."

≈ ≈ ≈

The first thing the next day, after eating a large breakfast, they went to the bank to see if the money had arrived. It had.

They bought a used 1928 Ford Model A roadster, in good condition, for two hundred dollars.

"Okay," said David. "Now that we have a car, I want to stop at a market and buy a few cured hams and a sack of potatoes."

"Why?" asked Ben.

"I don't think the Negroes in the South trust whites all that much. And with good reason from what I've seen and heard. I thought if we passed around a ham or two, people might be more apt to talk to us. Besides, times are tough. I'm sure a lot of 'em are out of work and could use a decent meal. I haven't seen any soup kitchens since we've been in town. Have you?"

"No, I haven't. And you make a good point. So, let's go shopping and then let's go get our story."

The small trunk of the two-seater barely accommodated the fifty-pound sack of potatoes and four of the seven hams they bought. Ben held one ham on his lap; the other two sat on the floor at his feet.

David pulled the car up in front of a house where two men were sitting on the front porch.

"Might as well start here," said David.

"What do I do with this ham?" asked Ben.

"Put it on the floorboard with the others. This may be a long day. We'll have to choose carefully who we give 'em to."

They approached the men and Ben said, "Hello."

The men said nothing. One of them nodded. But that was the extent of their greeting. Under his breath, Ben whispered, "This isn't going to be easy."

And it wasn't. The men knew nothing of Rosewood or people coming up from Rosewood. One of them said, "You say this thing happened eight years ago?"

Ben said, "Yes, in January of '23."

"That's a long time ago, mister. Why you tryin' to find out about it now?"

"We're from up North. We want to print the story in the newspaper so the world can know about it."

The other man said, "Sometimes it's best to let sleeping dogs lie."

Back in the car, Ben asked, "What do you think?"

"I don't know. Maybe they were lying or maybe they weren't. Let's drive around some and see who else we can find to talk to."

David was surprised at the squalor the Negroes lived in. All the houses were little more than shacks with tin roofs. Hand pumps and outhouses denoted a lack of running water. And none of the streets were paved, as opposed to the rest of Gainesville.

Two hours later, they had spoken to twenty-three people, but no one knew anything about a town called Rosewood, or at least that's what they said.

"This isn't getting us anywhere," said David.

Ben was a bit more optimistic. "Sometimes when you're on a story, everyone wants to talk to you. Other times, you really have to dig to get to the truth. It's well past noon. What do you say to grabbing some lunch and then coming back to work through the afternoon and evening? And we still haven't given out any hams. Perhaps that will work. We can try it when we come back."

David was about to swing the car around when they passed an empty lot with a large shade tree smack in the middle of it. But it wasn't the tree that captured David's attention. It was the ten or so men sitting under the tree.

"I have an idea," he said. "I need to get something at the hotel."

When they arrived back at the hotel, David asked Ben to go into the restaurant and order for the both of them. "Get me a ham sandwich. I have business to conduct with the clerk. If I'm not there by the time the food arrives, go ahead and eat without me. No need to stand on ceremony."

Twenty minutes later, David walked into the restaurant cradling a brown paper bag in his left arm. His sandwich was on the table waiting for him. Ben's plate was empty.

"Ben, you pay the bill and have the waitress bag up my sandwich. I'll eat it in the car. I'll see you outside."

When Ben came out, David was sitting in the passenger seat.

"Looks like I'm driving," he said. He got in the car and tossed the bag with the sandwich in it to David. "So, what now?"

"Go back to that empty lot we saw. I wanna talk to those men."

"Anything else?"

"Yeah. If you don't mind, I'd like to do most of the talking this time."

"Sure. By the way, you wanna tell me what's in the bag?"

David shifted the bag so he could get at his sandwich.

"This bag holds two bottles of gin. The desk clerk secured them for me for a two-dollar tip. All hotel clerks and bellboys know bootleggers."

They drove up to the lot and saw that the men were still there. Most of them were sitting on overturned wooden crates. A few were standing, and one man was sitting on a seat that had once graced a 1919 Nash Touring Car, but now sat on the ground under a large, beautiful banyan tree.

The men grew quiet as Ben and David approached.

"Remember, let me do the talking," said David.

"Gotcha."

David walked up to the edge of the shade, Ben held back a little. "Hello, gentlemen," said David. "My friend and I are from up North. We're newspapermen and we've come to write stories about the

410

South. We were passing through Gainesville and thought we'd get the Negro perspective on things."

No one said anything. David stood there holding his brown paper bag, feeling kind of foolish. Ben came up next to him and said, "Do you mind if we join you in the shade? Even though it's a cool December day, it's still a little warm being out in the sun ... for us Yankees."

Someone said, "You say you're from up North?"

"Yes, we are," said David and took a few steps into the shade. Ben followed.

Another man asked, "Why do you want to talk to us? White folk don't usually care what us colored folks think."

David said, "Up North, newspapermen talk to everybody." Then, with a pronounced flourish, like a magician pulling a rabbit out of a hat, he pulled a bottle of gin from the bag. "And we usually like to do it over a drink or two ... if that's okay by you gentlemen?"

The man who had spoken first stood up and said, "Come on in. You can have my seat."

Another man stood to make room for Ben. David introduced himself and Ben and handed out the two bottles to the two men who had relinquished their seats. "You boys take a good healthy swig and pass 'em around. We can talk newspaper business once we quench our thirst."

The bottles went around once and ended up back with David and Ben. All eyes were on the two white men. Would they drink from the same bottle that a colored man had put his lips to? David knew what they were thinking and did not hesitate. He gulped down the hooch without bothering to wipe the mouth of the bottle. He was praying that Ben, even though he was a non-drinker, had the smarts to know it would be an insult not to take a drink from the bottle. He need not have worried. Ben saw the expectant looks on the black faces surrounding him and did what he had to do. He hefted the bottle, took a small sip, and as soon as it hit bottom, he started coughing. All assembled broke out in laughter.

The ice had been broken.

Ben and David spent the afternoon drinking and swapping stories with the Negroes, trying to gain their trust. When the bottles were, at last, empty, David said, "I forgot. We have some hams in the car we don't know what to do with. Do you fellas think you can help us out by taking them off our hands?"

The conclave crowded around the Model A as David handed out the hams. Ben opened the trunk and encouraged the Negroes to help themselves to all the potatoes they could carry.

Everyone was in good spirits. By then, the sun was nearing the horizon and David figured it was now or never.

"Excuse me, my friends. We have heard tales, dark tales, about a place called Rosewood and we were thinking that, if true, that story would play well in the papers up North. My friend and I were told that some people from Rosewood might have relocated here in Gainesville. You boys wouldn't know where we could find any of those folks, would you?"

The camaraderie between the white men and the black men suddenly vanished. The Negroes mumbled their thanks for the booze and the hams and ambled off in all directions, leaving Ben and David by themselves as night descended on the little town of Gainesville, Florida.

"Well, that didn't turn out exactly like I thought it would," said David.

Ben said, "I'll drive. You look a little wobbly in the legs."

As Ben cranked the engine, a figure emerged from the shadows and stood silently in front of the Model A, impeding its forward movement.

"Who's that?" asked Ben.

"Only one way to find out," said David. "You stay here. I'll handle it."

The figure turned out to be a young Negro girl. No more than eighteen. She stood tall and erect; her deep-set brown eyes glimmered in the failing light.

"Can I help you?" inquired David.

The girl bit her lip and fidgeted with her hands.

David asked, "Is there something you want?"

The girl took a deep breath and said, "Word's going 'round that ya'all are lookin' for some of the people that come up from Rosewood. Is that true?"

"Yes, miss, it is. Do you know any of those people?"

"What do you want 'em for?"

"We want to talk to them about what happened eight years ago. Then we're gonna put the story in newspapers up North so that everyone will know what happened on that horrible night."

The girl's shoulders relaxed. In the gathering darkness, she looked relieved.

"My name is Minnie Lee Langley and I can tell you anything you wanna know. 'Cause I was there."

42

"The first I knew of any trouble was when my cousin Robie and me was playing out in the yard. A carload of white men came down the street. There was so many of 'em in the car they was spilling out, and they was all carrying guns. When they saw us, the car slowed and they gave me and Robie mean looks as they passed."

≈ ≈ ≈

David and Ben were sitting with the Negro girl, Minnie Lee Langley, in the house where she now resided. They sat at the kitchen table to be near the warmth of an old wood stove. The house had no electricity; however, a kerosene lantern gave off sufficient light for Ben to take notes.

Minnie Lee lived with a woman whom she called Aunt Betsy. She wasn't actually a relation, simply a kind-hearted woman who had taken in a scared little nine-year-old girl who had just lost her entire family. Aunt Betsy had said nothing when Minnie Lee brought home two white men. She welcomed them into her home, served them sweet tea, and then retired to the front room to read her Bible before going off to bed.

Minnie Lee had not wanted to be seen talking with the white men, so Ben had suggested interviewing her back at the hotel where they were staying, but she set them straight on that account. "No colored folks are allowed in that hotel unless it's for working."

She had been more concerned that members of her own community would see her conversing with the newspapermen than she was about white people seeing her.

"Why is that?" asked David.

"We was lucky to get away. The people up here took us in, but most folks are afraid them white men from Sumner and Cedar Key is gonna come and get us."

"It's been a long time. Do people really think those men will come here to finish the job?"

"That's not it. They'll only come if we start talkin' about it. They don't want nobody to know what they did."

David only had to think back to hiding behind a cypress tree, knee deep in a snake-infested swamp, to know that Minnie Lee was right. Certain people did not want the unpleasant truth to come out. He asked her, "Why are *you* talking to us?"

" 'Cause ya'all are gonna tell them people up North about Rosewood. I sure don't want those men from Sumner and Cedar Key to come looking for me. But I'm willing to take my chances. I miss my mama and my papa, every day. I miss my cousin, Robie. Those men took everything I had, everyone I loved. No one else will talk to you, so *I'm* talkin' to you."

"We're glad you are," said Ben. "And you have our solemn promise that your story will be printed up North. If we're lucky, maybe newspapers all over the country will print it. Then you won't have to worry anymore. The story will be out and there will be nothing anyone can do about it."

Minnie Lee sipped her tea and said nothing.

"Why don't you continue where you left off," said David. "You tell it in your own way and Ben will write down what you say."

Minnie Lee's dark eyes grew distant and her heart began to race as she thought back to her last days in Rosewood.

"As I was sayin'. Those white men drove by looking mean, and it was right after that my mama come running outta the house and told us to go inside. I was only nine and Robie was six, but we knew things was serious because of the look on Mama's face.

"Mama worked as a maid for Missus Richards over in Cedar Key. And Papa worked at the pencil mill. When they was at work, I'd look after Robie. She was my cousin, but we were like sisters. Both her parents were dead and Robie had been living with us from way before I could remember.

"Mama and Papa had to go off to work, but before they left, Mama told us not to go outside the house. She didn't tell us why. She didn't have to. When Mama told us to do somethin', we did it or else we'd get our fannies whomped. But I knew it had something to do with those men.

"I had a rag doll and Robie had one, too, and that was all we had to play with. After a little while, I started to get bored. I said we should go outside and play in the woods. At first Robie didn't want to 'cause she was afraid of what Mama would do. But I told her Mama would never know. We'd be back long before she or Papa got home. It was a beautiful, sunny day. You gotta remember it was January, it was cool and pleasant. Sorta like it is now.

"I knew where there was a patch of blueberries. It was kinda early in the year for blueberries, but you never know. I took Robie by the hand and we cut through the woods, heading for the patch. After a few minutes, we heard someone screaming. And there was a whole lotta noise, a whole lotta voices.

"I wanted to see what was goin' on. Still holding onto Robie's hand, we crept up to a small clearing. We kept to the trees, but we had a clear view to what was happening. There was Sam Carter, surrounded by white men. Maybe twenty of 'em.

"Sam was all bloodied and his clothes were ripped and torn. He was on his knees begging for somethin'. We couldn't hear what he was saying, but he had his hands together like he was praying. I could tell by his face that he was crying.

"Robie and I was scared to death. We wanted to get away from there real fast, but we was afraid to move. We was afraid we'd make noise and be found out. All we could do was hope they'd go away, so we could go home. I swore if the good Lord would just let me and Robie get back to our house, safe and sound, I'd never leave it again.

"Then one of the men put a rifle on Sam's forehead and pulled the trigger. It was horrible. The back of his head exploded, and Sam keeled over. He didn't move after that.

"Robie started to scream, but I got my hand over her mouth just in time. I hugged her to me until I was sure she would be quiet. She was shaking real bad, and I was too.

"One of the men put a rope around Sam's neck and threw the other end over a high branch. Then they hauled him up like he was no more than a side of beef and tied off the end of the rope. They was all laughing and whooping it up like they just won a baseball game.

416

"They left Sam hanging there with blood and bits of his brains spilling out of the wound. I didn't want to look, but I had to. As soon as we was sure they was gone, Robie and me ran all the way home.

"I didn't want to tell Mama we went out, but Robie wouldn't stop crying. So Mama knew something was up. I had to tell her the truth. I told her what we had seen. Mama surprised me. She didn't whomp us for disobeying. Instead, she hugged us to her, and I could feel her warm tears as they fell onto my face.

"When Papa got home, he looked real concerned, not happy as he usually was. He took Mama into the bedroom so they could talk without us kids hearing what they said. But I went up to the door and listened. Papa was tellin' Mama about Mingo Williams. I didn't hear all of it, but it seems Mingo was on the side of the road collecting pinesap to take to the turpentine still when a carload of white men drove up and just shot him dead. Papa said there was no reason for it, no reason a'tall. He said all the white people of Levy County had gone plumb crazy and until things calmed down, none of us was leaving the house.

"Then Mama told Papa what me and Robie had seen and asked him not to question us about it because we was already shook up enough.

"When they came out of the bedroom, Papa sat down at the table with his shotgun and started cleaning it. Mama called us girls to the kitchen to help out with dinner. But I think that was just to keep us busy."

Minnie Lee paused to take a sip of tea. Ben took out his clasp knife and sharpened his pencil. The shadows were deepening in the corners of the small room, so David reached over and gave the lantern a little more wick and the room brightened. Minnie Lee took another sip of tea and went on with her story.

"Usually, me and Robie slept in the front room, but that night we slept with Mama. Papa didn't sleep a'tall. I heard him going from window to window all night long. In the morning, we didn't have to be told not to go outside. Mama and Papa said they wasn't going to work but was gonna stay close to the house. After breakfast, we went over and sat on our bed and kept quiet. Robie had a picture book she liked. She looked at that as I watched my worried parents

417

try not to look worried for our sake. Mama kept busy in the kitchen. Papa sat at the table, holding his shotgun with a grim look on his face.

"At one point, Papa said he was going out to talk to some of the other men. He wanted to get news of what that posse was up to. They said they was looking for an escaped convict, but that surefire didn't explain why they killed Mingo Williams and Sam Carter like they did.

"There was no word 'bout nothin'. Everyone was stayin' close to their homes. We spent the day as best we could, for being cooped up. By sundown, we thought everything would be all right. No white men had come to Rosewood since the day before. Maybe they had caught the convict. I could see Papa was starting to relax as he stood his shotgun in the corner and told Mama to get dinner on the table. With Papa relaxed, so was the rest of us.

"We said grace and dug into the fried offal and collard greens Mama had been cooking all day. It was a Saturday night, and Mama told me and Robie that, when we was in church the next morning, we had to thank the Lord for sparing us from the trouble. She had just finished tellin' us that when we heard cars comin' down the street.

"Papa went to the window. I don't know what he saw, but when he turned back to us, he had a bad look on his face. He shouted to Mama to shut off the lights and told us kids to get in the firewood closet and get down behind the wood, fast!

"Me and Robie did as we was told and sat in the dark waiting for something bad to happen. It seemed like a long time coming, but then we heard the boom of Papa's shotgun. Then we heard rifle fire, and a bullet came through the door of the closet.

"There was more gunfire and then the second barrel of Papa's gun went off. I was praying that he was giving those crackers what for. Suddenly, everything went quiet. I reached out to take Robie's hand, but she wasn't there. I whispered her name but got no answer. I felt around, using what little light that came in from the bullet hole to find her.

"She was lying on her back. I shook her and told her to stop playing, that she was scarin' me. That's when I felt her warm blood on my hands.

418

"I burst outta the closest and found the house on fire. Papa was over by the table, Mama was right next to him. They was both shot up real bad. They was both dead. Three dead crackers lay scattered about, so I knew Papa went down fighting. I went back to the closet to check up on Robie. With the door open and by the light of the fire, I could see that she, too, was dead. The bullet that had gone through the door had hit her square in the eye."

At this point, Minnie Lee grew quiet and began to cry. Softly at first. Then the dam burst wide open and she was crying her heart out. David reached out to put a hand on her shoulder but drew back. He wasn't sure she would want to be touched by a white man. Tears rolled down Ben's cheek. They waited for Minnie Lee to work through her feelings. There was nothing they could say to alleviate her pain. Clichés and platitudes would not bring her family back.

The sobbing eventually gave way to sniffles. David handed Minnie Lee a napkin. "Here. Dry your eyes and blow your nose."

She looked at David and said, "Thank you. I'm all right now. It's just that I try to keep those thoughts outta my head or I'd go crazy."

"We understand," said Ben. "We can come back tomorrow, if you like."

"No. I have to finish this tonight. I can't have you comin' back 'cause then people will know for sure that I'd been talkin' to you about Rosewood. Anyway, ain't that much more to tell."

Ben nodded and turned to a clean page in his notebook, pencil at the ready.

"Go on, Minnie Lee. What happened next?" prompted David.

Before she had broken down and started crying, Minnie Lee had been speaking in a whisper. But now her voice, although not loud, was strong. It was as though she had come to terms with the horror and was not going to hide from it any longer.

"The front of the house was on fire. I knew I had to get out, but I was afraid those men would be outside waiting for me. I went to the back door and looked out. I didn't see anyone. A ditch ran behind our house and I thought if I could just make it to that ditch, then I could go up the other side and get into the woods.

"Then part of the roof crashed to the floor, right close to me. That sent me running. I was halfway to the ditch when I tripped over something. In the light of the fires, I saw that it was the body of

419

Lexie Gordon. Her face had been blown off by a shotgun. But I could tell it was her by her grey hair and the dress she wore. It was her favorite.

"I made it into the woods and went in as far as I could before I collapsed. I lay on the ground and cried until I had no tears left. The next thing I knew, it was daylight and the birds was in the trees, singing their morning songs. That's what woke me up.

"I was cold and hungry. I was hoping the night before was just a bad dream, but I knew it wasn't. I heard some thrashing off to my left and froze. I thought the men who had killed my people was comin' after me.

"As the noise got closer, I could tell they was colored folks by the way they talked. There was five of 'em, two women and three children. They had done the same as me, run for the woods. They was happy to see me and I was glad to see them. Two of the children, both girls, was younger than me. The other one was just a baby who clung to his mother.

"We sat there for a while and swapped stories. The women were trying to decide if it would be safe to go back home. One woman wanted to wait. The other one, the one with the baby, said she didn't know what to do. She was mostly crying. Finally, I told them that I was gonna sneak up to the town and see if anyone was around. If it was safe, I'd come back and get them.

"When I got to the ditch, I could hardly believe what I was seeing. The whole town ... all the houses and the two churches ... they was gone. All that was left was the still-smokin' ruins. Lexie Gordon's body was gone, too.

"Then I heard one of them caterpillar machines. I moved down along the ditch, keeping my head low, until I saw a group of white men standing around. They was watching a bulldozer dig a big hole. But what stopped me in my tracks was all the dead bodies lined up near the hole. It looked like those men done collected all our dead and now they was gonna bury 'em in one big grave.

"I went back to that place in the woods and found that more people had showed up while I was away. There was some men there, too. I told 'em all what I had seen. Some of the women started in to crying.

"We stayed there for three days and nights and not one of us had anything to eat except the baby, who suckled on his mama's teat. For water, we would lick the morning dew off the leaves. All night long we shivered in the cold. During those long days, as we cried for our dead, we prayed to the Good Lord Almighty to deliver us from this nightmare.

"That's what those white men done to us. And now I'm here to tell about it. I only wish others would speak out. But they're afraid, and I reckon I don't blame 'em."

Ben looked up from his notebook and asked, "How did you get to Gainesville?"

"We wasn't the only ones hiding out in the woods, there were lots of others. On the morning of the fourth day, when we could hardly stand the hunger no more, word spread that a train was picking up folks and getting them out of the county. The signal was two short blasts on the horn and one long. We didn't know if it was true or not, but we prayed that it was. We had to believe there was some hope.

"It turned out it was the Bryce brothers. They was conductors or somethin' for the railroad. They had heard what happened at Rosewood and when their train passed nearby, they'd slow down, sound the horn, and pick up people as they come running out of the woods. The train went through Gainesville, and it being the first town of any size we came to, most of us got off here."

Ben closed his notebook. "That's some story, Minnie Lee. And we thank you for having the courage to tell it to us."

"That's alright. You just make sure you tell those people up North what it's like for colored folks in the South. Our lives don't mean spit to white people. Oh, there's good white people like the Wrights and John and William Bryce, but most of 'em just as soon lynch you as look at you."

Ben looked over at David. "Anything else you think we need to know?"

David roused himself from deep, dark thoughts.

How could anyone treat other human beings in such a way?

"No, Ben, I guess not. I've heard enough. However, I would like to say to Minnie Lee that, on behalf of the whole white race, I apologize for what happened to you and your family. At the moment, I'm thoroughly ashamed of my race."

Minnie Lee cautiously took David's hand in hers. She had never touched a white man before. "I thank you, Mister Mahoney. It's like I said, there are some good white people. Just like there are some bad colored people. It's the way things is, is all."

David reached into his pocket and pulled out sixty dollars and placed the bills on the table. "You're a good-looking young woman, Minnie Lee Langley, and I think you should have a new dress and a new pair of shoes. Whatever is left over, you give to Aunt Betsy for the use of her kitchen tonight."

Back at the hotel, Ben went over his notes. After comparing Minnie Lee's testimony to what Brady had told them, he said, "Well, David, I think we have enough here for one hell of a story. I'll have to flesh it out, of course, but that's all. People will be outraged when they read what really happened at Rosewood. It's just too bad we couldn't get some pictures of the place, or what's left of it. But it's probably overgrown by now, anyway."

David sat across from Ben in the hotel's restaurant. His thoughts were elsewhere.

"I'm sorry, Ben. What did you say?"

"I said we have our story. Tomorrow, we can head back to New York."

David slouched back in his seat, his face clouded by doubt. "I don't know, Ben. I was thinking I might head out west. Maybe take your advice and see what I can find out about my father in Las Cruces. There *might* be something about him in an old newspaper. I never gave him a chance while he was alive. I think, late as it is, I'd like to get to know who he really was.

"Anyway, I got nothing and nobody waiting for me back in New York. You take the story and get it printed. You don't owe me anything. I've been paid in full just by the honor of meeting people like Brady and Minnie Lee. And you, too, my friend. It was a privilege to know you and to work with you. But for now, I'm heading west. And later, I'll just have to see where the winds of chance take me."

"You're a strange one, David Mahoney. But likewise, it's been a pleasure to have known you. I'll get my train ticket in the morning and we can say goodbye then."

"Hold on, Ben. You take the car. I don't need it or want it. I intend to hitchhike. I want to meet people, get to know their stories. I can't do that while cooped up in an automobile. It's a big country out there, of which I know nothing. I have a lot of catching up to do."

"I can't take your car."

"You're not taking it. I'm giving it to you. I've had it with cars for the time being. Did you know I once owned a Duesenberg?"

"No, I didn't."

"Well, I did. And it was a complete waste of money. Think of what I could have done with the thirteen thousand dollars I laid out. How many hungry people could I have fed?

"Here's how we're gonna work it. You take the car. I'll sign the paperwork over to you. And I'm giving you two hundred dollars to hold you over until you can sell the story. Then you're going to New York and become a famous newspaperman and I'm going out West to learn about my father, and by doing so, perhaps learn a little about myself."

David rode with Ben as far as Jacksonville. He got out when they came to US Highway 90. According to the map, that would get him as far as West Texas.

As they shook hands goodbye, Ben said, "When I found you in that soup line, I never thought things would turn out like this."

"Me either, Ben. Now get to New York and tell the world about Rosewood."

David watched the Model A recede into the distance until it was enveloped by the early morning mist. He then hefted his new suitcase and started walking west. One hope-filled step at a time.

423

43

For the first time in his life, David Mahoney was truly happy. It was a crisp, cool morning, ten days before Christmas, 1930. He had money in the bank and money in his pocket. But it was not the approach of Christmas, nor the beautiful morning, nor the money he possessed that brought joy to his heart. It was the fact that he was free. He was finally free from fear.

All his life he had been afraid of one thing or another, but the dread he felt when he realized he had gone through his inheritance had set his world on end.

The humiliation of losing his posh Park Avenue apartment, and then the indignity of being thrown out onto the street from a third-floor walkup was just too much. He had not believed that he could sink any lower. But the flophouses and soup lines soon taught him otherwise.

As he walked the highway under a startling blue, cloudless sky, he gave thanks that he had met Ben Shahn and, through him, Minnie Lee Langley. She had been his salvation. After hearing what she had gone through, he doubted he'd ever sweat the small stuff again.

That first day, he caught a series of rides that took him into Tallahassee. He stayed the night at a motor court and was on the road bright and early the next morning. David's first ride of the day left him off outside of Pensacola, opposite a small roadside stand. Seeing as how he had foregone breakfast, he crossed the street and ordered a hotdog and a Coke. He had his choice of any of the five stools lining the counter. Instead, he opted for the shade of a large oak tree located in an adjacent field.

He was sitting on his suitcase, preparing to take his first bite of the mustard-covered delicacy when a voice from behind him said, "Mind a little company?"

David turned to see an older gentleman, a thin man in his fifties, his hair beginning to turn grey, his face grizzled and lined. He carried a rolled-up blanket, tied up with a length of rope.

"Not at all," answered David. "Come on in and sit down."

"Thanks. The name's Joe Turner."

"I'm David Mahoney. Glad to meet ya."

Nodding towards the hotdog, Turner said, "Don't let me interrupt your meal. Have at it."

In between mouthfuls, David answered a few questions.

"You on the road?"

"Yup. Hitchin' west."

"I only ask because your clothes are clean and you're clean-shaven."

"I've been traveling for only two days."

"What happened? You lose your job?"

"Something like that," said David as he popped the last piece of hotdog into his mouth.

"That hit the spot."

"It looked as if it would," agreed Turner.

It was then that David gave the guy sitting across from him a closer examination. He was more than thin, he was downright emaciated. And his clothes were threadbare and worn.

"When was the last time you had anything to eat?" asked David.

Turner looked down at his veined, bony hands and mumbled something.

David said, "I'm sorry. I didn't catch that."

"I said, not since yesterday. But I don't want you worrying about it. I just got into town and wanted to rest up a spell before I went foraging."

"Foraging?"

"Yeah. You know, hitting back doors and offering to work for a little food. Sometimes you get chased away. But that only happens in the better neighborhoods where the swells live. In the poorer neighborhoods, people are always happy to share with you what little they have."

David did not hesitate. He reached into his pocket and came out with a dollar bill. "Here. Take this and go buy yourself a hotdog … buy two."

Any pride Turner might have possessed had long since deserted him. He reached out his hand, tentatively, almost as if he expected it was some kind of a trick. His eyes glistened with moisture as his fingers embraced the bill. Whispering a quick, "Thank you," he hurried over to the food stand.

David called out after him. "And get a Coke!"

Turner returned with two hot dogs in one hand and an unopened bottle of Coca-Cola tucked up under his arm. In his other hand, he held three quarters. "Here's your change."

David waved him away. "You keep it. Now sit down and eat."

Turner sat down and placed the Coca-Cola bottle on the ground next to him. Nothing was said for the next few minutes. David delighted in seeing Turner wolf down the food. When the dogs were no more, Turner pulled out a clasp knife and popped the cap off the bottle and drank down its contents in one long swallow. He used his coat sleeve to wipe his mouth and said, "That sure was good. I can't thank you enough, mister."

"You're welcome, Joe. And you can call me David. Where are you headed?"

"I'm on my way down to Tampa to pick oranges."

A truck passed by, loudly working through its gears as it climbed the slight grade. When things had quieted down, Turner ventured to say, "So, you're headed west. What's out there?"

"I'm not rightly sure. I'm trying to get a lead on my father."

"You're trying to find him?"

"No. Nothing like that. He's dead. It's just that I didn't know him very well. I want to find out who he was. It might turn out that I didn't know him at all."

Joe nodded as though he understood what David was talking about.

It was getting on near noon and business at the hotdog stand had picked up; people were coming and going, most all of them in automobiles.

"A car ain't a bad way to move about," observed Turner, his voice tinged with longing.

"No, it's not," agreed David, as he stretched out his legs and leaned back against the tree. "Ah, that's better. I was getting a bit stiff. You hitchin', Joe?"

"Naw. I'm riding the rails. When you're old like me and dressed as I am, it's hard to get rides."

For the moment, neither man seemed eager to leave the comforting shade of the big old tree. They would be on their respective ways soon enough, but right now was a time to rest.

"If you don't mind me asking, Joe, what drove you to riding the rails?"

Turner rubbed the grey stubble on his chin, frowned, and looked off into the distance.

"We were farmin' on the shares up in Oklahoma, me and the wife. It was a hardscrabble life, I can tell you that. It was just the two of us. We never did have any kids.

"We did all right year in and year out. Never got rich. But after the landowner took his share of the profits, we did all right. We were on that farm nineteen years. Then, four years ago, there was a drought. Nothing grew. The landowner was understanding, but that was about all. My wife had to take in laundry and sewing, and I had to hire out to a well-drilling outfit just to make ends meet.

"Come spring, the landowner bought the seed and what else we needed for planting a crop. He even advanced us a few dollars to eat on because I told him I couldn't drill wells and plant a crop at the same time.

"Because I wanted to make up for the losing year, I asked if we could plant an additional forty acres on the fallow quarter section next to ours and the owner said yes. Well, my wife—her name was Eva—and I set out working like we had never worked before. We worked from before sunrise until long after the sun had gone down."

Joe Turner's voice started to waver. "Just before we finished with the planting, Eva took sick. A week later she passed over. I believe I worked her to death. I should never have wanted to plant those extra acres. I thought we had to make up for the previous year's loss. But we didn't. It was just greed on my part.

"I couldn't work the farm by myself. For that matter, I didn't want to anyway. There were just too many memories of Eva. I couldn't bring myself to sit in the parlor at night and look at her empty chair. I couldn't lie in our bed at night without crying."

Joe's voice trailed off as though he might have said too much. As though he might have let too much of his deep-buried anguish come to the surface.

An awkward silence followed. Eventually David said, "That's tough, Joe. I'm sorry about your wife. And it's not fair that you put in all those years of farming only to end up with nothing. It's just not fair."

Joe gave a rueful smile. "Who ever said life was fair?"

David smiled back and said, "Nobody."

Traffic had ceased on the road. The hotdog stand was quiet now that lunch was over, and the wind that had been blowing in from the northwest had slackened to a gentle breeze. The two men sat under the oak, lost in their separate thoughts. Joe thinking that David was right. Life was unfair. David thinking that life had been *very* fair to him and he had blown it.

At length, Joe said, "What do you mean, you're looking to get to know your father? Was he killed in the war?"

"No. It's just that I never got to know him very well because I was a spoiled idiot. I thought of no one but myself. However, in a way, the war did contribute to the estrangement with my father."

David went on to tell how he had never forgiven Dillon for not trying to get him out of the draft. How he had moved to New York City to be around people just as spoiled as he was. How he had chased an empty life until his money ran out.

"I was so wrong. I never once thought of my father's feelings. He practically begged me to call him on the phone once in a while. But I never did, and now I regret that, too. Well, that's my story and I'm not very proud of it."

Joe stood up to stretch his legs. "I don't understand. You didn't want to fight for America?"

"With a passion, I did not want to go to that damn war. Did you?"

"Yes, I did. I wanted nothing more than to fight for my country, but I couldn't leave Eva alone. It didn't matter anyway. Farmers were considered essential to the war effort, so I had a deferment. Plus, I was forty-one at the time."

David's laughter indicated his incredulity. "*Fight for your country?* How in God's name was marching off to France gonna help America? The Huns were not coming over here and attacking us. It was a war between France and Germany. And then England got involved. Those three countries had been feuding like the

Hatfields and McCoys for centuries. The whole thing was none of our damn business!"

David grew fervent at this point. "You ever hear of Verdun?"

"Sure, everyone has."

"Yeah, the battle was fought just before the draft was enacted. I read about it at the time. It lasted eleven months, and at the end, not one inch of ground had been gained by either side. Do you know how many men's life-blood was shed in the town and forests of that godforsaken place for no reason whatsoever?"

David did not give Joe a chance to answer. "I'll tell you how many. One million men died in those eleven months, and all for nothing. Then, when England and France started running low on cannon fodder, they asked the United States to send over our boys to die in the trenches for no goddamn good reason that I could see."

David calmed down. In a somewhat introspective voice, he said, "My mistake was in directing my anger at the whole situation towards my father."

Joe said, "I kinda see your point about going off to France. Now that you've explained it to me. And I'm sorry that you and your father had a falling-out about it."

It was getting on to three o'clock. David had dallied long enough. "I gotta be hitting the road. It was nice talking to you, Joe."

"Likewise. But let me give you some advice, if I may. You're young. You still got some life ahead of you. After you find out about your father, settle down and get yourself a good job so you don't end up like me. This depression can't last forever."

David fished around in his pocket and came out with a ten-dollar bill. "Please take this. It will save you from having to forage for a while."

Joe could not believe his eyes. "I haven't seen a ten-dollar bill since our last good harvest. And that was five years ago. But I can't take it. You'll be needing it yourself."

"What I need, Joe, is to get hitchin'. Now, take this so I can be on my way."

Joe accepted the bill with a shaky hand. "God bless you, David. No one has been this kind to me in a long time. But can I ask you one question?"

"Sure."

429

"If you got money to be giving away, why aren't you taking a train? Why the hitchhiking?"

"So I can meet people like you, Joe. Now if you'll excuse me, I've gotta get a move-on."

≈ ≈ ≈

The asphalt highway ran straight and true. To the west, cottony white clouds were turning to grey. Ethereal pinks and flaming reds fought for supremacy with a brilliant orange sky. Soon, the staggering colors would fade, bringing on twilight, which, in time, would be replaced by the night.

David had been on the road for four days—three since he had parted ways with Joe Turner—and he was getting to know his fellow Americans. The men who had picked him up did so mostly for conversation, someone to talk to as the miles passed by. They did most of the talking and David did most of the listening. They talked of their lives and their jobs, their hopes and their dreams. David figured it was easier for them to open up to a complete stranger who would soon be left on the side of the road than to someone they knew.

Earlier in the day, David had been let out at a crossroad. After an hour without having caught a ride, he started walking, not knowing how far it was to the next town. As he walked the mostly deserted highway, he occasionally looked over his shoulder, hoping to see a car coming his way. The land was flat, the sky, endless, and the going, slow.

If he did not get a ride soon, he'd be stuck out in the middle of nowhere for the night. But he was not worried. He had discarded his suitcase two days ago. Now he carried his few belongings in a rolled-up blanket, tied off with a length of rope. Just like Joe Turner.

If he did not secure a ride by the time it was full dark, he'd go a ways off to the side of the road to find his bed for the night, just as he'd done the night before. It had been a little chilly sleeping out under the stars, but wrapped up in the blanket, he had survived.

The last of the daylight finally surrendered to the night. David was about to call it quits for the day when, way down the highway, far to the east, he saw a set of headlights coming his way.

430

He stood on the shoulder with a smile on his face, his thumb out, and the blanket tucked up under his arm. Ready to go.

The car was moving slowly, and it took forever for the light from the headlights to wash over him. He leaned his upper body out over the road. He wanted to make sure he was seen.

The car passed by without stopping.

It was time to search out a place to bed down, but then David noticed the car had stopped after all. It was pulled off to the side, about a hundred yards away. David hurried in its direction. When he got close, he saw that it was not a car at all, but an old Ford Runabout with a pickup body.

"Hello. Need a ride?" asked the man behind the wheel.

"I sure do."

"Then hop in."

David threw his bedroll into the back and climbed into the small cab. The driver was a man of about forty with a full head of dark hair. He wore a beard that carried a little grey in it and his smile was genuine. "I'm sorry I didn't stop right away, but I didn't see you until I had passed by. It took me a minute to realize what I had seen." He spoke with a slight accent, which David could not place.

The driver put the truck in gear and pulled out onto the lonesome road. David leaned his head against the back of the cab and sighed. Perhaps this ride would get him into a town with a hotel and he could sleep in a warm bed tonight. Perhaps the hotel clerk would be able to supply him with a small bottle of spirits. Gin would be nice.

"Where are you headed?" asked the driver.

"Las Cruces, New Mexico. How far are you going?"

"Not that far, I'm afraid. I'm turning off up ahead a ways."

"By any chance, will we pass through a town before you turn off?"

"Nope. The closest town is Brackettville, and that's ten miles past where I'll be letting you out."

The driver concentrated on working through the gears as they went up a small hill. Then he introduced himself. "I'm Otto Fischer."

"My name's David and I really appreciate the ride. It gets kinda lonesome stuck out there at night."

431

"Sure enough, David. It gets kinda lonesome on this stretch of road, and I've driven it many a time. I got a farm a few miles northwest of here. Today, I had to go to San Antonio to get parts for my windmill."

They made small talk as they cut through the dark, peaceful night. "You going to Las Cruces for Christmas?" asked Otto.

"No. I'll just be passing through on my way to California."

"You got family out there?"

"Nope. I gotta see a lawyer in Los Angeles. After that, I don't know where I'm going."

Otto Fischer took his eyes off the road for a moment and studied David. "At loose ends, are you?"

"I guess you could say that. I gotta figure out what I want to do with the rest of my life."

"You married?"

"Haven't had the pleasure, as of yet."

Otto chuckled. "Then it's easy. Find yourself a good woman and get married. Then have lots of kids. After that, you won't have time to worry about what you're gonna do with the rest of your life."

To change the subject, David said, "You said something about a windmill?"

Otto grumbled, "The bane of my existence!"

Having successfully redirected the conversation, David pressed home his advantage. "Why's that?" he asked.

"Our well ran dry and I had to dig a new, deeper one at a different location. That means I'm gonna have to move the windmill. Anyway, when I pulled up the equipment, I saw that the check valve was almost shot, and I needed a new seal for the top of the drop pipe. That's what I've been doing all day, running down parts."

David had no idea what Otto was talking about. But just to be polite, he said, "Then you should be all set."

Otto snorted. "You would think so, wouldn't you? But I still gotta dismantle the windmill and then move the tower to the new well."

"Is that a problem?" asked David.

"Not for two men. But there's no getting help right now. It being Christmastime, all my neighbors have their own problems. My wife

432

isn't strong enough for the job and my boys are too young to be of any help. But not to worry. After the first of the year, I'll round up someone and get it done."

Otto then tried to steer the conversation back to David. "You got any family at all?"

"No relatives that I know of."

Not much more was said after that. Otto was thinking about his windmill and David was thinking of a thick, juicy steak. He hadn't eaten since early that morning.

Out of the blue, Otto asked, "You hungry?"

"Funny you should ask. I was just thinking it would be nice if there were a café where you turn off. There isn't, is there?"

"There isn't *anything* where I turn off."

"I figured that."

"Well, that's what I was getting around to. It's desolate out here and we've seen only two cars since I picked you up. And they were both going in the opposite direction. Look behind us. Do you see any headlights?"

David craned his head out the window. "Black as pitch back there."

"I thought so. How about coming home with me? You can get something to eat, and sleep in the barn. I'll drive you back to the road in the morning."

David did not have to think about it. "That would be great. I appreciate it."

"Good. The turnoff is right up ahead. The road to the farm is a little rough and the springs on this old truck are a little worn, so be prepared."

Otto had been right on the money about how bumpy the ride would be from highway to farm. David had to grip the dashboard hard just to keep from being thrown about.

They pulled into the yard, and, from somewhere in the darkness, a hog snorted. A soft, yellow light emanated from the front window of the house. The only light for miles around.

As though reading David's mind, Otto said, "Electricity hasn't made it out to the farms yet, just the cities. Come on in and meet my wife. The boys are probably in bed by now."

Otto went in first and David followed. An attractive woman, about thirty-five years of age, sat in a wicker chair, reading a book by the light of a lantern. Without looking up, she said, "I'll get your supper in a minute, dear. I just want to finish this chapter."

Otto cleared his throat. "Karin, I've brought home a guest for supper and he'll be sleeping in the barn tonight."

The woman lifted her emerald-green eyes and smiled. She was absolutely beautiful in spite of what she was wearing—dungarees and a man's red flannel shirt with the sleeves rolled up to her elbows. Her blonde hair was pulled back in a no-nonsense bun.

She rose from the chair and approached David with her hand extended. "Welcome to our humble home. I'm Karin." She also had a slight accent.

Her hand was dainty and small … and calloused. It was obvious from the clothes and the calloused hands that she did her fair share of work around the farm. But you'd never know it from looking at her lovely face.

David gripped her hand. "My name is David Mahoney and I thank you for allowing me into your home."

The corners of Karin's mouth turned up in a smile. "You men sit down at the table. I've kept the supper warm. I hope you like *pichelsteiner*, Mister Mahoney."

David looked to Otto for an explanation. "*Pichelsteiner* is a traditional German dish. It's basically a beef and vegetable stew."

Karin served David and Otto and then sat down with them at the table. "You men go ahead and eat. I've already had mine with the children."

The stew was good and David said as much.

Karin accepted the compliment, then turned to her husband. "Did you get the parts for the well?"

"Yes. I'll get them installed tomorrow. But we still won't have water until I get the tower moved."

David asked, "What do you do for water now?"

"There's a little creek a hundred yards out back. Until the pump's working again, we haul water up from there for what we need in the house and to water Karin's garden."

Karin gave Otto a wifely look and he amended his statement. "Well, the boys do most of the hauling. And, I must say, they keep busy at it; the buckets are kinda heavy for the little fellows, so they carry only half a bucketful at a time."

Pride flashed in Karin's eyes as she said, "You will meet the boys in the morning. Joseph is nine, and Peter is seven."

The talk then turned to David. He explained to Karin that he was traveling west, and Otto had been kind enough to offer him food and lodging for the night. She asked the same questions Otto had asked. But for some reason—it might have been because of her penetrating green eyes—he opened up to her more. He told her about his relationship with his father and how he was now trying to learn something about the man, admittedly a little late. He did not say anything about Dillon perhaps having been a gun-fighting marshal, because he didn't quite believe that himself.

When they had finished eating, Otto said he'd take David out to the barn and get him settled. Karin went into the bedroom and came out with a blanket. "Here. I'm sure you can use this. It gets a bit cold this time of year."

"I have a blanket, ma'am."

"A second one can do you no harm," she insisted.

David accepted the blanket and thanked her for the meal and her hospitality.

Otto stood by with a lantern in his hand. "You ready?" David nodded and followed him out the door. As they passed the truck, he grabbed his kit.

Inside the barn, Otto pointed to a pile of hay. "That should make a good bed."

"I'm sure it'll be a hell of a lot more comfortable than what I thought I'd be sleeping on tonight."

"Okay then. I'll leave you the lantern and I'll see you in the morning. We get up early, before sunrise. I'll come and get you, and you'll have breakfast with us. Then I'll drive you back to the highway."

Otto was just about out of the barn when David called after him. "Once you get some help, how long will it take to get your windmill up and running?"

Otto turned around. "Two men could have the job done in three or four days. Why do you ask?"

"I was thinking I might like to help out. That way, you folks could have your water back by Christmas. Besides, I'm in no rush to get anywhere."

"That's mighty nice of you. It would be a great Christmas gift for Karin. But I won't be able to pay you anything. Things are a little tight right now. The best I can offer is to feed you and let you sleep here in the barn."

"Then it's settled. I assume we'll get to work in the morning."

"First thing," said Otto.

"Then I better get some sleep," said David.

44

At breakfast, Karin introduced her children to the stranger. "Joseph, Peter, I would like you to meet Mister Mahoney. He'll be staying with us while he helps your father move the windmill."

The boys were enthralled. Here was something new. Joseph, by dint of being the older of the two, asked the first question. "Where are you from?"

"Right now, I'm traveling. But my last home was in New York City."

Joseph's eyes grew wide. "Have you ever been up in an elevator?"

"Yes. Many times. I lived on the tenth floor."

Joseph's eyes grew even wider.

His younger brother, not to be denied, asked, "You ever been on a streetcar?"

David smiled at a forgotten memory. "Not if I could help it."

Karin spoke to her sons. "Now you boys leave the man alone. Let him eat his eggs in peace." She pointed to a plate holding thick pieces of bread. "Help yourself, Mister Mahoney."

Before David could reach for the bread, Joseph, trying to be helpful, snatched it up and held it in David's direction.

"Thank you, Joseph," said David.

Otto entered the fray. "You boys eat up. You have to bring the horses down to the creek for their morning watering and then get about your other chores."

In unison, but looking a little disappointed at not being able to engage the stranger in further conversation, the boys said, "Yes, sir," and went about finishing their breakfast.

David used the bread to mop up his egg yolks and said, "I'll tell you what. Tonight, after supper, we can talk about New York and I'll answer any questions you may have. Is that all right?"

Both boys nodded their heads vigorously.

437

≈ ≈ ≈

Out at the windmill, David asked Otto, "Okay, what do we do first?"

"First, we dismantle it from the top down. I hope you're not afraid of heights. The tower's forty feet high."

"I'll be all right."

They worked through the morning, and, by noon, when they were called in for dinner, they had gingerly, with ropes, pulleys, and horse power, lowered the fan and rudder to the ground. The afternoon went as smoothly as the morning had, and by suppertime, the windmill had been dismantled. Tomorrow they would tackle the tower.

After supper, David kept his promise and regaled Joseph and Peter with tales of the Big City. Most of them true.

By the end of the next day—with the help of Otto's two horses—they had the tower lying on its side, ready to be sledded to its new location.

As they washed up for supper, Otto said, "That's half the job done. But I'm gonna have to go into Brackettville tomorrow. We're gonna need new lengths of angle iron for anchors. Did you notice how the old ones were almost rusted through?"

"To tell the truth, no."

"Well, they were. Maybe it's a blessing in disguise that I had to move the windmill. If a winter storm were to come through like the ones we had last year, the tower might have toppled and that would have been the end of everything."

"Why do you say that?"

"Most certainly the fan and rudder would have been destroyed if the tower blew over. And right now, I can't afford to replace them. But that's not going to happen. The day after tomorrow, the windmill will be securely fastened to the earth with new anchors and we'll have water again."

At supper that night, in between answering questions from Joseph and Peter, David asked a few questions of his own.

"So, Otto, are you folks from around here? I only ask because both you and Karin have a slight accent that I just can't place."

Otto was focused on slathering a thick slab of white butter onto a square of yellow cornbread, but not too focused to address David's question. "Karin and I were both born in Germany. My parents brought me to America when I was ten. Hers, when she was eight. But we didn't meet until years later. I was twenty-seven and working at a steel mill and Karin was a beautiful *mädchen* of twenty-two, working as a teacher. It was love at first sight. Wasn't it, Karin?"

Karin reached over and patted Otto's hand. "Mister Mahoney only asked about our accents. I'm sure he does not want to hear our entire history."

"On the contrary, Missus Fischer," said David. "Until recently, I've led a rather sheltered life. I'm just beginning to realize it's a great big world out there. That's why I'm traveling as I am. To meet different kinds of people. Good people such as yourselves. And I'd be happy to learn as much about you folks as you're willing to tell me."

Karin looked over at Otto. "As long as you don't bore Mister Mahoney to death, why don't you tell him how we met and came to live here. We've never told the boys. We kept putting it off because we didn't think they were old enough to understand. It will be good for them to learn where their parents came from and how they met."

"If you'll be kind enough to pass the potatoes," said Otto, "I'd be more than happy to tell David and the boys how we ended up here on a small farm in Kinney County, Texas."

Karin passed the potatoes with the admonition, "Go lightly with the butter, or else it won't last until next churning."

"As I said, Karin was teaching, and I was working in a steel mill. This was in Pittsburg. Well, one night there was a dance at the German-American Club. I wasn't much for dancing, but it was a Saturday and I didn't have to work the next day, so I thought I'd go just to have something to do.

"I stood against the wall with the other men who had come stag. However, unlike the other men, I didn't go over to the far side of the room to ask a girl to dance. I was too shy. But I enjoyed watching the other people dance and have fun. And the music was lively."

"I'll say he was shy," said Karin. "I was watching him for the longest time, hoping he would come over and ask me to dance. All the other boys had. Finally, out of desperation, I marched right up to him and said, 'May I have the pleasure of this dance?' " Karin smiled at the memory. "You should have seen the look on his face!"

"You can't blame me for that look," interjected Otto. "You were the prettiest girl there. And here you come, bold as brass, and ask *me* for a dance. Of course I was surprised … and more than a little nervous."

Karin reached out and took Otto's hand in hers. "You were, by far, the handsomest man there."

Under his sun-bronzed skin, Otto might have been blushing, but it was hard to tell in the dim light of the lantern. He picked up the story from there. "I *wanted* to dance with her, but I was afraid of making a fool of myself. I didn't know what to do."

Karin cut in. "He didn't stand a chance, Mister Mahoney. I took him by the hand and dragged him out onto the dance floor." Both she and Otto had a faraway look in their eyes as they relived the memory.

Joseph and Peter sat in rapt attention, mouths agape. They had never seen this side of their parents before.

"That's about it," said Otto. "One thing led to another and we got married and then we ended up here."

Karin withdrew her hand from Otto's and said, maybe a little too harshly, "*Men!* That's not how it happened at all, Mister Mahoney. Otto courted me in the most romantic way. He brought me flowers every time he came to visit. On Sundays, he'd take me for long rides in his dilapidated automobile, which was held together with baling wire."

Otto laughed. "It wasn't that bad, but almost."

"It *was* that bad, Mister Mahoney. But I didn't mind. To me it was a golden chariot, and Otto, my prince come a calling.

"I was waiting for him to work up the courage to ask me to marry him. He got close a few times, but at the last moment, he'd sigh and look at me with those big puppy-dog eyes of his and my heart would melt. Finally, one day when he was stuttering and hemming and hawing, I didn't give him a chance to falter again. Before he could give me that long sigh of defeat, I said, 'Of course I'll marry you.' He gave me a cute, lopsided grin and then took me in his arms, and we kissed for the very first time. It was so very romantic. And that's how I caught him."

"Yup, that's how she caught me alright," joked Otto.

Karin playfully slapped at Otto's hand. "Someone had to take the bull by the horns, or I would have died an old maid."

They had spoken of this many times before, but only between themselves. This was the first time they had let anyone else in on how their betrothal had come about. David could see that they liked telling the story.

The boys were aghast at hearing how their parents had met. Parents were not supposed to be in love. They were supposed to be parents!

"So, how did you end up in Texas?" asked David.

Otto exchanged a look with Karin and said, "Why don't you tell him? It was originally your idea to come here."

The dishes were still on the table, although they had finished eating a while ago. Karin moved her dish to the side, straightened in her chair, and folded her hands before her.

"You must remember that I only saw Otto on Saturday nights and on Sundays. I had never seen him come straight from the mill. But that changed once we were married. I saw a different man than the man I had married. He was worn and his skin was red and blistered from feeding a blast furnace all day. I knew if he stayed at the mill, he would pay dearly for it and die long before his time. And I wasn't about to let that happen.

"One day, I came across a small advertisement in the newspaper for a homestead in Texas that was for sale. It had never occurred to me that we might be farmers. I had been looking for a position for Otto—something that would not be so physically demanding.

"Without telling Otto, I corresponded with the man in Texas, and after many letters back and forth, we worked out a deal. He was desperate to sell. He was not married and was lonely on the farm. He wanted to move back East, and he was willing to take very little money down *and* allow us to make payments.

"When everything had been arranged, I informed Otto that we were going to Texas and become farmers. That was eleven years ago. When we first came here, the farm did not look anything like it does now. The house was only one room. The first thing Otto did was build a kitchen for me. Over the years, he's added on to the house and built the barn. He's worked very hard. We both have. But at the end of the day, we're working for ourselves, and that is very satisfying."

Otto leaned over and kissed his wife on the cheek. "Isn't she a gem?"

Karin stood and began gathering up the supper dishes. "Okay, boys. Say goodnight to Mister Mahoney and get ready for bed."

After the boys had gone, David thanked Karin for supper and said to Otto, "If you don't mind, I'd like to ride into town with you tomorrow. I need a few things from the general store, assuming Brackettville has a general store."

"The very best," said Otto.

"Then I'll see you in the morning, Otto. Goodnight, Missus Fischer."

"Goodnight, Mister Mahoney. Sleep well."

Otto and David were on the road to Brackettville just as the sky was turning gunmetal grey in the east.

"Will the store be open this early?" asked David.

"This is farming country. It'll be open."

Nothing else was said for a few minutes until Otto broke the silence. "I figure we should have the windmill up and operational by tomorrow night."

"I was thinking the same thing," said David.

"Yeah. But what I wanted to say was, the day after that will be Christmas Eve and Karin and I would like you to stay over for Christmas."

David was touched. Christmas was a time for family. To invite a stranger into their home on that sacred day was a kindness indeed. Especially because he knew things were not going well for the Fischers. He had been on the farm for only two days, but in that time, he got the sense they were struggling. At meals, the family's portions were always a little smaller than his. That first morning, he had two eggs on his plate while the others made do with only one. After that, he always refused seconds, telling his hosts that he was too full to eat anything more.

Otto and Karen grew cotton and corn, but that year's crop, while not a disaster, had been a disappointment. Then, to make matters worse, the well had gone dry.

"I don't know, Otto. I don't want to intrude."

"You won't be intruding. The boys like you. And, of course, Karin and I like you. You've worked hard, and because I can't pay you anything, the least we can do is see that you have a Christmas that's better than standing on the side of the road waiting for a ride. Now, I admit, it won't be anything fancy. But we're going to have a turkey and Karin is gonna bake an apple pie."

"Sounds good. But do you mind if I ask you something personal?"

"I reckon that depends on what you want to ask. But go ahead."

"It's not *that* personal. I was just wondering if you had time yet to buy presents for the boys."

"Don't you mean if I can afford to buy presents for the boys?"

"I'm sorry, Otto. I meant no offense."

"That's alright. And the answer is no. We've already told the boys that Santa might miss our house this year. We wanted to get them ready for the let-down. While we're in town, I'm gonna get a yo-yo for Joseph and one of those little toy trucks for Peter. But truth be told, that's all I can afford."

David nodded. "What about Karin? What does she want for Christmas?"

Otto laughed. "That's easy. All she's wanted for the longest time has been a bathtub. As it is, we have to bathe in an old wooden washtub that you can barely get your butt into, never mind the rest of your body. The boys and I don't mind, but you know how women are. Now, don't get me wrong, she has never once complained, but I know."

Things were quiet for the next few miles. At length, in a wistful voice, Otto said, "The general store has one. A bathtub, that is. It was a special order for someone who never picked it up. It's a real beauty, made of cast iron and porcelain-enameled. Mister Benjamin, the man who runs the store, said he'd give me a good price on it, and I had planned on buying it right after the harvest. But things didn't quite work out that way. I'm hoping to get her one next year."

443

Otto pulled up in front of the blacksmith's shop. "This might take a while. If you want to get what you need at the store, I'll meet you there. It's just down the street on your right."

Forty-five minutes later, Otto walked up to see David sitting on the bench in front of the store wearing his best Cheshire cat grin. "What are you grinning at?" asked Otto.

"Oh, nothing. I was just thinking how wonderful life can be at times."

"Maybe sometimes, maybe most of the time. But at other times, life can surely wear on a person's soul."

David nodded in agreement.

"Are you ready to go?"

"Almost. If you'll give me a minute, I'll run in and get those toys I mentioned for Joseph and Peter."

Once inside, Otto stopped flat in his tracks. Right there—*right there!*—next to the counter, stood *his* bathtub filled with parcels wrapped in brown paper. Benjamin was behind the counter putting grocery items into a woman's shopping basket. Otto patiently waited while she paid her bill and left the store. Then he said, "Are you selling the bathtub?"

"I'm sorry, Mister Fischer, but its already been sold. I just sold it to that gentleman standing next to you."

It took a moment for the information to register. When it did, Otto quickly turned to David and stammered, "What? … Why? … How? … How can you afford it? Why would you buy that for us? I assume you're not buying it for yourself."

David wanted to get Otto moving before he had time to think things through and flat-out refuse the gift. In the short time he had known him, David knew Otto to be a proud man. "All fair questions, Otto. But can we talk about it on the way back to the farm?"

Bewildered, Otto said, "I reckon so."

As they loaded the bathtub onto the back of the truck, Otto asked about the packages.

"Just a few things I picked up for the boys," said David.

"That reminds me. I still have to buy that yo-yo and toy truck."

"I already got 'em."

Otto shook his head but said nothing.

444

Once out on the highway, Otto spoke up. "When I stopped to give you a lift, I thought you were a forgotten man. One of those guys roaming the country looking for work. I figured you were broke. So, how can you afford to buy a bathtub that I know cost at least eighty dollars? And that was *my* price because I know Benjamin. You probably paid more."

David explained that money was not a problem for him. And he was not looking for work. He was exploring America. He went on to say that he appreciated Otto taking him home to feed him and give him shelter for a night; in his eyes, that was no small kindness. That's why he bought the gifts. It was his way of saying thank you.

Otto said, "You've more than made up for anything I may have done for you. Karin will be beside herself with joy when she sees the bathtub. And the boys ... I guess they'll keep believing in Santa for at least another year. By the way, what's in the packages?"

"Just stuff I would like if I were a kid." A faintly whimsical smile played across David's face as he enthusiastically recounted a few of his purchases. "I bought an erector set, a gyroscope ... a model airplane that you wind up with a rubber band and the propeller turns. It says on the box that it will roll across the floor on its own power! Oh yeah, I got a Morse Code telegraph learning set. I think the boys will like that."

As they approached the turn-off to the farm, David asked, "Where are you going to put the bathtub?"

"When I was building out the house, I added on a bathroom, anticipating the day when we'd finally get indoor plumbing. There's nothing in there right now but the washtub. But you know what? I'd like to surprise Karin. When we get home, I'll pull straight into the barn and we'll unload the tub and hide it. Then, on Christmas Eve, when Karin is out back tending to her garden, we can sneak it into the house and put it in the bathroom. Boy! Will she be surprised."

They hid the tub under a pile of hay and went to work on the windmill. They worked the remainder of the day and all of the next. By Christmas Eve, the pump was once again pumping water into the water tank.

After supper, David said his goodnights and went out to the barn where he nailed two one hundred-dollar bills to a post where they were sure to be seen. He then rolled up his blanket and started for the highway. The Fischers would wake up the next morning surprised to find him gone. But Christmas was a time for families, not for interloping strangers.

≈ ≈ ≈

The ride let him off in front of the offices of the *Las Cruces Daily News*. The woman at the counter told him she knew nothing about past issues. Her job was to take orders for classified ads and that was all. Perhaps he should speak with the editor.

"Perhaps I should," said David.

"If you'll have a seat over there," advised the woman, "I'll tell him you're here."

Fifteen minutes later, a man wearing a green eyeshade visor came up to the counter. "May I help you?" He wore no coat. His tie was loosened, and his shirt sleeves were rolled up to his elbows. He managed to look both busy and annoyed at the same time.

David stood and went to the counter. "I was hoping to look at some of your past issues, if I could."

"I suggest you seek out the library down the street. They have past issues. What we have is called a morgue. It's where we keep issues of every edition we've ever printed. But it's for the use of our employees only. Now, if there's nothing else, I have a paper to get out."

"Would the library have issues going back to the 1880s?"

The editor regarded David warily. "What are you looking for?"

"I heard there may have been a gunfight in the early 1880s that might have involved my father. I don't think it did, but I'd like to know for certain."

The editor removed his eyeshade and rubbed his brow. "There were a lot of gunfights in Las Cruces back in those days. What makes you think you could pinpoint *your* gunfight even if you had access to our morgue?"

"I understand this was a rather famous gunfight. It was between someone named Luke Short and a man named Dillon Mahoney."

"And which one was your father?"

"My name is David Mahoney. Dillon Mahoney was my father."

446

The editor replaced his eyeshade and pushed open the swing-gate at the end of the counter. "Why don't you come back to my office?"

They made their way through the newsroom to a glass-enclosed office at the back. The editor pointed to a chair and invited David to sit down. "The name's Keith James, but everyone calls me Buddy."

David waited.

"Okay. Let's cut to the chase. I wasn't entirely honest with you out there. The issues in our morgue date back only to 1914. We didn't exist before then. Before us, there was the *Rio Grande Republican*, and before them, the *Borderer*. If it were still around, that's the paper you'd want. But unfortunately, they're long since gone, and so are all their back issues. The place burned down sixteen years ago."

"So, why am I here, sitting in your office?" asked David.

James leaned back in his chair and smiled. "Because I just might be able to help you."

45

Keith James reached into his side desk drawer and came out with a bottle of scotch. The real stuff. "Living so close to the border has its advantages. Care to imbibe?" he asked.

"Don't mind if I do," said David. "Got any ice?"

"I wouldn't think the son of Dillon Mahoney would need ice."

David stiffened in the chair but said nothing.

James poured out two healthy shots into two semi-clean glasses and handed one to David.

"Why don't we drink to your father. Then I'll tell you where you might find a treasure trove of information pertaining to the matter at hand. Fair enough?"

"I'll drink to my father. I owe him that. But I want you to know this: My father was a meek and mild man. He was a business man. He was no gunfighter. *And* he always put ice in his drinks."

James shrugged and downed his scotch. He started to reach for the bottle, but then thought better of it. He still had a paper to get out. "Okay. Maybe the Dillon Mahoney who took down Luke Short was not your father. But you're searching for the truth. So, here's how you can find it."

David took a sip of the contraband liquor and nodded his approval. It was good.

James went on: "That shootout is still talked about to this day. I don't mean all the time. But we have this thing called Frontier Days. It's a celebration of the Wild West. It's held in November, just before Thanksgiving when things have cooled down a bit. One of the highlights is when the old-timers get up and talk about 'the good old days'."

David leaned forward a little.

"Well, there's this one old-timer, Frank Evans is his name. And every year he tells the same story. Can you guess what story that would be?"

David finished off his scotch and placed the glass on the desk. "Why don't you enlighten me."

"Frank Evans was a witness to the shootout. He's the only man still living who actually saw it. Some of the other old-timers claim they did, but they didn't. Frank Evans is the real deal. He'll suit you better than an old, dried-up piece of yellowed paper with faded newsprint on it."

David asked the obvious question. "How do I find him?"

"I'll tell you in a minute, but first I have a proposition to make."

"How about you refill my glass first? I haven't tasted booze this good in a long time."

James said, "I knew there was something about you that I liked. I think I'll join you."

The two men took a moment to savor the illicit booze before resuming their talk.

"I didn't bring you back here, Mister Mahoney ... do you mind if I call you Dave?"

"My name is David."

"Fair enough ... David. I didn't bring you back here into my office for altruistic reasons or to ply you with booze. I'm a newspaperman first and foremost, and this is one hell of a story."

"What do you mean?"

"From what I hear, Luke Short was a real bad hombre. The town's folk lived in fear of him. If you somehow offended him, you'd most likely end up dead out on the trail with a bullet in your back and no witnesses as to what had happened. Then, Dillon Mahoney rides in from out of nowhere and saves the town from Short and his gang. Strangest thing is that, afterwards, he just disappears. Everyone wants to know what became of him. Don't you see what a story this would make? I can picture the headline now: *Las Cruces Daily News Solves Mahoney Mystery!* Or something along those lines.

"We could make this a series. It could run for a week. Three days at the least. Think of the papers we'd sell!"

David stood up. "I didn't come here to sell papers. Now, if you'll be kind enough to tell me how I can find Frank Evans, I'll be on my way."

James slumped back in his chair. "Okay. You're right. I got a little carried away. But if *our* Dillon Mahoney turns out to be *your* father, the *Las Cruces Daily News* is gonna write about it. Or my name ain't Keith James!"

"That's fine by me. But you'll have to do it without my help. Now, how do I find Frank Evans?"

Frank Evans lived at the hotel. Room 301. David asked at the desk if Mister Evans was in at the moment.

"You probably passed him on your way in. He spends his days sitting out on the porch. Says he likes to watch the world go by."

David retraced his steps through the lobby and out the front door. There, to his right, sat a man slouched down in a padded wicker chair, wearing an old, beat-up, straw cowboy hat tilted down over his eyes. He looked to be asleep.

"Excuse me. Are you Frank Evans?"

The man looked up from under the brim of his hat. "The very same, son. What can I do ya for?"

"Rumor has it that you witnessed the shootout between Luke Short and Dillon Mahoney. And if you don't mind, I'd like to talk to you about it."

Evans pushed his hat back and sat up straight. His eyes fairly twinkled. "Don't you know that old men like nothing better than telling stories from their misspent youth? Are you from some newspaper or somethin'?"

"Nothing like that. It's personal with me. My name is David Mahoney."

Evans' eyes flashed with interest. "What relation would you be?"

"I don't know if I'm any relation. That's what I'm here to find out ...if you can help me."

"Why don't you take a load off and we'll talk."

"I have a better idea. How about if I buy you lunch and then we'll talk? I just got into town and I'm kinda hungry."

Evans stood up. "Well, if that ain't the best goldarn idea I've heard all day. And I know just the place. Follow me."

They waited for a break in the late morning traffic, then made their way across the street to a small, run-of-the-mill restaurant.

"You see this hole-in-the-wall?" asked Evans. "It used to be a saloon. Its name was The Green Cactus. But it got shut down when Prohibition came along. Later, someone up and made it into a restaurant."

David looked unimpressed.

Evans quickly added, "This is where the shootout took place."

"Looks like a good place to eat," said David.

"I thought you might think so," said Evans as he led the way inside.

After their order had been placed, David said, "I thought you might be older. I mean, what we're talking about took place fifty years ago."

"I was only twelve at the time. But tell me, what do you want to know?"

"I want to know if my father was Dillon Mahoney."

Evans' eyebrows rose. "You don't know who your father was?"

"My father's name was Dillon Mahoney. *A* Dillon Mahoney had a shootout with Luke Short. I want to know if they were one and the same."

A half-smile escaped Evans' lips. "How many Dillon Mahoneys do you think were roamin' the West back then?"

"I just can't believe it was him. He never once spoke of it. Can you tell me what he looked like?"

"Well, when I saw him, he was wearin' a beard. His hair was long. Almost down to his shoulders. And it was dark. I would say black. He was tall. Of course, I was only knee-high to a grasshopper back then. That's about it. Any of that ring a bell with you?"

"I never knew my father to wear his hair long and he was always clean-shaven. But he was tall ... as tall as I am. And his hair *was* dark. Anything else you can think of?"

"No. I reckon not ... wait a minute! I just thought of somethin'. He had a mole on his neck, on the left, no ... it was on his right side, under his ear. Does that help?"

David's face went blank. He was in shock. His father *had been* a gun-wielding U.S. Marshal who had helped tame the West! He just could not believe it.

Thankfully, just then their food arrived. David took a bite of his hamburger. He had no desire for further conversation just then; he could not trust how his voice would sound.

For his part, Evans was content to munch on his French fries, in between taking bites of his tuna fish sandwich. Very little was said while the two men ate.

After the dishes had been cleared away, David said, "Mister Evans, would you please tell me about my father?"

"Why not call me Frank?"

"Alright, Frank."

"I'll tell you what little I know. Like I said. I was just a kid at the time. The only reason I was there at all was because my father was the county sheriff.

"This is the way it happened: Your father and his deputy were hanging around waiting for Luke and his gang to show up. When they finally hit town, my father, your father, and the deputy met up at the jail. I was in the back sweeping out the cells. That was my job. I had to do it once a week. Anyway, I don't think anyone knew I was back there. So, when they started talking about taking down Luke, I quietly leaned the broom against the wall and crept up to the door leading to the office so I could better hear what was being said.

"Your father was chasing Luke because Luke had ambushed him and left him for dead. So, even though my father was sheriff and it was his town, he let your father run the show.

"I heard Marshal Mahoney say he wanted to take Luke by himself and that he was planning on taking him alive. He only wanted my father and the deputy for backup, if they were needed.

"When they had their plans laid out, and they were armed up, they started for the saloon. I waited a few minutes and then followed them up the other side of the street. When they came in here ... I mean, when they went into the saloon, I crossed the street and tried to see what was going on by getting down on my knees and looking in under the swing doors. But all I could see were men's legs. Everybody was standing bunched up by the door ... to get out of the line of fire, I reckon. So I went over to that there very same window."

Frank halted his narrative to point to a window on the left side of the room. David looked to where he was pointing.

"And this is what I saw: The deputy was at the door, holding a shotgun. My father was off to the side, his hand hovering over his six-shooter. But it was your father who was front and center, facing down four dangerous men. And I gotta say, he looked cool and calm as could be.

"I couldn't hear what was being said, but two of Luke's gang peeled off to the right, like they wanted no part of what was coming. Now it was just Luke and his side-man, Patrick Hawke, facing your father.

"Your father said something, then Luke said something. Then everyone froze. It was Luke who made the first move and Hawke was right behind him. Luke got off the first shot but missed. Your father didn't. Hawke had barely cleared leather when he went down. They were both deader than a jack rabbit at a coyote convention. And that was all she wrote.

"But one thing that really sticks out in my mind is how your father acted when it was all over. While everyone else was talkin' and congratulating him, some of 'em even slappin' him on the back, he didn't say anything. He stood there in the middle of all that ruckus, by himself, all isolated like, and calmly opened his gun, dropped the two spent cartridges onto the floor, and replaced them with two new ones. Never once did he acknowledge those around him.

"It was about then that I thought I'd better make myself scarce. If my father had seen me, I would have gotten the walloping of my life. I hightailed it back to the jail and went into the cells. But I didn't do any more sweeping. I couldn't, after what I'd just seen. I sat on one of the bunks and shook a little. It was the first time I had ever seen a man killed."

David found it hard to reconcile the man he knew with the man Frank Evans was describing. All he could think of was that time in New York when his father had asked for a hug. Back then, David had been put off by what he perceived as a weakness in his father. But now he realized that any man who could stand up to four men with guns probably did not have a weak bone in his entire body.

"Is there anything else you can tell me about him?" asked David.

Frank rubbed his grizzled chin in contemplation. "There's just one thing that stuck with me from that day ... I mean besides the gunplay. It seems that your father was put out that he'd had to kill Short and Hawke. It had not been his intention to do so, he said.

"My father and the deputy tried to reassure him that it *had* been necessary. But I could tell that no amount of talk was gonna make him believe killing another man was okay. I gotta say, that really stuck with me. Especially after what I had just seen him do."

David called the waitress over and paid the bill. As they walked out of the restaurant, David took one last look at the far corner where it had all happened, so long ago.

Out on the street, David thanked Evans for talking with him. "You've given me new insight into my father, and for that, I sincerely thank you."

"That's alright, Mister Mahoney, but I would like to ask you something that's been bothering me for nigh on fifty years now."

"I'll answer if I can."

"Well, it's just this. Other lawmen, like Pat Garrett, the Earp boys, and Bill Hickok, we all heard about them up until their dying day. But your father just disappeared. Like he never was. Can you tell me what ever happened to him?"

"He fell in love, settled down, and had a kid."

"Is he still alive?"

"Sadly, no. Thanks again, Frank. Now, if you'll excuse me, I have a train to catch."

David had an uncontrollable desire to visit his father's grave. He did not understand it. It was just something he had to do. Then he did understand it. He had to beg his father's forgiveness before he did another thing in this life.

The day was Friday, the 26th. If he could get to Los Angeles by Monday, the 29th, he would be able to visit with his father, so to speak, *and* see the lawyer, Lane, before the first of the year. Then, he could start 1931 with a clean slate. The only problem was, he would have to hitchhike up to Albuquerque to catch a train to Los Angeles.

He got to it and stuck out his thumb.

≈ ≈ ≈

The train pulled into Central Station at 1:03 a.m. on the 29th, twenty-three minutes behind schedule. Having slept on the train,

454

David was well rested, and seeing as how the cemetery was only three miles away, he decided to make the pilgrimage without delay.

Every Sunday when he was young, his father would take him to visit his mother and sister. His father had paid for a marble bench to be installed opposite the graves, and there they would sit for, what seemed to his younger self, an interminable length of time. His father in silent contemplation of what might have been, and David, bored with the whole thing, thinking: *What a waste of time.*

He had never known his mother and sister. To him they were just names carved on white stone. As soon as he was old enough, around fourteen years of age, he had refused to accompany his father on his Sunday visits. And now here he was, twenty-two years later, in the early morning hours, making his way down dark and empty streets to visit that very cemetery.

He was thankful the bench was still there. It was now his turn to sit and think of what might have been. Tears streamed from his eyes as he said over and over again, "I'm sorry. I'm so very sorry."

As his tears slackened, and the sky lightened in the east, and the birds started in with their singing, the noise of an awakening city intruded into the quiet of the cemetery. David had things to do, but before he left, he promised his family that before the day was done, there would be fresh flowers on their graves.

David met with Lane later that afternoon.

≈ ≈ ≈

"Come on in, Mister Mahoney, and have a seat."

"It's good to finally meet you, Mister Lane."

The two men shook hands.

Once David was seated in the comfortable client chair, Lane opened the conversation. "I assume you're here to claim your ten thousand dollars."

"We can get to that in a minute. What I'd like to talk about right now is my father."

"What about your father?"

"You were his attorney for forty years. What can you tell me about him?"

Lane's brows knitted, and he squinted through his bifocals as he sized up the man sitting opposite him. "If you don't mind me saying,

455

Mister Mahoney, you were his son for almost as long as I was his attorney. What could I possibly tell you that you don't already know?"

David's voice was barely audible as he said, "I regret to say that I was not that close to him. A far cry from the son he deserved. And, although it's now too late, I'm trying to get to know the man. I've already found out one astounding thing about him, but I want to dig deeper into his life. And I don't know where to start."

Lane's expression softened. "There isn't much I can tell you. My relationship with your father was strictly business. I was invited for dinner a few times and I met your mother. Of course, this was before you were born. She was a beautiful and charming woman. But to answer your question, your father was an honest man. He never asked me to do anything underhanded to gain him an advantage in business."

David had been hoping to learn what made his father tick. He already knew him to be an honest man. He also knew he had been a man of great forbearance. *He would have to have been to put up with me all those years.*

He tried to mask his disappointment but failed miserably. In a hollow voice that rang with regret, he said, "Thank you, Mister Lane. Now, if you'd like, we can talk about the money."

Lane leaned both elbows on his desk and steepled his fingers. "I just remembered something. Your father had a business partner. His name, as I recall, was John Elroy. They split up their holdings and he moved away before you were born. But he was close to your father. If anyone knew Dillon Mahoney, except for your mother, of course, it would have to be Johnny Elroy."

"Do you know where I can find him? Is he still alive?"

"Wait a minute. I've got the particulars right here. I pulled your father's file in case there was anything we needed to discuss."

A surge of hope flared in David's heart.

"Okay," said Lane, "here it is. He lives in New York City. At least he did. I'll write down his phone number and address and you can take it from there."

"Thank you, Mister Lane. Now, as to the money. I don't really need it right now. I was wondering if you could hang onto it and send me a thousand or so at a time, as I need it."

456

"I'll be retiring soon. And anyway, the money should be in an account of your own. The bank is right around the corner. When we're done here, I'll walk you over and introduce you to the manager. He'll set you up with an account and you can make arrangements with him to send you funds as you need them."

"That will be fine. Now, what about the gun you mentioned?"

Lane reached into the bottom drawer of his desk and pulled out the old six-shooter. The leather of the holster was dried and cracked. David cautiously accepted the weapon into his hands. He had never held a gun before.

"Is it loaded?" he asked.

"I took the precaution of removing the bullets when I took possession of it," answered Lane.

David slipped the gun from its holster. There were a few flakes of rust here and there; however, for being over fifty years old, it was in remarkably good condition.

"It looks like he took good care of it," mused David.

$$\approx \approx \approx$$

"Long distance, please."

"Yes, sir. How may I help you?"

"I'd like to make a person-to-person call to John Elroy at Circle 7-0224 in New York City."

"One moment, sir."

Less than a minute later: "Go ahead, sir."

"Hello? Mister Elroy?"

"Yes. This is Elroy speaking."

"Mister Elroy, you don't know me. My name is David Mahoney, Dillon Mahoney's son."

David heard an intake of breath on the other end of the line. Then silence.

"Are you there, Mister Elroy?"

"Yes. It's just that you took me by surprise."

"I'm sorry about that. But I'd like to talk to you about my father."

"What is it you want to know?"

"I don't mean over the phone. I'd like to come and see you."

"I know you're calling long distance, but from where?"

"I'm in Los Angeles."

"And you want to travel three thousand miles to ask me a few questions about Dillon?"

"That's about the size of it, Mister Elroy."

"Well, then you're in luck. I'm sitting here alone in this big old house, and a little company would be most welcome. When are you planning on being in New York?"

"I could leave right away and be there in three days. That's Friday, the 2nd, the day after the New Year. Is that all right with you?"

"That's fine. Do you have my address?"

"Are you still on 5th Avenue?"

"Yes."

"Then I'll see you on Friday, Mister Elroy."

"I look forward to meeting you, David."

"Same here. Good-bye for now … and thanks."

"Good-bye. And Godspeed."

46

The houses and commercial buildings gradually yielded to soft, umber-colored hills which, in turn, gave way to towering mountains. On the far side of the Colorado River, a serene desert, graced with cactus and stately Joshua trees, ran on for miles, eventually coming to another set of mountains whose height infringed upon the pale-blue sky's infinite domain. Thenceforth came the open plains, where tawny waves of winter wheat, bent sidelong by a blustery northwestern wind, fought to maintain their hold upon the earth.

A thick blanket of virgin-white snow covered the landscape. Newly frozen streams and rivers glistened in the weak winter sun. On the far horizon, ominous ebony-grey storm clouds gathered, readying for an onslaught against the conveyance as it raced across a continent.

The last time David made the trip from California to New York, he had been too preoccupied with his impending poverty to appreciate the scenery. A wide, beautiful country existed right outside the window of the speeding train, and this time he enjoyed watching the miles roll by. However, he preferred the America he had experienced while driving with Ben Shahn, and while hitchhiking. For it was then he had the opportunity to mix with the common man and woman, the ordinary and the downtrodden.

The train pulled into Pennsylvania Station at 10:20 a.m., right on schedule. David wasted no time. He hailed a cab and told the driver to take him to 51st Street and 5th Avenue.

As he stepped from the cab, he marveled at the four-story structure that Johnny Elroy called home. It was one of the few remaining houses on the block, the others having been replaced by apartment buildings. Unbeknownst to David, his grandfather had worked at that very house as a bricklayer's assistant back in 1850. It had been his first job in America.

David knew the neighborhood; he had passed this house many times on his jaunts around the city, a lifetime ago. In those days, he had been driving his Duesenberg with a giggling bottle-blonde sitting on the seat next to him. He shook his head at the memory and pushed through the gate.

His knock on the door was answered by an older gentleman with a full head of white hair. He was thin, but, overall, looked spry and healthy. When he saw who was standing on his stoop, his mouth twisted into a smile. "You must be David. Come in. Come in, young man. It's so good to see you."

David took a tentative step inside. "Yes, I am David Mahoney. And it's a pleasure to meet you, too, Mister Elroy."

They shook hands and Johnny closed the door. "Come. We'll sit in the library. Would you like a beverage, some tea or coffee?"

"No, thank you."

Johnny led the way to the library, situated on the second floor, and once they were settled in comfortable, high-back leather chairs, he said, "So, how was your trip?"

David answered simply. "Uneventful."

An awkward silence hung in the air. Finally, Johnny said, "I know it's early, but I'm going to have a brandy. Would you care to join me?"

"I'd love to."

David was nervous and not quite sure how to open the conversation. He was hoping the booze would calm his nerves.

When they had their brandies in hand, Johnny raised his glass. "To your father. One of the finest men I have ever known."

David saluted and downed the brandy in one gulp. When its warmness had settled in his stomach, he expressed his apology. "I know you're not supposed to drink good brandy that way, but, in all honesty, Mister Elroy, I'm a little nervous."

Johnny said, "That's alright, son. I'm a little nervous myself. Let me refill your glass."

"I'm okay for now, Mister Elroy. We might as well get down to business. I came here to learn about my father. I know it's a bit late. I should have gotten to know him while he was still alive."

Johnny took a sip of brandy and said, "I think I knew him as well as anyone, and better than most, in fact. There was a time when we were very close. While we were drilling those first oil wells, we had nothing else to do at night but sit around our campfire and talk. He told me all about himself. However, as most often happens in life, once I moved away from California, we weren't in touch all that much. Maybe a letter or two every year ... a few phone calls over the years. But I don't believe he ever changed. He was a man of principle, through and through."

David looked uncomfortable. "I know he was a principled man. Of that I have no doubt. I don't know if I can explain it, but I want to know *who* he was."

Johnny nodded his understanding. "To know who he was, you have to know where he came from. And, indeed, where you come from."

"What do you mean?"

"I'm talking about your Irish heritage. I'm talking about your grandfather."

"My father told me about him when I was little."

"What did he tell you?"

"That he came over here from Ireland and worked hard to get ahead and then lost his life in the Civil War."

"Well, that's probably all you would tell a kid. But there was a lot more to it than that. As you know, Dillon never knew his father, who was killed when Dillon was only a year old. Everything he knew about his father came from his mother, your grandmother. She made sure to tell it all. The horrors as well as the high points. She wanted Dillon to pass the story down to his children, and for them to pass it on down to their children, so the Mahoney clan would never forget how they came to be in America. Now here you are, the entire Mahoney clan. And here I am, not of the clan, but the holder of the truth. Funny, ain't it?"

Johnny finished his brandy and refilled their glasses. "After this one, we'll have some lunch. How does that suit you?"

"I don't want to put you out. I just came to see what you could tell me about my father and then I'll be on my way."

"Do you think I could tell you about your father and grandfather in one setting? There's a story here, young Mahoney ... and also a moral. I owe it to your father to tell his son what he himself would have told you if things had worked out differently."

That stung. "What do you mean, '*if things had worked out differently*'?" asked David, even though he knew the answer.

Johnny sighed. "We might as well get to it and get it out of the way. What I'm about to tell you, your father would have told you if he had had the chance. He had intended telling you about your grandfather … and about himself, his younger days before he met your mother, when you were a little older. But then you went off to college, and time and circumstance never offered him the opportunity. Dillon told me about it, that time he was here in New York to see you."

David swallowed hard. "What did he tell you?"

"Just that he had been to see you and you were busy living your own life. He was worried about you, but he knew you would eventually find your footing. And he was right, because here you are. He also said that he loved you very much and always would. Now let's go get that lunch."

"Are you sure I'm not imposing?"

"You see this big house we're in? It sits on prime New York City real estate. Developers are knocking on my door day and night trying to buy the lot. They want to tear down the house and put up an apartment building. They're offering ungodly amounts of money for this small parcel of land.

"I really should sell. I live here alone. My wife, Virginia, died eight years ago. My kids, all five of 'em, are spread out to hell and back, busy raising families of their own. But I don't complain. I've had a good life. I had enough money to raise my five children in a decent manner. To send the boys to the best schools and get the girls married off to men of distinction, men with good family names.

"And you know who I have to thank for all that? That's right. Dillon Mahoney, that's who. When I first met your father, I didn't have two cents I could rub together. I was a bellhop. Then I was selling lots in a newly laid-out city by the name of Hollywood." Johnny chuckled to himself. "I couldn't *give* them away back then. If you can believe that.

"Dillon had an idea and he put every cent he owned into it. Then he brought me in and made me a partner. The next thing I know, I'm a rich man. So, no. You're not putting me out."

While David looked on, Johnny puttered around the spacious kitchen, eventually coming up with two ham and cheese sandwiches and two glasses of cold milk.

"If you don't mind, we'll eat here in the kitchen. It's the warmest room in the house."

In between bites of his sandwich, David asked, "This *is* a big house. Do you have servants? I mean, like a cook or a maid?"

"A woman comes in once a week to clean, but that's all. We used to have a live-in maid and a cook to help Virginia when the kids were young. But all things being equal, I prefer doing for myself."

They made small talk until the sandwiches and milk were but memories. Afterwards, they retired to the library.

With snifter in hand, Johnny resumed the conversation. "I'm going to tell you the story of how your grandfather came to America. I heard it from your father, who heard it from your grandmother. There might be some pieces missing. But I'll tell you everything I know, as best I can recall."

David leaned back in his chair, made himself comfortable, and waited.

≈ ≈ ≈

"It all started in a miserable, squat, dark hut, on an English Lord's landholding somewhere in County Kerry, Ireland. Devin, your grandfather, near death from hunger ..."

Johnny went on to tell how Devin had to walk to Cork with nothing but a few days' supply of cornmeal. How he was shipped out to America on a coffin ship. How half the passengers died en route from various diseases. He told David about the little girl, Hannah, whom Devin had taken care of after her parents died. How he had looked after her until she, too, died and was buried at sea.

He told of the ship losing its mast and being caught in the doldrums, while the emigrants starved and were denied water. Then limping into New York Harbor only to be quarantined because of the disease onboard. How Devin had to jump ship and swim to shore to begin his new life in The Promised Land. And how he was robbed of all his money on his first day in America.

463

Johnny told of how Devin had worked hard at a menial job and saved his money, and when he was just getting ahead, how he ran afoul of a murderous gang and had to run for his life. How he ended up in Pennsylvania and worked for the railroad at back-breaking labor until he was rewarded for his hard work with promotion after promotion until, ultimately, he was running an office in town.

How he fell in love and married the beautiful Mary Callahan. How he built a house with his own two hands for his lovely bride, and then settled down to raise a family.

"With the American Dream within Devin and Mary's reach, the war broke out. Devin felt it his duty to go and fight to free the Black Man. Mary begged him not to go. But a man has to do what he thinks is right, or he's no man at all.

"Devin wrote long, detailed letters home telling of the battles in which he fought and of the everyday life of a soldier. He shared his thoughts as related to war and conveyed to Mary the loneliness he felt at being away from his loved ones. Mary kept his letters and … in time … Dillon read them all. It was how he got to know his father.

"And as you know, Devin never made it home from the war. Mary never recovered from his death, and she died relatively young, leaving Dillon on his own at the tender age of twenty."

$$\approx \approx \approx$$

The late afternoon sunlight slanted in through the large library windows. Diminutive dust mites danced in and out of the shafts of light. As David listened to the details of his grandfather's life, he would occasionally study the sunlight through the dark, amber-colored liquid filling his glass. He did not believe himself to be half the man his grandfather had been.

"I must say, my grandfather was nothing if not tenacious. I don't think I could have gone through half of what he went through and come out the other side in one piece."

Johnny declared, "Don't fool yourself, David Mahoney. You have his blood flowing through your veins. Now tell me, have you made arrangements for where you're going to stay while in the city?"

"Not yet. I came here straight from the station."

464

"That settles it. You'll stay here."

"I can't do that. I've imposed enough already."

Johnny laughed. "This house has nine bedrooms. When you told me you were coming, I had the cleaning lady make up the bedroom next to mine. So I won't take no for an answer."

"Then, I thank you very much."

"Good. It's been a long afternoon. I'll tell you about your father tomorrow. Come with me. I'll take you to your room and you can freshen up. There's a bathroom down at the end of the hall. When you're ready, come downstairs and we'll go out to dinner. I think we'll dine at my favorite restaurant. It's been a long time since I've been there."

"I don't exactly have the right clothes to be seen in a fancy restaurant."

Johnny gave David the once-over.

"I see what you mean. You can borrow one of my suits. We're about the same size. The pants might be an inch short, but no one's going to notice."

Over dinner, David asked Johnny if The Crash had affected him.

"Can't say that it did. I've kept my money in oil stocks, and it looks like people are always going to need gasoline. I don't think we'll be going back to the horse and buggy anytime soon."

"My father diversified into banks and insurance companies. He lost everything when the bottom fell out."

"Yes, I know. I spoke to him shortly before he died. He really didn't mind except for the fact that he'd be leaving you with nothing."

"He left me the house. That's more than I need ... and more than I deserve."

"I'm sure your father would be quite proud of you. He told me how you blew through your inheritance. And how spoiled you had become, and how you believed you were entitled to the good life without having to work for it. So, he devised a little plan to nudge you into becoming a man."

David stopped cutting his steak; looking directly into Johnny's eyes, he asked, "What do you mean?"

Johnny couldn't help himself, he had to smile. "Your father instructed his attorney to stall on the probate. He didn't want you to get your hands on the house until you were absolutely flat broke. He knew you'd lose your phony friends and all your play toys. He was hoping you'd be thrown out of your fancy-dancy apartment. He did not want you to take possession until your desperation to do so had subsided to a casual interest. That would mean you had gotten yourself a job and had grown up."

David threw back his head and laughed. He laughed so long and so loud that many of the other patrons in the restaurant stopped with their own conversations to look over at the uncouth young man who had not the manners he was born with. Johnny noticed their disdain and started laughing also.

At length, David got himself under control and said, "That old son-of-a-bitch! And to think I thought he was a doddering old man."

Back at the house, they partook of a digestif in the form of a *very* rare Cognac Johnny had been saving since before Prohibition. "I don't know what I'm saving this for," he said. "When I'm gone, the kids will probably throw it out. None of 'em are big drinkers."

David lifted his glass in salute. "Thank you for dinner, and thank you for sharing your liquor and your home with me. But most importantly, thank you for telling me of my family."

"It's been my pleasure. Sometimes I get lonely in this big old house. We'll continue with this in the morning, and I'll fill you in on your father. If you get up before I do, go down to the kitchen and help yourself to anything you want. The coffee pot is on the stove and the coffee is in the cupboard right above, and there's plenty of food in the ice box."

"Thank you, Mister Elroy."

"Might as well call me Johnny at this point."

≈ ≈ ≈

The next morning, after a filling breakfast of fried eggs, sausage, and coffee, they reconvened in the library. Settled once again in those comfortable leather chairs, Johnny continued with his chronicle of The Clan Mahoney.

"All your father wanted to do was experience the West for a few minutes while his train took on water and coal. But instead, Destiny played its hand."

Johnny told of how Luke Short had started a fight with Dillon for no reason other than the fact that Dillon was a tenderfoot. And after he had thoroughly hammered Dillon until he lay bloodied on the rough wooden floor of a two-bit saloon, Short had pulled his gun and was about to shoot the unarmed boy when someone stepped in and saved his life.

"Your father, being your father, was not about to leave town with his tail between his legs," said Johnny. "He was going to settle things with Short, but first he had to learn how to fight. He hired on as a cook's helper for a cattle drive and by the time he returned, he had become proficient with both his fists and a gun.

"But by then your father had matured some and decided to let bygones be bygones. However, Luke thought differently. He gunned your father down, putting two bullets in his back and then leaving him for dead.

"When your father recovered, he set out after Luke, but did so under the auspices of the law. He had secured a commission as a Deputy U.S. Marshal. And remember, he was only twenty-one years old.

"He admitted to me that when he started out, he thought he might have to shoot Luke if the man did not submit to an arrest. But he didn't look forward to killing Short. Then, along the way and through no fault of his own, he had a shootout with the outlaw Heck Thomas and beat him to the draw. That set tongues a waggin' that there was a new fast gun in the territory. But it also solidified Dillon's aversion to killing.

"He told me he did try to take Short alive, but it wasn't to be. He ended up beating Short and another man in the same shootout. That cemented his 'reputation' as a fast gun." After that, he was challenged a few times, but was always able to talk things down so he didn't have to go to the extreme of having to shoot anyone. He had killed three men and it rubbed on him. He never wanted to be in the position again where he had to pull his gun on another man. That's why he came to California, to get out of that life.

"It was about that time I met up with him, and the rest is history. He fell in love with your mother, got rich in the oil business, and you were born. I do know this: Your father was a lonely man after your mother died. And I hate to say it, but he became lonelier still when you would have nothing to do with him."

That tore at David's heart. He carried so much regret.

Johnny saw the pain in David's eyes. "I'm sorry I had to say that."

"Don't be. It's the truth. I want to thank you for seeing me and telling me about my father and grandfather. It's good to know from where I came. Now, I just have to figure out where I'm going."

"I can tell you where you're going. You're going with me, to lunch. There's a speakeasy around the corner that serves a mean Lobster Newburg and their booze is top notch. But what else would you expect on 5th Avenue?"

"Sure, Johnny, but only if I pay this time."

"You're a guest in my home ... but if you insist."

The Lobster Newburg was excellent, and so was the booze. When they had finished eating, Johnny signaled the waiter to remove the dishes. Leaning back in his chair and patting his belly with contentment, he said, "This place knows the right cops to pay off. There's never any trouble. And you sure as hell can't complain about the food."

"I've got no complaints," said David.

"Good! Now, if you don't mind, I'm going to give you a lecture and then I'm going to make a suggestion about what you can do with the rest of your life. Would you rather hear it here or back in my library while we partake of that fine, smooth, and very old Cognac?"

With a grin, David said, "The library sounds good to me."

"I thought it would," said Johnny with a grin of his own.

$$\approx \approx \approx$$

To begin with, I'll stipulate that old men are infamous for sticking their noses in other peoples' business. As I happen to be an old man, I'm sure you'll give me leeway to stick my nose into yours. And please, do not interrupt until I have finished. That's another thing about us old men, we don't like to be interrupted."

David chuckled. "The floor is all yours ... old man."

"Thank you. Now listen to me, young man. Did you know that you are descended from kings?"

468

David was about to say something, but Johnny cut him off. "Tut … tut, that was a rhetorical question. According to Dillon, who heard it from his mother, who heard it from Devin, Southern Ireland was rife with Mahoneys. They were the first kings of Ireland. Mahoneys led the clans that threw out the Danes. They were born with fighting blood in them. As is evident with your father and grandfather. Well, you have the same blood flowing in your veins. So now it's high time you put some of that fight you inherited to good use.

"Last night, at dinner, you told me about your trip down South and what you encountered there. You said you came away from that experience wanting to help people on the lowest rungs of society. Well, that's all fine and good. But how are you going to support yourself? How are you going to eat?"

David interjected before Johnny could go on. "I have a little money. Ten thousand dollars."

"Yes, I know. You told me. But that's not going to last. You need a job … a profession. Something to bring in money while you're helping people. The ideal solution would be a job that in and of itself helps people."

"That would be nice. Any ideas?"

"As a matter of fact, yes, I do have an idea. You gave it to me yourself when you told me why you were hired by that newspaper man. Do you remember?"

"I was hired to drive his car. You want me to get a job as a chauffeur?"

"What else were you originally hired to do?"

"Oh, you mean take pictures. But that didn't work out. The camera got burned up and then we realized there weren't really any pictures to be taken."

"Have you ever heard the old adage, 'one picture is worth a thousand words'?"

"Of course."

Johnny took a moment to refill their glasses. Once the stopper was back in the carafe, he continued. "It's funny, but just the other day I was reading an issue of *Life Magazine*. Are you familiar with it?"

"I've heard of it. As a matter of fact, if we got any good pictures down in Florida, we were going to approach them to see if they were interested."

"Right. Anyway, I was reading this piece by one of their lead photographers, and in it he laid claim to the principle that the aim of photography is to move people to action."

Johnny leaned back in triumph. He wore a broad smile on his face.

It took David a moment, but it finally dawned on him. "Are you saying I should become a photographer?"

Johnny spread his arms wide. "You would be a natural. You said you wanted to travel around and meet people. You said you'd like to help as many people as possible. Look, get yourself a camera and take it with you on your travels. When you come across people like you were telling me about—that farmer and his wife, that hobo, and that little Negro girl—take their pictures. Show their circumstances. Show their reality in stark, black-and-white realism. Move people to action, son.

"If you have an ounce of empathy in you, it will come across in your photographs. Then take those photographs and sell them to magazines and newspapers and tell the stories behind them. The untold truths that many of us rarely get the opportunity to hear … or see. You'll be making people aware of what's going on out there. And, unfortunately, there's no shortage of misery in this country right now.

"That way, you'd be doing what you want *and* be making a living."

David was warming to the idea. "Maybe you're right. I think I'll give it a shot."

The two men celebrated David's plan of action by having a little more Cognac, then went downstairs to the kitchen and had hotdogs and fried potatoes for dinner.

The next day, David bought his camera and went around the city using up rolls and rolls of film. When he got back to the house, he suddenly realized he was going to need a darkroom to process the film.

"Don't worry about that," advised Johnny. "You can get film developed anywhere. You sure as hell can't carry a darkroom

470

around with you. You just concern yourself with getting the right pictures."

While he was in town, David tried to run down Ben Shahn, but couldn't find him. There was no telephone listing for him and no one at any of the larger newspapers had seen him. David wasn't worried, though. It had only been a few weeks since they parted ways. He figured Ben was putting the finishing touches on the article before he went out and tried to sell it.

The day came when it was time for David to get on the road. He was going to take a train to Florida, probably all the way down to Miami, and then work his way up the peninsula. He would hitchhike throughout the South during the winter. When spring came around, he'd see what was doing up north.

At Penn Station, just before David boarded the train, Johnny offered one last piece of advice. "Don't you ever forget that you are a Mahoney, and you are every bit the man your father and grandfather were. Now, go out into the world and make a difference. Make them proud."

Epilogue

David did go out into the world. He rode the rails, capturing images of desperate men as they gathered in their pathetic hobo camps and while riding on top of boxcars. His camera caught the fear and sense of abandonment in their eyes as they moved from place to place, always hopeful the next would be better than the last.

At first, he sold very few photographs. Then, in March of 1931, the article about Rosewood came out in a New York paper. Ben had graciously added David's name to the byline. The story itself did not make quite the splash that David and Ben had hoped for. It was old news as far as most people were concerned. But those in the newspaper business knew it for what it was, good solid reporting. After that, when David approached an editor with pictures to sell, he was not rebuffed as he had been.

About a year later, he landed in the small town of Sturgis, Oklahoma, just before a massive dust storm hit. His stark black and white pictures of the aftermath were picked up and syndicated throughout the country and started a national conversation regarding the farmers so grievously affected by the capricious whims of nature.

He traveled with those who had been displaced by the dust, those windswept souls, as they headed for the Promised Land known as California. His images of the migration and the ensuing suffering of those people brought home to many Americans—in a way that mere words could not—the tragedy taking place within their own country.

David Mahoney had found his calling as he traveled the railways and highways, seeking out the disadvantaged, the weak, and the oppressed, telling their stories through his pictures. Newspapers and magazines alike vied for his powerful and emblematic photographs.

Near the end of 1936, he met the love of his life and married. By then he was a well-respected photojournalist. During World War II, the New York Herald put him on payroll and sent him to the Pacific

Theater. Although his views on war had not changed since his college days, he believed the war against fascism was one that had to be waged.

As the American Navy went from island to island, liberating them from Japanese control, he waded ashore with the Marines and chronicled the fighting in pictures so vivid, the people on the home front could not help but know the sacrifices being made on their behalf.

In 1950, his only daughter was born. That brought the grand total of Mahoney children to five—four boys and a girl.

In 1955, he covered the Mississippi murder trial of two white men who had killed a fifteen-year-old black boy by the name of Emmett Till. His thoughts harkened back to Minnie Lee Langley and what had taken place in Rosewood.

In 1956, he went to Montgomery, Alabama, to cover a boycott staged by the black residents of that city in protest of the arrest of a black woman for not giving up her seat on a bus to a white man. Four years later, he was again in Mississippi, documenting the various sit-ins taking place in protest of segregated lunch counters.

On a clear, hot August day in 1963, at the age of sixty-eight, David Mahoney found himself in Washington, D.C. He was there to attend the March on Washington. He knew many of the organizers from his days covering their protests in the South and wanted to show his support for them and their movement.

The closest he could get to the Lincoln Memorial was the far end of the Reflecting Pool. But he could still hear the music and the speeches through the loud speakers. When the words of the Reverend King carried to where he was standing, he thought of his grandfather, who had also had a dream.

It had taken three generations for the Mahoneys to get a firm foothold in America, but now that they were here and well-established, the progeny of Devin Mahoney would fulfill his dream.

Of that, David John Mahoney, son of Dillon Mahoney and the descendant of kings, had no doubt.

I would like to thank you for buying my book. If you enjoyed it, please leave a review on Amazon. Reviews are very important to authors as they are a tremendous help in stimulating sales.

The next few pages showcase a few of my other books. If you're interested, please turn the page.

Once again, thank you,

Andrew Joyce

Redemption:

The Further Adventures of Huck Finn and Tom Sawyer

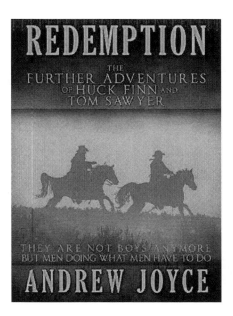

Winner of the 2013

Editors' Choice Award for Best Western

Three men come together in the town of Redemption, Colorado, each for his own purpose.

Huck Finn is a famous lawman not afraid to use his gun to protect the weak. He has come to right a terrible wrong. After his wife's death, Tom Sawyer does not want to live anymore; he has come to die. The third man, the Laramie Kid, a killer Huck and Tom befriended years earlier, has come to kill a man. For these three men, Death is a constant companion. For these three men, it is their last chance for redemption.

Molly Lee

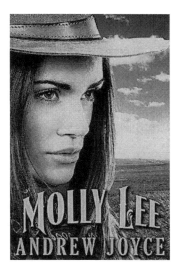

Molly is about to set off on the adventure of a lifetime … of two lifetimes.

It's 1861 and the Civil War has just started. Molly is an eighteen-year-old girl living on her family's farm in Virginia when two deserters from the Southern Cause enter her life. One of them—a twenty-four-year-old Huck Finn—ends up saving her virtue, if not her life.

Molly is so enamored with Huck, she wants to run away with him. But Huck has other plans and is gone the next morning before she awakens. Thus starts a sequence of events that leads Molly into adventure after adventure; most of them not so nice. She starts off as a naive young girl. Over time, she develops into a strong, independent woman. The change is gradual. Her strengths come from the adversities she encounters along the road that is her life.

We follow the travails of Molly Lee, starting when she is eighteen and ending when she is fifty-three. Even then, Life has one more surprise in store for her.

Resolution: Huck Finn's Greatest Adventure

It is 1896 in the Yukon Territory, Canada. The largest gold strike in the annals of human history has just been made; however, word of the discovery will not reach the outside world for another year.

By happenstance, a fifty-nine-year-old Huck Finn and his lady friend, Molly Lee, are on hand, but they are not interested in gold. They have come to that neck of the woods seeking adventure.

When disaster strikes, they volunteer to save the day by making an arduous six-hundred-mile journey by dog sled in the depths of a Yukon winter. They race against time, nature, and man. With the temperature hovering around seventy degrees below zero, they must fight every day if they are to live to see the next.

On the frozen trail, they are put upon by murderers, hungry wolves, and hostile Indians, but those adversaries have nothing over the weather. At seventy below, your spit freezes a foot from your face. Your cheeks burn. Your skin turns purple and black as it dies from the cold.

They cannot stop or turn back. They can only go on. Lives hang in the balance—including theirs.

Yellow Hair

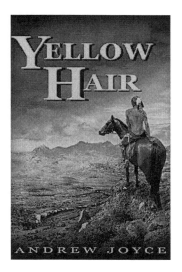

Awarded Book of the Year by Just Reviews

Awarded Best Historical Fiction of 2016 by Colleen's Book Reviews

Through no fault of his own, a young man is thrust into a new culture just at the time that culture is undergoing massive changes. It is losing its identity, its lands, and its dignity. He not only adapts, he perseveres and, over time, becomes a leader—and on occasion, the hand of vengeance against those who would destroy his adopted people.

Yellow Hair documents the injustices done to the Sioux Nation from their first treaty with the United States in 1805 through Wounded Knee in 1890. Every death, murder, battle, and outrage written about actually took place. The historical figures that play a role in this fact-based tale of fiction were real people and the author uses their real names. Yellow Hair is an epic tale of adventure, family, love, and hate that spans most of the 19th century.

This *is* American history.

About the Author

Andrew Joyce left home at seventeen to hitchhike throughout the US, Canada, and Mexico. He would not return from his journey until years later when he decided to become a writer. His books have won various awards and become best-sellers on Amazon. He now lives in Gloucester, Massachusetts.

Made in the USA
San Bernardino, CA
02 August 2020